BAKER, REBEL, SPY

A Historical Novel of the Revolutionary War

MARK ALAN LESLIE

ELK LAKE PUBLISHING INC
PUBLISHING THE POSITIVE
Plymouth, Massachusetts
A Christian Company
ElkLakePublishingInc.com

COPYRIGHT NOTICE

Library Cataloging Data
Names: Leslie, Mark Alan (Mark Alan Leslie)
Baker, Rebel, Spy / Mark Alan Leslie
364 p. 23cm × 15cm (9in × 6 in.)
ISBN-13: 9798891343016 (paperback) | 9798891343023 (trade
paperback) | 9798891343030 (e-book)
Key Words: Historical; American Revolution; spy; baker; faith; hero;
Philadelphia.
Library of Congress Control Number: 2024948148 Nonfiction

DEDICATION

To the men and women of faith, then and now, who have braved the dangers of imprisonment and death by crossing enemy lines. May God be with them, as he was with Christopher Ludwick.

ACKNOWLEDGMENTS

Some researchers dig as with a shovel. Others grab a backhoe and frontend loader. The latter is my wife, Loy. This story is due to her massive-sized backhoe. She needed no persuasion for me to jump on board to tell Christoff Ludwig/Christopher Ludwick's story.

Most of all, this is a "novelography," my new word for a novelized biography wherein there is enough historical proof for what is most important to Ludwick's tale. (Much like *A Cause Most Splendid: The Battle for the Bible*, which the American Family Association Journal named Best Novel of the Year in 2022.) What a legacy Christopher Ludwig left behind!

Christopher's exuberant bravery and love of God, Philadelphia, and his adopted country filled his spirit such that, even today, the Christopher Ludwick Foundation carries on, providing free education to poor children of all denominations in Philadelphia. Christopher's bequest of $13,000 has grown to almost $6 million, with grants amounting to some $250,000 awarded each year.

Coincidentally, an old friend, Brent Wadsworth, passed on not long before this book was published. Brent and Christopher shared the dream to help disadvantaged youth.

Brent established the Wadsworth Golf Charities Foundation in Illinois in 1997 along with his wife, Jean—its focus: self-improvement and building character through the game of golf.

I would be remiss if I did not mention Dr. Benjamin Rush's *An Account of the Life and Character of Christopher Ludwick*, found in the Library of Congress. Dr. Rush's thirty-page, heart-felt mini-biography of his dear friend is poignant and was very helpful in my research. Rush's missive ends with: "He lived and died respected for his integrity and public spirit by all who knew him. Reader, such was Ludwick. Art thou poor, venerate his character. Art thou rich, imitate his example."

My special thanks to my editors, Peggy Ellis and Cristel Phelps, for their diligence and grand advice. Kelly Artieri's cover design is catching and right on. Meanwhile, Elk Lake Publishing, Inc.'s head honcho, Deb Haggerty, waived her magical wand over the entire process, somehow fitting all the pieces into the puzzle with none missing.

My gratitude also to Don Pauley, who is not only a close friend but whose bilingual German-English expertise came in handy.

Thank you, all. Yet, as always, the greatest gratitude is saved for the One who defines excellence and grants to each of us who love Him a portion of His creativity.

CHAPTER 1

War! Its blood-thirsty tentacles had found Christopher Ludwick again.

A sudden chill rippled down his back. He glanced at his wife, Catharine, to see if she felt it too.

No. The chill was not from a draft through the sitting-room window but from an article in *Pennsylvanischer Staatsbote*. He glanced back at the headline in Philadelphia's German-language newspaper: The Hessians Are Coming. They're coming even here to America, a world away from his homeland, an eternity away from nightmares that still sometimes invaded his sleep.

The sharp crack of rifle shots, the wailing cries of anguish from wounded men knowing they were drawing their last breaths. Christopher, the former Christoff Ludwig, the former Hessian, felt again the sting of a sword to his stomach, the prick of the bayonet to his forearm, leaving wounds visible forty years later.

He skipped a breath at the newspaper's revelation. Icy tendrils trickled along his back, turning to an iron grip on his stomach. Yes, war had once been his companion. He'd joined willingly, expecting adventure and excitement, but he'd dug too many graves. Lost too many friends. Squandered too much time, not to mention treasure. The companion of his youthful dreams had now turned nemesis, staring him down again. A relentless predator, demanding attention, commanding submission. A perverse, rabid beast—like a fox throttling a rabbit.

Only I've always been the rabbit. No more.

The difference today? Until now the American enemy had worn a red coat, carried a long rifle, and spoken English. This morning, another enemy was joining the fray, a foe who wore green with crimson facing, brandished death, and spoke his native German.

Christopher finished the article, folded the newspaper, and laid it atop the latest *Pennsylvania Gazette*. Turning to the love of his life, he said in a hushed voice, his heavy accent heightened by the burden of his decision. "My dear lady, I must take my actions to Congress, then to the battlefield."

As if she read his mind, Catharine nodded. More than once, they had discussed what Christopher would do if Hessians ever stepped foot on American soil.

Catharine's delightful dark eyes locked on his, then, downcast, she dropped her gaze to her hands, laid her knitting on a side table, and whispered, "I know."

CHAPTER 2

PHILADELPHIA, PENNSYLVANIA
FRIDAY, AUGUST 9, 1776

Two days later, Christopher stepped out the door of their Race Street home. He turned to his wife, shared a prayer, a kiss, and off he went to persuade the leaders of this would-be nation. His was a wistful walk along Fourth Street past Arch and High Streets.

Mrs. Strong and Mildred something-or-other nodded and smiled as he passed a haberdashery on Arch Street. He tipped his tricorn hat.

"Morning, Christopher," said Archibald Newman as Christopher crossed High Street. Archibald served with him on the Philadelphia Society for Assisting Distressed Prisoners.[1] A good man, him. Christopher nodded.

As he approached Independence Hall, *Congressional Journal* editor Robert Aitken, himself heading to the meeting, nodded and smiled.

These were a few of the Philadelphians who had not long ago elected him to the committee planning the city's defense—one of several on which he served to lead the city into an unsure future.

"Good day," Christopher said, his cheery voice belying a certain trepidation that had crept into his mind. Would Congress approve his dangerous plan? Well, dangerous for him alone.

As he reached Chestnut Street and approached Independence Hall, a tall young soldier stood at the door, musket held against his chest, trying to look "official" while guarding against intruders.

"Carl," Christopher acknowledged.

"Mr. Ludwick!" The young man pushed his rifle out from his chest with pride. "One of the rifles you bought."

"I hope you never have to use it, son. But if you do, pray first, then shoot straight."

"Good advice, I'm sure." Carl smiled and stepped aside.

The conference room was buzzing, animated. These were men of distinction, or at least they were dressed as such. The Second Continental Congress was about to go into the day's session. Christopher hoped he could inject himself into the agenda unannounced.

He spotted Benjamin Franklin holding court with several men, among them George Clymer of Philadelphia, Congress's co-treasurer and one of the first to advocate for complete independence from England. Robert Livingston and Roger Sherman were also in Ben's orbit—for he was like the sun around which planets revolved. And there was John Dickinson, another Philadelphian some were calling the Penman of the Revolution because of his *Twelve Letters from a Farmer in Pennsylvania*, which were published ten years ago and united the colonies in protesting the British Parliament's Townshend Acts, a series of taxes and regulations. Dickinson acknowledged him with a nod.

Franklin spotted Christopher, who, at six-foot-two, was taller than most anyone here, except perhaps Thomas

Jefferson, and nodded hello. Christopher held up his pointer finger, signifying he wanted a moment alone. Franklin excused himself and approached. "Yes, my friend."

Christopher told Franklin his plan—an idea that secured the older gentleman's feet to the ground, unmovable. He cupped a hand to his chin, looked to the ceiling, at his feet, then straight into Christopher's eyes.

"Inspired," he declared. "A dazzling idea." He considered for a moment. "Perhaps a deadly idea. Lethal to you, my dear man."

Christopher shrugged. "Mine is but one life."

Franklin nodded. "Once Mr. Hancock gavels us to order, I'll stand and ask the floor of you."

Christopher could not contain a wide smile. "Thank you, Ben."

He turned and scanned the hall looking for John Hancock, the forty-year-old and ever so dapper man in charge of this session. He was about to step onto the short platform at the front of the hall. Christopher felt a special affinity for the man who had lost a fortune at the hands of the British-appointed Massachusetts governor.

Christopher hustled around cliques of men to be near the head of the room. Getting there, he stood off to the side, waiting.

When Hancock noticed this, an edge of doubt, if not concern, entered his countenance. However, he said nothing and, moments later, ascended the platform. He gaveled the meeting into session as four dozen delegates scuffled to their seats.

Not a second later, Franklin stood. "Before we start matters, our friend Mr. Ludwick has a proposal I believe deserves our attention. But before you hear him out, let me remind you all Mr. Ludwick partnered with Dr.

Benjamin Rush and others to finance the United Company of Philadelphia for Promoting American Manufacturers,[2] which already employs four hundred."

Franklin looked skyward as if scouring his recollection. "Further, two years ago, Christopher raised the idea of founding a society to help poor German immigrants[3] who needed to sign contracts of indentured servitude to immigrate to America. His wife, Catharine, did him one better, suggesting he create a school[4] to teach these people the English language, reading, writing, and arithmetic. And that school is with us now.

"So when Christopher speaks, I listen. Please hear him out."

Muffled exchanges circulated around the hall.

Christopher squared his shoulders and walked to the front of the platform, comfortable in his extrovert self.

"Christopher Ludwick," he said in his heavy German accent, "had a past before he came to America and to Laeticia Court, before he built the Ludwick Bakery Shop, and before his involvement in the affairs of our wonderful city. He was a German. What's more, a Hessian soldier who fought in two wars."

A hushed rumble of surprise echoed in the room. Surely, most of these men who knew Christopher considered him as "the gingerbread man," the light-hearted, good-mannered though serious friend of all, whom the people who lived near him called the Lord of Laeticia Court.

Not even one of these members of Congress knew this Hessian Christopher. No. This Christopher—this Christoff— was a part of him he'd suppressed, one of which shocked Catharine right out of her seat, when he'd exposed all to her during their courtship.

Not even one of these members of Congress knew this Hessian Christopher. No. This Christopher—this Christoff—

was a part of him he'd suppressed, one of which shocked Catharine right out of her seat, when he'd exposed all to her during their courtship.

He plowed on. "Yes, I was Christoff Ludwig then—my head full of promises of adventure, new lands to see. A rifle in one hand, a sword in the other. I was trained to kill, but I was almost killed myself."

Christopher looked over the delegates. Such a diverse group—from zealots like Sam Adams to mild-mannered bankers like Robert Morris, farmers like John Morris whose property was near one of the Ludwick farms, and in the back, his young friend Benjamin Rush.

Foreheads frowned. Lips sealed tight. Yet, all were attentive, which energized Christopher.

So, he went on. "The German emperor has hired out thousands of soldiers to the British. Those Hessians are about to join the fight in New York. Not hundreds, but thousands. At least eight thousand at first."

Heads nodded. These men knew this much.

"These German soldiers are professionals who prepare tirelessly. Christoff Ludwig would arise every day before sunrise, with all his comrades, to train, train, train. Load-ramrod-fire. Load-ramrod-fire. Parry-and-thrust. Parry-and-thrust." He stopped and shrugged. "America's army? Admit it, ours is not truly an army. Brave men, yes. Zealous for our country, yes. But trained?"

Heads shook.

"You men know better than any, when you asked Mr. Washington to lead the troops back in May 1775, you were dropping on the man's shoulders a task equivalent to harvesting a field of corn before a kernel had been buried in the ground."

His analogy drew a few chuckles but they were doused with cruel reality.

Christopher continued, "You ask, what does Christopher Ludwick propose?"

"Yes, man, speak!" an anxious voice said from the back. Christopher spotted the red face of a fellow he did not recognize but who was without doubt eager to get to the scheduled business of the day.

Christopher eyed him. "Every Hessian soldier who joins this fight, sir, will take at least one life of our own. It could be your son, your nephew, your cousin. Perhaps you. Remove a Hessian from the fight and—you see what I mean."

The man sat back in his seat, his scowl replaced by a look of "oh-yes, point-well-taken."

Christopher spread his hands. "My proposal is simple. Allow me to go behind enemy lines, speak to these Germans, persuade them that if they desert the British ranks, we will accept them, open-armed, into our country."

Silence.

To his left, a man scoffed. Christopher raised an eyebrow at him, inviting his complaint.

The man rose to his feet. "Accept them? With welcoming arms?"

Christopher nodded. "Nothing less."

The man harrumphed but sat back in his seat.

Another delegate, whom Christopher recognized as Stephen Crane from across the river in Elizabethtown, New Jersey, stood.

"Christopher," he said, his high forehead wrinkling, "if as you say, these Hessians are trained fighters, why on earth would they leave their comrades, their employers?"

New Jerseyite John De Hart sitting next to Crane, said, "What about their families? Their homes back in Germany? Or the laws jailing or executing them as deserters?"

Christopher locked his eyes on Crane's, then De Hart's. "Life in Germany, whether in the country or the cities, is difficult, often grueling, my friends. None among the Hessian soldiers are lawyers like yourself, John. They are a far cry from the noblemen in Germany, who live in extravagance in grand homes. No, most people live in the country as farmers. Theirs is a desperate struggle. A great many are serfs with no personal freedom, not able to marry without their sovereign lord's approval, not allowed to sell or buy land, not permitted to move elsewhere." He shrugged. "The life Christopher Ludwick lives here is not possible where they come from."

"But, if they are confident in British victory, they wouldn't hitch their horse to America," De Hart retorted. "They must think this a swift fight."

"Overcoming such a thought would be part of my task, would it not?" Christopher asked. "To persuade them we will prevail. We, whose land, whose possessions, whose families and personal futures are at stake."

"My dear man," came the voice of Benjamin Rush, "the British shoot spies, do they not? I count you as more valuable to us alive than dead."

"Thank you, Benjamin," Christopher turned his palms upward. "However, I am of little value to myself if I do not do this. If I do not, at least, attempt to convince them. I feel God compels me. With Him as my shield, I will escape the executioner."

Benjamin hung his head and did not respond.

Christopher contemplated his many times together with this man, building a friendship close to one of a brother. Gathering himself, he looked with affection at Rush. "Please, Doctor, allow me to go with a promise of hospitality, to tell my old countrymen about our fine German churches, how our tradesmen eat good beef, drink out of silver cups, and ride out in chairs in the afternoon. They will all soon run away, come and settle here, and be as good Whigs as any of us."

Chuckles spread around the room at the mention.

***

Two hours later, when Christopher burst through the door of the Ludwick Bakery Shop, Catharine looked up from behind the countertop. His smile was so broad she knew he had won his way.

Oblivious of the dozen or so customers sitting around the shop's small circular tables, Christopher blurted out, "Mr. Hancock gaveled the room to order. Mr. Franklin, my favorite lover of gingerbread, a wise man ..." His eyes sparkled. "... stood and said, 'A friend has a proposition we ought to listen to,' and my dear Catharine, his words were equivalent to an endorsement. They carried the day."

She shook her head in admiration. The customers frowned in bewilderment.

"But more," he said, pointing skyward, the sparkle now a glow.

"More?" Catharine's eyes widened.

What more was possible? She must speculate.

"Yes, more. Mr. Jefferson and Mr. Franklin are devising an incentive to persuade them. Cease fighting for the British, my friends, and we'll give you free land."

Seconds later, they met in the middle of the room and embraced. He leaned back, examining her countenance. The look on her face revealed all he needed to understand. Though afraid, she acquiesced. The best of helpmates, the truest of companions.

Catharine had made his life complete—something he knew would be the case in 1755, when he'd first met and courted the young widow here in Philadelphia. He was fresh off a boat from England then, with gingerbread molds in his hand and dreams of success in his head.

Behind them were twenty-one years of faithful devotion. He hoped there would be many more.

But maybe not.

"I must prepare my departure," he said, looking about the bakery shop forming the foundation of his business world.

"Of course," Catharine said, her voice just above a whisper. "I'll see you later at home."

He smiled, nodded, and hurried out the door, his mind overflowing with ... what? Joy? Yes. Apprehension? Yes. Anxiety? Anxiety too.

Fear? He tried to leave such an emotion out of the equation. Fear, like war, was an old companion. Only this one, he'd all but vanquished. He'd revealed all to Catharine before their marriage. The memory of their interaction flashed back at him as he walked the short distance home, and though her relentless questions had disturbed him at the time, he thanked God for them now. Though painful, the answers had also been cathartic.

"If I am to know you enough to continue our relationship, I must know you thoroughly," she had said. "Nothing less, Christopher. For in knowing everything about you, then I can trust you. Trust is about as important as love. Love is empty without it."

He'd relented and confessed, with reluctance relating his vagaries, his faults.

Though educated in a *Freischule* (free school), learning reading, writing, and arithmetic along with catechism in the Lutheran Church, he'd later drifted far from God before finding his way back. Seeking adventure in 1737, he'd left his home in Gießen, Landgraviate of Hesse-Darmstadt.

"Christoff Ludwig abandoned his widowed father to operate his bakery alone," he'd said, hanging his head. "My seventeen-year-old self was restless, heady with excitement. Enlisting as a private in the Emperor of Germany's army, I fought with the Austrians against the Turks in the Austro-Turkish War. Merciless Turks." He'd shook his head, trying to erase the blood, the death. "Our army was pummeled, but I was still besotted with the idea of being a hero. So, I then joined the King of Prussia's army in the Russo-Turkish War."

Catharine had sat quietly, letting him ramble, absorbing his angst.

Sitting on a swing outside her home, he had gazed at her, the curls frolicking over to her shoulders, the eyes swallowing him. She was so easy to speak with, to release his dark memories.

"But dreams of glory are fleeting when lead buzzes by your head." He'd said this with an accompanying chuckle, but it was nonetheless a terrifying truth.

"I survived those wars by sheer luck, not by my own skill or cleverness," he said, waiting a moment before continuing his confession. "Yes, perhaps there was an Invisible Hand to thank. Which of course I did not do—not at the time."

As the courtship continued, Catharine had dug deeper still, and Christopher had disclosed more, clutching at whatever dignity he could hold onto while relating he had beat a further retreat into moral depravity.

"After the wars, I was begging for pocket money for bread and beer in Berlin. The last time I ever begged. The last time I will ever borrow. Penniless, I joined the crew as a baker on the Royal British Navy's *H.M.S. Duke of Cumberland* in early 1743."

Christopher had apprenticed at his father's gingerbread shop, he told her, and he used those baking skills as a cook the next two years, sailing to the East Indies and China.

Once the name "China" left his lips, Christopher had hopped up, grabbed his satchel, and retrieved his treasured china bowl with silver rim he'd bought on one of his trips and with his name and the date 1745 engraved on it.

"Dear Catharine, this bowl will toast us on our wedding day," he'd declared.

"You presume too much, Christopher, Christoff ... Mr. Ludwick," she'd sputtered, storming off inside her home, slamming the door behind her.

She'd rebuffed his repeated overtures for a dreaded fortnight afterwards. A sleepless fortnight.

Torment!

Finally, she'd relented, "but only with a chaperone to control your advances, sir."

When Catharine resumed her queries, Christopher had continued his revelations.

"When I at last returned home in 1745, I found my father had died, leaving his home, his business, and heaps of money to me."

"But I left God," he confessed, admitting he'd squandered his inheritance in London in Royal Greenwich.

Tears had stung his eyes. "The prodigal son, but without a father."

Catharine had startled him by leaning into him and hugging him as he cried silently.

Finally, he'd sat back, deciding to unload his wonderful revelation.

"Then one day, my hungover head aching as though in a vice, depression drove me to the edge of the Thames River and challenged me to end it all. Then, dear Catharine, I heard a voice."

Catharine shook her head, bewildered.

"*A Voice.* I rediscovered the God of my childhood. Up close. Personal. Challenging. 'Christoff,' the Voice said, 'awaken. Fulfill your destiny!'"

The next eight years, 1745 to 1753, he'd turned his life around with a plan, he'd told her. God's plan, which revealed itself one step at a time, not prodding but persuading.

For grace does not condemn—it persuades.

"While sailing merchant ships to the West Indies, Ireland, and the North American colonies, the realization of my purpose blossomed: amass a fortune, not for myself, but with which to do good, then to do so and do so well."

His life had changed, he said, when he off-boarded in Philadelphia on one trip. Here he noticed a need for fine suits among the genteel class.

"In London, I bought chests full of suits, returned to America, and sold them at an enormous profit. While strolling one night through this modern city—like London, or Paris—I realized another scarcity. No, a void."

Catharine smiled, for she knew where the story was going. Philadelphia, a city complete with lamplight at night, cobblestone streets, merchants of all sorts, and men of distinction, had no fine pastry and confectionary shops. Not one.

"Nichts. Null. *Leer*," Christopher had said.

Nine months later, having again returned to London, but this time to master the fine art of confectionary and gingerbread baking, Christoff, now with the Anglicized name Christopher, possessed the skills as well as baking equipment—extravagant mold too—to start a new life.

"I was free from the past, free from lost expectations, free to flourish, free from war," he'd said. Then turning full-on to her, he added, "Free to find a wife with whom to share my life."

The words had escaped before he slapped his mouth shut.

But this time, Catharine had not balked at his bold proclamation. She'd tilted her head, eyes penetrating. Then, seeming to like what she read in his face, she smiled. Yes, finally, she had relented, agreeing to marry him in the summer of 1755. Joy!

Her smile had not waned in the years since. Not only did they share love, they shared beliefs. God, charity, and patriotism.

The loss of an infant son had been the lone mire, though dreadful, in their life.

A sharp crack from somewhere in the distance startled Christopher. When he looked up, he was standing at the front of their home.

★★★

The next nine days, Christopher and Catharine prepared for his absence.

Catharine would manage their flourishing gingerbread shop and catering business. Their handyman, seventy-something-year-old Maynard Knowles, would deal with the nine rental homes they owned around the city. A man of many talents, Maynard only begrudged the fact he couldn't go fight "them mangy Redcoats."

Christopher and Catharine had driven their carriage out to their farms in Germantown and Lancaster, spent a couple days at each one, leaving comfortable the properties were in good hands. An Amish couple, Aaron and Sarah Hostetler, operated the Lancaster property, while Hermann and Elli Meyer ran the Germantown farm.

The farms filled the Ludwick kitchen and bakery with pork, beef, chicken, and eggs as well as an orchard, beehives for honey, plus wheat for the flour. Combined with molasses, they had stockpiled from the British West Indies, ginger from Jamaica and spices from Asia, they had everything required to bake their famed gingerbread creations and feed the hungry among them.

Finally came Christopher's last evening at home.

Catharine cooked the dinner for two, complete with two candles atop the dining room table, flowers in a vase, and wearing her—his—favorite dress.

Christopher absorbed every nuance of his darling wife's countenance. Hers was more a beauty of spirit. She possessed a sort of atmosphere which effortlessly engaged everyone around her. Theirs had been a blessed union, but a fragile future loomed before them.

He cut into the roast beef and devoured the potatoes and acorn squash before him, wondering when he'd see his next homecooked meal. Catharine was more subdued, nibbling at this and that. Pondering. Always contemplating, this lady.

Finally, she broke the silence. With eyebrows raised, she asked, "Have you any idea we might lose this war? Thirteen colonies against the world's greatest military power?" She hesitated, then added, "Even great nations cower at the notion of facing Great Britain. And we're—well ..."

"But, my lady, this fledgling country—I'm sure she justifies this definition—is full of individual aspirations. When England battles France, the soldiers on each side are fighting under their king's orders. We're fighting for our homeland, our homes, our families. The British in this war? Their homes, their families are on the other side of a wide ocean. America means nothing to them personally. We are their king's personal treasury."

"But if we lose, we may lose everything," Catharine said, her voice faint.

"If we don't fight, we've already lost everything. At least what we hold most dear—our freedom."

Silence covered the next several minutes as Catharine rose and served slices of his favorite pie, strawberry-rhubarb, with tea.

As they enjoyed their dessert, Catharine raised her eyes. "Will you be wielding musket and charging with bayonet?"

He felt mirth in her voice but saw none in her visage.

Hiding her concern, my Catharine.

Christopher patted his paunchy stomach, allowing a soft smile.

"You jest." He raised an eyebrow. "Though I could indeed revisit some tricks learned the hard way." He wrinkled his nose. "But I have a better idea. Perhaps two."

Catharine tilted her head, a question on her brow.

"First, think of all the Germans who live here. I'll wager some of these Hessian soldiers have relations all around us. I'll raise the issue with them. Second, they're uninformed, fighting for the wrong side. They do not know their alternatives. I'm certain I can convince them America is their future, not their enemy, so they should lay aside their weapons, join us, and pick up a plowshare here. Literally."

Doubt did not occupy her look, rather the acceptance he'd perhaps had one of his revelations, and he felt secure in his plan.

CHAPTER 3

PHILADELPHIA, PENNSYLVANIA
MONDAY, AUGUST 19, 1776

With Jefferson and Franklin's plans in hand, plus a mountain of prayer under his belt, Christopher stood in the threshold of their home. As the yellow hints of sunrise flirted with the treetops, he stood rod-straight, a rifle cradled in one arm, two large sacks slung over a shoulder. He caressed Catharine's cheek, leaned down, and kissed her. She struggled to hold back tears.

"Do not worry, my love," he said. "Christopher Ludwick will return to his bride intact and of sound mind ..." He raised an eyebrow, a twinkle in his eye. "Perhaps with some German friends at my side."

Catharine nodded, swept a strand of curly hair from her eyes, and conjured a soft smile. She studied him a moment, his pleasant face, the seldom-fading smile. His mere size sometimes made her feel safe, though she knew his faith secured such confidence.

She sighed as he stepped along the walkway, turning westward toward Douglas Bradford's Livery a few blocks away. There he would mount Hugo, one of the horses they boarded, and ride out of the city.

Catharine pulled in a deep breath. At this moment, Christopher appeared to be marching. No doubt to his own beat, she opined with close to a giggle.

She could not prevent a tremble in her hand, a sigh in her throat. Was the man invincible?

Self-determined, for certain.

She spoke to herself. "My husband. My hero."

If you put a goal in front of her husband, he'd see it done—wrapped in a package, delivered on time.

Catharine had been dismayed over the years at how Providence seemed to hover over him, directing and blessing every move he made. Did he have an ear to God? Without doubt.

Christopher had risen from an immigrant to a trusted member of the community and the Lutheran church, a man full of stories of sailing the world to a loving husband filled with passion for his wife and compassion for the poor.

Yes, he made friends like he made gingerbread—hands-on, with gusto, honesty, love, and trust.

Catharine wrapped her arms around her shoulders as he walked out of sight, chin high. With certainty, a smile brightened his face. He seemed as calm, as self-assured as he would if he were off to a normal day at the bakery, not a care on his mind for his own life, armed with a firm notion he'd make a difference in the war—a revolt defying prediction.

Would she lose him? Her lip quivered. A tear formed in the corner of her eye.

Dear God, I can't lose him!

Christopher had come into her life at the perfect moment. His joviality had lifted her spirits at a time when the memory of her deceased husband still lingered. His sheer persistence was a compliment, surpassing any flattery.

His love of God proved his character. Never borrowing money, yet with an open hand to the penurious.

"A person's reputation goes before them—good or bad," he'd said to her one day. Christopher's—no, theirs—had soared over the years.

If only every couple were lucky enough to be so compatible! From their devotion to the Lord to enjoying their flourishing bakery. From their shop's popularity among Philadelphia's substantial German population to its equal esteem among aristocracy whose dinner parties highlighted Christopher's pastries. From the many friendships around Laétitia Court to befriending the tenants in the nine rental houses they owned around the city. From sharing Christopher's common ancestry with neighbors around their Germantown farm to Catharine's family ties around their one-hundred-and-twenty-three-acre farm in Lancaster County.

As Christopher walked out of sight, Catharine was certain he was fine-tuning his plan to somehow reach those untold numbers of his countrymen. As he did with his recipes, he'd experiment in his mind until perfecting the "taste"—in this case, a winning strategy.

A teapot whistled in the distant kitchen behind her, so Catharine turned and closed the door. She had time for a cuppa, then off to the bakery.

The Morrises have a soiree tonight. Perhaps their last.

Mary Morris had told her Robert believed this would be their final evening of dancing before the certain battle for Philadelphia became serious. Ludwick Bakery had been engaged as the caterer. Work called. Good. She needed to keep busy—to calm her mind more than anything.

CHAPTER 4

Robert Aitken hailed Christopher as he approached Douglas Bradford's Livery.

"So you're off," Robert guessed.

"Yes. To find the Flying Camp."

"They're entrenched in Perth Amboy, New Jersey. You've had a long ride ahead."

"Hugo will rise for the challenge. My Narragansett Pacer," Christopher said. "After the trouble riding I've had with Morgans with their bouncy four-beat trot, I find he's a smooth ride for his master."

"God be with you," Aitken said.

"I'm depending on that."

"Christopher," Aitken locked him in his gaze and with a wide smile added, "be as careful as you are putting cinnamon in my favorite treat."

Christopher let loose a hearty laugh.

Shortly afterward, leaving the livery, Christopher was saying his goodbyes to Douglas.

"All hell might break out any day," Douglas said. "I have my sources."

Douglas indeed did have a close cousin high up in the military.

"General Washington's twenty thousand troops are camped on Manhattan Island," he continued. "Putnam's six thousand-plus men are at their ready in Brooklyn. Meanwhile, the British troops under General Howe are positioned around Staten Island. Generals Grant, Von Hester, and Alexander are spread around Long Island.

"Word is, six days ago, several thousand Hessians landed on Staten Island amid fierce artillery attack. They're bivouacked with Howe's troops near Dennyse Ferry, which they would take to cross to Long Island."

"Indeed," Christopher said," the last issue of *Pennsylvanischer Staatsbote* reported one Hessian ship has been sunk."

With this news filling his mind, Christopher settled into his saddle and considered what lay ahead. Under the command of General Hugh Mercer, Flying Camp's battalions were culled from the militias in Pennsylvania, Maryland, and Delaware for rapid aid to troops in dire straits.

Mercer, a few years younger than Christopher but also a veteran of wars—fighting for Bonnie Prince Charlie in Scotland against England, then for Britain in the Seven Years' War—was charged with the defense of Philadelphia and New Jersey while assisting operations around New York. This Christopher knew. Colonel Joseph Hart's entire Bucks County militia were there in the Flying Camp as was Colonel William Montgomery's Chester County Battalion, which had marched past the Ludwick Bakery a month ago.

★★★

Hours later, Christopher rode over a bridge across the Lehigh River, which alerted him to one of his favorite sights. To his left, about eight feet tall, stood a sturdy little tree, rooted in the rocks in the middle of a waterfall. How on earth did the tree get there?

A mystery, no?

Over the years, this tree's existence had preached to him a different sermon every time he'd passed.

The first time he spotted the anomaly, the message was "stand on the rock, not sifting sand."

Next came when a driving, pelting rainstorm was swelling the river to flood stage. He had pulled his coat high to cover his neck. The message: "When the enemy comes against you as a flood, the Lord will rise and defend you."

Today the exhortation was without debate: "Be anxious for nothing, but in everything, with thanksgiving, make your request known to the Lord."

Christopher smiled at the encouragement.

★★★

The day of travel had given Christopher time to think through his coming conversation with the general. A brilliant man, Mercer—a physician now living in Virginia and commissioned to fight this revolution.

Christopher would fight, if need be. He would feed, if need be. He would do whatever task was set before him, with vigor.

As he approached Perth Amboy in a steady rain, a real-life terror from his past flashed across his memory.

"Christoff!" called a familiar voice behind him. "Christoff, help!"

Starving and on the edge of exhaustion, Christopher had wiped the raindrops from his eyes, turned, and felt a cloak of dread at the sight of his friend, Otto. His face white, shoulders slumped, knees bent, Otto looked at him with eyes wide. Fear filled his face.

Christopher hurried to Otto's side, wrapped his arms around his shoulders, then lowered him to the ground, to sit on a flat stone at the side of the road.

They and two score others with them were another eighty miles from Vienna, the destination of their lethal trek from Turkey after their devastating defeat in the Austro-Russian-Turkish War. They'd lost the battles, the war, and in the end their will. Now, they were a motley gang of Austrian soldiers, unarmed, their clothes in tatters, the soles of their boots worn paper-thin.

"I'll never make it," Otto croaked. He choked out a fearsome cough such as had plagued him for several days. Christopher noticed a gurgling sound in his friend's chest.

Not good.

"You can make it, my friend," Christopher said in his native German. "Think of your beloved. Think of Frieda. You survived the Battle of Banja Luka. You endured the Battle of Grocka. You can beat this."

Otto moaned and coughed again. A rattle echoed in his chest. It was cold, their clothes drenched, yet Otto was sweating.

Afraid of losing their comrades, Christopher had pulled Otto to his feet and lugged him along the muddy road for miles until he too collapsed, exhausted. He'd lost consciousness for a time, lying there, with Otto stretched out beside him.

When he'd awakened, he'd turned to his friend. Otto was white as a sheet. Dead.

Christopher cried out, "Otto!"

Three others died during the night.

Several days later, Christopher and a mere handful of his party arrived in Vienna. All the others of the thousand had perished. Every one of them. Gone were Johann, Reinhold, Gustav, Willi—so many friends in arms.

Starvation. The frigid cold besetting them near the end of their trek. The demoralizing oppression of defeat.

Remembering this thirty-year-old trauma, Christopher squeezed his eyes shut, shaking his head in grief. He did not want such depravation to visit itself on any more of his countrymen—whether from his new nation, America, or his old one.

No, this was not 1740. He was neither unarmed, freezing cold and starving, nor blurry-eyed from walking through snow and mud forever. This was 1776, he was well-covered from the rain with a slicker over a warm coat, riding Hugo, with his rifle attached to his saddle, a large ration of food in two saddlebags, and his destination was ... what? Right ahead!

As Christopher rode on, the rain stopped, a sliver of sun shone through an oblong hole in the clouds. He was struck by the scene before him.

Like vegetable plants sprouting out of the ground, small tents made of hemp, some with toppers, or valances, created from painted fabric, encircled a large encampment. The site filled about an acre of land along the banks of Raritan Bay.

A pair of soldiers, rifles held to their chests, stood guard, eyeing him warily.

As Christopher drew closer, the older one shouted out, "Christopher!"

The other, a young man trying against odds to grow a beard, raised his rifle high. "Mr. Ludwick! This is one of the guns you bought. Thank you."

Christopher beamed at the continuing proof his money was put to good use. True, he'd had a hand in transporting gunpowder to Fort Ticonderoga the previous fall. But what good is gunpowder without rifles?

Or rifles without gunpowder, eh?

Christopher's happiness ended then, for behind the two soldiers a scrum broke out. Faces red with anger, a dozen men or more pushed and shoved each other. Grunts, grumbles and growls exploded into screeches.

"Deserters!" one man yelled.

"No, we're not!" another cried back.

"You're leavin', you're desertin'," was the rejoinder.

"What we're doin' here is starvin'," was the response. "Not gettin' paid, neither."

"Men! Men!" Christopher called out.

He scrambled down from Hugo—so nimble!—and went to his knees.

Sudden silence.

A quick prayer for direction, then Christopher raised his eyes. "Brother soldiers, listen for one minute to Christopher Ludwick. When we hear the cry 'fire' in Philadelphia, on the hill at a distance from us, we fly there with our buckets to keep it from our houses. So, let us keep the great fire of the British army from our land."

He scanned the men around him, then smiled. "No one's starving. Ludwick the baker is here."

Christopher stood. Patting the bulging canvas bags draped over his horse's loins, he declared, "Bread and cheese for all!"

Hoorahs greeted him, the storm was quelled. Christopher found more volunteers than he needed to help with his preparations. A miracle.

He spotted several cast-iron Dutch ovens made for outdoor cooking, sitting empty around a smoldering fire.

They were made with short legs to hold the pots off the coals.

Better still, because army "kitchens" had no roof, soup was too often left inedible because falling leaves and dirt too often found its way into an open pot. Ovens had no such problems.

Thank you, Abraham Darby, for inventing the Dutch oven.

"Catharine and I use indoor Dutch ovens in our bakery, but these would do fine," he said to one young man eager to help. "Perfect, in fact."

"Get the fire blazing," he said to no one in particular, but everyone together. "We'll be enjoying the finest bread you ever tasted—all of us." He pointed to another satchel on Hugo. "A wheel of the best Butterkäse cheese in America."

He motioned toward the nearest firepit. "We want round wood. Oak or ash if you can find it. We want hot-hot embers. Place a layer of small twigs in the bottom of each oven."

The men all around stared at him, mouths agape.

Christopher tilted his head and raised his hands questioningly. "Well? You want to eat?"

A sudden burst of energy sent the soldiers hustling about, picking up whatever dry wood they found, grabbing sticks. The word spread, "Ludwick the baker is here!"

Meanwhile, Christopher pulled the mammoth bags of flour out of his saddle bags.

"Help me out here, boys," he said. In moments, he had helpers galore. All arguments were forgotten—at least for the moment.

He enlisted several men and set about preparing his creation.

After a span of twenty minutes, a corporal hustled over to Christopher. "When will we know the fire's ready?"

"Hold the back of your hand one foot from the flames. When it takes three seconds to become uncomfortable, she's ready."

The young man's face went ashen. "Hand to the fire?"

Christopher smiled, offering a "yes-I-know" shrug.

This younger generation.

He shook his head and murmured, "I'll do it." The soldier sighed in relief.

Once the dough was in the ovens, Christopher found himself surrounded by comrades—many he knew, many he didn't. Many had questions.

"What have you heard about the Redcoats and Philadelphia?"

"Not there yet," he replied. "We're preparing defenses."

"Any word about Congress?"

"They're still in our fine city."

"Did ya' bring any Bibles?"

"No. Sorry."

"How 'bout a preacher?" another added with a laugh.

"None of them, either, I'm afraid. Gone back to England, most of them, those who weren't born here."

"How much flour'd ya' bring?"

"Enough for the bunch of you."

Laughs all around at his good-natured reply.

"What the heck is a man your age doin' joinin' the fight?" one young man asked.

"I'm fifty-six, not an old man!" Christopher replied to the jab. "I've shot more bullets in battle than you."

Not a memory you want in your 'old age,' son.

"Slept more nights on the cold, hard ground."

Christopher winced at the memory. This boy was about seventeen, the age he himself was when he left home to fight—one of those wars a stunning defeat to France. Now, here he was in another country, hoping France's young King Louis would see fit to send his navy and army to the rescue. His other hope was France's allegiance would be the end of kings in his life—except, of course, for the King of kings.

Before long the entire camp was buzzing as a slight breeze spread the dazzling aroma of fresh baking bread.

Soon, the bread was ready, the cheese sliced into slivers, and hungry mouths were fed all over the Flying Camp.

***

A shadow hovered over Christopher as he sat on a log, enjoying the final morsel of his bread. He put a hand over his eyes to shade them and looked up.

"General!" The words escaped his lips as he scrambled to his feet, then saluted.

Hugh Mercer stared at him, shaking his head with a smile of disbelief.

"Mutiny avoided, with your help, I hear." Mercer's Scottish brogue made understanding him a bit difficult for Christopher—English being his own second language.

"Feeding the troops, no more." Christopher raised an eyebrow. "Odd, isn't it, how grumbling stomachs so easily master clear-headed minds."

The tall redhead nodded, then motioned for Christopher to follow him.

They trudged along, skirting puddles and areas still muddied from the rain. Men stopped and saluted Mercer along the way, but he kept his eyes stayed on his destination. He appeared single-minded, determined. Silent. So, Christopher allowed all sorts of scenarios to play through his mind.

Mercer turned and in a low voice asked, "Has General Washington contacted you yet?"

"About what?"

"He's naming you Baker General."

Christopher took a step back. He did indeed recall George's off-handed mention of something of the sort, in a vague way, in a distant conversation over a meal together in the Ludwick home. The notion had intrigued him, but he'd soon forgotten the idea. A whim wafted away by a morning breeze.

But now he found he must consider such a job.

But beforehand.

Christopher reached into his breast pocket, extracting a sealed envelope.

"Congress has another idea first," he said. He passed the envelope to Mercer.

★★★

The general read the dispatch, then scanned the page again. He shook his head in dismay.

Mercer knew little of this man standing before him but admired all he had seen and heard. A cheery man, obviously. An intelligent man, indeed. He chuckled to himself, thinking of General Washington's plans for Christopher. He was also a man whose girth and occupation suggested he appreciated good cooking.

He again examined Congress's letter. But this?

Finally, he peered at Christopher. "You persuaded Franklin?"

Christopher nodded with a slight smile.

His voice a bit higher, Mercer added, "And Jefferson?"

Christopher again nodded, and his smile widened.

"As well as land?"

Christopher shrugged, "We have plenty to give, sir. Fifty acres or more, according to the Hessian's rank."

"I can't argue your point." Mercer hesitated, then, his eyes afire, he said, "Are your affairs in order, your goodbyes said? The British shoot spies, my friend."

But Christopher was determined—a man with a steel edge despite his appearance.

"We all die sooner or later," was his response, spoken with the tranquility of talking to a Sunday school class. "The question is, have we done all we can for all we met?"

An uncomfortable question. This Ludwick fellow might be a baker by trade, but if he returned from behind enemy lines—after accomplishing his purpose—he'll be what in Scotland we call a sheòid, a hero and inspiration to the rest of us.

Mercer folded the letter, crossed his arms, and put his chin in his right palm. Moments later, he nodded a determined bob.

"Then we shan't stand in your way." He hesitated, "But first, a surprise may delay your plan."

★★★

Christopher turned to try to read the general's expression.

A surprise?

What surprise?

He remembered a commanding officer leading his troops, including Christopher, straight into an ambush in the hills of Moldavia. The man's face was set the same as Mercer's. No mirth. Gravely sober. Even moments before the slaughter.

He and Mercer came upon a canopy about ten-foot square with no walls. At the four corners stood four

American soldiers, their rifles steady and aimed inside. Beneath the canopy sat eight Hessians, six in their blue uniforms and two Jägers in their green. The looks on their faces were half-disdain, half-defeat, half-fury.

No, too many halves. Christopher allowed a wry, silent chuckle, remembering once when he over-spiced an experimental concoction.

Let's say these ones are troubled, sprinkled with a mixture of despair, despondency, and anxiety.

When the Hessians spotted them, one of the Jägers rose to his six-foot-something height, stood erect with his feet planted below his broad shoulders, crossed his arms, and glared. Imposing.

Wenn Blicke töten könnten. If looks could kill.

Mercer turned to Christopher. In a low voice he said, "We sank their ship as it came into the sound. But as you can see, we're not prepared for prisoners of war."

"Yet here they are," Christopher said.

"Yes." Mercer shrugged, then met the tall Jäger's glower with one of his own.

"You brought me here to translate?" Christopher asked.

"Maybe you don't have to cross enemy lines to weave your magic. I've learned only one thing in the six days we've held them. This big fellow is Captain Schäfer. I've tried to treat him with dignity with deference to his rank, but ..." Mercer's mouth twisted as if he'd lost a third straight game of Whist.

With a deep breath, Christopher looked over the prisoners, one by one. They reminded him of his young self. Marching off to war with hopes of glory or forced off to war to avoid a prison cell for some minor infraction of the law. This might be their first taste of battle. Christopher commiserated with failed expectations. Moreso, with capture. Moreso still, with fear and anguish.

Except for the massive Captain Schäfer, who looked as if he'd have no trouble challenging a charging bull, these men appeared "normal." Country boys from Hallertau, probably. Or mountain boys, from Lower Saxony, perhaps. One or two from a city. Heidelberg, maybe. Out of their depths, without question.

Opportunity!

An eyebrow raised, Christopher locked eyes with Mercer. "Let me speak with them."

Mercer seemed relieved. "Have at it." He pointed southerly. "Headquarters. Our Sons of Liberty flag flies atop it—the one with five red stripes. When you're done, find me."

Mercer strode away. Christopher bent his head toward the Hessians. Approaching them, he focused his attention on Schäfer.

"*Moin*," he said.

No one replied.

"*Wie geht es dir?*" asking how they were.

"*Alle sist in Butter,*" Schäfer said in a tone as dry as a bone. His intent—sarcasm. The term meant "everything is in butter," or "everything is fine."

Christopher approached the man, extending a hand. "*Mein name ist Christoff Ludwig. Ich komme aus Gießen, Landgraviate of Hesse-Darmstadt.*" Revealing his name and hometown was a good thing, correct?

"*Hau ab!*" (Go away!)

"*Lass den mann sprechen,*" urged the other Jäger, a rugged man of middle age, secure he would keep his head despite obstructing Schäfer's hostility. His words suggested they let Christopher speak.

Schäfer raised his arms in acquiescence. *"Alles klar."*

The comment was Christopher's go-ahead. He plunged right in, speaking German. "I too fought for the emperor. Twice. Against the Turks. Nothing to show for it but these."

He removed his jacket and lifted his shirt to disclose an ugly scar along his abdomen, then pulled up a sleeve where a jagged wound along his forearm was still a gruesome reddish brown.

Several sets of eyes went wide.

"My reward?" he said. "Not a 'thank-you.' Not an extra ration of bockwurst. Not a Knackwurst. Null."

"Ich habe gesagt, du sollst abhauen," Schäfer said. (I told you to get lost.)

Christopher did not step back, but instead allowed a crooked smile, and with a twinkle in his eyes, responded in German, "Let me first extol this country—America. These people, Americans, whom Emperor Joseph the Second would have you kill while, for your efforts, he pours British coins into his treasury."

Schäfer took a giant step toward him with danger in his demeanor, fists clenched. But the other Jäger held forth his arm in a motion to wait.

"Let him go on," he said in a voice under control.

Schäfer harrumphed and stalked to a log on which he sat without ceremony. His stare went to a distant spot.

"Germans are everywhere in America," Christopher said. "Even among the men whom you were brought to fight. Maybe from your own hometowns. Undoubtedly, Munich, Hamburg ... I know families who moved here from Wilhelmshaven and Schwerin and Weser. A whole region, Germantown, close by the city where I live, Philadelphia, is filled with our countrymen. Maybe your family, your cousins. Eh?"

Christopher had their attention—well, not Schäfer's, perhaps—even some nods recognizing his suggestion was possible. Maybe they would be shooting Cousin Bruno or Uncle Ernst.

"My hometown is a bit north of Frankfurt. Is anyone here from Frankfurt?"

One young soldier raised his hand.

"Would you take aim at a man who immigrated here from Frankfurt, perhaps a friend of your parents?" he asked, trying to keep no tone of accusation but simple inquiry. The young man squirmed along with several others. One nervously scratched an ear.

"Friends," Christopher said, "I came to this country with a bit of money and a few gingerbread molds. I now own a bakery, my home, nine other houses, and two farms with more than two hundred acres."

"*Ach nee!*" one Hessian exhaled, surprised by the revelation.

"You toy with us!" Schäfer interjected in German, then pointed to his head, adding, "*Es ist niemand zu Hause.*" (No one is at home, inferring Christopher was crazy.)

Apparently, you have been paying attention, Captain.

With incredulity written across his face, an infantryman added, "*Dir haben sie wohl etwas in den Kaffee getan.*" (You're kidding, without doubt.)

Christopher stiffened. "I swear to God, who is my king, my emperor. I speak not to emotions but to truths."

"Then prove it," said the second Jäger.

Good point. Prove it. Hmmm.

"I can, and I will," he exclaimed, wondering how.

"*Das Blaue vom Himmel versprechen,*" Schäfer spat out. (Promise the blue of the sky, meaning "make a promise you can't keep.")

The challenge swirled through Christopher's head. He looked at the prisoners. Then, an idea taking form, he said, "I will return."

★★★

Christopher found General Mercer under the canopy sporting the Sons of Liberty flag, with vertical red and white stripes and two black crossed muskets.

The general was among several men huddled over a map. Noticing Christopher, he turned his attention to him.

"Well?"

Squaring his shoulders, Christopher pressed in on Mercer, taking him into confidence.

"Let us," he said, "take them to Philadelphia. We can show them the life they could lead if they exchange weapons for plows, war for peace, and live with us as Americans."

The Scotsman had been thinking the same, for he answered without hesitation.

"You, two wagons with five of my men. All I can spare."

Christopher was beside himself.

So quickly, this?

God's timing?

Could this dream, so soon after being hatched, burst into reality?

Lieber Gott. (Dear God)

"How soon?" Christopher asked.

"Very," Mercer said, motioning him to the map. "Maybe tomorrow. Come see."

Mercer waved Christopher to the table, where two of his officers stood waiting, intent on the matter before them.

"Gentlemen," Mercer said, "I want you to meet Christopher Ludwick from Philadelphia." He introduced

Colonel Henry Haller of the Berks County Battalion, Major Hays, and Lieutenant Colonel Lawrence.

Haller was the first to extend his hand, saying, "Your dear wife treated my battalion with kindness on our way through your fair city a month ago."

"Gingerbread for all," Christopher recalled. "She told me."

Hays and Lawrence stepped forward to shake hands.

Christopher turned to Mercer. "I believed Colonel Montgomery, Colonel Hart, and Captain Jacob Clotz were stationed here too." He referred to the commanding officers of the Chester County, Bucks County, and 2nd Lancaster battalions.

"I've deployed them north to Fort Lee on the New Jersey bank of the Hudson," Mercer said. "We have twenty-six hundred of Pennsylvania's Flying Camp troops stationed at various points in New Jersey, two thousand of them the primary garrison at the fort."

Mercer proceeded to tell the officers about Congress's plan.

"You got this past Franklin?" Haller asked.

Christopher nodded.

"And Jefferson?" Hays said.

Christopher nodded, his smile widening. It was déjà vu, he thought, recalling Mercer's reaction. Only missing the last question.

"And land?" Lawrence said.

There you are. A trio of disbeliefs reiterated yet accepted.

Mercer motioned everyone toward the map on the table.

"Christopher, we've lost two good men gathering this information inside enemy lines."

Christopher stepped to the table. A map hand-drawn on a cloth.

Perth Amboy, where they stood, was designated by an "X" at the bottom of the map. Beyond a sliver of water to the northeast was Staten Island, shaped like Italy.

There a steady hand had penned General Howe, 35,000.

Mercer pointed. "Troops. Thirty-five thousand."

Christopher blew out a heavy breath.

Beyond Staten Island was another short stretch of water called The Narrows, then Long Island, a behemoth of land along which was a line of circles containing the names of generals and their troop numbers—Grant, 7,000; Von Hester, 5,000—and an unknown number of troops under Alexander (Lord Sterline). All British.

And then Israel Putnam (American, "Old Put," a hero of Bunker Hill) on the land designated Brooklyn, whose troops numbered 6,000-plus.

North of Long Island and across the East River, the long, narrow Manhattan Island contained one general, Washington, with the number 20,000.

Christopher's shoulders slumped. Memories of his former lost wars hovered like pests, tiny gnats, in his mind.

"These are not good odds," he said in a low voice laden with pain.

Mercer shifted on his feet. "The next battle could come at any moment. We believe the one thing delaying Howe's attack was the arrival of the Hessians. Now they're here ..." He shrugged. "So, the sooner we get you and the prisoners out of camp the better for all of us. We can do without distractions."

***

As nightfall overtook Flying Camp, Christopher was restless. Wednesday nights in Philadelphia meant attending mid-week services, enjoying a rousing sermon, food for the soul, refreshments for the flesh as well—often pastries from the Ludwick Bakery—and coffee or tea.

But here he was with hundreds of men, yet no chaplain. He found himself fiddling with his grandfather's coin in his pocket.

His father's face flashed before him, then his grandfather's kind brown eyes. Christopher's father had inherited the French coin from his grandfather. Now Christopher carried it everywhere. The currency was no memento but held deep meaning.

One side was marked in bas-relief, a representation of John baptizing Jesus, with the words below in German: "The blood of Christ cleanseth from all sin"—from the First Book of John chapter one, verse seven.

On the reverse side was a depiction of a newborn infant lying in an open field, with the words below—"I said unto thee when thou was in thy blood, live"—from Ezekiel chapter sixteen verse six.

Clearing his voice, Christopher stood in the middle of the camp. "Friends. Comrades!"

Eyes turned toward him. He prayed to have words fill his mouth. Pulling out the coin, he reread its inscription for the umpteenth time— but in this instance aloud to a group of men outside a church, on what could soon be a field of blood. Yes, a field of blood.

"With no pastor to preach, Christopher Ludwick has something to share on this fine Wednesday," he called out. "Please draw near."

Some of the soldiers did so, others stood their ground, but paid attention. Awareness was all he wanted.

"In the days ahead—perhaps even today—we may be shedding our own blood. We may shed others' blood. Remember one thing—the One whose shed blood changed the world was our Savior, Jesus Christ. He died on the cross as a sacrifice to cleanse us of our sins.

"Whether we live or die in this war, all who believe have a bright future. Here on earth or with Him." He pointed skyward. "Aways remember this from Psalm 27. 'Though an host should encamp against me, my heart shall not fear: though war should rise against me, in this I will be confident.'"

Christopher let his eyes roam over the crowd. Men's lips were pressed tight together. Many eyes were on the ground before them. Many hands were fidgeting.

He spoke a volume louder, wanting those on the periphery of the crowd to hear: "The Lord said, 'Trust I will never fail you or forsake you.' He is God. He does not lie. He protected me in two wars. He kept me alive on a torturous trek during which many friends died. Yet even if He hadn't, I would still trust in Him. In the end, His will is loving and His plan is perfect."

Christopher returned his coin to his pocket, bowed his head, then raised it, and with glistening eyes, finished, "Christopher Ludwick thanks you for listening, my friends."

Pats on the shoulder and well wishes followed Christopher as he settled upon a blanket under the stars. No tent cover for him. Not tonight. He wanted to contemplate the universe, the future—the continual mystery of tomorrow.

CHAPTER 5

THURSDAY, AUGUST 22, 1776
PERTH AMBOY, NEW JERSEY

Breakfast in their bellies, the Hessians climbed aboard a horse-drawn wagon driven by an American soldier and escorted front and rear by four other armed troops. Eight prisoners, five guards led by Lieutenant August Fischer, a man in his forties whose parents hailed straight from Munich, who had attended Christopher's church until moving to Germantown a year ago. He spoke German fluently.

In fact, all the soldiers whom General Mercer had chosen to guard the prisoners on the excursion were of German descent and spoke the language. So, the conversation would all be in German, all the way to Philadelphia, where—hmmm, a bridge to cross when you get there.

Fischer—Gus, as everyone called him—was a solid militia member worthy of leading the excursion. Christopher corralled him. In a conspiratorial voice he said, "You know what the name Fischer means in German?"

"Fisherman," the young man replied.

"Yes. In the next few days, you will be a fisher of men."

Fischer frowned. "We're here to guard, not proselytize."

"Your parents taught you to listen to God." Christopher pointed to his right ear. "Do so and obey. Would these men prefer to be in a free country, free to worship, able to make their own choices, unfettered ... or subject to an emperor who has no regard for their lives but sees them as chattel to rent out to fill his money vaults?"

Fischer twisted his mouth as if he'd swallowed something sour.

Christopher persisted, "I want them to hear straight from our friends and neighbors—from customers, city dwellers, farmers. You have guards. Let them guard them. But if I'm effective in persuading them, there'll be no need."

Fischer nodded in slow motion as if having an inward debate.

This, Christopher knew, as they left the encampment: most of the men—guards and Hessians alike—were glad to be away from the fighting, though the two Jägers might be the exceptions—Schäfer, in particular.

Sitting on the buckboard beside Private Nikolaus Bohn, the soldier fingering the reins, Christopher looked over his shoulder. The faces revealed a range of emotions from malaise to malice, Schäfer's stare equivalent to daggers.

Christopher cringed as he pictured his throat in Schäfer's hands.

Ach-h!

Christopher had requested—and Mercer had acquiesced—in a show of kindness and trust they would not tie the prisoners' hands.

Now he wondered to what degree they trusted these men.

They headed westward, led by Fischer on horseback in front of the wagon. Corporals Luka Meyer and Jacob

Hoffman trailed behind on horseback behind. Riding on Bohn's left was Private Anton Wagner.

We'll pass beautiful farmland, Christopher thought. Well-kept villages and, finally, the American jewel—Philadelphia. All of these were positives in swaying the Hessians.

He had learned their names now as well as a bit about each.

Two—Hans, a seventeen-year-old infantryman, and Emil, a nineteen-year-old grenadier—were from the Rhine and Nectar River valleys, many of whose residents had emigrated to America since the 1720s.

Johann, in his mid-twenties and a hussar from the Hessian light cavalry, hailed from an equestrian family in the Black Forest.

Rudolf, a chasseur or sharpshooter, was twenty-two, his father the gamekeeper for a wealthy landowner in the Baden-Württemberg area. In his last hunt in the beautiful dense forest, Rudolph had taken a mammoth wild boar. The feat was so newsworthy, he carried with him a newspaper clipping recounting the story. He'd removed the folded paper from his pocket and shown the story to Christopher, his chest out a bit further—depression having a bit less hold on him.

Bernhard and Heinrich were friends from childhood who both had figured they'd either get killed or caught together. Such seemed to be their troubled history from some industrial city in the north.

The Jägers? Schäfer couldn't be trusted to not strangle any American soldier he put his hands on, if given an ounce of a chance. Incongruous, wasn't it, he'd been given the name Kristian?

Ha!

But Schäfer's compatriot, Karl Blum? Though it wasn't difficult to imagine him impaling an enemy on a sword, he at least showed signs of humanity. Hailing from Frankfurt, he had once traveled through Gießen and even remembered Christopher's father's shop there.

Blum, at least, laughed at a story about the town's Burgermeister.

"One day," Christopher had told him, "Our Burgermeister, Herr Kuenning, travels to Poland. At the border they ask him his nationality. He says, 'German.'

"They ask, 'Occupation?'

"He says, "No. A short visit.'"

Blum had burst out laughing, along with all the others. Except Schäfer.

After a moment, Blum added with a broad smile, "Good he didn't tell them Kuenning means clan of warriors."

Christopher joined in another round of chuckles, then said grimly, "We lost every fight I was in. Those Turks! Phew!" He shook his head.

"My father read to us the accounts," Johann, the horseman, said.

Christopher let the mood fade, allowing the men, first, to think about the possible horrors of war—second, to admire the beauty they were passing. Through Brunswick. Then Pennington.

"Tidy farmhouses," Johann remarked.

"Painted barns," said Bernhard.

As they took the ferry across the Delaware River, Emil, the nineteen-year-old grenadier, remarked, "Reminds me of home. The Rhine in its lower reaches. Broad. Smooth flowing."

Landing on the Bucks County side of the river, eyes went wide at the sight of the bounteous river land with fertile soil evident in vibrant green fields blooming with vegetables of all sorts. Corn stalks high. Potato plants a healthy dark green.

Christopher allowed himself a smile, observing the reactions. All positive. Even Schäfer's. And they didn't yet know about the coming offer of free land for the taking. Leave your weapons, join our citizenry, enjoy a life of fulfillment.

What an enticement!

***

When night fell, they camped below the hills outside Bristol in a meadow surrounded by fir trees. The aroma of pine permeated the field.

Pennsylvania. Penn's Woods. A fitting name. Not mountainous like Burgberg but long inclines to hilltops with spectacular views. The forested area sported all the species they'd find back in Germany—spruce, pine, beech, oak, and with hemlock too.

So, if these soldiers preferred forest, they would be impressed. If they preferred farmland, its splendor was all around them.

Lieutenant Fischer ordered Privates Bohn and Wagner to gather enough deadwood to have a good-sized fire, and before long, Christopher had baked more than enough bread for everyone.

"I was thin like you, Hans, when I came to America," Christopher said, patting his belly.

Laughs greeted the revelation.

"But America!" he said, his eyes ablaze, "she captivates you with her splendor, her opportunity. Whatever you desire, she possesses in abundance. Whatever direction you want to roam—north, south, west—not east, or you'd run into the ocean ..." Christopher allowed a round of chuckles. "This land needs people of all types, all nationalities. I will show you."

"Pshaw!" Schäfer spat.

"You don't yet see, Captain?" Christopher asked. He eyed Jäger Blum. Blum shrugged with the look "I agree, but my teammate here is an impenetrable block of hardwood."

"Hirsch!" whispered Rudolph, pointing.

They all looked. A buck, an adult doe, and two fawns had stepped into the meadow. Their heads were lowered, munching on the lush meadow grass. Rudolph stood. The buck noticed, turned then bound into the forest, followed by his family.

"Ah. Sorry," Rudolph said.

"They're four of thousands," Christopher said.

"Any boar?" Rudolph asked.

Christopher shook his head. Looking at Fischer, he said, "No boar. But more deer than people, for sure. Am I not right, Gus?"

"Shot a few deer myself," Gus said with a grin, "at my parents' farm in Germantown."

The revelation drew a smile to Rudolph's face.

"Besides deer?" Johann asked.

"Bobcats, raccoons, turkeys," Gus said.

"Don't forget ducks and geese," said Luka Meyer.

"Or partridge," added Jacob Hoffman.

Christopher smiled. He had told all the guards about his mission in taking the Hessians to Philadelphia. They had tuned into what was happening in this conversation.

The talk evolved into what rifles were used for what hunting—Luka showing off his musket and Gus holding his smoothbore flintlock fowler, adding with a smirk, "Good for takin' down men too."

A couple of gulps cut the exchange to the quick. Then Jäger Blum peered at Anton's rifle, inquiring as to its caliber. The question started a long discourse on ignition systems, calibers, lengths and weights.

By the end of the banter, eyes were weary, and men were nodding off.

Until Blum noticed Christopher toying with a coin in his hand.

"A good luck charm?" he asked.

"I don't believe in luck," Christopher said. He looked with fondness at the piece of silver.

Christopher lifted his gaze to Blum, and his voice became animated. "This coin has been present in all my voyages to Asia, Europe, the East Indies, America ..."

Other eyes turned to Christopher, so he continued, "This coin reminds me of my beloved father, my grandfather, and our shared faith in our Savior. When my Hessian comrades and I struggled through snow and ice with barely a boot on our feet or a coat on our backs, I put this coin under my sock so I wouldn't lose it, my hands were so stiff and freezing. I was among two dozen of us out of one thousand who survived.

"When the HMS Cumberland was being bashed about by a fierce storm off Cape Town, I held this coin tight in my fist, hanging on to a length of rigging, praying for a miracle. A sudden calm fell upon the ocean all about us."

Christopher shrugged. "So, no, this is no good luck charm. It serves as a reminder who my refuge is amid the valley of death or anything else the devil throws at me to make me stumble or die."

"Amen," Blum murmured.

"I pray this for every German parent, Jäger Blum ... may religion, industry, and courage be their children's inheritance." Christopher dropped his head in the shame of the memory of one dark part of his life.

"When I fell away from God, squandering my inheritance on drink and merrymaking, this coin was the one possession I would never part with. Its inscription is what saved me in the end—when I reread the Scriptures, I realized the gift of salvation Christ offered me. Our price was paid by Him, through the shedding of His blood on the cross ... His gift. The two are incomparable."

Dead silence covered the camp. What other response was possible to this testimony?

CHAPTER 6

When the sun rose, so did the campsite, though Luka Meyer and Anton Wagner needed to suppress yawns after standing the third watch of the night.

After a quick breakfast of sausage and German pancakes over a flaming fire, Christopher climbed aboard the wagon. He and Anton Wagner again bracketed Nikolaus Bohn at the reins.

Within minutes, they were crossing the Lehigh River. Christopher motioned Bohn to stop the wagon. He pointed to the tree in the middle of the river.

"I've seen floodwaters surge over her," he said. Turning to the Germans, he asked, "What do you think? Is there a lesson in the tree?"

The men looked in awe.

"Many, I'd suppose," Blum said.

"Then why don't you preach us one." Schäfer spoke with a crusty edge.

"I'll leave the homily to your own imagination," Blum retorted.

So will I, Christopher thought, then motioned for Bohn to drive on.

Sometimes we try in vain while God alone can reach a dark heart.

***

Midday sun glistened off the majestic oak trees lining York Road, the stretch of King's Highway leading into Philadelphia. Beautiful fieldstone houses dotted the landscape as did fields of cabbages. Rows of corn were waist-high and taller.

There was Joseph and Betsey Galloway's Growden Mansion. Then came Manor Moreland. Loyalists.

Better keep quiet about them.

But then came the Jacob Telner farm.

"My neighbors!" Christopher declared, pointing to Telner's stunning granite farmhouse. Smoke drifted from a chimney on a tiny stone building behind the house.

"Jacob's smoking something," Christopher said. "Venison, perhaps. The Telners are good Germans, but their loyalty is to their adopted country, not an emperor three thousand miles away."

Schäfer grunted, but Blum appeared to accept the statement as truth.

Next came Samuel Tyson's fertile acreage behind a two-story wooden house painted white, with a porch sweeping around the front and sides.

"Hammer geil," young Hans muttered, thinking the place awesome.

"Samuel Tyson and his son are both on Long Island, I believe, fighting for freedom," Christopher said. "Such freedom has allowed them to become landowners, but not threatened by King George's tyranny."

Again, a grunt from Schäfer, but a nod from Blum.

The Coender and Hendrick farms followed. Both good German stock.

"Ah!" Christopher said, pointing to Rudolph. "The Coenders are from Stuttgart, near your home. Moved here nine or ten years ago. Look at their farm." He waited a few seconds, then asked, "Would you desire such a place, Rudolph?" He moved his gaze to Emil. "You, Emil?" Then to Johann. "You?"

None bellowed, *"Ja, Herr Ludwig. Wirr denken schon!"* (Yes, Mister Ludwig. We're on board.) But by the looks on their faces, he had them thinking more deeply.

"One of my farms is a mile or so over there." Christopher pointed westward.

But the roadway took them southwestward, closing in on the Schuylkill River and Philadelphia beyond.

Christopher also pointed out farms owned by Dutch families.

"Earlier this year the Updegraeffs, Kunders, Pastorius, and others instigated the process of banning slavery within the Society of Friends and all besides," he said.

The prisoners, aware of the Quakers, absorbed this information with satisfaction. All except Schäfer, who released his trademark grunt.

Christopher wondered what could break through the Jäger's armor. Perhaps he had a loved one at home whom he would never consider abandoning.

Hmmm.

I have the answer.

"Some of the men I've met from our homeland," he said, "came here, earned some money, then sent back home to bring their family to join them." He pointed behind them.

"August Coender, for instance. He brought his young bride, Marta, here after six months."

There's a seed planted.

***

Now comes the *coup de grâce*, the fetter Schlaganfall, Christopher considered as their wagon drew up to North Two Street.

Funny, we have First, Third, and Fourth streets, but amid them is Two Street. And I believed I'd learned English.

"Philadelphia!" he declared with his arms spread wide. "Forty thousand people. The second largest city in the British empire."

He searched for impressed expressions and found a few. Schäfer scowled.

Christopher gave Lieutenant Fischer directions to his home, a short distance away. Minutes later, they arrived, a wagon full of Hessians and a packet of American soldiers, in front of his fine house.

Christopher checked his watch. Noon. He hoped Catharine was home but doubted so. She'd still be at the bakery. In charge. Always in charge. His woman.

While wondering this, the front door burst open. Out she came, her face full of happiness at seeing him—followed by astonishment at the spectacle before her.

He had planned out this moment on the way here. He stood, arms wide. "My darling Catharine, we have guests!"

Her response was as he had imagined—for she had long ago ceased to surprise him with her determination to seize any challenge with gusto, often with no hesitation. The Hessian uniforms were a giveaway to their identities, but did she flinch? Not a twitch.

This response? The same as the evening he'd brought George Washington home in May 1775, unannounced, for dinner. Christopher had witnessed Congress name the Virginian commander of the rebel army—a post he'd accepted though aware there was no actual battle force.

Today, her response? Catharine lifted her skirt to ankle height, then quick-stepped along the pathway to the street.

"Let's have a look at them," she said, a smile widening as she approached.

Christopher hopped to the ground, embraced her, then with the sweep of an arm introduced, first, Lieutenant Fischer, the other Americans, then the Hessians, beginning with Schäfer and Blum.

Was she surprised he was so familiar with everyone? He doubted so. He'd always been good with names.

"And what are we to do with everyone?" she asked.

"Feed them, house them, then show them the city, the countryside," he said.

She frowned. "How about clothing them with something less conspicuous?"

Aha. Something he hadn't considered. Christopher sighed, then grasped the answer at the same moment as Catharine.

In unison, as if rehearsed, they pointed index fingers skyward and said, "The church."

St. Michael's Lutheran Church, around the corner at Fifth and Arch streets, stored used clothing in a back room to help immigrants.

"I'm sure they have enough, and if not, we can check out the new church," Christopher said.

"Zion," Catharine agreed. Zion Lutheran Church, built in 1769, stood at Fourth and Cherry, closer, but catering to Swedish congregants, in particular.

"Pastor Mühlenberg may even help me show the men around, steer them to America ... to God," Christopher said.

Catharine nodded. She had held Henry Mühlenberg in high esteem ever since she had first met him.

"If he's not out in Trappe," she said.

"If he's in Trappe, then Provost Wrangel will be in the city." Christopher referred to Karl Magnus Wrangel, who had come from Sweden sixteen years earlier.

"Surely."

"But he's not German."

"No."

"Then pray Henry is here."

She nodded. "But first, they all can fit into the house on Quarry Street. With Cecil gone to war, Evelyn has taken the children to her sister's home in Wilmington."

"Good."

This was his notion exactly. Quarry Street was a short distance to the east. The house contained four large bedrooms, sleeping three or four per room, if need be, plus a three-seat outhouse beyond a kitchen boasting a woodstove equal to his own.

"Can you spare Lina to help with the cooking?" he asked.

"I need Lina at the shop. Marta will do."

"Agreed. We'll have to get supplies to fill the pantry over there to feed this group."

"I'll take care of it. You have your hands full."

"Martin running the bakery, is he?"

"Doing a fine job too."

Christopher smiled at having such an able wife.

My Proverbs thirty-one woman.

He stepped over to Lieutenant Fischer.

"We'll take the men to St. Michael's to clothe them, then get them settled at the Quarry Street property."

"Clothe them?" Fischer said, his face reddening. "If we do, what's to prevent them from slipping into a crowd, then masquerading as Americans, never to be captured again? We need to be able to distinguish them."

Christopher deliberated on this.

Good reasoning. He could argue either side in a debate.

He hesitated, then, "Yes, but do we more want to make them feel welcomed as if they were about-to-be-new neighbors? If so, won't their Hessian uniforms scare Philadelphians to the other side of the street instead of engaging with them as merely immigrant Germans?"

While Fischer considered this, Christopher exchanged looks with Catharine, who was beside and behind him but close enough to hear the interchange.

"Do you want my input?" she asked.

"When have I not?"

Catharine crossed her arms, caught his eyes in hers. Meticulously choosing her words, she said, "Straight talk. No innuendo. A few things I've discovered from all you Germans is you're direct. You love rules, structure. You're industrious, sometimes brilliant mechanically, always detail-oriented and efficient. Never ever late." She hesitated, then, a twinkle in her eye, added, "Plus you love gingerbread."

Christopher tittered. "Don't forget sausage."

Catharine joined his laugh, but she then turned serious. "Most stereotypes are clichés," she said, "but these are ninety-percent true. Then there are some, like you, who are funny, who love to joke, laugh, make others chuckle."

"So, in one short sentence what are you saying?"

"Tell all. The good, the bad, whatever is true. Stick to those, and with your personality, my love," she put a tender hand to his cheek, "you will win them over."

Christopher placed his hand on hers, squeezed it, smiled, then turned to Fischer.

"Gus, I agree with your concerns, but I believe they're outweighed by the real possibility we'll succeed in our mission if we treat these men as friends—recruits we want to convince to move to our land, live next door, work with us, buy from us, sell to us."

Fischer shook his head, unconvinced.

"If you had a choice," Christopher asked, "would you opt to fight a war with the fear of being killed at any moment, or accept an offer of free property and sunny prospects?"

Fischer failed at trying to cloak his agitation, pondering the question. Christopher jumped ahead, "When I came to Philadelphia, I saw a simple need I could fulfill—baking gingerbread. If free land does not inspire them, perhaps there is a clothier among our friends here. Perhaps a blacksmith. Perhaps an artisan. Perhaps ..."

"Okay. Okay." Fischer raised a hand to stop him. "We'll try this your way, but at the first sign of escape ..."

Christopher winked at Catharine, squaring his shoulders. "Then follow me to St. Michael's, Lieutenant."

He kissed Catharine on the cheek and climbed aboard the wagon.

***

St. Michael's Church was an impressive structure, a stone's throw from Robert and Mary Morris's manse as well as the Pennsylvania State House on High Street. The church was inspiring. Built of stone, the structure was three stories high, its gold-gilded spire aimed toward heaven whose Creator Christopher trusted with his every breath. Inside, deep mahogany walls and pews welcomed all to sit, pray, and feel the comfort of the Lord throughout the day.

But when they arrived at the front of the church, Christopher motioned for everyone to stay with the wagon. He had noticed a knot of women who had been walking along Arch Street had spotted them, then crossed to the other side, hurrying along North Fifth instead.

He motioned to Lieutenant Fisher, nodded toward the women, and said, "You see, Gus, those ladies knew the soldiers are Hessians, and fear sent them scurrying away. I'd expect the same reaction everywhere they go, if they keep their attire status quo."

Fisher waved toward the church, urging Christopher to continue on with the plan.

He walked along a pathway by the side of the building to Pastor Mühlenberg's office door at the rear corner. Knocking first, he entered.

Mühlenberg sat at a wide desk piled in a haphazard melee of books and papers. He was bent over a document, gazing.

Hearing Christopher at the door, Mühlenberg glanced up, startled. "Christopher!" he exclaimed.

Christopher smiled.

"Catharine told me you were away to Flying Camp. She told me of your mission. We prayed for your protection."

"It worked—so far," Christopher said. "But now I need your help."

"Of course," Mühlenberg said, "but first, read this."

He waved Christopher over to his desk, pointing at the document.

"A copy of our Declaration of Independence. 'Self-evident,' they wrote. 'Self-evident that all men are created equal, endowed by their Creator ...'" Mühlenberg smiled broadly. "This infant nation? She ... will ... survive. She will flourish. She will be God's city on a hill, but on another continent a world away from Jerusalem."

"Unlike the morass of provincialism in which our old homeland has been living?" Christopher said. "I hope so."

"I know so, Christopher. Such a bold pronouncement." Mühlenberg tapped his index finger on the Declaration. "Bold, unashamed, indelible."

"A firm foundation, you're saying?"

"Definite. Absolute."

"So you think you can persuade other Germans to your line of thinking?"

"An odd question." Mühlenberg tilted his head and peered at him.

"The help I mentioned?" Christopher nodded toward the front of the church. "We have eight Hessian prisoners of war outside."

Mühlenberg sat back, a stunned expression across his handsome face.

"Out ... outside this church?" His voice scratched across the words. He pointed to the floor. "Right here?"

"In a wagon, surrounded by several of our armed soldiers."

"You want me to help persuade them of the rightness of what—quitting soldiering for a life in America?"

"To join me in this effort, yes." Christopher raised a finger. "But first we need to clothe them."

The reasoning took a beat to dawn on Mühlenberg. But when he understood, he leaped from his chair.

"Bring them to the clothing hall. I'll meet you there."

Christopher hustled out to the wagon. "Follow me," he said.

The Hessians needed little prodding to climb from the wagon. They'd had enough of a ragged ride to last a lifetime, Christopher reasoned.

Lieutenant Fischer ordered his men to both lead and follow a double line of prisoners as they trekked behind

Christopher to the other side of the church. Ahead, a door opened and Mühlenberg stepped out to motion them inside.

"Pastor Mühlenberg," Christopher said in way of introduction.

Mühlenberg waved to them.

"Moin. Moin." He directed the men past him into a room filled with racks of clothing.

Several men returned his "good morning."

Jäger Blum offered an *"entschuldigung"* to excuse his passing by the pastor. Schäfer grunted.

Lastly, Christopher stepped inside. He was proud of this accomplishment of his church. He and Catharine had contributed heavily to its success. The clothing hall was open various evenings for people—anyone—needing clothing. Church members volunteered their time to help.

Speaking in German, Mühlenberg told the men there was clothing of all sorts, of all sizes. Even shoes and boots, though not with such a variety.

"Choose what you want," he said. "You can try on the clothing behind the screen over there." He pointed to a corner of the hall.

Scattering his men to the four corners, Fischer sidled next to Christopher by the doorway.

"I'm still wary of this," he said.

"But you saw the women scurry across the street as if fleeing a fire when they spotted the uniforms."

The corner of Fischer's mouth turned up. He realized the importance of this endeavor.

"Give us a chance. We'll win them over."

I pray.

Christopher turned his attention to the Hessians roaming around the room as if they were inspecting the wonders of Schwerin Castle.

"Discerning shoppers, them," Christopher said. With a chuckle, he added, "Now, Christopher Ludwick? He'd be out of here in a minute, clothed, ready to go."

Fischer laughed, then with a dubious look, offered, "Discerning? Or on the lookout for such as would make them unrecognizable?"

Christopher shrugged. "Time will tell. I believe these men's eagerness and soberness in this simple chore is a good omen. This I know—they'll notice good German workmanship in some of these clothes. Gifts from our friends around the city."

"This ought to suit you," he heard Mühlenberg say in his native language.

Rudolph, the sharpshooter from Baden-Württemberg, sheepishly stepped beside Christopher.

"Sir," he said, *"Ich will nicht mit in des Teufels Küche sein Jäger Schäfer und Jäger Blum."*

"There is no worry about getting into trouble with them," Christopher replied. "Doing this will allow you to experience our city as though you were a visitor, not a prisoner. You will fall in love with this place." He smiled mischievously. "Maybe with one of its fine ladies."

Rudolph's countenance brightened. His face was an uncomplicated one to read. Christopher had considered him an easy recruit. Perhaps he was right. If "getting into hot water" was the main obstacle to the young man trading rifle for land then this could be another portent of success.

"There are many fine women here," Christopher said, "and unlike Germany, there is no impediment to a poor man marrying a woman of stature. No unwritten law. No hierarchy of certain men over other men. No entrapments of society as you have in Baden-Württemberg."

Rudolph scratched his chin, thinking, considering, weighing options. He nodded, turned on his heels, and headed straight to a selection of shirts through which he'd been rummaging.

Mühlenberg disengaged from a conversation with Bernhard and Heinrich, then sauntered over to Christopher and Fischer.

"So nice to see you, Gus," he said. "How are your parents? Are they well?"

"Concerned for the future," Gus said.

"As are we all."

Christopher cut in. "Henry, what are your impressions of our guests?"

"Our countrymen are serious people. Good and bad, it's one of our traits," Mühlenberg said. "The English would call it 'resolute.' This in mind, I believe they're impressed with our selection, with the generosity of our people." He glanced at Fischer. "And, Gus, likewise with your willingness to allow this amount of freedom to a military adversary."

Fischer nodded toward Christopher. "I had little choice in the matter. Our friend here is persuasive to the point of exasperation."

Mühlenberg chuckled. Christopher recalled the times when they had debated various topics of concern, including the large loan he had granted the church a few months ago. The pastor didn't yet know the loan was interest-free. A surprise for the right moment.

"The problem," Mühlenberg had told him more than once, "is you see the good in people too often."

"How often is too often?" Christopher had responded.

"Oh, tosh!" Mühlenberg had said. "You win on points."

A hassle broke out on the other side of the room. Johann, who stood over the younger Hans, was pushing the infantryman in the chest.

"I chose those trousers!" he said in German. "They wouldn't fit you unless you put on twenty pounds."

"I'll have them altered."

"I'll have *you* altered, Private."

Christopher rushed over, stepping between the two men. "Gentlemen. Countrymen. Let Christoff Ludwig help. Both of you can have what you want."

Christopher gestured toward the far side of the room. "I volunteered here the other day and happen to know there is a replica of these trousers over here. They might fit Hans."

"There!" said Johann, full of bluster. "Head to the little boys' section, chum."

"Johann." Christopher put a hand to the man's chest. "We're all here as brothers, with one thing in mind."

Jäger Schäfer hurried to confront him. "Oh? What's the one thing?"

Christopher refused to retreat. The other Hessians formed in a semi-circle around them.

Christopher locked his eyes on the big man, who stood as tall as he did. "My 'one thing' is simple. I want to challenge you to think of your options. Think of the feudalism back home, where you work on someone else's land to gain a meager pittance to sustain your family. Compare Germany's system to the land here in America you get to call your own. I want you to consider Germany's dark life to this bright one. With no emperor at his whim, forcing you or your child to join the military at the age of sixteen."

Christopher held out his arms, hands up. "I want you to see how our tradesmen eat good beef, drink out of silver cups every day, ride out in chairs every afternoon.

"Think of all this, Kristian. Ponder. Dream. Your own land, your own business, your own choices."

"*Pshaw! Wieder, Das Blaue vom Himmel versprechen.*" (Again, you promise the blue of the sky.) You say 'your own land' as if such is the case. As if we can stay here and with ease ..." he snapped his fingers, "have our own land." He jerked his head toward the others. "Hans? Emil? Johann? Their own land? Ha!"

Christopher hadn't planned to reveal his surprise yet, but decided this was the optimal moment. If not now, facing Schäfer's condemnation, he might lose his cause before the first day was out.

Out of a pocket, he pulled the notice from Congress. He waved the paper before Schäfer.

"Friends," he said, gazing at each one in turn, "this is a promise from the American Congress—our ruling body—a guarantee to give each of you as many as fifty acres of land, free of charge, if you leave the British tyrants and join in the grand future of America. Fifty acres. Twenty *hectares*."

A hubbub echoed across the large room. All sorts of questions and excitement.

"Our leaders give their collective pledge to you. I also give my personal oath. You will be given property—not scrap land, not marsh and wasteland, but good, fertile soil." He eyed Rudolph. "Or forest if you wish. All you need do is stay here with us, not return to your comrades, not resume arms against America. Until the war is over, we have plenty of jobs for you because so many young men are off fighting. Once the war is over, you can claim your land. Then you may send for any family you want to bring to our country."

Jäger Blum raised his voice above the din. "This offer is unbelievable."

Christopher nodded.

"I don't have any fifty acres, though I was born here," grumbled Bohn. "Born and bred."

"Think of this, Nikolaus," Christopher said to the private, "for every soldier not fighting for Britain, one less man taking aim at us. Are not lives worth property when we have such an expanse of land—from here to who knows how far west?"

Bohn's face turned contemplative.

"You guarantee this offer?" Blum asked.

Before Christopher answered, Schäfer grabbed Blum's elbow. "Desertion!" he exclaimed. "You'd entertain such a traitorous offer?"

Blum squared his shoulders to his comrade. "Traitorous? What have you received from our dear emperor? So, he lowers our families' taxes a bit for our fighting. Did he ask your input to his decision to order us here to fight for a country not our own—against a country with whom we have no hostilities?"

"I live to fight." Schäfer snorted. "I know nothing else."

"But is warfare all you want to know?" Blum asked. "After all our battles, are you not sick of death? Have you not suffered enough wounds? Did I not nurse you back to health in Italy?"

Johann spoke up. "These people have done us no harm, Jäger. Not in the Black Forest where I come from. Not Hesse-Cassel where most of our troops live."

Schäfer shot a staggering look at the young hussar. "If we were in our camp, I'd ship you to the brig for such a remark, Corporal."

Blum held up a hand for silence. Peering at Christopher, he asked, "Is this a promise not only to the eight of us, but to others back in the camp?"

"Karl!" Schäfer objected.

Blum steeled his gaze on Christopher.

Is he thinking ...?

Christopher gasped at the implication behind the question, what might be going through Blum's mind.

Would the Jäger return and recruit?

Christopher gathered himself. "As many as want to come. We have land beyond the horizon for willing hearts. Jobs?" He looked around at all the men. "We need craftsmen, workmen, horsemen, farmers, farriers, clothiers. I, myself, need cooks for my bakery, farmhands for our farms." He eyed Blum, then Schäfer. "We need leaders to explore the unexplored. And you, Kristian, if soldiering is what you want, we need such a skill too."

"But we don't even speak the language," Blum said.

Christopher offered a broad smile. "My wife and I created a school where men and women, boys and girls are taught English and mathematics. Most of our students are Germans."

"Our church," Mühlenberg said, "is filled with Germans. We have two services every Lord's Day—one spoken in German, one in English."

Schäfer aimed a scathing scowl at Blum. "I cannot believe you are considering this, Karl. A Jäger. The best our emperor has in his army."

Blum crossed his arms in front of his chest. "I will listen. I will learn. I will take Herr Ludwig's 'tour,' as he calls it, to see whether what he tells us is true. Men drinking from silver cups, eating good beef, riding off into the beauty of the countryside in the afternoons."

Schäfer's glower intensified.

"Kristian," Blum said, "what is there to lose? We're not chained in a dungeon here, are we?"

No reply.

"We're not beaten or harassed, are we?"

No reply. The other Hessians' ears were up. They were contemplating, for sure.

A wrinkle of exasperation touched Blum's intonation. "Kristian, these people are clothing us, with the promise of a good meal. You've been a prisoner of war before. Were we fed decent meals then? More akin to gruel. Were our hands free, or were we chained?"

Fischer nudged Christopher. "For goodness' sake, tell them they have a choice. No one's twisting their arms to accept the offer."

Christopher nodded. "Friends, here is my challenge. At least let me show you our city, its shops, markets, homes, and churches. Let us ride through the country. When done, decide for yourselves.

"I'm guessing once this war is over, and America has won, many of you will decide to stay here, or go to Canada. So why face death if you don't have to?"

Blum shared a look with Schäfer. "*Er fällt immer mit der Tür ins Häuschen.*" (He always falls into the house through the door, or he always gets right to the point.)

Christopher guffawed and the younger Hessians joined him. Schäfer's grunt was less hostile.

After a few moments, Schäfer blew out a breath, shrugged, and grumbled, "Okay."

"Done," Fischer said to Christopher. "Let's get these men dressed, get going with your tour."

Blum ordered the men to be quick about finding clothing. They all spun on their heels, hustling off. Schäfer muttered to himself but followed.

★★★

Twenty minutes later, the Hessians, looking like civilians, filed toward the exit. Mühlenberg said, "You are all welcome to our services on Sunday mornings, and of course, the church is open for prayer all day long."

He received smiles and nods from at least half the men.

When Christopher brought up the rear Mühlenberg put a hand to his shoulder.

Speaking in English, he said, "Bring them Sunday. I'll be sure to preach a sermon aimed straight to their better selves."

It's Friday, Christopher thought.

Lord, in these next two days prepare these men's hearts to leave a life of warfare for one of peace.

"We'll see," he said. "God willing. I can only promise Catharine and I will be here."

Mühlenberg nodded in understanding.

Approaching the wagon, Christopher told Lieutenant Fischer the location of the house in which they'd be staying.

"Room for us all?"

"A large family, the Frosts, has been living there. Cecile had born six children for Henry in the span of eleven years."

CHAPTER 7

Quarry Street was little more than a half-mile away, north of the Laétitia Court area where the Ludwick Bakery stood. Christopher would not reveal that people called him King of Laétitia Court.

Far too prideful as well as too close to 'emperor.'

The thirteen-man contingent arrived at a three-story home where several men were bustling about, unloading a wagon, and carrying furniture inside.

Oh, the place is barren. Christopher's shoulders shrunk. No beds, kitchen table, couch or chairs. He had not considered this, but of course Catharine had. Christopher chuckled to himself. Sooner than he got eight men clothed, she had seen to this business.

What a wife!

One of the men unloading the furniture nodded to Christopher. "Another load will be on the way in a couple hours, Mr. Ludwick. Of course, we do not have the beddings with us, but they will."

"Thank you, Harry," Christopher said.

Lieutenant Fischer ordered two of his men to help the movers, while the others guarded the Hessians. An hour later, the job was done, Harry and his crew were leaving. Christopher led everyone inside.

As he showed them through the first floor and Fischer assigned bedrooms, excited women's voices came from the front door. In bustled Catharine with two young ladies who worked part-time for the bakery. Behind them was a donkey-led cart filled to the brim—but with what?

"Food," Catharine said. "Bread, sausage, eggs, potatoes, carrots ..."

Catharine had planned ahead, even though he had not.

"Gingerbread?" asked Christopher.

"Of course." Catharine flashed a look of exasperation.

As if she'd forget such an important ingredient to life itself!

She smiled. "Your favorite mold, my dear. The queen's crown."

"We'll need pots, pans, kitchen utensils," he said.

Catharine glanced at one of her companions. "Marta?"

"I have a frying pan and two large pots," the twentyish girl said.

"I have flatware and silverware," said the second helper.

"Excellent, Hannah," Christopher said.

"Gretchen is coming with flour, spices, and such," Catharine added, "all from the storehouse."

The storehouse was in Laétitia Court, which explained how the ladies had gotten here so fast.

You are an amazing God, planning everything out far before we would if left on our own.

"You do have an extraordinary wife, Herr Ludwig."

Christopher spun around, eyed Jäger Blum, and winked.

"What did I tell you?" he said.

"The truth, for sure," Blum said.

"I will not lie to you, Karl—about anything—ever."

"You can depend on his promise," Catharine said in German (for she had learned his native language well). "Isn't that right, ladies?"

Marta and Hannah nodded with such enthusiasm Christopher had to smile. Reputation was important. Character. What was a man's legacy—besides being a follower of Christ? Marta and Hannah were pleasant, cheery young women. Catharine wouldn't hire anyone otherwise. Both were blue-eyed, flaxen-haired. Everyone would say "lovely." Many would say "beautiful."

Christopher turned to the Hessians, who had followed him to the front room. "Young German ladies, these," he said, "so one wouldn't need to learn English before meeting a companion with whom they could converse."

He knew the young ladies were blushing, but why not plant a seed in both genders?

Rudolph, Hans, and Emil nodded, Rudolph with enthusiasm. Christopher would have to keep Rudolph's reaction in mind. The gamekeeper's son was a few years older than the other two, so must have reflected about marriage.

"Ladies," Christopher motioned Hannah and Marta to come closer, "meet our friends."

When they'd drawn close on either side of him, he introduced the Hessians, adding morsels he'd learned about each one.

The soldiers were all pleasant, nodding at their introduction. Even Schäfer forced himself to keep his manners. Etiquette prevailed even with a hardened warrior, it appeared. Or perhaps the beauty of the women was the catalyst to winning over the Jäger.

Yet another enticement, perhaps.

Insight, Lord. I need insight. Your discernment.

"Girls, girls," Catharine called. "Let's put the pots and pans on the stove and the food in the cabinets here and the pantry." She pointed to a room behind the kitchen.

As Christopher turned to continue the tour of the house, he noticed several of the Hessians—Rudolph and Hans, in particular—held their gazes upon their new acquaintances. He smiled.

Work Your magic, Father.

Christopher led the procession through the house, with Fischer's men giving them a comfortable latitude.

Exclamations echoed from the mouths of the "guests" as they looked in each room—four bedrooms, a dining room, sitting room, parlor .... They gasped as one, when he walked them to the back of the house—the three-hole water closet with a large water tank above.

Christopher was proud of his rented homes, always ensuring their upkeep. He'd wished he and Catharine had been able to have children enough to fill this large a house.

When they returned to the forward rooms, the delightful aroma of sausage with onions filled the air. Tantalizing. Before anyone knew it, they were seated around a long dining table, enjoying a meal from Catharine and the girls.

"Sauerkraut!" remarked Blum. "My first in many months."

"Truly?" Catharine asked.

"Drought back home. Fields are dry as a bone. No cabbages."

"Little of anything in the city," said Bernhard.

"Because we rely on the country," Heinrich added.

"Complain. Complain," Schäfer said with overt testiness. "Remember the good. Remember our beautiful country. The mountains ..."

"Seldom saw them," Bernhardt murmured.

"You never will either," Schäfer said. "Not if you take this man seriously. Not if you abandon your brothers in arms. What about your family you'd never see again?"

Christopher bristled, thinking "This could be bad."

But Bernhardt merely shrugged.

"Maybe we'd make a family here," Heinrich said. "Besides, Bernhardt hates his father. Mean man."

Bernhardt nodded, chagrin written across his handsome face.

"Rules with a rod," he said.

Christopher breathed a sigh of relief. Keep those notions churning, he urged in his thoughts. A new life awaits. New freedom.

Quiet consumed the next few minutes as the men—Germans and the Flying Camp troops, all but two who kept guard a few feet away—launched into their meals. In particular, the Hessians scarfed up the dinner.

Between chews, Blum glanced at Catharine, a sheepish look on his face. "Six weeks aboard a war ship with merely enough vittles to keep us alive."

Schäfer interrupted, his tone defensive, "The captain didn't want to drain all the food supplies, in case of a storm."

"Plenty of food in America," Catharine said with a broad smile tickling Christopher's heart.

"Ja," added Marta, eyes twinkling.

"You should see our table on Sunday after church." Hannah's spirit sang the scene.

Christopher absorbed the conversation as if it were a maneuver on a battlefield of words. Marta and Hannah had both learned from their elders about life in Germany—the reason they'd fled for America.

Good girls. You're part of the persuasion brigade. Ha! Persuasion Brigade. Ladies may not be fighting in the front lines, but still taking arms of another sort.

"True, unless the Redcoats come crashing in, absconding with the harvest," Fischer said.

"My uncle and aunt's farm in Rhode Island," said Luka Meyer, the young corporal who stood eating at the countertop. "They're worried because they live near Newport where the Redcoat navy is headquartered.

"So," Christopher said, his eyes on the Hessians, "the British, whom you'd be fighting with today, have not only taxed us to pay for the French and Indian War along with uprisings in India and Africa—they've closed our ports, forced us to provide barracks and supplies for their troops, regulated our export of lumber and iron. We've been given no self-rule unless approved by their surrogates."

"Don't forget they put tariffs on imported molasses, sugar, and coffee," Fischer said.

"Right, Gus." Christopher winked at the lieutenant sitting across the table. "Since the molasses comes from the British West Indies, King George is certain to be taxing the sugar cane growers there as well—for exporting the stuff."

"So, he's making money both leaving the Indies and entering America?" Blum asked.

"He's our king." Jacob Hoffman puffed out his chest in mockery.

"Not anymore." Christopher's reaction was sharp.

Jacob's shoulders slumped. He blushed. "Right."

"A true king does right for his subjects," Christopher said. "A true king reigns justly, righteously."

"A dream," Schäfer scoffed. "If you even win this war, which is doubtful, who's to say your American king doesn't act the same?"

"We're not going to have a king," Christopher said.

"Men *of* the people will rule *for* the people," Fischer cut in.

"Oh? Who will decide who that is? You?" Schäfer pointed to Fischer. "...you?" He pointed to Luka, then Jacob.

Before any replied, the sound of the front door opening was followed by a female voice calling out, "Hello?"

"In here," Catharine called.

A moment later Gretchen Miller, one of their bakery staff, entered the kitchen, holding a large tray brimming with gingerbread, whose special aroma preceded her. The tall, lithe, golden-haired young lady was stunning. Christopher heard young men catching their breath, their tongues tied in knots.

My Catharine, my brilliant wife, saved the most beautiful young woman in Philadelphia for last. Gretchen, in her mid-twenties, was a widow, her husband having died two years before in a forest accident.

Her appearance was an exclamation point—culinary as well as beauty-wise—to America's attractions.

Christopher exchanged glances with his wife. She winked in return, then announced, "Dessert."

Looking about the room, Christopher couldn't tell what was getting more attention—Gretchen or the gingerbread. Oh, yes. Gretchen, for sure.

She lit the room with an ear-to-ear smile.

"Straight from the oven," she declared, green eyes alight.

She set the tray in the middle of the table. Quick hands emptied half the goodies in a moment. Sounds of delight soon followed.

"We baked our most favored recipe," Gretchen said in German, her bright voice like a fine-tuned wind instrument. "With Mr. Ludwick's secret ingredient."

Though most of the eyes around the table remained glued to Gretchen, a few turned his way. Christopher murmured, "A secret between us—carrot juice."

"Carrot juice?" remarked Blum.

"Complements both the cinnamon and molasses," he explained.

Satisfied murmurs sounded around the kitchen. Soon the entire contents of the tray had been devoured.

Christopher settled back in his chair as all the young men commenced conversations with each other, and with a bit more eagerness, with the young ladies. He caught Catharine's eyes again. Their speechless "conversation" was filled with congratulations.

Each girl's family, upbringing, education, work, living arrangements, so ons and so forths were revealed and explored. The young men from both countries exchanged pleasantries, the Americans extolling the weather conditions for farming. Men from both armies bantered about their hunting explorations, jobs, and pastimes.

"Brilliant," Christopher repeated to himself. Again, he looked at his wife. Her smirk confirmed how he himself felt.

But it is only round one, he cautioned himself. We have a distance to go.

He walked to Fischer's side. "How about the ladies clean up, the men settle into the house, get a good rest tonight, and tomorrow, we'll explore Philadelphia, then take a ride to our farm in Germantown?"

Fischer nodded. "I'll take charge here. You can sleep in your own bed tonight."

Christopher shook his head. "Christoff Ludwig will sleep with his countrymen tonight—I should say, men of both my countries—here in Laétitia Court."

***

In the evening, Fischer stationed Privates Nikolaus Bohn and Anton Wagner at the outside doors. Fischer and Corporals Luka Meyer and Jacob Hoffman semi-stood guard in the large sitting room, near invisible to the Hessians, who sprawled on the couch and chairs. arguing about their situation. Christopher sat on the edge of the sofa, absorbing every word, every nuance.

The discussion was spirited.

From the beginning, Christopher gauged where the men each stood along the spectrum of zero to ten—zero being staunchly opposed to switching sides in the war, ten being doubtless on board with the idea.

Hans, the seventeen-year-old infantryman, and his friend, the nineteen-ear-old Emil, weren't far from ten, he surmised. Emil ventured they'd find relatives from those Germans, who had left the Rhine and Nectar River valleys for America forty years earlier.

Rudolph, the handsome sharpshooter who was a few years older, was a solid seven, inching closer to ten each time he mentioned the divine Gretchen—perhaps his way of staking claim to being first to court the beauty.

Johann, the horseman, had inquired with Christopher about the need for farriers in Philadelphia.

"When I saw Douglas, who owns the livery, four days ago," Christopher recalled, "he said he'd have to hire extra help to handle all the needs of the growing city. But don't forget your twenty hectares."

Johann had smiled.

At least a six on the spectrum, for sure.

Bernhard and Heinrich? Both with a troubled past as well as the possibility of escaping the drudgery of the industrial city from which they came. Christopher speculated: nine for each one.

The Jägers were another story. As he considered them, their voices exploded from the far corner of the room.

"You wouldn't!" Schäfer roared, face-to-face with his comrade.

"I would!" Blum countered.

"Your name will be erased from the town rolls of Düsseldorf."

"Town rolls? Do I care?"

"What is there more important than reputation?"

"Life. Liberty. Salvation. Maybe next would come reputation." Blum put his hand to his hips. "I can't believe many will be thinking of me when they're scrambling to survive meal to meal."

The rest of the room had turned quiet. Christopher scanned left to right. All eyes were on the Jägers.

"What of your family?" Schäfer asked.

"My family, Kristian? You were with me when I received word my Isabell was dying of influenza. Captain Schmidt wouldn't allow me leave to be with her."

Schäfer shrugged.

"And do you know what Isabell's name means?"

Schäfer shrugged again.

"Abundance. Tell me, where was the abundance for her? Where was the abundance in Düsseldorf?"

Before Schäfer responded, Blum plowed on. "My grandparents all died in the Great Northern Plague—all of them. Yours too. My parents? Perhaps I'll write for them to join me here. Yes. A fine idea."

Schäfer fumed but lowered his voice to a deep growl. "You're a leader of fighting men. You're supposed to lead, not desert!"

Blum met spark with spark. "Maybe I should lead them here to Philadelphia, my friend."

Schäfer tightened his hands into fists.

Fischer started out of his chair with a sense of urgency, but Christopher grabbed his wrist, motioning for him to stay put. "Give them a minute," he whispered. "Let's see where this goes."

"Kristian. Kristian," Blum said, frustration filling his voice. "As soldiers, we've always been told what to think. This is our chance to think for ourselves, not the entire company. For our own futures, not for victory in a battle or a war. Our Savior said there will be wars and rumors of wars. He didn't say we had to fight them all."

"Our Savior." Schäfer hissed the name. "You know I don't believe."

"You believed the day of the miracle."

This caught Schäfer unawares. He stepped backwards, his back against the wall. His eyes, afire a moment earlier, watered.

"You don't deny it," Blum said, his voice lowered, "do you, Kristian?"

The big man's broad shoulders shivered. He drew several staccato breaths.

Blum moved closer. "He, Kristian. He, Jesus, wants the best for us. Is the best back there in Germany where poverty reigns? Is the best on the battlefield, taking aim at men fighting for their families, willing to die for their country, while you're fighting for an emperor you've never met? A ruler who wouldn't know you from Adam?"

Schäfer stood silent, not even mustering his patented sneer.

"The Bible tells us to choose life," Blum said. "Now, here we stand. We can make this choice for ourselves. *For ourselves!* Not made for us by someone living in a castle with venison, lamb, and beer on the table at the snap of his fingers."

Blum shrugged, then continued, "The choice lies right here before us. Shouldn't we even consider grabbing hold?"

Schäfer noticed all eyes in the room were on them. He stiffened his back and stood erect.

"What are you all looking at?" he demanded, his voice husky with emotion, his eyes piercing.

To a man, the Hessians averted their attention, and after a moment, returned to their earlier discussions. But Christopher knew their thoughts were elsewhere. Their contemplations, he hoped, were taking them to this country's green pastures, its vibrant woodlands.

CHAPTER 8

PHILADELPHIA
SATURDAY, AUGUST 24, 1776

Later, as he lay on the sofa attempting to sleep, Christopher replayed the Jägers' altercation in his mind. Nikolaus Bohn was sitting in a chair by the front door, half-awake. A full harvest moon lightened the room enough to distinguish the furniture.

Sometime in the middle of the night, Blum descended the stairs, saw Christopher awake, and asked, "Can we talk?"

Christopher leaned forward, motioning him to a chair next to him.

"Herr Ludwig," Blum said, "is this all true, or a dream?"

"This?" Christopher wanted to hear between the words, the unspoken, the heart of the man before him.

Blum looked out the window. Gesturing toward the outdoors, he said, "Your talk is eloquent. I want to believe America is willing to offer us freedom for nothing other than not fighting against you. The idea you would even come close to trusting us, eight different men—soldiers—you've never met before. Me, a prisoner, can sit here with you with the out-of-doors at arm's length. If I were in Johannesburg Prison, I'm certain the dungeon would be dark and dank. I'd have to fight off the rats trying to nibble bits of flesh flogged off my ragged bones."

Christopher chuckled.

True.

"In fact, if I were to do as you offer, and if America were to lose the war, I'll likely be captured and deported back to Germany. Torture's my future. If not Johannesburg, then even worse—Stuttgart."

Christopher shook his head. "America will not lose. Her cause is just, her future bright. Our men are fighting for their own homes, their families. The Redcoats' homes, their families are in London, Manchester, Liverpool." He gazed at Blum. "Or Munich, eh?"

An eyebrow raised, Blum questioned, "So, we take our chances and throw in our lot, our futures, with an untrained bunch of revolutionaries?"

"Trained enough to capture you, eh?" Christopher chuckled, then took a breath, serious in his response. "I hope so. We hope you will accept our welcome. No strings attached except leaving the fight."

Blum lowered his head, cupping his chin in the palm of his right hand.

"Karl," Christopher said, "sixty years ago a group from the Palatine region, next to Frankfurt, journeyed here. They were risking their lives. Indeed, many died aboard the crowded ships. But more than two thousand survived, settling in Pennsylvania and New York. In fact, today you may meet some of their grandchildren."

Blum was paying close attention. An eyebrow rose.

"America's German countrymen, we Deutschamerikaner," Christopher continued, "have been instrumental to her growth. We're good citizens. Hard workers. Industrious. My success is not an exception. It's a rule. I'll prove so today."

Blum nodded. "I believe you."

Simple. Declarative.

Thank You, Lord.

Blum turned toward the stairs. "I'll try again to catch some sleep."

"Before you do," Christopher said, "the miracle. What was it?"

"Miracle?"

"Jäger Schäfer's miracle."

Blum glanced at the stairway, checking to make sure no one was coming, then retook his seat.

"First, I must tell you," Blum said, "Kristian is a warrior of warriors—the one man I want by my side in the battlefield. The. One. Man."

Even in the gloom of the room, Christopher read the earnestness in Blum's eyes.

"Five, six years ago, we were in hand-to-hand combat in the battle of Kagul in the endless of hostilities, the Russo-Turkish War, taking orders from Russian Field-Marshal Rumyantsev. Rumyantsev was famous for his strategy in war. He might have cared for the lives of his men—Russians. But we Hessians? He sent us straight into the teeth of the enemy."

Christopher winced. "I know the Turks. I have scars to prove our acquaintance."

"So, too, does Kristian. There's the miracle. At the same moment, a musket ball to the chest missed his heart by a centimeter and a vicious stab from a bayonet missed a lung by less. Kristian lay dying on the hard ground of Kagul. Blood was everywhere. I killed the man who stabbed him, then knelt to the ground. I lifted Kristian to a sitting position, so he wouldn't drown in his own blood. Yet, I still heard the gurgle."

The hardened Jäger struggled to continue.

Christopher moved to the edge of the couch, no more than three feet away.

"He gazed at me," Blum said, "his eyes losing focus, and muttered, 'I have no one to remember me, Karl. Will you?'"

Blum sniffled.

"You see, Kristian has no family. None. He was such a hellion in his youth ... you see the result, the grown man."

Christopher nodded. "Go on."

Blum swiped the back of his hand across his nose. "'Will you remember me?' he asked. It was then I heard from heaven, Herr Ludwig. From heaven. I know so, though I didn't think about it then. I simply reacted. 'You won't die, Kristian," I said. "You. Will. Not!'"

Blum peered at Christopher. "Still, I saw his eyes dimming, his lifeblood seeping out of him, soaking my shirt and trousers. Musket and cannon smoke was everywhere. Men screamed in anger or in pain all around us. An extraordinary calm enveloped me, then I did something I'd never done before nor since."

His hands shaking at the memory, Blum said, "Laying a hand on his chest, I screamed to God." A soft chuckle escaped him. "As if God needed me to holler because of the noise all about us."

Christopher leaned closer to study Blum's face. Elation was imprinted across his features. He nodded as if imparting a "yes" to the memory, to the magnificence of what transpired next.

Finally, he coughed in embarrassment. "Heat, Herr Ludwig. Magnificent heat raced down my arm, through my hand and fingers ... and into his chest. In an instant, Kristian's eyes shot wide open—he gazed at me with a look of wonder. 'Am I in heaven?' he asked.

"I said, 'You're in Kagul, my friend. On the battlefield.'

"'But I feel no pain,' he said. 'I was dying, yet I feel no pain. So, this must be the afterlife.'

"I unbuttoned his shirt, scrutinized his wounds. The blood had stopped pouring out and had already begun to congeal. I shook my head. 'No, Kristian,' I said, 'God has healed you.'"

Christopher blew out a breath in amazement.

"Later, after I carried him to the field hospital, the doctor examined him, declaring it a miracle, estimating how close the musket ball and knife had come to ending his life," Blum said. "So, when I mentioned this miracle last night, it struck a chord."

"You'd think such a deliverance would have sent Kristian straight to the cross."

"It did—for a few days. But a week or so later, restored to health, back on the battlefield, he was the old Kristian again. Grim, determined, battling. Lethal as ever, as if the episode had never happened."

Christopher leaned back in the sofa, put his hands on his knees, and breathed out.

"So, now you've brought the miracle back to his attention, we pray the Holy Spirit will minister to him. He will give our friend direction."

"'Our' friend?" Blum snickered.

"Ha! You see, Karl, your friends are now mine."

Blum smiled, lifting himself out of the chair and preparing to leave.

Again, Christopher raised a hand. "So, Karl, are you closer to your own decision?"

His mouth twisting at one corner, Blum shrugged, then turned and ascended the stairs.

Christopher scratched behind an ear and lay back, resting his head on a pillow, determined to get, at least, a couple hours sleep on this enlightening night.

***

A couple of hours of satisfying sleep followed for Christopher. Then the front door creaked open, awakening him. Corporal Meyer, who had taken over sentry outside, peeked inside, spotting him. "Misses Ludwick and her helpers are here."

"Thank you, Luka. Let them in if you please."

Bustling in, Catharine flashed him a broad smile.

"You, my dear, are a sly lady," Christopher said.

"You think?" she replied, eyes alight. She turned, made a motion, and in came Gretchen, Marta, and Hannah. Expectation was written on their faces. Expectation of what, Christopher wondered. Then ...

Of course.

"We'll put together breakfast for everyone," Catharine said.

A few minutes later, mouth-watering aromas from the kitchen were drawing the men from their rooms, stifling yawns.

The odors weren't the one thing enticing them, for sure.

A few minutes later, the young women served breakfast of pancakes made with zwieback toast, along with omelets of bacon, potatoes, and Emmenthaler cheese.

"How are you this morning?" Rudolph asked.

The banter was more relaxed, more comfortable than yesterday. Further familiar questions—relaxed, sometimes comical answers. The eye contact was perhaps most revealing, and again, Catharine and Christopher were unobtrusive, observing and exchanging satisfied glances with each other and Gus Fischer.

Loud shouts outside the house interrupted the conversation. The front door flew open. A frantic Luka Meyer called, "Lieutenant Fischer!"

Christopher jumped from his chair at the same moment Fischer slid away from the table. His voice calm, Fischer asked, "Corporal?"

"A group of men." Meyer's voice was filled with trepidation. "Some are armed, sir."

Fischer hurried to the front door, Christopher at his hip with Corporals Meyer and Hoffman in tow.

Outside the threshold stood Joseph Galloway. Behind him, a dozen or more other men. Galloway himself held no rifle. Christopher knew the man well.

Feels armed combat is beneath him.

Galloway was not a large man, but one of authority who knew how to wield it. He was first introduced to Christopher by their mutual friend, Benjamin Franklin. He was a former speaker of the Pennsylvania Assembly as well as member of the Continental Congress.

In September 1774, Galloway had introduced his Plan of Union, wherein the colonies would remain under the British Empire, but have a Continental Parliament elected to three-year terms overseen by a President General appointed by the crown. The proposal had merit, but when it was narrowly defeated, Christopher staunchly stood with the revolutionaries while Galloway was fierce, declaring himself a Loyalist.

Christopher and Galloway had not spoken with one another since.

Galloway glared at Fischer. "We hear you have a bunch of Hessian soldiers."

Fischer nodded. To his credit, he remained calm, but his right hand was on the hilt of his sword. Meyer and Hoffman, meanwhile, stood to Fischer's sides, their rifles across their chests.

Christopher peered over Galloway's shoulder at the crowd. Worry edged into his thoughts.

Galloway shifted his gaze to Christopher.

"I suppose you have something to do with this, Herr Ludwick."

Emphasis on the "Herr." *So nice of you, Joseph. How long have we been countrymen together?*

Christopher determined to retain a good-natured conversation. He smiled. "You could speak to our friends, Mr. Franklin and Mr. Jefferson, or the rest of the Continental Congress," he said. "They've given full approval to our visitors."

"Folderol!"

"No such thing, my friend."

"What, exactly, do you think you're doing?"

"Offering these men a welcoming—and land—if they leave the battlefield."

"Land?!" A tall, stout behemoth behind Galloway bristled.

Thomas Crouch. Oh, my! Thomas "Misery" Crouch, the man who created "the box" all clever people said we must think outside. Misery lived ensconced inside his box, never to peer out to investigate unexpected possibilities, novel ideas. A stone mason, Crouch would have thrived in the Stone Age.

The man stepped along beside Galloway, then past him, mammoth muscles flexing beneath an open-collared shirt. He bent forward so close Christopher smelled tobacco on his breath.

"Grant them our land?" he fumed. "Give it away?"

"Not yours or mine," Christopher replied. "Nobody owns it now. The British have laid claim to this continent, but when the Revolution is won, the land is Congress's to keep, Congress's to bestow. It won't be land you or I live on, but their own—as fellow citizens of this baby country."

"New country?" Crouch spit out the words. "You've always been a dreamer, Ludwick, with your school for immigrants, the company for manufacturers, giving away your own good money for this cause and that. If you do win this war, you'll be left destitute, with a country in ruin, a demolished Philadelphia, maybe your bakery a pile of ashes."

"You're admitting your British friends would destroy our city?" This was a quarrel better argued later.

"Gentlemen," Lieutenant Fischer broke in, "let me end this, er, dialogue." Authority oozed from his pours as he spoke. His voice seemed to deepen. His eyes narrowed on Crouch. "First, Mr. Crouch, please take a couple of steps back. Intimidation won't work here."

Crouch prickled, noticed Meyer and Hoffman closing in with muskets at the ready, then retreated beside Galloway.

Fischer turned his gaze on Galloway. "Second, I know who you are, sir, your standing in this city. So, with respect, I appreciate your concern. I share your unease. Well, I did, until a day ago."

"Sure." Disbelief filled Galloway's response.

Disregarding the sentiment, Fischer plunged forward. "Now, I realize this is a good idea. A wonderful experiment, even. If Congress—notably Mr. Franklin—is behind Mr. Ludwick, the plan is worthy of our support. He hesitated, peering at Galloway, Crouch, and the armed men behind them, and asked, "Don't you think?"

"My wife, Lieutenant," said one man whom Christopher recognized as the owner of a garment store, "was scared half to death when she and her friends saw those Hessians in front of the Ludwicks' home. Those women fear for their lives. We've all read about those mercenaries. Blood-thirsty killers."

Christopher lost himself. "Mercenaries, Mr. Alonge? Blood-thirsty killers? Simply because they're German? What if I identified you with Caligula?"

He turned his attention to another of the men. "Or, Monsieur la Porte, if I characterized you with Gilles de Rais, or the Marquis de Sade?"

Both men appeared bewildered.

"Caligula, a cruel, sadistic tyrant, demanded to be worshiped as the Sun God," Christopher said. "And, Mr. Alonge, he reigned in your homeland, did he not? Italy?"

Alonge, a tall, skinny, long-faced man, shrugged a "so-what?"

Christopher didn't waste a moment, raising his voice as he eyed le Port. "Gilles de Rais—from France like you, Monsieur—enjoyed killing children, while the Marquis de Sade ..."

"I know who the Marquis de Sade is!" La Porte's face erupted into shades of red. "To make such an allegation ..."

Christopher motioned to stop la Porte.

"You see, Monsieur la Porte, these Hessians are not the German emperor. You call them 'mercenaries,' 'blood-thirsty,' 'soldiers for hire.' But they," Christopher motioned inside the house, "have no choice. They are in the army of their emperor. It is he who decided to rent their services. They have no voice in the matter, no vote."

Galloway peered at Christopher. "I know you're a righteous man, Mr. Ludwick. Can you guarantee there will be no problem from these Germans?"

Moments ago, in the kitchen, Christopher had looked each of the Hessians in the eye. He'd seen no sliver of animosity. What he had discerned was acquiescence, even from Schäfer.

"Jäger Blum," Christopher said in German, "these men are concerned you endanger the city. What do you believe?"

Blum, standing in the threshold between the sitting room and kitchen, said in German, "We will be peaceful, respectful, just as we are being respected by our keepers, you and Lieutenant Fischer."

Turning back to Galloway, Christopher said, "Our guests will act as gentlemen. They will comply to our concerns."

Galloway nodded. "Very well, then." He turned to the crowd around him.

"Let's all disperse," he said.

"But the land give-away—" objected Crouch.

"A matter to discuss with Mr. Franklin and Mr. Jefferson," Galloway said, leaning a hand on the man's shoulder. "Let's go."

Once they'd gone, Lieutenant Fischer eyed Christopher. "Word spreads fast in this city."

"The women who spotted us yesterday," Christopher said. "They're a conduit faster than Mr. Franklin's lightning strike. But think about it this way. Think of persecution as an opportunity to be a testimony."

CHAPTER 9

An hour later everyone was ready for the day.

"Itinerary?" Lieutenant Fischer asked Christopher while they stood in the sitting room, sharing a look out the front window.

Sun splashed the trees and lawns outside. Christopher hoped this portended a day of sunny results in their endeavor.

"First, our bakery," he said, "then a stroll down High Street to show off our bustling city—industrious even during a revolution, productive because our people are so."

Fischer nodded in agreement.

Eying his men, he said, "You heard our host."

"Follow me, my friends," Christopher declared, beating everyone to the front door.

The men filed outdoors behind him as he turned south, proceeding to Ludwick's Bakery a couple of blocks away.

As they approached the thirty-by thirty-foot building, Christopher's expectations proved correct. First, the fragrance of warm bread straight out of the ovens.

Second, nine o'clock. The place was active already. Despite all the apprehension because of battlefields not far distant, the business was outdoing any dreams he'd had when he'd opened the doors.

People looked up from several of the small round tables dotting the shop. A couple others who were standing in line at a counter near the rear turned to look. He knew them all, of course. By the looks on their faces they were in a combined state of surprise and curiosity about his companions.

Marta and Hannah stood behind the counter, taking orders, preparing to serve customers. Their faces lighted at the sight of the men who entered behind Christopher.

Stepping into the room from the kitchen in the rear, Martin Ross waved to Christopher. Martin was managing the shop because Catharine had left the rental house to ride out to the Germantown farm to prepare the employees there for an afternoon visit by Christopher's entourage.

Christopher nodded, then waved toward the soldiers around him.

"Moin, good friends," he announced, his eyes roaming the room. "Please say 'Hello' to new acquaintances of mine from my homeland." He pointed to a couple at one table, "Alfred and Elli, two young gentlemen here are from your old city of Hamburg."

Bernhard and Heinrich took notice of the mention of their hometown.

Alfred, a tall, jovial man, stood, motioned to chairs at their table, saying in a most welcoming tone, "*Kommen Sie zu uns.*" (Come, join us).

The Hessians hesitated. Christopher encouraged, "Go on, if you prefer."

The two glanced in unison at Blum for approval. The Jäger shrugged a "go-ahead." A moment later, there were four seated at the table. Alfred asked, *"Welche Nachbarschaft?"* (What neighborhood?)

Christopher turned his gaze to a couple standing in line near the counter. "Herman, Matilde," he said, "you came from near Buchenwald, didn't you?"

Matilde raised an eyebrow. "Offenburg. Not far away."

"I've cousins in Buchenwald," Herman offered.

Christopher's eyes widened. He locked them onto Johann. "Fellow Black Forestians, my friend."

Herman extended his hand to the young man, then said in German, "Please, tell us what's happening back home."

A few minutes later, Christopher had connected every Hessian to a person whose family, or they themselves, had emigrated to America from the Hessians' native areas.

All but one.

Christopher flashed Lieutenant Fischer an "allow-me-this" look, then sidled next to Schäfer, who was glaring at Blum, seated with an elderly man near one of the two front windows.

Christopher tugged at Schäfer's elbow. "Follow me, Kapitän Schäfer." He took two steps toward the counter. Schäfer didn't budge. Christopher gave an encouraging tug. The Jäger, appearing in disdain, capitulated.

Christopher led him past the counter to meet Martin Ross. Martin had worked for the Ludwicks for several years, becoming a stern student of the German language purely to further his knowledge.

After introducing the two, Christopher caught Schäfer's eye. "Martin here was a career soldier in His Majesty's British army. Lost his leg in the Seven Years' War, or what we called over here the French and Indian War. What did the king give you for your service, Martin?"

Martin offered a gruff laugh. "Gave me the boot faster than lightning. Showed me the door, he did." He tapped his leg with his knuckles. "Had to buy this wooden appendage on my own."

"No severance?" Christopher asked.

Martin chuckled, turning his gaze on Schäfer.

"You're a career soldier?" he asked.

Schäfer nodded.

"You think there's nothing else you can do?" Martin asked.

A shiver rattled Christopher's back. What a perfect question to pose. Did Martin somehow know things about the Jäger?

Of course. Catharine had filled in her manager on Christopher's "guests." The wisdom of Solomon.

Schäfer's jaw was set, but he seemed struck by the question. As if he'd been struggling with it since last night when Blum had raised the specter of an after-soldier life.

Christopher grabbed the moment of silence.

"I'm going to show everyone our beautiful city as well as countryside today."

Martin, his gaze still on the Jäger, smiled. "While doing so, check around you for all the opportunities Philadelphia has to offer. You might be surprised." He hesitated. "I was but am no more. Found my niche. Maybe you'll find yours."

Schäfer grunted—but it was an odd neutral grumble carrying no disdain. Was his hardened veneer softening?

Martin cocked his head and waited a beat. When no response came, he nevertheless smiled again. "Enjoy your visit, my good friend."

Martin's "guter Fruend" meant not just "friend" but "good friend." Schäfer's expression showed he took notice of the cordiality. The warmth behind it wasn't forced.

Martin nodded to Christopher, then returned to the kitchen.

Christopher took the cue. He walked Schäfer to the table where Blum sat with Arnold Klein. Klein grinned. "Christopher, we're having an interesting discussion."

"Oh?"

"Seems my poor harvest of potatoes the last couple years was because of lack of good goat manure. Goats!"

Blum laughed. "Toggenburg, in particular. Or Thuringian, if you can find them—a cross of Toggenburgs, Harzerziege, Rhönziege, and Thüringer Landziege."

"Oh?" Christopher said. "I didn't realize they had goats where you live in Düsseldorf, Karl."

Blum shook his head. "My Uncle Max and Aunt Mimi had them at their farm in Altstadt, where I spent summers growing up. Goats. Poor peoples' cows. I helped milk, cleaned the horses' stalls, helped till the fields, sow the seed, whatever they needed, including cutting the potatoes and planting the eyes." A smile filled his face. "I loved every minute of those summers. Early to bed, early to rise. Work hard, sleep solid. Watch the vegetables grow."

Taking a seat, Christopher motioned for Schäfer to join them. He did. Reluctantly.

"The secret to potatoes?" Blum said. "Plenty of manure. You can't beat goat droppings."

"Nein. Sheep," Schäfer said, his voice deadpan. "Friesian sheep to be exact. And you can add rabbits—German giant grey rabbits. Both are better than goats."

"Pshaw!" Blum responded. "We have this argument. I say goats, Kristian says sheep. We go back and forth. He never relents."

"Doesn't matter, does it?" Schäfer said. "We'll never settle the argument. Will never have sheep or goats or rabbits."

"Why not?" Christopher said. He laid a hand on Schäfer's arm, to which the Jäger flinched. But Christopher persisted. "Why not do so? Right here. Right out by my farm in Germantown. There are two plots of land—one for each of you. Get your goats, Karl. Get your sheep and rabbits, Kristian. Have a competition. In the meantime, grow some potatoes. I'll buy as many as you want to sell."

Brows knit on both Jägers. They exchanged a look. Eagerness? Enlightenment? Gears were whirling in their minds.

Making progress here, Lord.

All the while, Marta and Hannah roamed the room, offering coffee and tea and gingerbread and pastries whose beauty matched the aroma filling the cafe. Christopher sensed a different kind of aroma—one of growing friendships. The place was warming up and not just temperature-wise.

★★★

A half-hour later, the men rose to leave the bakery and follow Christopher and Lieutenant Fischer.

"Do come and visit us," Elli said to Bernhard and Heinrich. "I'll bake you a strudel you won't soon forget."

Smiles filled the faces of the two young men.

Herman hugged Johann like he was a long-lost relative, and Matilde grabbed at Johann's elbow, whispering as though her comment were mother-to-son, "You look so tired. Get some sleep."

Blum shook Arnold's hand. "Thank you for reminding me of the joys of growing things, sir."

"Arnold," Klein corrected.

"Arnold." Blum smiled as he turned to leave.

Neither did Christopher miss the furtive looks Rudolph, Hans, and Emil gave to certain young ladies.

"Gus," Christopher said to the lieutenant, "you lead the way along High Street. We'll follow."

Fischer nodded agreement, beginning the westward trek. Christopher took a post amid the Hessians.

This was a busy street, even with a revolution being fought a short distance away. Saturday was market day. Horse-drawn wagons and carriages rolled by them, their riders gazing with curiosity at the double line of men strolling along the sidewalk.

There were pedestrians as well, though far more women than men.

To their right stood the London Coffee Shop, then the Quakers Great Meetinghouse.

To their left, from Front Street behind them to Third Street South ran a head house, an enclosed structure filled with vendors on normal days—before the revolution.

"The largest head house in the colonies," Christopher said. "Before so many of our men went off to the battlefield, this place would be bubbling with people. Still, see all the tables for artisans and craftsmen of all sorts to sell their wares—myriad creations from quilts to leatherware to jams, jellies."

"Yum," said Hans.

"You just ate," Emil chided.

"I wonder if anyone makes harnesses or saddles," Johann said.

Christopher peered inside. "A-ha," he said, pointing. "Randall is away with Washington, but his wife, Lyn, is here. Go see for yourself."

Johann hastened to a booth some twenty feet away. Luka Meyer took a cue from Fischer to follow him. Christopher held his breath, hoping for constraint on the corporal's behalf.

Indeed, Luka pulled up short, rifle across his chest, paying attention as Johann spoke to Lyn Middleton, a middle-aged woman whose young daughter sat on a stool beside her, reading a book.

"Exquisite craftsmanship," Johann said in wonder, running a hand along a mahogany-shaded saddle. The lady cast a puzzled look at him, not understanding his German.

Luka stepped up. "He said your saddle shows exquisite craftsmanship, ma'am."

Lyn broke out in a smile. "My husband's. He does beautiful work. You must see his men's belts. So intricate. But he is proudest of his saddles."

Luka translated. Johann responded, "Tell her she too ought to be proud. Staying at home with a wee one can't be easy."

Luka's translation drew a wide smile. "Oh, I'm running the shop now. Have always done the books."

Hearing her response, Johann was taken aback. Women in Germany weren't known for such a thing.

Women also manned the next few stalls.

Christopher introduced each of them to one or two of the Hessians, who were taking interest.

"This is Cornelia Smith, whose teas we sell at the bakery," he said.

"Let me introduce Deborah Connolly, whose molasses we use in our gingerbread," he said.

"Hannah Weston," he said, "these gentlemen might, someday, be here to buy some of your lavender for certain young ladies."

In each case, the women showed no fear or anxiety. They were pleasant, even joyful. Deborah even exchanged glances with Bernhard, or was it Heinrich? This was a good thing.

Several minutes later, the entourage strolled past Two Street. Christopher pointed to the tall, magnificent Christ Church, its spire reaching toward the heavens.

"Our brothers in Christ fill this church all the time," he said. "They hold joint Christmas and Easter celebrations with St. Michael's along with our other Lutheran church, Zion. A joyous time."

The impressive District Court House dominated the street front to their right all the way to Third Street, where two stone buildings constituted the jail. Or had constituted the jail. Once hostilities erupted, the prison served as a military headquarters for the Colonial Army.

"Justice will be meted here once we win this war," Christopher said. "True justice. Not the king's twisted version."

Christopher felt agreement in sentiment around him, but then he noticed two soldiers, rifles across their chests, who fronted the steps into the building. Christopher cringed at the portent of peril.

Lieutenant Fischer nodded to them. They saluted in return, curiosity in their visages.

Go ahead, be curious, boys. But do nothing brash.

He drew the Hessians' attention away by pointing across the street to the four-story brick home of Benjamin Franklin. The unassuming structure did not impress the Hessians.

"Our greatest thinker lives there," he said, "and he does not distinguish between rich and needy. In fact, he publishes a periodical he calls *Poor Richard's Almanac.*"

Christopher straightened his shoulders when they crossed Fourth Street. Next came the *Pennsylvania Gazette.*

"My good friend Robert Aitken's newspaper," he declared with a smile. "Aiken is the publisher of Thomas Paine's *Common Sense.* You may have heard of this pamphlet."

He looked around him. Finding some shrugs, some bewildered looks.

"*Common Sense*," he said, "may be the mightiest public cry lighting the idea of independence on fire. This Revolution might not exist without it. Liberty, not the iron-fisted domination of a king or emperor."

Nods of appreciation replaced the vacant visages.

Next came the Indian King Tavern, an establishment drawing oh's and ah's from the younger Germans, plus chuckles from their American counterparts. Several people in the city, mostly women, had turned empty rooms in their homes into makeshift taverns, but this was the real thing.

"Junto meets there," Christopher said, "a group of men dedicated to improving Philadelphia's civic life."

They passed Fifth Street. There it was—Robert Morris's home, across the street from the Bank of North America. None of the eyes were on the bank. All were riveted to the show the Morris home displayed. Bracketed by a tall brick wall on each side, the brick home was at once simple and stylish, with symmetry on display. Four ceiling-height windows allowed outside light to flood the second floor as well as two small dormers above them.

"Our bakery often caters here," Christopher said. "You ought to see the grounds behind those brick walls. A haven from the world."

The ooh's and ah's from this view were a different appreciation than those for the tavern.

High Street indeed proved Christopher's point—Men of purpose, men of dreams, men from another world accomplished much here they'd never achieve as subjects to an emperor.

When they reached Eighth Street, they turned north.

"I want you to see something of which I am very proud," Christopher said. "Our school, which is closed for the summer."

A two-story wooden structure lay ahead to the left. When they reached the building, he dug into a pocket, pulling out a key to open the front door. As he reached for the knob, the door opened.

There stood Didi Schneider, the headmistress who, despite being seventy-something years old, was as full of vigor as anyone half her age. Tireless, relentless in her desire to fill her students with the knowledge to be successful, she was a pillar.

Christopher considered her the minor cornerstone of the building, next to the Major Cornerstone of Christ himself. Didi used the Bible to teach English, history, and mathematics, not to mention geography.

Spotting the men coming along the street, she set her smile of greeting to its highest brightness, which was sometimes blinding.

"Herron!" she spoke the German for "gentlemen," for she had determined half the men with him shared his heritage ... or perhaps she had heard about them through the Philadelphia grapevine, which made the rounds three times in the span any newspaper was published.

She made a dramatic sweep of an arm, inviting them inside.

"A tour?" she asked, eyeing Christopher.

He nodded agreement, then introduced her to the group.

"Didi," he then said, "is our inspiration. She has taken our seed and has nurtured the seed into full blossom."

She smiled a thank you, then declared, "English. You will learn America's language so you will be our friends, able to enjoy a life unlike back home, I assure you."

She swept ahead of them into a room filled with perhaps thirty desks facing a three-square-foot blackboard. Christopher was proud of this blackboard, for it was perhaps historic to have such a large piece of slate. Even students in Europe more often used small pieces of slate or squares of wood coated with paint and grit, framed with wood. With the blackboard, the teacher instructed the entire class at once instead of doing so individually. This had hastened the learning process for the growing number of immigrants.

A small slate lay atop each desk. There were inkwells, also. But with the price of scarce ink, blackboards were more useful—indeed preferred.

"Our main classroom," she said, "for the bulk of our students are young, but ..." She breezed past them all, heading to an adjoining room half its size with a couple dozen chairs facing a small desk.

"Here we teach young and old from Germany. Next door," she pointed to her left, "are rooms where we teach French, Spanish, and Swedish speakers, thanks to Mr. Ludwick, Mr. Morris, Dr. Rush, as well as others in the community."

Christopher felt the eyes looking his way. This school was his brainchild. But others, Didi for instance, deserved the credit for making the enterprise work smoothly.

Suddenly, he knew Didi's "lesson" had been taught and consumed. Time had come to return to the Quarry Street house, then take these men to Germantown, to his farm, to land these men might claim for their own. The penultimate enticement, second to their personal freedom.

He thanked Didi. Turning to Lieutenant Fischer, he said, "Time to take them home, Gus."

Fischer nodded consent. Several of the Hessians thanked Didi on their way out the door.

On their return, up Seventh Street then back along Arch Street, he pointed out George Mason's clothing store.

"George and his wife, Helen, dine with us once a month. A wonderful time."

Next a haberdashery.

"Best hats in America, no doubt. The owners came here from Scotland. Wonderful people, the MacLeans."

Then a tailor.

"A fellow from Brussels owns this business. Arrived not long after I did, twenty-two years ago."

A hairstylist, outside which he raised an arm to gain everyone's attention.

"Mind you all, women also have rein here in America. Our dear friend, Margaret Duncan, when her husband died six years ago, announced she would carry on business as usual, offering a large assortment of goods. She has.

"Also, merchant John Rhea's widow, Mary, has carried on their business since he died three years ago."

Yes, each of these businesses was an accomplice in Christopher's mission.

Am I a salesman? No, an ambassador.

★★★

An hour later, the Ludwick farm loomed a short distance from the wagon. Again, Lieutenant Fischer rode on ahead, Private Nikolaus Bohn feathered the wagon's reins, Corporal Jacob Hoffman and Private Anton Wagner rode on board with the Hessians. Corporal Luka Meyer trailed on his horse.

Christopher looked around him. What he observed confirmed the nature of the group was less cautious, far less wary. Anxiety had slackened. The young men on both sides of the war were more apt to dispute the pronunciation of a German word than oppose each other in combat.

He chuckled to himself. He hadn't yet reached a state of jubilation or euphoria, but he felt triumph was on the horizon. The sensation escalated as they drew nearer to his farm. A batch of teenagers was harvesting summer squash in the southeastern field. In the distance beyond them, others were on ladders picking Winesap apples—harvested in September in normal years. But troops were hungry now. His plan was to ship as many as possible to the Flying Camp and perhaps even to Washington's army on Long Island.

Catharine, in on his plan to come here, was at the end of the drive beside their farm manager, Hermann Meyer. She waved. Christopher waved back. If he had any nervousness at all, it was calmed at once.

Even Fischer, some of his men and several Hessians waved back.

My, my. What has my wife prepared?

Catharine and Hermann walked toward the farmhouse. Christopher motioned Private Bohn to follow but not overrun them. When they reached the front porch, he rested his hand on Bohn's. "Stop right here, Nikolaus."

Christopher exchanged a look with his wife, then climbed from the buckboard, waving for everyone to join him.

When everyone was gathered, he whispered to Hermann to tell everyone about the farm.

"In German?" Hermann asked.

"The one tongue these men understand."

Hermann nodded, then let his eyes roam over all those before him. "From here to as far as you can travel in two days, the soil is rich." He pointed to the youths gathering squash in the land adjacent to the road. "From squash and cucumbers to other vegetables, including Christopher's carrots." This last was said with a smile.

Hermann aimed a finger to the north. "An apple orchard and plum trees over there," he said, then gesturing to the northwest, added, "In fields on the other side of the house, we grow potatoes, corn ... everything anyone wants."

Catharine stepped between Hermann and Christopher, her grin something to behold. She winked at her husband. "Don't forget my garden of herbs on the other side of this porch."

"Plus, a hundred acres of wheat on our Lancaster farm," Christopher said.

At the end of the drive rose a fifty-fifty-foot, two-story barn. Blum pointed. "What's in the barn?"

"Draft horses, dairy cows, dairy goats," Hermann said. "They share a large fenced-in pasture behind the barn. The small stone building to the right of the barn is a milkhouse. Behind it is a stone smokehouse. Also back there is a large chicken coop, with more than enough laying hens to supply the bakery."

A tall, lanky woman emerged from the house, peering out at the mob of visitors. Hermann waved her to him. "I might have the title of farm manager, but my wife, Elli, runs this place. Our daughters, who are somewhere out there in the fields, help with the milking and other chores."

"Hard work," muttered one of the Hessians.

"The German way," Hermann said. "We come from farming families. From the Rhineland, as do many of our neighbors out here in Germantown."

Elli turned to Catharine. "Can you help me inside?"

"Of course." She cast her eyes toward Christopher, raising four fingers.

Christopher took his cue—continue his tour of the surrounding land before returning for a hearty lunch in forty minutes.

"All aboard," he said as he walked back to the wagon. Sitting tall on his roan, Lieutenant Fischer pulled alongside the buckboard. "We'll amble along beside you, Christopher. You lead the way."

Several minutes later, Christopher gestured for Private Bohn to stop the wagon. They could see perhaps a half mile to the north. Fields stretched a distance until running into a deep forest.

He stood, turning toward the Hessians.

"Look about you," he said. "We have a continent to fill. I don't know how big she is, but she offers something for everyone. There's enough right here on this property before us for my good friends, Jägers Blum and Schäfer, to settle their dispute of various growing powers."

He chuckled as did a few others, including Blum. Schäfer?

Yes! Schäfer's laugh was rueful, perhaps. But still ...

"This property is available. I'm certain Congress can make it yours. Come. Look."

He climbed down and walked several yards to the meadow. Blum trailed behind him.

"Stick your hands in the soil," Christopher said, pointing to the ground.

Blum knelt. Driving his right hand into the earth like a trowel, he pulled it out, holding forth a palm full of dark, rich soil.

"Perfect," he said. "All it needs is a healthy helping of goat dung."

Christopher laughed aloud.

Behind him the response came. "Rabbit."

He turned. Schäfer still sat with the others in the wagon, but a crooked smile crossed his face.

Then, as they were all about to reboard the wagon, Christopher raised an arm to get their attention.

"William Penn, for whom this colony of Pennsylvania is named, declared: 'Men must be governed by God, or they will be ruled by tyrants.'

"You'll see no tyrants here, my friends. At least not in the public realm, not where all men are created equal."

"Christoff," said Blum, who was climbing back into the buckboard, "how did you finance your home, your many houses, this farm? How much did you borrow?"

"Not a British pound, nor a German mark," Christopher said. "Christoff Ludwig borrows nothing." He shook his head. His stance was firm on this. Buy what you can afford. Nothing more. Be frugal with yourself, liberal with others.

But this might pose a problem for men accepted into this fledgling country with no means of support. He cupped his chin in his hand, pondering.

Then, "*Alles ist in Butter*," he said, meaning "everything is in butter," or "everything is fine." "I did come here with money in my pocket—something you're not able to do. So, this, I'm sure, we can deal with."

"*Das Blaue vom Himmel versprechen*," Schäfer said, warning Christopher not to make an unkeepable promise.

"I am not promising the blue of the sky," Christopher said. "If Congress doesn't help financially, Christoff Ludwig will, personally. I said I will never lie to you, and I won't."

He scanned the faces before him, wondering at the considerations going through their minds. Concerns of many kinds, of course. Their own lives as well as their families in Germany. Their plans, if, and when, they returned from war. If they stayed here, was it possible to immigrate loved ones here too? What work would they have?

He thought of his own sister, Helena, with her husband and children in Amsterdam. He remembered their parting hugs when he left to live in America. Two orphans, she and him. Yet she had resisted his repeated letters imploring her to come to America. Weightless missives. Would these men have better luck in persuasion with their loved ones than he?

He had shown them the city as well as country—proof there were all sorts of opportunity. Though America was a strange land to them, many of her residents were Germans, who had found joy, success, bounty, and Godliness here, as he himself had.

The breath he took was deep, fresh, heartfelt. Then, *"Bringen Sie auf die Beine,"* he said. "We want you to get your feet on the ground quickly. This means more than land of your own. You've seen the free school we created to teach the language, the customs of America."

"Do we spend time in prison before this would happen?" asked Johann.

Christopher shook his head. *"Nein."*

"We wouldn't have to fight for you Americans?" Bernhard asked.

Christopher smiled. "Not even fusiliers."

"I'm sure you're short of sharpshooters," Rudolph said.

"Use your skills to hunt deer and rabbit." Christopher offered a crooked smile. "I'll even buy the venison along with the Jägers' potatoes."

Chuckles met this promise.

★★★

Minutes later, they were back at the Ludwick farm. As they rode into the driveway, Schäfer pointed to the orchard.

"I see two African women." He glared at Christopher. Accusingly, he said, "So you—who speak with such liberality of freedom, of everyone having the ability in America to earn their way, show their skills—have slaves."

Christopher did not respond to Schäfer but motioned for Bohn to stop the horses. He then climbed from the wagon. "Chloe! Lucretia!" he called out, beckoning for the two women to come.

Chloe was around forty years old, Lucretia a teenager. Full of smiles, they sauntered toward the entourage of men—neither in haste nor dawdling. So not fearful, not responding to the call of an overlording master.

"Mr. Christopher," said the older woman, "wonderful to see you."

Christopher smiled broadly. "Chloe, I want you ladies to answer these men in whatever they ask."

"Of course." The two women turned their attention to the Hessians.

Lieutenant Fischer offered to Schäfer, "I'll act as the interpreter."

Schäfer shrugged an "okay," then jumped from the wagon and confronted Chloe.

The following exchange worked smoothly, with Schäfer speaking in German, Chloe and Lucretia answering in English, and Fischer interpreting. Schäfer stared at Chloe. "You work the orchards?"

"Yes," Chloe said, "as well as the garden ... sometimes in the kitchen."

"Hard labor. Long hours. Little sleep."

Chloe looked at him in astonishment. "Why would you say such a thing?"

Schäfer straightened his shoulders. "Am I wrong?"

"Yes. Yes. And yes. Elli, the lady who operates the farm, works alongside us often—as do her husband and daughter, Clara."

Schäfer's brow knitted. He studied her for a moment. "Your pay is a roof over your head, a couple meals a day?"

"No. We're paid the same as the others here, equal to the workers at farms nearby."

Schäfer guffawed. "You expect us to believe a slave is paid?"

"Slave?" Chloe's eyes went wide. "You think us slaves?"

Schäfer coughed a nonresponse.

"Sir, we are free women. Mr. Christopher bought us and several others at a slave auction in Virginia, then set us free moments later. We can leave whenever we want. But why would we?"

Lucretia cut in, "We love this place. We live in a house, have our own bedding and kitchen. I have my own tree in the orchard here. Whatever apples grow on it are mine. The same with all of us. We can each claim a tree in the orchard."

Schäfer turned to look at Christopher. His gaze was inscrutable. Did he not believe such forthright answers? Was it a look of dissatisfaction he had not unveiled a dark side of Christopher?

"Any other questions?" Christopher asked, his eyes passing over the Hessians.

Emil said, "One. Are you married, Lucretia?"

When Fischer interpreted, Lucretia blushed despite the molasses color of her skin. She lowered her eyes and shook her head, but her lips parted in a smile.

Johann and Hans, sitting on either side of their friend, both chuckled. Hans poked Emil on his shoulders.

"Very brazen of you," Johann said.

Emil shrugged. "Can't hurt a guy to ask."

Appreciative laughs broke out, for Lucretia was indeed pretty. She also appeared to be within a few months of Emil's age.

"Agreed," Blum said.

Schäfer kept silent.

Christopher spoke up. "Thank you, ladies. You're always a pleasure."

Their faces remained bright as they turned back to their work.

***

Minutes later, the group was inside the Ludwick farmhouse, seated around two long tables pushed together. Tantalizing aromas had met them even before they stepped through the door. Christopher's nose told him Catharine was at her culinary best. She and Elli had spared nothing in their preparations.

They had plucked Hilde Becker and Anna Neumann from their apple-picking duties to help in the kitchen. Both women were close in age to the Jägers. The four women, along with Elli and Hermann's daughter, Clara, delivered hot platters of food—the meal a feast for kings.

Christopher wondered if anything was left in the larder.

Beef roulade, an onion pie called Zwiebelkuchen, and appropriately, Jäger Schnitzel, which featured pork steaks pounded thin, sour cream, mushrooms, and butter.

What was baking in the large wood stove? He discerned cinnamon and cloves. Apple streusel pie.

Oh, my!

Christopher contemplated deep friendships so often born through dining with one another. True community sometimes becoming even intimate. This, he had discovered in their gingerbread bakery. He pictured the many times Jesus reclined at one table or another, engaging, sharing, loving. Then, he prayed the Lord would accomplish great things in these next moments—an elaborate meal but on a simple table in a simple farmhouse in Germantown, Pennsylvania. Fostering simple friendships lasting forever.

Anna, Hilde, and Clara poured milk in everyone's glasses. Christopher noticed Blum's steady eye on Anna, a golden-haired widow who lived nearby with her parents. She returned Blum's look with a half-smile.

True, he was handsome, while she a full-figured mother of one young boy.

Then Christopher asked, "Jäger Blum, will you lead us in grace?"

The soldier was taken aback. He glanced around the table, at his comrades, at Schäfer, in particular. He hesitated, then folded his hands, bowing his head. *"Lider Vater im Himmel, Lafs eshier weder Hafs noch Streitgeben Und nur Freude, Liebe und Grite walten."*

Christopher thanked God for this blessing, asking him to let there be neither hate nor quarrels, may love and joy reign.

Blum looked at Catharine, who was standing with her back to the counter. He shook his head in wonder.

"Mrs. Ludwick," he said, "this is a banquet beyond belief. I'm in amazement. We can't thank you enough."

Catharine caught Christopher's eye. She smiled, then, "Herr Blum, food is at the heart of feeling at home." She put a hand on Elli's shoulder. "For many, many of our neighbors out here, Germany was their home. They brought its tradition, foods, culture, and religion with them. This meal before you," she waved her hand over the feast, "is not unusual—"

"Yes," Elli cut in, "we would have served Sauerbraten for you, but we didn't have the four hours to bake it."

Rudolph chuckled at this, his face lighting up. "The beef roulade would have been more than enough."

"Or the Zwiebelkuchen," Hans blurted out. There were hugs, thank you's, smiles, and handshakes—not one of which appeared pretense.

"You're a big onion," Emil said, swatting Hans on the shoulder. "You don't need any more."

Laughs around the table set the mood for a joyous meal. Every plate was finished, every serving bowl empty. Then came dessert.

When they had finished the pie, Schäfer pointed to the bit left on the pie plate, caught Hilde's eye, pointing to his dish. "A dollop more of the Apple Streusel."

"Do I hear a 'please'? I'm not your servant," she said. Her glare would wilt even the strongest man.

"You're theirs," he said with a nod toward Christopher and Catharine.

"I am not!"

Schäfer was taken aback. "I apologize."

She hesitated, made him wait a few beats, appeared to be scrutinizing him—his appearance as well as his mind. Finally, she set her shoulders and whispered, "Apology accepted."

"Truly, miss," he said, "I am sorry—both for my attitude and my misunderstanding."

Now this was a different Schäfer. Perhaps the hidden Kristian Schäfer.

"None of us here are servants or slaves," Hilde said. "Such a thing is frowned upon both by my faith and my family."

Schäfer placed his fork across the back of his plate, indicating he was done with his meal, then offered her an oblique smile. But not before she ladled the last piece of pie onto his dish.

He laughed, offering a "thank you" as he scooped it into his mouth with a satisfied smile.

Christopher nudged Lieutenant Fischer to get everyone out to head back to the city. The breakup reminded him of a large family leaving after a Christmas meal.

As the Hessians filed out the kitchen door, Jäger Blum tapped Anna on the shoulder. In a low voice he said, "Thank you for your hospitality and helping Mrs. Ludwick and Mrs. Meyer."

"My pleasure" was followed by a look certain to win the hearts of half the men there.

Schäfer tipped his head to Hilde. "Auf Wiedersehen, Fräulein."

She frowned in return.

Christopher, trailing behind all the other men, cupped Catharine's elbow in his hand, pulling her to him. He hoped his kiss told her all he felt but couldn't say with everyone nearby.

"Smashing," he said to Elli with a grin.

"I pray we helped."

He whispered to Catharine, "Why Hilde?"

"She's as stubborn as the Jäger. You'll see." Her eyes sparkled.

A perfect match then.

★★★

Christopher instructed Lieutenant Fischer to lead the caravan westward, past Germantown, through pastures and forests toward Lancaster, then circle back to Philadelphia.

On their return to the city, they rode along Chestnut Street, parallel to High Street. They caught the attention of pedestrians all along the way. Christopher nodded to some, waved to others.

They passed the one-hundred-foot-long Independence Hall. The Georgian-style brick building, with wooden, winged buildings on either side, appeared more a country house than an urban public building. The symmetry had always impressed Christopher.

"Where our Congress has been meeting," he told the Hessians with a wave of his hand, keeping to himself the amount of time he'd spent there, serving on various continental committees. "The peoples' house."

"Men meet to discuss what actions the city and the country should take?" Johann asked.

Christopher nodded.

"What they decide is what is done? Truthfully?"

"Normally."

"I don't know how you do it without an emperor or king," Hans said.

"Proverbs tells us to seek the counsel of many, not one," Christopher said. "Unless, of course, the one is Jesus."

Beside him, Private Bohn nodded with vigor.

A good Christian.

Soon they reached the Quarry Street house. Everyone unloaded and walked inside.

Lieutenant Fischer held back Corporals Luka Meyer and Jacob Hoffman.

"Lax!" Christopher overheard Fischer say. "These men are under orders to fight for the Redcoats. Until they agree to Congress's land grant, they're not our pals." He spat out the last word, adding, "I want your eyes vigilant, or the two stripes you have will be ripped from your uniforms."

"Sir!" the two replied, saluting.

"Then go do your duty."

Fischer's face was scarlet. Christopher waited until the two soldiers were out of hearing. He gazed at the lieutenant. Fischer read his displeasure. "What!?"

Christopher lifted his hands in front of his chest. "I agree, but you've noticed, as I have, we're winning them over. Maybe we shouldn't 'cozy up' to them, but don't you think rubbing elbows is okay?"

"I don't want my men to get lackadaisical. Lord's sake, they're carrying weapons! Those Hessians, in particular the Jägers, wouldn't be patsies in hand-to-hand combat."

Christopher turned the page. "Gus, what is the most powerful personal relationship in the world?"

Fischer laid his chin in the palm of a hand, then replied, "Between a man and a woman."

"So, what would be most persuasive thing in these men's minds—even more so than the land grant?"

Fischer looked over Christopher's shoulder toward the house. A beat passed, then, "A woman they fancy?"

"Right. Well, have you noticed any fancying going on the last couple days?"

"I'm not blind."

Christopher shrugged a "well-there-you-are" then headed toward the house.

***

In the evening, sitting around the parlor, with men drinking tea and munching on gingerbread with warm butter spread over it, the home appeared like a lodge.

Christopher sat on the couch, amidst the swirl, the topics ranging from hunting and fishing (talk dominated by Rudoph and Johann), to the sweltering heat of a foundry (wisdom from Bernhard and Heinrich, whose fathers worked at such a place), to pretty ladies (comments from all the men).

Christopher wondered at no one mentioning homesickness. There seemed to be little allure to return to previous lives.

Then the discussion turned to risks versus rewards, above all the choice before them of changing their lives by jumping into the unknown.

"A risk not taken is a reward not received," said Blum at one point.

"Assuming there is a reward at all," Schäfer countered. "Maybe a penalty awaits. Maybe death."

"If you don't go after a reward, you'll never get one—no?" Blum said.

"All of a sudden you're certain of many things."

"I'm certain of this—if you want something you don't have, you must do something you've never done."

Crossing his arms in front of him, Schäfer set his chin. "Such is why they call the dilemma 'risk-reward,' mein Freund."

Rudolph injected, "The reward being to take America's offer, thus risk being caught after the war, then tried for desertion?"

"Or," Johann said, "staying here could be both a risk and a reward. Your reward is a risk. Is our new life worth leaving our present life in the past?"

"I've been to Wiesbaden House of Corrections," Schäfer said. "You don't want to spend a day there. An hour."

"As a deserter, you wouldn't," Blum said. "You'd never be sent back to Germany. You'd be flogged and shot right here."

Schäfer bowed his head. He uttered a silent "Risk-reward."

Christopher sensed a turning of the tide against accepting America's offer.

The ominous threat of death tends to have this effect.

He jumped in with, "I know crushing defeat from not one but two wars. I know the sound of cannon balls crushing the fortification I assumed safe. I know the horror of a dear friend dying in my arms, others an arm's-length away, the fright of the musket balls meant for me missing by a hair's breadth. I know the feeling of wishing I were anywhere else—anywhere—but dodging a bayonet from an enemy as frightened as I was."

He felt a drop of perspiration on his forehead, but continued, "These memories sometimes burst into my sleep. They shake me awake drenched in sweat—even after three decades. Is this what you want? Your 'payment' for serving your emperor—a surrogate for King George?"

The question was met with silence. The silence stretched through a time that saw everyone climb the stairs to bed— their minds swirling, Christopher was certain.

CHAPTER 10

A cool mid-morning breeze soothed the certain coming heat as the Hessians moved along Arch Street toward St. Michael's Lutheran Church for the German-language service. They were unconsciously marching, it appeared. Christopher was in the midst of them, chatting away, attempting to slow them, to distract their "left-right-left" into more of a casual stroll.

Good luck.

Yet, this exercise was not about appearances. To a large degree, the experience was about continuing to make the Germans feel comfortable in their surroundings—at home.

Walking along before and behind them, the American guards were trying to appear inconspicuous, despite rifles held tight to their chests.

"A finer Philadelphia day you won't experience," Christopher said to Rudolph beside him. He had taken a particular liking to the proud young man, considering hiring the sharpshooter to live on one of his farms and hunt for him. Philadelphia was overflowing with deer.

Venison was never declined at any dining table with which Christopher was familiar.

He continued, "Our fields are full of choice squash, cucumbers, green beans. Besides deer, our forests with turkey, black bear, elk, fox ..."

Rudolph nodded. "Still, deer are the most graceful, fast, cunning, elusive. I enjoy the challenge. They're the greatest test. What I live for."

"You live for the challenge?" Christopher asked.

"Ha!" said Johann, who was walking in front of them. He turned, eying Rudolph. "Your greatest challenge is Gretchen. Good luck with that hunt."

Laughter erupted from those nearest.

Christopher smiled to himself, knowing Gretchen would be at the service, perhaps singing in the choir.

People were pouring into the church. Many of the able-bodied men were away fighting the war, leaving St. Michael's with pews half-filled with women, children and older folks.

Several of them waved to Christopher, but with odd, questioning looks on their faces.

Who are these men I'm accompanying? You'll soon find out. But don't be alarmed.

When they entered the large front double doors of the building Christopher scanned the pews, spotting a familiar blue bonnet near the front in the second row, right side. Catharine. Sitting in their spot, but with three beside her.

Christopher wasn't certain but would wager those three were Hannah, Marta, and Gretchen.

Sweetheart, you are brilliant.

Lieutenant Fischer, leading the entourage, stepped to the left. He motioned for all the men to sit in the rear two pews.

"Rudolph." Johann elbowed his friend. He pointed. "Your prey."

"Prey?"

"Challenge, then."

"Challenge?" Rudolph puffed out his chest. "My bride-to-be."

Christopher listened with care as a moment clicked by. Two moments.

Then Johann understood his friend's comment and whispered shallowly, so only the two of them heard.

But Christopher's sharp hearing allowed him to discern a crow cawing a half mile away.

"'Bride-to-be'? So you're staying? You're deserting?"

"Not deserting. Escaping."

Christopher glanced over to see Johann leaning back in his pew, a somber look on his face, perhaps pondering the impact of Rudolph's decision on his own situation. He prayed, wondering if the same type of conversation might be taking place between Emil and Hans, who was besotted by Marta. Radiant girls attracted young men as he had been drawn to his own Catharine—in her case charisma more than any other trait.

The choir, a couple dozen teenagers to great-grandparents, stood from their three pews along the front-left wall, then sang Nun freut euch, lieben Christen g'mein, one of Martin Luther's hymns, meaning "Now rejoice, my dear Christians."

As the words passed by, Christopher wondered if Henry Mühlenberg had selected the song for him—"Let's jump happily, that we confidently sing with pleasure and love"—or perhaps their special guests—"To the devil I was trapped, in death I was lost; my sin tormented me night and day, in which I was born."

Perhaps Henry chose this hymn for both purposes. "The Lord said to me, 'Hold on to Me, you shall succeed now; I give myself completely for you, I will wrestle for you; for I am yours and you are mine, and where I abide, there shall you be, the enemy shall not separate us.'"

The hymn was written two hundred years earlier, yet still held a place in the first Lutheran hymnal, *Achtliederbuch*. Luther's lyrics served a further purpose.

Christopher bowed his head, his hands folded together at his waist.

Draw these men to You, Lord. And to this land of Yours.

★★★

When the last word was sung, Mühlenberg, in full regalia, loomed over the congregation from the pulpit raised three steps higher than the altar.

"Threat assessment!" he declared, looking down his long thin nose at his congregants. "A military term meaning, well, what it says—assessing a threat. A threat against you, your family, your city, your country, your army, or navy unit.

"Americans assessed the threat of King George against our colonies and determined to respond. Now we're paying the price. So is England. Death reigns on both sides. Musket shots know no names, no nationality. They take lives on both sides. Yet we can, we must respond to the threat."

He scanned the congregation. "Ideals! When making our threat assessment, we must weigh its impact on our ideals—as a people, as a culture, but with utmost importance as the body of Christ. Would our Savior urge us to trade musket ball for musket ball? Would He suggest living in silence? Like He himself did on the cross before Pilate?"

Where is this going? Christopher wondered.

"Yet here we are," Mühlenberg said, "embroiled in life-and-death battle. America assessed the threat and responded. A national thing. I want to discuss the personal threat assessment.

"I must tell you, dear friends, our greatest threat today or any day is not England, not her allies. Our greatest threat is not even the enemy of our souls, Satan. No, it's easy to blame him when our greatest threat is ourselves—the weakness of our flesh to resist his temptations. Sometimes, even our determination to obey our own inner desires instead of God's commands."

Mühlenberg leaned forward, hands gripping the sides of the podium, eyes intense. "The devil's temptations—either toward pride or power, or a million other impulses or appetites—will come our way, sometimes in waves. Expect them. Our response lies within us. Yes, the greatest threat is ourselves—our belief or lack thereof, our trust or lack thereof, our knowledge of our Lord or lack thereof."

The preacher drew a deep breath, eased back on his heels, and added, "Assess yourself today. Are you your own worst threat? It should not be, because, loved ones, when we ask Jesus in—into our hearts—He cannot coexist with the enemy. One or the other must go!"

Christopher recalled Joshua, Caleb and the other Israelites who went to spy out the Amalekites and assess their threat. The Jews' greatest threat was their own unbelief God would go before them to conquer the enemy.

Mühlenberg was unrelenting.

"Too often, we blame someone else for our sins," he said. "I did this because my father was too stringent. I did that because my mother was too lenient. My brother was obnoxious. My friends were pushing me there. He-he. They-they. Satan-Satan. Everyone but me-me.

"No, you did so because you were a self-indulgent sinner; now, you're full of excuses."

A sniffle at Christopher's side drew his eye to Johann. The young man was trying to hide it, but he was swiping his nose on his shirt sleeve.

Next to him, Rudolph appeared stoic. But Christopher stole a glance in the other direction. Emil's eyes were red as were Hans's.

He dared not look toward the two Jägers in the row behind him. Schäfer wouldn't be touched. Right? Christopher considered—then prayed.

Mühlenberg reached below the Bible on his pulpit to the cubbyhole beneath, extracted something, and set a box atop the Bible.

The box was beautiful, of obvious German artistry, about eight inches cubed, painted bright blue with images of finely dressed men and women.

Mühlenberg caressed the antiquity as if it were a treasure to hold dearly.

"We need to purpose to fulfill our purpose," Muhlenberg declared, looking along the front pews, then the back right corner where sat the dozen younger men as if they were at attention. "But what is your special reason for living?"

He leaned forward and tugged at an ear, letting his eyes roam. Then, "So many of us have been inside our own boxes—either ones we ourselves constructed, or others have built. We've allowed ourselves to be placed within. We may have come to adore our box, treasure its familiarity. We've allowed this box to define us, to perpetuate our condition because we've known no other life, or work, or mission, or specific purpose."

Feet seemed to be shuffling all around Christopher. Men anxious to be on the move. To be anywhere but here. They'd either heard enough or been convicted enough. Or bored, perhaps?

"Perhaps you," Mühlenberg said this word with tenacity, his eyes locked onto one of the Hessians—Schäfer? This was something Mühlenberg never did, focusing on one obvious person. Never.

"Perhaps you have been in a box," Mühlenberg said. "You've lived there as long as you can recall. You're comfortable there. Miserable, but comfortable, in your familiar circumstances. Comfortably miserable, let's call it."

Christopher's senses heightened. He hoped Mühlenberg was certain in what he was doing. Otherwise ...

"But!" Mühlenberg picked up the box, extended his hands, and allowed it to hover for several long moments above and beyond the pulpit. Then, he let go. The beautiful wooden box, its painted images so delicate, so precise crashed to the floor, splintering. The clatter echoed around the church.

A stunned hush overwhelmed the congregation. Then, in one united response, mumbling erupted all around.

Christopher groaned at the loss of the beauty.

Agh-h! Henry, what have you done?

Mühlenberg bowed his head, shook his long locks, and murmured, "God does not live in a box, dear ones. Neither must you."

He looked again. This time his eyes encompassed everyone in the sanctuary.

"Was God thinking inside the box when He delivered manna from the heavens to feed the Israelites, or water from the rock to give them drink? Or when He spoke to Moses through a burning bush, or held back the waters of the

Red Sea?" Mühlenberg lifted an index finger. "Or when He Himself left the comfort of His own heaven, descending to a new 'home'?"

"And, allow me, but who thinks of using a whale to swallow a prophet to get his attention?" He waved his arms in the air. The congregation blew out in group laughter and relief from the angst over the broken box.

"No, our Lord allows no box to contain Him or His way of doing things. Nor should you."

Mühlenberg's eyes were imploring. "In your own lives, your own circumstances, break the box, wreck the mold."

Mühlenberg laid a hand upon the Bible, allowing his eyes to roam to the Hessians.

"Ephesians 3:20," he said, "tells us the Lord is able to do far more abundantly than we ask or think. So don't be surprised when some solution for your life falls into your lap. A gift from heaven."

He took a half-step backwards, straightened his shoulders. "Remember, there is a king, but His name is neither George nor Ferdinand. His name is Jesus Christus—the way, the truth, the life. Gott mit Uns."

Mühlenberg gave a blessing, but Christopher didn't hear. Not a word. His mind was consumed with wondering how his Hessian friends had received the message. Thumbs up or thumbs down?

★★★

During the singing of the doxology, Mühlenberg walked along the center aisle to the front door where he stood outside as was his custom. As the congregation exited, he greeted everyone.

When the soldiers walked out, he shook each one's hand, thanking them for attending the service. Except for

Schäfer, the men nodded pleasantly. Schäfer grunted, "Too bad about the box" and walked on.

Mühlenberg shook his head, sighed, and turned to face Christopher.

"Well done," Christopher said.

"Will it change a heart or two?"

"We'll see ... soon."

Christopher stepped to one side, waiting for Catharine and the young ladies to file out. He sidled close to his wife. *"Es geht um die Wurst,"* he whispered. "It's the moment of truth. Do or die."

"Were you able to gauge their reaction to Henry's sermon?" she asked.

"I saw red eyes, heard a half-sob, caught a couple eyeing your fine young ladies who, I'm certain, have stirred more than one heart. Rudolph and Hans, in particular. Blum too. Maybe even Schäfer."

She smiled, then reached up, planting a kiss on his cheek.

"Why don't you bring everyone to our house? The girls and I will cook another feast.

"The way to a man's heart—" Christopher commenced.

"—is through his stomach," she finished and, with a mischievous look, patted his belly.

"Not fair," he quipped.

"But so true," she replied in a girlish tease.

He laid a loud kiss on her forehead. "See you in what, an hour?"

"Make it two."

CHAPTER 11

Two hours later, as they rode to Christopher's house, the prevailing mood among the Hessians seemed an odd mix of excitement, anticipation, and trepidation.

Christopher found it difficult to discern, but guessed the excitement was spurred by the prospect of seeing Marta, Hannah, and Gretchen.

"I'd love a piece of land on a river," said Hans, who sat dangling his feet over the side of the wagon. "Not wide as the Reine, but one you could fish in every day."

"Posh!" said Emil. "You never caught a fish in your life."

"But I'd like to."

"I'd show you how," Rudolph chimed in. "I've caught plenty."

"Ha!" Johann said. "You'd be too busy regaling Gretchen with your mighty conquests of deer and bear." He waved his arms, feigning fright. "The bear was huge, Gretchen, and his teeth were this big. And his claws were this long. And this sharp—"

"And saliva drooled out of his monstrous mouth—" Bernhard interjected.

"And his eyes," Heinrich said. "His eyes were red with hatred as they drilled though me as if I were a tasty morsel to devour—"

Laughs abounded. Even Shafer emitted a short chuckle.

"Okay. Okay," Rudolph said. "Make your fun, but I was serious with our young friend, Hans."

Blum squashed the joviality with, "Yes, but if America loses the war, you could end up dying a slow, torturous death in prison—"

"Or a quick death in a firing line," Schäfer said.

The wagon went silent, everyone lost in their own reflections.

Christopher's thoughts went to the upcoming dinner, itself an enticement for men relishing a true meal after months on a ship. Remembering wartime rations, he doubted 1776's fare was any better than when he served. Here in Philadelphia, these men were better fed than at home in Germany, no doubt. Conditions throughout Germany were grim, he'd read.

Emperor Joseph the Second had achieved two purposes by enlisting these Hessians for England. First, he'd filled his near-barren treasury. Second, he'd lowered the number of mouths needing to be fed.

When Private Bohn pulled the wagon to a stop in front of the house, Christopher lowered himself to the ground and hurried ahead. He opened the front door to a waft of delicious smells. Ester Kocht, or roasted duck. Warming cranberry sauce and cloves. Potatoes. Even the cabbage smelled good.

Besides the three young women he knew would be present, there stood Hilde, the lithe young lady who had turned Schäfer's head at the farmhouse.

Again, my discerning wife outdoes herself.

Two large tables had been pulled together, an enormous tablecloth covering them. After the men were seated and the meal served, the women didn't stand by, but took seats along the other side of the table.

The afternoon passed in extraordinary fashion.

Christopher pulled Fischer aside. "Not one mention of the Revolution," he said. "That's good."

"A score of questions about our politics and who rules over who," Fischer said.

"Your men were terrific, mentioning the wide breadth of careers available—"

"And that our citizens are from all over Eastern and Western Europe as well as the British Isles, Germany, and Austria," Fischer added.

"I haven't spoken as much German in years," Christopher said with a chuckle."

"Fingers crossed," Fischer said.

"No, Gus. Prayers lifted. At this point, I'd trust any one of these six Hessians—even Schäfer—to live near us, work for us, whatever they chose to do."

Christopher returned to his chair, feeling a strange comfort. He was surrounded by "enemies of war" turned friends.

When the crowd of men stepped out the door to return to Quarry Street, their reluctance was real, their goodbyes forlorn, the brightness of their attitude startling in the fact they were prisoners of war.

***

In the evening, Christopher lounged on the couch, reading the latest edition of *Staatsbote*, with the American soldiers stationed strategically. The Hessians sat about casually, lost in their own deliberations.

The newspaper was full of the looming Das Schlacht on Lange Insel, or the Battle of Long Island. He considered sharing the article with the men but decided to wait for the moment, to gauge the tenor of the room. He folded the broadsheet, tucked it under his arm, and observed.

Silence reined as the men seemed lost in their thoughts. The gears churning as the Germans weighed their options on a scale with various measures of fear balanced by hope, apprehension counterpoised by boldness. He wouldn't say the atmosphere was grim—rather, hesitant.

Then Blum, who was leaning on the Newell post of the stairway, cracked a joke breaking the unspoken question wide open.

Christopher later wondered if Blum was being surreptitious on purpose or meant it as a mere ice-breaker.

"My neighbors' boy, Anton," he said, "was saying his prayers one night 'God bless Mom, God bless Dad, and please make Hamburg the capital of Germany,' he said.

"So, my neighbor Carl said to Anton, 'Why do you want Hamburg to be the capital of Germany, son?'

"'Because I wrote Hamburg in my geography test,' the boy said."

A burst of laughter echoed around the sitting room. Then Schäfer said, "I don't care if I ever see Hamburg again."

"Never been there," deadpanned Emil.

"Me neither," Hans echoed. "I don't care to, either."

"Have family in Hamburg," Blum said. "An uncle, aunt, two worthless cousins."

"Explains why you used Hamburg in the joke," Rudolph said. "Instead of, say, Munich."

"Don't care for Munich either," said Schäfer.

Everyone laughed, including Christopher.

This is good.

Christopher so wanted to add his two bits to the conversation—about both the Battle of Long Island, how it might factor into their decisions, and about the bounty of reasons to leave the war for the prospect of peace and prosperity. Instead, he decided to let the conversation play out among those to whom this issue counted most.

He eyed Lieutenant Fischer, who exchanged the look. Both would keep mum.

I hope all our soldiers are paying attention.

"If I were to stay, I'd miss my mother, but not my father," Emil said.

"I'd miss my father, but not my mother," rejoined Hans who was sitting on the floor beside him.

"Ha!" Emil poked Hans on the shoulder. "How long have we dreamed my father and your mother would get together?"

"What a match!"

"Like you and Marta," Emil kidded.

Hans threw back his shoulders. "Or you and the African girl in the apple orchard."

"Right. I don't even recall her name."

"Sure, you do. Lucretia." Hans eyes went wide in mirth. He fluttered his eyelids. "First you were gawking at her, even asked if she was married. You don't recall? Ha!"

"Can't stay here because of some *mädchen*." Emil cupped his chin. "She was no mere girl, though. She was a, a—."

"A comtesse?" Hans suggested.

"A duchesse?" Rudolph submitted with a laugh.

"No, no," Emil said firmly. He put the tips of three fingers to his lips and smacked them with a flourish. "An empress. Alexandra of Russia."

Chuckles echoed around the room because everyone knew Empress Alexandra to be a beauty on any stage.

"Christoff," Emil asked, serious, "would such a union be outlawed in America?"

Christopher hesitated, thinking the question through. "A white man with a black woman?"

"Yes."

"In God's eyes there is no black, white, male or female, no Jew nor gentile. In America there is no law of which I'm aware."

Bernhard broke the ensuing silence, saying, "Can we make a decision to stay here based on a pretty face?"

"Did you recall such a pretty face as Marta or Hannah in our streets back home?" Heinrich asked. His tone was half-jesting.

Bernhard shrugged and answered in a whisper, "No. I was only asking."

"I see many reasons besides marriage prospects," Rudolph said. "Wild game. Rich pastures."

"Sure," Johann said. "Your sights, Rudy, are more set on Gretchen than a buck in the woods. You're so obvious."

Rudolph scoffed, but blushed.

Christopher recalled Blum's steady, interested gaze on the golden-haired widow Anna and Schäfer's connection, be it ever so limited, with Matilde.

Blum took a half-step forward, pointed upward and said with an air of authority, "Many women who claim no beauty of face have captured the hearts of many a man by the beauty of their form and the temple of their soul."

"Leave it to Jäger Blum to attempt injecting wisdom into a conversation about beautiful women." A twinkle belied Schäfer's passive expression. "Who are you quoting, Karl?"

Blum shrugged and put his hands in his pockets. "Don't recall." Then, shoulders back, he stepped into the middle of the room, eyeing each Hessian, his face abruptly somber.

"Listen, men, we can talk about Germany, about beautiful women, land grants, hunting, riding, about warfare and all elements of life and death, love and allegiance." He stopped, his eyes narrowing, then, "Allegiance. There's a word central to this dilemma, eh?"

Christopher held his breath, feeling a tension in what was coming.

"This decision we face must be personal not collective," Blum said. "Outside the battlefield, we must answer to ourselves alone. But I will ask you to consider this—Does your allegiance sit with our emperor? Do you owe him fidelity, commitment?"

"How about duty?" Schäfer interjected.

Blum glanced at Schäfer. "Obligation too. We each must be led by what is in our hearts. Regardless of my rank, I hold no man guilty, no matter his decision."

"Have you made your decision ... comrade?" Schäfer's question was a knife, perched at the ready, it seemed. But was his inquiry a veiled threat? Or perhaps a probing query—decisive for Schäfer, if Blum's answer was what he expected, what he hoped.

Christopher envisioned future side-by-side Blum and Schäfer farms in Germantown.

No, no, no. This was not Schäfer being his old self—the belligerent, snarly, disagreeable Jäger. This was Schäfer deciding whether to forsake the military. He needed confirmation, subtle as it may be, from his friend, his peer in peril and his equal in any civilian life they might pursue.

Christopher looked from one Jäger to another. The question—"Have you made your decision ... comrade?"—hung in the room. A specter.

Seconds ticked by as Blum said nothing, returning Schäfer's gaze with his own. Self-reflective. Both their futures hung on this moment for all to see.

Peace. Be still.

The level of the silence grew from awkward and prickly to unnerving, bordering on distressing. Then Christopher received a prompting to speak up.

He leaned forward, displaying his newspaper for all to see.

"Gentlemen, I've read the Battle of Long Island is imminent—perhaps today, perhaps tomorrow, or Tuesday."

All the soldiers, American and German, groaned.

"Many men will die on both sides," he said. "God willing, America will prevail. But, even if the Redcoats, with Hessian help, are victorious, what would you gain?"

His answer was another stretch of silence. Christopher glanced at his American comrades. They were intent on the Hessians' reply.

Then the seventeen-year-old Hans asked, "Why do you care, Heir Ludwig?"

Christopher scratched his chin and smiled, catching the young man's eyes in an iron gaze.

"Ephesians two verse ten," he said. "For we are God's workmanship, created in Christ Jesus unto good works, which God hath before ordained we should walk in them."

Hans's head shot back and he exhaled. "So, we're your 'good works'? Getting you into heaven?"

Christopher shook his head. "Faith alone gets you into heaven, Hans," he said. "No good works will do it, so no man can boast. But, yes, I'd think saving your lives from battle by offering a fresh life here in America would be a good work."

Hans shrugged, his mouth twisted.

"I know this," Christopher went on, "I don't want you to die, Hans. Or any man here—" He glanced around the room. "On either side of the battle."

"I don't want any of my friends in our battalion to die, either," said Emil.

"Nothing you can do about that," Rudolph interposed. "You can't prevent it."

Silence again.

Then Johann, the hussar corporal, leaped out of his seat. "Maybe yes. Maybe we can!"

"What?" Rudolph replied. "Not possible."

Johann peered at Christopher then at Lieutenant Fischer.

"What if we went back to our camp and told our comrades about America's offer? About what we've seen?"

"Yes," Bernhard said, "about how many of our countrymen live all around here."

"About all the opportunities," Heinrich added.

"About a future." Emil's expression had transformed from one of distress to palpable optimism.

"You'd desert." This from Schäfer, who folded his arms in front of him, his eyes boring into the others, one by one. "You, a hussar, Johann? You fusiliers, Bernhard and Heinrich? You two grenadiers, Hans and Emil?"

Then he looked hard at Rudolph. 'You, a chasseur whose father has the favored position as gamekeeper to a wealthy landowner? A young man who does have a certain, fine, future back home."

Rudolph stared back. Christopher knew the young man's response. Inside, he rejoiced in anticipation. Not for Rudolph's sake alone but knowing the other four younger men respected him.

Rudolph shot a look at Christopher, then back at Schäfer. He gave a firm nod. "Me too."

Fischer, standing at Christopher's side, reacted with a "Yes!" The utterance seemed to surprise Fischer as much as Christopher.

Schäfer, his features stern, even harsh, looked back, staring at Blum.

Blum glared back.

Two seconds expired. Three. Then both men broke out in the broadest beams Christopher remembered witnessing, then embraced.

"Soldier!" Schäfer exclaimed.

"Neighbor!" Blum responded.

Blum's entire face radiated. Now the Jägers had joined the others.

Then, it seemed, in unison they turned to Christopher and Fischer.

"The next question remains." Blum said. "Can we ask the opportunity to go back into our camp to persuade our comrades to leave?"

"Greater love has no one than this: to lay down one's life for one's friends." Christ's words from the Gospel of John slipped out of Christopher's lips before he even conjured them up. Immediately, he thought he'd overstepped his bounds. For where would he be when these men were putting themselves in danger? Here in Philadelphia, or at the Flying Camp?

No. He'd proceed with his initial plan—pass behind the British lines by himself.

I'd be right there with them. Instead of me alone as I'd planned, there would be eight others besides.

But first ... Christopher looked at Fischer for the lieutenant's response. Fischer shrugged, raising his hands in wonder.

"We'd have to ask General Mercer."

"Then what are we waiting for?" Blum said.

"Morning light," Fischer said. "We'll leave at sunrise."

CHAPTER 12

Monday, August 26, 1776
Philadelphia

"If only I had a bugle!" Schäfer bellowed loud enough that Christopher could hear from his place on the couch in the sitting room early the next morning. "Get up, you lazy sloths! You're still in the military and not basking in the light of freedom, either."

Blum came bounding down the stairs. "At least not at this moment," he said, eyeing Christopher. "Not yet."

A minute later, all the Hessians descended to the first floor.

The mood was convivial, animated. Not fearful, but eager to get moving, Christopher thought. He was sure each man must feel apprehension, or a bit of unease if not angst. But, if so, they weren't showing the emotion.

"I need to find my cousin, Jonas," Heinrich said. "He's with the Third Fusiliers."

"Persuade him well," Rudolph said. He shot a mischievous look at Bernhard and Heinrich. "Fusiliers are an obstinate gang."

The two friends from childhood took the ribbing, shaking their heads but smiling all the while.

A knock came at the front door, and Christopher edged by Private Bohn. "I'll get it, Nikolaus," he said, and the young man stepped aside.

Pastor Mühlenberg stood there. Late last night, Christopher had skipped over to his house to tell Catharine the plans. A smooch, a prayer, and off he went, hustling down to the church parsonage to ask Henry to come by before they all left for Flying Camp.

Mühlenberg's face was as bright as a streetlamp. He'd been seriously alone with God.

So beguiled by his friend's countenance, Christopher only managed, "Thank you for coming, Henry."

"I appreciate you asking." The enticing aroma of coffee and gingerbread greeted Henry when he stepped inside. He surveyed the large sitting room. The Americans were standing a loose guard while the Hessians mulled about, drinking coffee, chomping on thick slices of gingerbread heated in the oven.

They all turned at the sound of Henry's voice. Blum walked over to shake the pastor's hand. The others also ambled over. Only Schäfer stood aloof.

"I hear you men are on a crusade, asking to go back to your ranks to persuade your countrymen to join you, to let the Brits fight their own battles," Henry said.

Blum nodded. The others muttered agreement.

"Despite putting yourselves in danger of subterfuge, of being discovered, even executed?"

Rudolph, standing behind Blum, stated matter-of-factly, "We don't want our friends to die fighting good people, folks battling for freedom."

"You're right," Johann blurted.

A curious smile edged across Henry's face—one Christopher had seen before, one exhibited when the presence of God was noticeable and victorious.

"Your willingness to risk your own lives reminds me of Jesus giving His life for ours." He followed his simple statement by looking one at a time at the German soldiers.

No words in response. Just nods.

There were murmurs of gratitude when Mühlenberg said, "I'm here to see you on your way with encouragement and a blessing."

Christopher knew Henry had made a distinct impression, when clothing the Hessians on Friday as well as with his sermon Sunday. His presence this morning would cement the personal connections, no doubt.

God, I see Your hand in this.

Henry continued after a quiet moment. "There's a Proverb which says if we commit to God things will go well. Proverbs 16 tells us while we see ourselves as pure, the Lord 'weighs the spirits'—which means He weighs the thoughts and intents of our hearts. If we roll our works upon Him—to commit and trust them wholly to Him—the Lord will cause our thoughts to become agreeable to His will. Then our plans will be established to succeed."

"You say He will cause our thoughts'?" Rudolph asked.

"Yes, if we trust Him with all our hearts, minds and souls."

"Never heard such a thing!" Hans said.

"You never read the original Greek," Henry replied.

Hans laughed.

"He can barely read German." Emil punched his friend on the shoulder.

"Bah!" Hans shrugged away from Emil.

Chuckling, Henry shook his head. "Well, we have free schooling in the city for anyone who wants it, thanks to Christopher."

Christopher eyed Henry, smiling. "But we don't teach Greek. Not yet anyhow."

The two men exchanged a laugh, then Henry looked about the room. "You are all certain? Committed?"

Mumbles of agreement were his answer. Schäfer remained remote from the conversation, but added a firm nod, nonetheless. Christopher had raised Schäfer's score on his "scale of persuasion" to a solid nine point five. He prayed again for the Jäger's salvation.

If one of the Hessians pulled out, it would mean peril for the entire group.

Henry interrupted Christopher's reflections. "Then let's pray." He bowed his head. "Father God, Your children are trusting You to guard them, show them favor, shut the mouths of any enemies who might confront or threaten them on their quest to set their friends free—liberated to seek a future here in America. Ensure our friends when they return, we will welcome them with open arms. The church, too, will help in every way we can."

As he and the others said, "Amen," Christopher thought *Henry, you've done it again—you and God.*

***

They'd gotten a quick start and were out of the city before most of the Philadelphians had awakened. The Hessians had donned their military uniforms, their civilian clothing folded into satchels, and they'd all traveled through Germantown and Bristol, fast approaching the Delaware River.

"We'll reach Flying Camp before noon tomorrow at this pace," Christopher said aloud.

Then our great—but dangerous—adventure.

Suddenly, calamity! The front right wagon wheel dropped into a deep rut, sending the wagon into an abrupt stop, tilting wildly to the right. Christopher and Nikolaus Bohn were thrown off their seat. They grabbed hold of the small steel handle at the end of the seat and held on for dear life.

There were screams behind them. Christopher glanced over his shoulder and gasped. A few feet away, a severe slope descended to a deep ravine, scraggly fir trees sprouting out of the ground along the way.

Maybe this was the end of his "dear life."

He glanced to his left where Private Bohn struggled to grasp the reins so he would not crash into him. Behind him, the Hessians tumbled about in a moment of haywire.

"Agh-h!" came one man's holler, followed the crashing noises and screams of pain as he slid down the steep incline.

Then Hans's tremoring voice lifted into the air as he, too, dropped out of sight.

Alarmed, Christopher turned to look ahead, praying he could hold on.

Lieutenant Fischer had heard the commotion, turned his horse around, and was dismounting, panic on his face.

The wagon settled with a shake—crippled, three-legged. The angle was too severe for Christopher to hold on longer. His left shoulder screeched in pain, twisted in a way it was never meant to.

Fischer scrambled toward him, and as the last of Christopher's strength failed him, Fischer grabbed him around the waist and yanked him free of the wreckage.

"Thank you, Gus!" Christopher gasped. Then, regaining his balance, he rubbed his throbbing shoulder and turned about to look into the ravine. Lying at the bottom, Rudolph groaned in pain, grasping his left leg, his face distorted. A meter away, Hans sat, rubbing his right shoulder and grimacing. Dirt covered both men.

Most startling, halfway down the ravine, Schäfer grasped a scrawny sprout of a fir tree. Silent, he assessed his situation. While the slope allowed the others to slide down, Schäfer hung over a sheer drop of ten feet or so. He was no lightweight dangling from the tiny bit of foliage.

What to do?

Christopher looked at Fischer, this question wrinkling his forehead.

Fischer was already checking about him. "The harness!" he called to someone, anyone. "Take the harness from the horses. We need to lower it to Kristian."

Fischer's use of Schäfer's first name didn't escape Christopher.

'Kristian,' he called him. Not 'Schäfer.'

Having extricated himself from his precarious spot on the wagon seat, Bohn was detaching the harness. Bloom and Luka jumped into the chore. In a minute, the three were standing atop the ravine above Schäfer.

"*Abwarten!*" Blum hollered. "Hold on!"

"You think I have something else in mind?" Schäfer responded.

Sarcasm. A cousin—not a true partner—of fear. A good sign of his state of mind. He was a warrior, after all, familiar with the prospects of death. When a soldier, Christopher himself had used sarcasm to ward off panic. Jäger Schäfer was the ultimate combatant.

Bloom and Luka held onto one end of the harness and dropped the rest. When it landed against the slope, it kicked a shower of dirt into Schäfer's face. He coughed, spit it up, and hollered an obscenity Christopher hadn't heard since the last days of the Siege of Prague.

"Sorry!" Luca shouted back. Blum smirked, shaking his head.

Holding the bit of tree with one arm, Schäfer reached for the leather strapping. His fingers were oh-so-close. Maybe a foot away. He pulled himself higher, hooking his elbow around the tree, and again extended his other arm. Six inches!

"Oh!" was the collective response of the men standing all around. They were as attentive as a crowd at a sporting event.

Leaving Christopher's side, Fischer stepped to the wagon where the horses still stood. He grabbed hold of one of the bellybands and unhitched it in one practiced motion.

"Pull the strappings back up," he ordered as he hustled to the top of the ravine.

Bloom and Luca did so and Fischer tied the bellyband to the end of the harness. Schäfer would be able to grab the bellyband and buckle it around him.

With a heave-ho, Bloom and Luca tossed the mass of leather into the ravine. Another shower of dust, another curse, and Schäfer clutched the bellyband, wrapped it under his arms and yelled, "Pull!"

Johann and Emil joined Blum and Luca in pulling Schäfer up the incline. He was a big man, the job was not easy, but a couple of minutes later, Schäfer stretched his arms to the ground and heaved a deep breath.

Hauling himself to his knees, he looked about him and sighed, "Danke. Danke, everyone."

"Now for Hans and Rudolph," Blum said, looking into the chasm. His forehead was wrinkled in concern, sweat on his brow—from heat or anxiety, maybe both.

The two young men—with Rudolph rubbing his knee and Hans cupping his right shoulder in the palm of his left hand—had both watched Schäfer's rescue and now looked expectantly.

"What we need is a length of rope," Christopher said.

"Maybe the farm back there a couple miles has some we can use," Fischer said.

"I'll ride back and find out," Private Anton Wagner volunteered.

"On your way, then," Fischer said. He turned and peered down the embankment. "Hang in there, men. We'll get you out."

In unison, they turned their attention to the wagon.

Christopher shook his head.

"We need a wheel," he said.

"At least the axle's not broken," Luka said. He was on his knees looking at the undercarriage.

Cheers all around greeted his revelation.

"We need another wagon altogether," Fischer said.

"A blacksmith or a wheelwright," Christopher murmured, thinking of who would be available. The massive presence of Douglas Bradford came to mind. The blacksmith, as loyal to the Revolution as any man, lived not a half mile west of the Ludwick home.

"We've a man near our home," he said.

"The trip will take two days there and back on horseback," Fischer said.

"It might take more at any rate," murmured Luca, "even if we had a smithy right here beside us."

"I'm sure Douglas has a spare wheel or two," Christopher said.

"It'd have to be the exact same size as the others," Fischer responded.

"Sir." Luca gazed at his lieutenant. "To fix this wheel, we have to break it apart, so we can remove the iron rim intact."

"And to do so," said Bohn, "we may have to cut off some good spokes to reduce the pressure holding the wheel together."

"Right," Luca agreed. "Also, we'd have to make spokes to replace broken ones."

"Then reassemble the hub and spokes and rim sections," Blum continued.

All eyes went to the Jäger, whose eyes went straight to Fischer.

"We'd need a chisel, hammer, grease, a fire, blacksmith tongs, and a bucket of water to cool the rim." He shrugged. "Replacing the wheel is too difficult for us to accomplish out here in the countryside."

Fischer put chin to knuckles, groaned, and, with his eyes imploring, looked at Christopher.

"We'll have a long wait here," he said.

"We have food enough." Christopher hesitated and spun a look toward the back of the wagon, anxiety fingering along his spine. "Unless!"

The bags of food were gone.

"Food's all here in a couple of burlap bags," Rudolph called up.

"Then I guess we'd better get you men here," Schäfer deadpanned, a smile widening.

"Or drop the rope Anton's bringing back to haul up the food," Blum said with a chuckle.

"Luka," Fischer said, "take my horse and ride quick as you can back to Philadelphia and implore Mr. Bradford to come to our rescue."

"Use my name," Christopher said. "Douglas will respond."

"Ninety centimeters," Blum said.

Luka looked a questioning at the Jäger.

"The diameter of the wheel," Blum said.

"Ah."

Luka hustled to Fischer's horse. "I'll take good care of her, sir."

"Be quick, Corporal, and mind your way." Fischer shook his head, no doubt wondering if it were possible for this trip to go any worse.

***

Half an hour later, Anton returned with not one but two long lengths of rope.

"From the Brandt farm, Lieutenant," he said, handing the two looped ropes to Fischer.

Blum and Schäfer volunteered to rappel down and help Rudolph and Hans. Soon all four Hessians were sitting on the edge of the ravine, breathing hard but their faces relieved.

Christopher drew near. "Anything broken?"

"My feelings," Rudolph quipped.

"I'm not so sure," Hans said. "Dislocated, maybe."

"We'll have to have the Flying Camp doctor take a look," Fischer said.

Christopher sniggered.

Fischer shot him a look.

"These men would be better off seeing a mother or grandmother, Gus."

Fischer looked offended. "The Continental Army Medical Corps was formed more than a year ago. Our man will do fine."

"Oh?" Christopher's brow raised. "Ben Rush is a good friend, and he's been outspoken about the care our soldiers are getting."

"I'd prefer to stay at camp sleeping on a rock than see the army's quacks," Jacob Hoffman offered.

"Corporal!"

The lieutenant's glare caused Hoffman to stutter. "I'm saying what the men feel and what they've said."

Christopher stepped close to Fischer and spoke in a low tone only the lieutenant could hear.

"Dr. Rush told me, personally, the one prerequisite for an army doctor's apprentice is the ability to stand the sight of blood. The war's only begun, and John Adams said at one of Congress's committee meetings for every man dying from a musket ball, ten more are dying from infections. Even Mr. Franklin, who founded the colonies' first hospital in Philadelphia, has expressed he's appalled at the care of our soldiers."

Fischer lowered his eyes and at each of these revelations slowly shook his head in resignation.

Finally, he asked, "So what shall we do?"

"Drop in on an old lady somewhere along the way," Christopher responded loud enough for everyone to hear.

Anton offered, "Mrs. Brandt back there at the farmhouse fits the bill. She's old as my *großmutter*. Offered me a drink of milk straight from the cow, like my großmutter does when I visit her and my *großvater*.

"We have nothing better to do while we wait for Corporal Meyer and the smithy to return to fix the wheel," Fischer said. "Let's hike back to the farm. How far is it, Corporal?"

"A mile or two."

They set off from where they'd come, with the two Jägers letting Rudolph lean on them for support.

Christopher chuckled to himself about his idea of getting to the Flying Camp in two days.

What was the old saw? Our plans and God's will may quite different.

Twenty minutes along the road, Luka Meyer pointed to a well-kept farmhouse situated on a knoll and with a large barn attached.

"The place I mentioned," he said.

As they approached an elderly lady walked out of the barn, a basket hanging from her arm. When she spotted a dozen men walking toward her house, all of them besides Christopher in military garb, the lady set her basket on the ground, alarm on her face.

Then Anton waved and called out, "Mrs. Brandt! It's me, Anton."

With recognition came relief, and the woman smiled broadly. She was a tiny woman, dressed for farmyard chores—a rough-knit sweater and a dress hanging to her ankles, beneath which were a man's rubber boots.

"With a company of friends," Luka added in German now. "Hessian friends."

Mrs. Brandt took an anxious step backwards, a hand to her chest.

Responding to her obvious alarm, Christopher said in German, "We need your help. We've had an accident, and two among us are injured."

She hesitated, then, eyes narrowing as she peered at Christopher, she said, "I know you."

"Oh?"

"The gingerbread man, no?" she blurted, "In Laétitia Court?"

Christopher broke out in a loud laugh and nodded exuberantly.

"Yes," he said and proceeded to introduce Fischer, and one by one, all the others.

"Come on up," she said. She motioned for them to come to the house, then grabbed her basket, which Christopher now saw carried eggs, turned on her heel, and strode to the house.

A determined step, hers.

Once inside, the dozen men filled the kitchen. The aroma of bread in the oven was mouth-watering. Maybe she would cook some of the eggs from her basket.

"Not your gingerbread, mind," she said, "but ingredients are hard to come by nowadays."

"Smells wonderful nevertheless," Christopher said. "Mrs. Brandt, we're here on the blind hopes someone nearby would be able to mend a shoulder. May be dislocated.

She chuckled. "First, call me Helena. Second, you've come to the right place. My Klaw, bless his heart, was always dislocating his shoulder. Pounding a fence post—dislocate his shoulder. Tossing hay to the cows—dislocate his shoulder." She shook her head, lost for a moment in those memories. "Poor man."

Christopher and the others laughed as she spoke about her deceased spouse.

Then Christopher sobered. "Mr. Brandt is no longer with us?"

Helena shook her head sadly. "With the Lord. And our son's off to war, who knows where. Long Island, I've heard. So, too, is our daughter's husband. Off to war—somewhere. So—" her voice trailed off. After a moment, she said, "So, I'm here baking for myself, and I'd love to share the bread when it comes out of the oven. Two loaves ought to be enough, don't you think? But first who's this with a bum shoulder?

Hans stepped forward.

"Kneel, son," she ordered. She was all matter-of-fact, reminding Christopher of Benjamin Rush.

In command, always.

Hans knelt.

Helena placed both hands on his shoulder and worked her fingers as if kneading bread.

"Aha!" she said. "There it is." She stepped to his side, about two feet away. "Stretch out your arm."

Hans flinched as he obeyed.

The little lady grabbed his biceps in one hand, his wrist in the other, tilted his arm higher, at an angle, and braced herself.

"Count to three," she said.

Hans began, "*Eins... Zwei...*"

Helena yanked the arm. Everyone could hear a click. Hans's eyes went wide, his face broadened and he exclaimed, "*Verblüffend!*"

Yes, amazing, Christropher agreed.

Hans rose to his feet, lifted his arm straight toward the ceiling, turned, and gave the woman a hug.

Helena smiled. "My Klaw always hugged me afterward," she said, "then returned to his chores."

"You have chores you need done?" Hans asked.

"Yes, ma'am," Blum offered, "perhaps we can all pitch in to help before we leave."

Helena crooked her head. "Maybe I do. But first—" She walked to the oven, opened the door, peered in, and said, "Why don't you men all eat first?"

As they stood around the kitchen, munching on the hot bread topped with warm butter, the Hessians told their hostess about being captured, then being given the tour around Philadelphia and Germantown, and their decision.

Christopher noticed each man joined in the telling. He was flabbergasted.

Lord, You continue to amaze!

"Astounding," Helena said. "There's plenty of available land around here. You can travel east for miles of rich unowned land. And if not, I'm sure my son and I could use at least one of you gentlemen to help with the farm once this ... skirmish is over."

If it were but a mere "skirmish," Christopher thought. A brief interlude in the life of this fledgling nation. "Skirmish?" A dream, for sure.

★★★

The American and Hessian soldiers forked piles of hay into the barn, hammered in a couple of fence posts, repaired railings, and even milked the Brandts' three cows.

Then, knowing they had another day to wait for Anton and Bradford to arrive, they accepted Helena's invitation to fill her empty house overnight.

Christopher spent a couple of hours in the kitchen with the widow, divulging his secrets for the world's most delicious gingerbread. She shared her love for the Lord, and he his. They had other things in common as well, for instance when she told him she and Klaw spent their last day together visiting Philadelphia and enjoying a treat at the Ludwick Bakery.

"When I last saw you," she said. "Four months ago. And what a time we had. Of course, we didn't know he was going to have a heart attack the day we returned home."

Sorrow filled Christopher's heart, and he wondered what life would be without his beloved Catharine at his side. He quicky decided to bury such emotions deep.

Proverbs thirty-one came to mind as he considered his wife. "A virtuous woman who can find? Her worth is far above rubies."

"I'm sorry for you," he managed.

"Oh, don't be," Helena said. "We had four decades together. Our daughter, Gretta, she married a good man and moved to Boston. She has a son I've yet to meet. Our son, Diedrich, was married but three years before his wife died. In childbirth, it was. The babe perished too. When he returns from the war, he'll move in with me—at least until he finds another woman to love. The good Lord meant for a man and a woman to marry, to complete one another."

"Two are better than one," Christopher said. "They double the joy, halve the sorrow. Read it somewhere."

"King Solomon, I'd guess," she said.

He nodded. He thought of what it meant to share the joys of life. He'd pray for Diedrich tonight.

Boisterous laughs erupted in the adjoining sitting room while a comfortable silence reigned in the kitchen for a few moments as both reflected on life.

"Scripture says something about if one falls, the other is there to pick him up," Helena said.

"Or fix his dislocated shoulder." Christopher chuckled.

She joined in, adding, "That too."

During a lull in their talk, Lieutenant Fischer walked in, motioning for Christopher to join him outside.

As they stood on the porch Fischer said, "We're bunking here for the night. My job is to keep these Hessians under watch—"

"I hear a 'but,'" Christopher said.

Christopher believed he knew what was coming, so he was not surprised when Fischer said, "All my men need a rest."

"And?"

"What are your thoughts on the matter?"

"My thoughts," Christopher repeated. He took a long pause.

Somewhere, an owl hooted. Closer, a sweet aroma—a flower of some sort—reached him. Somewhere men were preparing for battle, wondering if their dreams for a full life would end, or if they'd end someone else's aspirations. Somewhere a woman was learning she'd become a widow, children were discovering they were fatherless.

Fischer's polite cough interrupted his revery.

Christopher pulled himself together. "I have come to trust these men, to believe them to be truthful, Gus. Even Schäfer has come around. His malice has turned to kindness, even bordering on good humor. But is one or more of them acting? Are they still soldiers in the end—still loyal of their emperor?" He shrugged. "We must wonder. So, this is a difficult situation. I do believe you have a conundrum."

Christopher studied the man. Fischer shrugged, scratched the stubble on his face, hemmed and hawed.

"How about this?" Christopher offered. "We can stand watch while your men get the rest they need."

Fischer nodded, squeezed his lips together so hard it must have hurt, then looked Christopher straight in the eye.

"An early watch, a late watch," he said. "Which do you want?"

"Sleep is more my companion than yours. You choose."

"I'll take the first."

Fischer checked his pocket watch. "Eight o'clock. I'll come wake you at two."

Christopher was fine with the arrangement. He had claimed those hours as his from those years long ago when he would rise from bed at four o'clock to begin preparations for the day at the bakery. In the city, the world would be asleep, dreams occupying their minds, while he was laboring to achieve his own aspirations.

Dreams. Dreams. Dreams. Was their realization the Lord's will? To what degree did hard work and dedication have to do with it? God did say, through Solomon: "Look to the ant."

One thing he knew about his German countrymen—they were intelligent, orderly, efficient, punctual, hard-working, and full of ingenuity. In his own case, those characteristics had meant initiative.

A sense of humor? Well, no.

Indeed, early on Catharine had so flummoxed him with her brand of jest and wit, he had sought refuge in developing his own. Jibe-for-jibe, the two had word-wrestled until, unlike the leopard, he had changed his stripes.

Stoic? No longer. Jovial? Yes, now.

Indeed, where did Ben Franklin get the joke so often retold—Any fool can criticize, condemn and complain, and most fools do?

Christopher chuckled to himself, looked around, stretched out on the floor next to a wall, and was asleep in moments.

***

After Mercer had wrestled him from a hard nap at two o'clock, Christopher pulled his chair beside the doorway and settled in for a six-hour watch. If he lowered his shoulders and looked up, he could see the stars. Where are you, North Star. Aha! There! A constant guide, set in place by the Creator.

As he gazed heavenward, Christopher heard a muffled conversation above him. The window of one of the bedrooms was open, and the voices of Rudolph and Johann wafted down.

"I will hunt game to my heart's desire," Rudolph said.

"Not the only thing your heart desires, eh, Rudy?" asked Johann. "I know how you feel about Gretchen."

Silence, then Johann continued, "What of your *fraulein* back home?"

"You know the story, Johann. We talked of marriage—seriously—but her father, the *bürgermeister*, whisked her off to Austria to marry a nobleman. Some count or other. I was beneath her. The son of a gamekeeper."

"*Quatsh*. (Nonsense)."

"She could have refused. She could have run off with me. We could be living in Switzerland or Liechtenstein. She didn't."

"Her family would have disowned her."

Silence rolled on for several seconds, then Johann blurted, "I'm excited ... and scared too."

"How so?" Rudolph asked.

"Herr Bradford offered me a job working with horses. Having land—near people who are already friends, and the couple I met at Christoff's bakery—Herman and Matilde Schneider? All of this excites me."

"But?"

"I'm frightened of getting caught. I envision being pushed against a brick wall and being shot. One musket ball and ... darkness."

"You don't believe?"

"Believe what?"

"In heaven."

Silence.

Finally, Johann said, "I do believe. But I want to live a life here on Earth first."

More silence.

Two intelligent, skilled, handsome young men, Christopher thought. One was from an equestrian family in the Black Forest, the other the son of a gamekeeper from Baden-Württemberg. Unlike the infantryman Hans and grenadier Emil, whose homeland offered little. Unlike fusiliers Bernhard and Heinrich, whose city offered little more than death by lung disease.

Rudolph and Johann were even unlike the Jägers— Blum from Düsseldorf and Schäfer, whose skills in warfare had earned them promotions into the middle ranks of the military.

Yes, if America's alluring treasure trove of abundance attracted Rudolph and Johann, she could draw anyone.

Yes, this mission has appeal.

Christopher decided to stroll around the house. A perimeter check, they called it. He rose from the chair and turned right. Beneath a second window, he caught another conversation. This between Hans and Emil.

Hans said, "Could I find my aunt and uncle?"

"The ones in Carolina?"

"Yes, a scary-sounding place."

"Cape Fear?"

"Yes."

"Your uncle a textile merchant?" Emil said.

"Last I heard."

"I talked to a private in the Scottish brigade before we set sail from England. He said many Scotsmen have sailed to the Carolinas."

"Oh?"

"'Highlanders,' he called them. "Protestants. He said his parents received a letter from relatives in Carolina asking them to come to America. Said they grow two crops each year."

"Two?" Hans harrumphed. "Not possible."

"This Scotsman claimed so. Lettuce, peas, and green beans in the spring. Turnips, beets, and Swiss chard in the autumn. He also said people there sell tar, pitch, turpentine, resin, and hemp to the British navy."

"Not now. I'll wager all those products are going into the American Navy."

"If there is an American Navy."

"Maybe there isn't."

"But if there is, it's being built up north in what they call New England," Emil said.

"Yeah?"

"My father's brother and his wife went there when they emigrated here years ago. Last we heard he was building ships in Massachusetts—up near Canada."

Hans laughed. "So, my uncle's friends might be selling products to your uncle. Ha!"

Emil chuckled. "You can have all the tar and turpentine you want. I'd choose growing food, my friend." He hesitated. "Which makes me think. What about the meals we've had since Christoff took us to Philadelphia?"

"Phew! Some cooks, eh? You suppose your Leticia can cook as well?"

"My Leticia?"

"Tell me you did not see her blush."

"I did. But we don't have to have girlfriends to stay here, you know."

"I know," Hans said. "There are plenty of other enticements."

"Your main motive being the food," Emil said with a chortle. "Empty plates in Germany, full plates here."

"No. My major reason," Hans said—and his voice left no room for argument—"is my father. I despise him as Bernhard hates his. If I were to stay here, I'd be sending a letter to my mother. 'Mutter, come join me in America. Leave your abusive husband behind.'"

Emil chuckled ruefully. "My letter home will be to my *vater*, saying 'Papa, come join me and Hans and Hans's mutter here in America. Unlike mutter, Hans has a fine temperament."

Hans laughed. "Ah, we dream."

"Not necessarily a dream."

Silence. Then, "Maybe not. Maybe the same as my other dream?"

"Marta?"

"Hm-m. Marta, the fairest of damsels."

Emil harrumphed. "You may be correct about Marta's beauty. But what do you think about my Lucretia?"

"Yours?"

"You called her such. Besides, I can dream too."

"A freed slave," Hans said.

"Won't you and me—indeed, all of us—in effect, be freed slaves, Hans?"

Silence again as the question hung in the air, and Christopher decided this was a good time to move on.

CHAPTER 13

The morning sun erupted over the eastern horizon, sending Christopher's mind to wondering if the sight portended a grand revelation ... or perhaps a frightening one. Did good or bad await them when they arrived at Flying Camp? Doom, gloom, or something in between.

First, they had to get the wagon repaired. He had never been one for waiting, something Catharine joked with him about.

"You're in a hurry to be in a hurry," she'd say. "God will deliver you when you're supposed to be there and not before."

She was right, of course. Except—was this the case now? *War waits for no man, I'm afraid, darling.*

This war was no different. King George had hired the Hessians. So how about Vikings, or Poles, or any alien individuals in love with war and killing?

Christopher had known more than one such man back in Austria. Blood lust. Those were the few who preferred bayonet and sword combat. Close. Personal. Violent. Even their laughs were chock full of venom.

Thankfully, they were on his "side," though he was certain similar men occupied the enemy camp as well.

Men were stirring in the house. Pots and pans clanked in the kitchen. Christopher decided to step inside and help Helena cook breakfast. They had brought with them the bags of food, but she refused.

"Keep it. Keep it." She slipped on an apron and tied it behind her waist. "My girls have been laying eggs and milking out for little old me. Gotta use them or lose them. One egg's enough for me in the morning. I share the rest with neighbors when I see them, and they reciprocate with a bit of ham or beef because we don't grow pigs or raise beef cows.

"Klaw?" An eyebrow rose and she added, "He'd gobble two eggs, or even three for breakfast. But, seeing as who my guests are, I'll cook some good old Pfannkuchen, German pancakes, this morning. Lots of eggs, butter and buttermilk."

"You have syrup?" he asked.

"Buttermilk syrup."

"How can I help?" he asked.

"Wait a moment," she said, and stoked the embers in the wood stove, adding a few pieces of kindling, then setting a mammoth iron frying pan over the fire. Then she turned and smiled at him. "Now you can help."

Helena was so nimble around her kitchen, Christopher figured she would be a good "hire." But she appeared capable of taking care of herself out here on her farm—husband or no husband. And in Germantown, neighbors were friends, and friends were family.

The tandem worked well together, Christopher catching on to Helena's process. And soon all the soldiers were gathered around waiting—expectant of something special.

Once seated and eating, the Americans and Hessians were indistinguishable, except for their uniforms.

Fischer stood at the door, his hand on his musket, but his demeanor offered little license for concern. A major difference from the previous night.

In fact, ...

Christopher rose from his chair. "Gus, I've had my fill. Take my seat for a helping of Helena's pancakes."

Fischer accepted the offer.

Blum was in the midst of telling a story about his youth spent in the bustling streets of Düsseldorf.

"My older brother, Nikki, was teaching me how to swim in the Düssel River, a small tributary, to the Rhine. Well, he tossed me over the bank into the river, and off I went."

The men around the table broke out in laughter.

"Funny, you think? I was horrified. Couldn't swim a lick. Never tried. But Nikki was adamant I'd learn—or he wanted to kill me. I'm not sure."

Another burst of laughter.

"So off I went. What saved me was I was wearing an old shirt far too tight. But somehow a bubble of air had formed beneath the shirt, causing an air pocket that kept me afloat. The air pocket and the current."

Eyes went wide.

"I'm gurgling and bubbling, keeping my head above water, and shockingly, I'm swimming. Kicking my legs and flying along like a fish."

Gus joined the others in cheers, and Christopher smiled to himself at the camaraderie.

"I lifted my head above the water and looked toward the shore." Blum chuckled at the recollection. "Nikki was crashing through underbrush along the shoreline trying to keep abreast with me—fright etched across his face.

"He taught me a lesson, and I believe my lesson taught him one as well."

"Yeah. Jump into a roiling river yourself, idiot!" Schäfer chortled.

Deferring to Blum, their superior, the younger Hessians stifled laughs, but their attempts went awry.

Christopher broke the moment, asking, "So what happened next?"

Blum again smiled at the memory. "After a few minutes, I swam right into a downed tree laying along the shore, gashing my forehead with a scar I still bear." He pointed. "I grabbed ahold of a branch and dragged myself to shore. A minute later, Nikki caught up, exhausted, eyes as big as Mutter's Christmas platter. Fell to his knees and cried."

Heads shook in awe around the table.

Christopher said, "I'd call it a miracle."

Heads nodded. After a few moments, even Schäfer nodded agreement.

Blum caught Schäfer in his gaze. "Yes, we all have at least one miracle in our lives, I imagine."

A few moments of silence greeted this remark, but no one opposed it or pondered it aloud.

Finally, Fischer asked Blum, "Your brother, is he always reckless?"

Blum turned somber and tilted his head to the side, fumbling for words. "Nikki is no more. Died in the Russo-Turkish War. A Jäger. The emperor reduced his widow's taxes for a year to 'honor' his death. He'd do the same for me, if I had a wife and died over here."

Silence again. A miracle on one hand, harsh reality on the other.

God is working.

***

Their plan for the day was for the American and Hessian soldiers to work together to strengthen and patch the Brandt barn. Helena made apologies for not being able to maintain the farm's appearances as well as her beloved Klaw had done.

As the men dispersed to carry out the job, Christopher took Hans aside, "Can I speak to you alone?"

Hans nodded. "Of course. What about?"

"Your father."

Hans threw back his shoulders and stiffened his back. "What of the man?"

"Whatever he's done, you must forgive him, Hans."

Hans's face skewered into a severe expression of disgust. "Never."

"Hans, our Savior said we must forgive as our Father has forgiven us, in order to be forgiven ourselves."

Hans objected: "A masochist. A wife-beater. A child-beater."

Now Christopher knew, but he pressed on. "No matter."

"I don't believe Jesus would say such a thing."

"He did."

"Where? Show me, and I'll believe it. Otherwise—"

Christopher scrambled to recall the Scripture.

"In the Sermon on the Mount."

"Show me."

Christopher raised a finger for Hans to wait and hustled to his satchel he stored on the wagon. He returned with a German Bible he treasured.

He prayed, opened the book, and found the Gospel of Matthew, chapter six. He held the Bible in front of Hans and pointed at verses fourteen and fifteen: "For if ye forgive men their trespasses, your heavenly Father will also forgive you: But if ye forgive not their trespasses, neither will your Father forgive your trespasses."

Hans read the Scripture and his eyes went wide.

"No way!"

"The only way." Christopher put a hand on the lad's shoulder. "Even if you were an atheist and didn't believe in God, hate accomplishes one thing—eats you from the inside the same as disease does from the outside. Hate festers and grows—from dislike and distaste to loathing and revulsion. Nothing good comes from hate, Hans. Only bitterness and darkness, and eventual death—eternal death because your Creator cannot forgive an unforgiver. Paul admonished us to think on the lovely, noble, and pure—and for good reason."

The anger on Hans's face was shriveling. He spun on his heels and stalked off.

Some things come hard, Christopher thought, and dispelling hatred perhaps hardest of all. But he wouldn't abandon hope for the young Hessian. No, never.

★★★

Shortly before noon the following day, August 28, Private Wagner, who stood at the end of the driveway keeping a watch on the highway, hollered, "Luka's coming ... and another man!"

The men were all milling around the farmhouse's massive porch, taking refuge from an unusual heat and playing some sort of newfangled German word game, with which Christopher was unfamiliar.

Everyone stood and headed along the drive, looking westward, shading their eyes from the glaring sun.

Christopher and the still-struggling Rudolph were late getting there, but sure enough along came the corporal and Christopher's friend, Douglas Bradford. He was unmistakable. As broad as the Arabian he was riding and about as tall. Behind him—strapped to his back?—was a wagon wheel.

The man would have been a mighty warrior but couldn't hit his own barn door from ten paces and—as only a few knew—stayed at his business to act as a spy for his cousin, Colonel William Bradford, commanding officer of Philadelphia's 1st Battalion. This was in case the Redcoats ever wrenched control of Philadelphia and the Americans needed a spy inside the city.

Had Douglas deferred from service out of fear?

Christopher chuckled at the thought, for this was a revolution, and during war, the spying business was a mortal affair, the offender hung from a short rope.

As the two men approached, Douglas waved a hearty hello, his face both sociable and showing concern. "Problems, I hear."

Fischer took charge. "Yes, sir, and we thank you for coming such a long distance, Mr. Bradford."

"Gotta leave the city once in a while to be reminded of God's glory," Douglas's husky voice went silent as he looked about the property. "The wagon?"

"Couple miles beside the road." Fischer pointed.

"Let's get her done."

The men gathered what little they'd brought with them, including a couple of bags of food goods, said their thank you's and goodbyes to Helena, and headed east.

Douglas dismounted and led his horse along, walking beside Christopher.

"Thought you were off to Flying Camp," he said. "Corporal Meyer—Luka—filled me in on what's happening here."

Christopher nodded.

"I've been thinking since you and the Hessians dropped by the livery the other day."

"And?" Christopher asked.

"And I'll be needing help now Matthew's gone to war." Matthew was Douglas's apprentice.

"And?"

"Well, Johann knows everything about horses. And he is a sturdy fellow."

"Yes?"

"What do you know of him?"

"I know he loves horses, and he has a grand knowledge of leatherworks and saddles. You should have seen him with Lyn Middleton at the stalls."

Douglas nodded in appreciation.

Christopher continued. "He connected at the bakery with Herman and Matilde Schneider whose family is also from the Black Forest. He is big and strong. Headstrong as well, but he's a good lad."

"So, you'd not object if I offered him a job, good wages, and a place to live? Unless and until he decides on taking some of the land Congress is offering."

Christopher smiled and pointed ahead. "Well, the young man is over there. Make your proposition. Do you think your German's good enough for the conversation? I'll interpret."

"I'll give it a try on my own," Douglas said. He handed the reins of his horse to Christopher and hurried ahead.

Christopher watched with intensity as Douglas shook hands with Johann, who was walking alongside Emil. All the others were in a strong walk, not marching but taking long strides.

Douglas tugged at the young man's elbow and maneuvered him away until they were a few feet apart from the others. Douglas spoke, Johann nodded. Douglas continued, and Johann's nod became more animated. Douglas turned his head to look more at Johann, said something else, and the equestrian stopped in his tracks.

Douglas stopped as well, and Christopher drew alongside them as Johann sputtered, *"Wirklich? Meinst du, dass?"* meaning, "Truly?"

"Ja!" Douglas said. "Ja!"

Johann turned to Christopher, a broad smile across his face.

"I have a job, Christoff!"

Christopher met the smile with his own and glanced a thankful look Douglas's way.

Douglas nodded, with a keen look of satisfaction.

Emil, several yards ahead now, heard the exchange and hurried back to inquire. "Is it true?"

"Yes. I'll be working at the livery, handling horses, learning how to make horseshoes and harnesses, all the things I'd love to do."

Emil wrapped his arms around Johann in a bear hug.

Christopher remembered when he was calculating where each Hessian stood in a zero-to-ten scale concerning whether they would leave their British comrades.

Johann had been a six on the spectrum. Emil and Hans had both been close to ten already. Rudolph had jumped from a seven to a solid ten now, being enthralled with a certain young *mädchen* hadn't lowered his number, for sure.

The fusiliers, Bernhard and Heinrich? Coming from the poverty of an industrial German city to this beautiful land and now knowing they had plenty of countrymen living here—a community of support—Christopher pushed his earlier speculation of nine on the ten-point scale to over the top.

Finally, Jägers Blum and Schäfer. Unless they were the best actors since British actor David Garrick—whom Christopher had seen play Richard III at the Theater Royal in London before sailing off to America—even they were solid tens. And solid bets to be his future neighbors by the Germantown farm.

But do not count your chickens, Christopher.

The warning was a whisper in his ear. Not a rebuke, but a reminder of a lesson he'd learned more than once. God alone is one-hundred-percent certain of affairs of the mind. The rejoinder prompted him to pray, right there and then.

Johann and Emil strode ahead to share the news with their comrades, and Douglas waited for Christopher, keeping hold of the horse's reins.

"A successful negotiation, then," Christopher said.

"Like you and Congress," Douglas replied. "I don't know how on earth you formed the idea, then won Congress over to your thinking, but you, Benjamin, and the others have fashioned a winning strategy."

"I believe you're right, Douglas. I pray you are."

***

Minutes later, they arrived at the wrecked wagon, with Christopher at Douglas's side.

Douglas took charge. "Someone, find a sturdy log to put under the wagon here where we're replacing the wheel. We'll need a couple of you men to lift this front-right part of the wagon, so we can rest the wagon on the log to replace the wheel."

Christopher chuckled to himself when Douglas said "a couple" for while it might take two Douglas Bradfords to do so, such a weight would take four ordinary men to lift.

Fischer motioned to nearby woods. "Private Bohn, Corporal Meyer, go find an adequate log to hold up this wagon."

Nikolaus and Luka hustled away.

Schäfer pointed to Hans, Emil, Johann, and Bernhard. "Prepare to lift the wagon, men."

A minute later, with the four Hessians grunting and groaning to lift the wagon, Nikolaus and Luka rolled a hefty log into place.

Douglas had pulled the spare wheel from his horse and a glass jar from his saddlebag. He motioned for Johann to kneel with him by the axle.

He opened the jar, stuck his massive fingers in, and pulled out a handful of lard. He slathered the lard on the end of the axle.

"When you do this, don't spare an ounce," he instructed.

Johann nodded and applied a handful on the wheel hub.

"Fill her as full as a tick," Douglas reminded him.

Though he spoke in English, Johann nodded.

"Hand me the wheel."

Johann lifted the wheel into Douglas's ready hands, who slid the wheel into place.

"Easy as pie," Douglas said, then winked at Christopher. "I would never say gingerbread."

Moments later, he'd tightened the wheel. With a smile of satisfaction, he stood, slapping his hands together. "Job done."

Douglas eyed Johann and said in halting German, "That's how it's done, son. You'll learn more."

Johann grinned.

"Private Bohn," Fischer said, "roll the log into the ravine."

Bohn did so, and Fischer ordered, "Load the food back into the wagon, get our friends back on board, and let's head out."

Several of the men shook Douglas's hand, thanking him. Johann gave him a hug—at least putting his arms as far around the massive man as he could.

Douglas tipped his cap to them, pulled himself atop his horse, and gazed at Christopher.

"Viel Glück," he said, meaning "good luck."

"Your German's getting better," Christopher said with a smile. "You and Johann will be teaching each other your languages."

Douglas nodded. "We will. By the way, my friend, success favors the bold. I count you among them. May the Lord confuse our enemies."

"Thank you," Christopher said. "Godspeed. Mind how you go."

As Douglas rode off, Christopher climbed onto the front seat of the wagon.

Fischer was atop his horse. The soldiers and Hessians were in place.

"Maybe we'll get to Flying Camp by Thursday," Fischer said. "Maybe not."

CHAPTER 14

"Maybe not" became the reality as a heavy rain pelted them, making slop out of several marshy areas. They found an abandoned shack in which to lay low and dry off, then waited out the storm for several hours.

"I can only imagine the condition of the Flying Camp in this weather," Christopher said to Fischer.

"If they're even still there," Fischer hesitated, "or otherwise engaged."

Christopher flinched at the picture of his friends in battle.

After the downpour, they started on their way, and in late afternoon, crossed the Delaware River at Wells Ferry. The water flow was so rapid Christopher prayed angels would prevent the ferry from being swept away downriver.

With a windless, cloudless night bore down on them, they bunked there under stars stretching to the horizon.

"Aquila, the eagle," Blum pointed. "My favorite constellation."

"The North Star." Schäfer pointed. "Ought to be yours. Then you'd never get lost." He chuckled.

"Me lost? Huh!" Blum responded. "Plunk me in the middle of the Black Forest, blindfolded. I'll find my way home."

"Jäger," Rudolph piped up, "you're our North Star."

A couple of the others snickered.

"You titter like little girls," Blum said. "Who here can pick out the Canis Major? For you bumpkins, it means 'big dog.'" His laugh doubled the challenge.

Yet no one accepted the test.

"Canis Major isn't visible this time of year," Fischer said matter-of-factly. "You asked an impossible question, Big Dog."

Everyone laughed at this.

Blum nodded. "I admit you're right. Didn't know there was another astrologer in our midst, professor."

"My father," Fischer said. "He was my personal Canis Major."

His use of past tense brought silence.

Christopher considered that perhaps they were all thinking of friends and loved ones gone. In this Revolution, some of these friends and family might not be long passed. He considered his father, whom he had left behind to join the army.

Sorry, Papa, for choosing adventure instead of staying with you.

Adventure, the promise of which had called many a young German into the ranks before getting conscripted.

"Lieutenant," Schäfer said, "I have a question for you." Schäfer lay on a blanket where he raised himself up on an elbow. "You colonists—"

"Americans," Fischer corrected.

"Okay. Americans. You live in a city comparable to the greatest of those of Germany and all Europe. Many of you are in comfortable houses surrounded by gardens and orchards. You're as affluent as German country gentlemen. Why revolt against a government under which you enjoy such lives?"

"Authority," Fischer said without hesitation. "Control. English kings have long treated America as a treasure chest. King George robs us to pay his debts, the latest being the French and Indian War—a struggle he claims was to save the American colonies when, in truth, it was to strengthen his empire, increase his wealth."

Fischer crossed his arms, his eyes boring into Schäfer's. "The king's laws and taxes—ever the taxes, the Sugar Tax, the Stamp Tax, the Currency Act, which made us dependent on British currency—all these combined are a dagger to the heart. How can we grow, how can we continue to prosper, with such a burden?

"The king and his Parliament," he continued, "have lorded it over us without a single vote. If he had allowed America a representative in the House of Commons to express our concerns ... If he had granted us a simple seat at the table ... then perhaps, I say *perhaps*, this whole revolt would never have happened."

Schäfer sat up. "You expect this from a king?"

Fischer's eyes were afire.

"Worst of all," he said, "we are a source of the king's utter contempt. The scorn pours from his veins. His derision is toxic in its virility. His royal governors in our colonies have shown the same disdain. Corrupt local officials charge exorbitant fees and seize our property."

Is Fischer a scholar? Christopher wondered.

The lieutenant continued, "An old farmer friend of mine, who's fighting under General Putnam, said to me a while ago, 'We always had been free. We meant to be free always. The Brits? They believed otherwise.' My friend had never read Thomas Paine, or John Locke, or any others about the principle of liberty. So, he wasn't driven by their words, by borrowed feelings, but his own experience. He said, 'The only books we've had were the Bible, Watts's Psalms, a few hymns and almanacs.'"

Fischer drew a breath. "Jäger Schäfer—Kristian—the Revolution is a medicine to eliminate an incurable disease, a malady otherwise leading to slow death."

Bernhard, lying next to his boyhood friend Heinrich, asked, "Has England's king ever hired Americans as soldiers as our emperor does?"

Fischer spat out the answer. "If slipping a coin into the pocket of a man in a crowd, then swearing he took the king's shilling and enlisted? Yes. A familiar trick."

His response drew ooh's and ahh's.

"Another hoax," said Christopher, "is when British recruiters declare you become a gentleman when you join the king's army."

"Oh?" Blum said.

"I joined the Royal Navy for a time," Christopher said. "Standing at the docks in Liverpool, I heard a recruiting sergeant declare, 'You're now a pack of dirty, meagre ragamuffin fellows. But join me, and with sword in hand, you'll be treated as gentlemen and provided for accordingly.'"

"Foolish," Schäfer said.

"If America wins the war, what will you do, Lieutenant?" Rudolph asked.

"If?" Fischer said. "Once we win, I'll return home, resume my life as a lawyer."

The sentiment answered Christopher's earlier question.

An orator, a lawyer, a fine soldier.

"Amen, Lieutenant," Luka said. "After we win."

Christopher enjoyed hearing the high hopes of these young men. He himself was firm in his faith. God supported freedom for the two and a half million Americans.

★★★

The next morning, August 29, after a breakfast of porridge and bread, the whole party was on the road. As dusk darkened the woods around them, they arrived at the Flying Camp at Perth Amboy.

But no one was there. Not one.

Tents and canopies stood abandoned. No smoke rose from the rings of rock where fires had burned. No horses, no cannons, no wagons.

Lieutenant Fischer led them right into the middle of the encampment, then motioned to halt the procession and swung down from his horse.

From his seat on the wagon, Christopher called out, "What do you think happened?"

"Off to the battle?" Fischer ventured, then stepped off toward what served as General Mercer's strategy tent. Christopher scrambled to the ground and followed him there.

The table where Mercer had spread the maps stood empty.

We're missing the fight, Christopher thought.

"Men must be dying," Fischer said.

Christopher froze at the thought and moaned.

There was no sound.

Then there was.

Faint at first. A rustling in the distance, a stir in the air, then a squawk from a rousing grouse a hundred or so meters away. A flock of birds fluttered from the treetops of the forest.

The size of the flock was startling. As if a thousand fowl had awoken from the same spectacle at the precise moment and had to scatter into the heavens quickly.

A portend? Christopher's muscles tightened. His breath caught. The enemy? Worse still, the Hessians?

Fischer ordered his men to take arms, then stared at Blum, asking, "Can you get your men behind the wagon, Karl?"

As Blum did so, Christopher ignored the bustling all around. He kept his gaze on the forest beyond the encampment. He narrowed his eyes, leaning forward, hoping even a couple inches would help him hear what was rustling there.

Then the sound of horses' hooves and the rambling of cannon wheels pounding the earth shattered the silence.

Out of the woods marched a column of soldiers, led by several horsemen, flying the Taunton Union Flag. Christopher couldn't read the words in the red section of the flag, but knew they were "Liberty" and "Union." He could breathe again.

"They're ours!" he shouted.

"Hold your fire, men," Fischer ordered.

As the troops drew closer, Christopher spotted General Mercer riding at the head. Behind on horseback were Haller, Hays, Hart, and Lawrence.

The nearer the troops came, the more exhausted they appeared, the more disheveled, the more ... depressed? Nevertheless, Christopher was heartened. Yes, they wore the dirt of many miles marching. But they were alive.

Decades had passed since relief had felt this good.

Praise You, God.

***

Minutes later, the encampment was abustle. Many of the infantry dropped to the ground. There they laid their heads against a stump or folded their coats beneath their heads.

Haller and Lawrence took charge, ordering tents to be raised and fires built. Hart and Hays headed to the headquarters canopy.

General Mercer motioned for Lieutenant Fischer and Christopher to follow him. Under the canopy, he grabbed a canvas pouch and removed a letter.

"This was intended for you, Lieutenant, informing you we were off to war. Didn't expect to return." Mercer shook his head, then, "I'm certain we've lost the battle for Long Island."

Fischer and Christopher groaned at the news.

"The Redcoats attacked early Tuesday before sunrise," the general continued. "Howe's army crossed over on the Doyles and Narrows Ferries across the Hudson and advanced by land, while his brother's warships blocked us from crossing in behind Howe and any of General Washington's and General Putnam's men from escaping off the island. The battle's been raging these two days. All we've been able to do is swap cannon balls at the warships. Lost seven men."

Mercer shook his head in disgust. "Our cannons couldn't reach the ships, so we retreated."

Two days! Christopher fumed. *And we were swapping family stories and enjoying Pfannkuchen!*

"We fear Howe will dig in for a siege, starving out Washington and Putnam. Twenty-six thousand men are stranded there. Potential prisoners of war."

"Never happen." Christopher's beliefs slipped out from his lips.

"What?" Mercer asked.

"We're going to win this war. There's no victory if Washington's lost." Christopher shrugged. "So, God's going to do something miraculous."

Mercer shook his head, dismissing the comment as frivolous. Behind him, Hart and Haller swapped looks of disbelief. Christopher wondered if any of them were men of faith.

"God has done so before," he said. "Remember, He had Gideon reduce his army to a mere three hundred, so no one could claim Gideon, not God, brought the victory. And Joshua at the battle of Jericho. Not an arrow was fired, instead shouts out of the mouths of His people."

Mercer blew out a breath and nodded as if—well, perhaps—such a deliverance was indeed possible.

"Praying men should pray. Believing men should believe," Christopher said.

"Then let's do so," Mercer said. He led the men in a soulful prayer for deliverance—somehow, some way.

When done, Fischer and Christopher told them all about the days spent exploring Philadelphia, touring the countryside, and meeting citizens at the bakery and church.

"Our reception was beyond expectations, sir," Fischer enthused.

Finally, Christopher said every one of the Hessians wanted to remain in America but had beseeched them to be able to return to convince their friends to join them in absconding.

"Are you serious?" Mercer asked. "You expect me to allow these Germans to—" he raised his voice several decibels, "return to the battlefield? Seasoned, proven, hired killers?"

Christopher resisted the urge to shrink at the dressing-down but nodded.

Mercer's eyes were bullets as he turned his gaze to Fischer. "Your assessment, Lieutenant?"

Fischer didn't hesitate. "I agree with Mr. Ludwick, General. I've paid close attention to the Jägers, listening to their personal conversations, gauging their reactions as we've inspected the city and met other Germans who've prospered here and spoke to them convincingly. I must say, Pastor Mühlenberg's impassioned sermon would convince the most passionate and partisan Hessians to come to America—perhaps even join our fight."

Mercer shook his head astonishment. He turned to his colonels. Hart shrugged. Haller did the same.

"Do you trust, can you be certain," Hart asked Christopher, "these men won't turn on us, their instincts won't get the better of them?"

"Instincts?" Christopher said. "With the exceptions of the Jägers, these young men have seen little of war, and what little they've experienced has convinced them they want no more of it. They have no devotion or loyalty to their emperor, who conscripted them to fight to fatten his own pockets. They possess no fidelity to King George."

"As a matter of fact," Fischer cut in, "they've gotten to know our soldiers pretty well, and what we've told them about King George has turned their stomachs against the tyrant."

"I started this experiment judging each man on a scale of one to ten, where they stood on the offer to leave the ranks of the Redcoats to live among us," Christopher said. "I've adjusted my grade every day."

"Yes, and—?" Mercer said.

"They'd top out at eleven, if I had such a measure."

Mercer's eyes moved to Fischer.

The lieutenant nodded agreement. "As astounding as it may seem, I have to agree, General."

"Let me consider your proposal," Mercer said. "I'll give you an answer in the morning."

Fischer and Christopher returned to the Hessians, who were gathered around a campfire wearing their uniforms and speaking in hushed tones.

Christopher delivered the news, leaving out the results of the Battle of Long Island. He stressed Mercer might acquiesce to their request. As he did so, a dense fog settled into the area—a fog even the campfire did little to dispense.

CHAPTER 15

Christopher spared no time rising from his one-man tent, beating dawn by a good half-hour, from years of practice operating the bakery with Catharine. He guessed the bugler was deep in sleep, perhaps playing taps in a dream.

The early bird gets the worm. Likely a British idiom, but one his father might have coined first. In this case, he hoped the early bird could travel incognito until he reached enemy lines. However, first he would prepare a good meal for the Hessians. God knew whether this was the last time they'd get such a treat.

Last night's fog was still about as thick this morning. The only light penetrating the darkness came from ambers in nearby fire pits.

Christopher was certain sentries were stationed around the perimeter of the camp, but they were invisible in the soupy environs.

His eyes adjusting, he pulled on his boots, wrapped his coat about him, found Hans and Emil, and asked them to stoke the fires to make breakfast. They were cooperative, energetic, thankful even. Anxiety was also written across their faces. Unspoken but there.

Others around the Hessians stirred as the three went about their business.

General Mercer walked out of the fog, startling Christopher.

"Can't sleep," Mercer said.

"A common malady during war." Christopher knew the problem well. A body craves comfort. Bitter cold, drenching rains, or blazing heat all plague the body in the search for sleep. The body often loses each of these battles.

So many nights sleepless and strapped of strength on the three-hundred-mile march.

Mercer nodded. "What're you all doing?"

"Going to get our foreign friends a good meal, which may be their last for some time." Christopher studied Mercer's response.

Must be a good card player. "Then, I plan to give Colonel Montgomery's battalion a special treat as well. He mentioned my wife had fed them when they rode past our bakery a month ago."

"His whole battalion?"

"His whole battalion."

Mercer shook his head but smiled. "I do believe General Washington has made a brilliant decision naming you Baker General. Perhaps 'co-general' would suit your wife.

"Thank you, General. And Catharine would be a grand choice all on her own." Christopher smiled broadly but knew something else was on the Scotsman's mind.

Mercer waited a moment, then opened his hands as if preparing to juggle balls.

"You have your approval," he said. "May God be with those Hessians."

"I'm going too."

"Excuse me?"

"My original orders from Congress were to infiltrate enemy lines to persuade my former countrymen to come over to our side. I have yet to cross those lines."

"But you've accomplished your goal."

"Eight men was not my goal," Christopher said, his voice rising. "Maybe eighty times eight."

"Then take my pistol." Lieutenant Fischer had walked up, unnoticed, behind Christopher. Now he offered his handgun.

Christopher caught his gaze. "Words will be my weapon of choice—the one firearm I'll need." He hesitated. "These eight men we took under our wing—they will be the musket balls, the cannonballs of persuasion. Better than me. I'll wait a few hours after their departure, then get on my way."

Fischer and Mercer nodded their approval. They had abandoned hope of dissuading him.

Christoff Ludwig is a man of determination. Dissuasion? Never.

Christopher looked at Mercer. "Do you have a dispatch heading to Philadelphia anytime soon?"

"A man leaves at noon to deliver our report to Congress."

"I've written a letter to my wife."

"I'll have the private find you before he rides out."

Christopher left Fischer behind to receive directions as how to release the prisoners.

***

Watching him stroll off, Mercer turned to Fischer. "This Ludwick fellow might be a baker by trade, but if he returns from behind enemy lines—having accomplished his purpose—he'll be what we Scotsmen call a *sheòid*, a hero and inspiration to the rest of us."

"Audacity," Fischer said.
"Audacity—and faith."
"Lavish faith."

★★★

Two hours later, his cooking duties dispatched, Christopher found a quiet spot to write Catharine. His final communication?

> My dearest Beloved,
> What an adventure we've had! What a wife you've been! What a partner!
> I'm off in a few hours to Staten Island to visit more of my countrymen. Along with those you've met and their persuasive power, I believe we will find success. God knows. He sees into the hearts of men, but I believe all men want freedom. All men want control of their lives, to live out dreams, to find happiness—temporal as well as eternal—without some emperor or king lording power over the air they breathe.
> America has so much to offer. She—and you, my dear— changed my life. God even more. So, I want this at least for these men, who have so little hope if they return to Germany. If they even were to survive this war, which promises to be so brutal.
> Please keep me and all our military in your prayers. Until I hold you again in my arms, I am ...
>
> > Eternally yours,
> > Christopher

He folded the letter, put it in an envelope, and at noon, handed the communication to a young soldier riding out with a pouch of important information for the leaders of Congress.

He was sure part of Mercer's report was an update on the Hessian prisoners. He was also certain Benjamin

Franklin, Thomas Jefferson, James Madison, and the others would take heart from the news. Something to keep in their "hope chest"—a way to save lives and help turn the war to America's advantage.

Fischer approached him. "Christopher, our plan is to escort our German friends as far as we can before reaching enemy territory. Then, they're on their own. So are you."

Christopher smiled. "Never 'on our own,' Gus."

Fischer smiled in return, knowing his meaning—and his faith.

★★★

Two hours later, Christopher approached the eight Hessians under their canopy. They were sitting in their uniforms, chatting, their civilian clothes in an orderly pile nearby.

Very German.

Christopher recalled a scene in Jonathan Swift's *Gulliver's Travels*, which he had read to hone his English-speaking skills. He had enjoyed the book because, the same as Lemuel Gulliver, he had sailed to remote regions of the world while aboard *The Duke of Cumberland*.

Like Gulliver, these men had been taken to their captors' capital, Philadelphia, then released. In Gulliver's case, he joined his captors in fighting another kingdom.

Could this be the case with Christopher's new friends?

Christopher had also appreciated the narrative, because he'd read it in the midst of England's escalating oppression. Swift used his story, written fifty years ago, as a satire against England. His lampoon of the British exacerbated Christopher's growing feelings of discontent with the monarchy and Parliament. For example, in Swift's story, political affiliations are divided between men who wear high-heeled shoes—symbolic of the English Tories—and those who wear low ones—representing the English Whigs. Court positions are filled by those who are best at rope dancing. Rope dancing!

Later, Gulliver sails to Brobdingnag, whose king describes the English as a race of "odious vermin." Gulliver's encounters mirrored what was a growing, sad predicament for American colonists, for sure.

Christopher looked over a group of men he'd first met as strangers nine days before. Now they were family. A dysfunctional family, perhaps, but close to his heart. Men from the Old Country. Men who loved gingerbread. And, at least, a few who loved God. A number which he hoped would soon grow.

Noticing him first, Rudolph waved a hello.

Christopher waded into their midst, catching their eyes individually. "I want to wish you Godspeed."

Nods of thanks.

"We'll miss you," Blum said.

"Until we see you again," Schäfer added.

Christopher's heart jumped at the comment. He caught the Jäger's eyes in his own. "Maybe sooner than you think, Kristian."

Schäfer and several of the others reacted with a "What?"

"I'm following you in."

Schäfer leaped to his prodigious height. "Too dangerous!"

Christopher shook his head. "Going there has always been my intention. When I first arrived, my plan was to cross over British lines to persuade your comrades to leave the Redcoats' service for a better life."

"They hang spies," Blum objected. "Or shoot them."

"So I've been told. General Mercer had the same response."

"You have a wife, a business, friends," Schäfer said.

"Yes. I also have a God I trust to protect me. If He doesn't, well, He has a reason. A better strategy."

Rudolph shook his head. "Mr. Ludwig, trust us to do this job. Please. We know these soldiers;—they know us and will trust what we tell them."

"Am I not a good persuader, Rudolph?" Christopher spoke with a chuckle.

Rudolph displayed some consternation, but after a moment's delay, nodded. "Yes," he said grudgingly.

"Then the two of us could double your effort. Now multiply by all seven of our comrades here." He waved his arm to include the entire group.

Blum stood now, next to Schäfer, placed his hands on hips, looking Christopher over from foot to head. "Christoff," he said, "there is one of you, just one. God made the mold like one of your gingerbread molds. But when He'd finished, He broke the thing ... never to be duplicated."

"Thank you, Karl ... I think." Christopher raised an eyebrow. "But do I have your approval?"

Before Blum responded, Schäfer asked, "Do you have a specific strategy. Are you going to stroll past the sentries, wallow into the camp of the army, and declare your proposal? Lieutenant-General Von Heister will have your head before you finish "Hallo."

"Kristian," Christopher said, "Pastor Mühlenberg once told me 'worry is an accusation against God.' I try to live this belief, but I trust it's veracity. So, I will approach them as I did you but perhaps with a bit more discretion ... given the circumstances."

"Big circumstances," Blum said. "We were prisoners in your camp. You will be a spy in ours. You won't be able to speak as candidly."

"I'm glad you used the past tense, 'were.'" Christopher smiled. "I understand your concerns, Karl. I do. Pray for me and I will pray for you. You, too, will face dire consequences if caught convincing other men to leave the emperor's service."

"We will be candid with friends, one-on-one," Schäfer said. "The British don't understand German. Our concern won't be with the old man, General Von Hester, but with those closest to the troops—Captain Wreden, who leads our own Jägerkorps, Von Donop, Von Bardeleben, and Lieutenant Rueffer of the Mirbach Regiment.

"They have a stake in the fight, so to speak," Blum said, "because the emperor has promised their debts have been paid and their families will be taken care of until they return. If they lose us, their heads may roll—and not figuratively."

Christopher nodded. "You've all talked this through, haven't you?"

"Yes," Blum said. "Ad nauseum."

"Until my stomach turns," Schäfer added.

Blum hit his friend on the shoulder. "That's what ad nauseum means, Jäger." He shook his head in feigned disgust. "Public schools in Germany ... what can I say?"

Schäfer harrumphed and the group laughed.

"The point is, Christoff," Blum said, "we can motivate, convince."

"So can I. So will I." Christopher turned to leave. His decision was nonnegotiable. "You go now. I'll come this afternoon."

"And find us?"

"Yes."

Christopher hurried out of the canopy before anyone else mustered another argument.

After all, he recalled a verse in Psalm 50 where God says, "You thought I was just like you."

We consider that He has the same worries we humans do. Well, He doesn't.

CHAPTER 16

FRIDAY, AUGUST 30, 1776
STATEN ISLAND, NEW YORK

Yes, indeed, war had again hunted Christopher Ludwick down, and yes, again, he had walked straight into its bony arms. On purpose.

He wondered if he would not learn its lesson. On the one hand, selfless love of country and adventure. On the other hand, distress, mayhem, even death. All the tortures and triumphs of life encapsulated in one sweeping, fateful event.

Men in high places were often the cause. In this case, King George III not allowing his subjects a say in their government, among other things. Not to mention head mercenary Landgrave Frederick II ordering his fellow Hessians to war for another country. An "enlightened despot," indeed. Filling his personal coffers with blood money from George.

Christopher saddled Hugo, and with a sack of goodies prepared for his task, headed north. Toward the enemy camp. Toward the company of trained killers—thirty-five thousand of them, both Redcoats and Hessians.

Among those Hessians, a handful were his now-fellow spies. But they were part of Jägerkorps, the most dangerous enemy of the American troops. Perilous because they were trained to fight as the Americans did—in scattered skirmishes. But, in their case, with rifles accurate from four hundred yards. Not all sharpshooters like Rudolph, but many were. When coupled with the regular Hessian infantry, who with speed loaded their long rifles and attached bayonets to those rifles, they were a staunch, sometimes invincible force.

Yes, Christopher was traveling toward all this, but he was in the hands of his God.

Remember this. Remember this.

***

As Christopher rode toward his countrymen, a sudden flurry of recollections rushed at him. Recollections he hadn't shared with General Mercer or any of the colonels at Flying Camp or even his dear Catharine. Recollections from his sessions with Congress, convincing members to support his idea.

Benjamin Rush, John Hancock, and John Jay all warned against the scheme. Benjamin, one of his best friends in all the world, had grabbed him by the elbow, pulled him aside, and declared in a guttural admonition only he could hear, "My dear Christopher, you are perhaps the godliest man I know, the most selfless. You are one we cannot afford to lose. You going into the enemy camp is foolhardy in its simplest form. If nothing else, think of your dear wife being left a widow."

Christopher had gazed back at Benjamin's kindly, imploring eyes. "I compare not myself to such a great man, but didn't the Apostle Paul know if he went to Jerusalem he'd be bound, imprisoned, delivered to the authorities? Yet he remarked, 'The will of the Lord be done.'"

As Benjamin pondered a response, Christopher had continued, "Sometimes God wants us to face danger, not shrink from it. Paul said he was bound by the Spirit, and though he knew 'bonds of affliction' awaited him, he held his life as no account."

"So, you're comparing your going into harm's way to Paul spreading the gospel." The words were flat. They might have been supposed scoffing if not from the lips of this one man.

Christopher squared his shoulders. "Shall I not try to save some of my old countrymen from death, lead them to greener pastures than they'd ever own in Germany, perhaps even lead them to the throne of God?"

Looking deflated, Benjamin had blown out a deep breath, his shoulders slumped. He knew he'd lost his argument.

They were interrupted by the voice of Patrick Henry. The forty-year-old Henry had earned everyone's respect, helping to draft, then sign, the First Continental Congress's Petition to the king two years earlier.

Having walked to the front of the hall, Henry stood tall, his arms crossed. "Would we deny the man his vision?"

Seven simple words ended the debate.

★★★

An hour later, dressed in his everyday garb, tricorn in place and trying to look as innocent as a German peasant, Christopher crossed Raritan Bay to Billops Point on the Long Ferry with little trouble. He was surprised. The ground was sloppy, but the sun was on its upward climb to noon, on its way to drying the land from yesterday's downpour. He passed Rossville, where the Continental Army had recruited heavily, then Richmond, closing in on Castletown.

Spotting an innocent-looking pasture with a couple dozen sheep, he dismounted, removed the saddle and blanket, covered them with branches behind an oddly formed tree he figured he'd find with ease later, leaving Hugo with a flock of companions. The stallion spotted a birch tree, stretched and chomped on a mouthful of tasty leaves. Between the plentiful hay a foot high, the birch and nearby dogwood and elm trees, Hugo would be happy here. A smart horse—he'd wait.

Hefting his sack onto his back, Christopher set off toward Dennyse Ferry, where he expected to find his friends among the Hessian forces. They'd be decked out in fine array—the infantry in their blue jackets, the Jägers with their green jackets with crimson facing.

★★★

"Halt!"

The command stopped Christopher in his tracks, but he was prepared. He thought.

Having seen the bustling encampment of troops from a distance, he had kept his steady pace, undeterred in spirit while dreading the malevolent possibilities. His determination was fueled by the empathy he felt for his countrymen since little was going well for Germany back home—yet his resolve was tempered by fears of discovery.

His ally, what he was relying on, was the idea of opportunity. Where did it exist? Not in Germany.

Prospects here? Categorically. He was proof.

Between what the Hessians had witnessed firsthand this last week, what he shared about his experiences the past two decades, the offer of liberty, self-determination, and free land, he felt the Hessians couldn't resist such a series of revelations. If he lived long enough to share.

A Redcoat wearing a stern expression and carrying an impressive rifle but too young to shave—therefore being designated for sentry duty—gazed at Christopher as if he were a long-lost uncle. Therefore, why even question his intent in entering the British encampment?

What else would he think? What sane person would attempt to walk in the "front door," so to speak, if he were an agent of the enemy?

"Why, son," Christopher said, "my name is Christoff Ludwig. I'm here to find my nephew, Rudolph, who is fighting under Captain Wreden's Jägerkorps. His dear aunt has baked him a treat." He pointed a thumb toward the sack on his shoulder. "A treat to add to the good food I'm sure he's being fed to strengthen him for the battles ahead."

"A treat, huh?"

Christopher nodded.

The soldier stepped forward. "Care to share?"

"Why, of course."

Christopher shrugged the sack off his shoulder and lowered it to the ground.

"Stop right there!" a gruff voice demanded. Christopher glanced up. A bearded, dark-haired, thirtyish sergeant—looking every bit a woodsman out of the forest—strode toward him with a musket at the ready. First, the man glared at the private. "Boy, what are you playing at? We're not in Liverpool or London. We're in a hostile land. Have you heard of spies? This place might be full of 'em. This man here might be one himself.

"So," he continued, "what must you be on the lookout for when someone asks entry?"

The private looked at his superior, wide-eyed, as if the answer lay somewhere in the heavens, not in his own head.

"Beware, private, not of those who stutter and stammer and try to look the innocent, but the smooth ones, those who charm, appeal, enthrall, and speak good, beguiling things."

"Beguiling?" the private asked.

"Enchanting. Attractive." The sergeant looked at him with wonder. "Where'd you go to school, private?"

"I didn't, sir."

The sergeant shook his head and muttered, "We'll accept anyone into this army." He steadied his glare on the private. "Listen, don't consider everyone our friend—even when they look unassuming like this man here, who with all innocence say they want inside our lines. Especially then."

The young man shrugged.

"Who knows what a 'visitor' might discover here? Who knows what information they might take with them upon leaving? If I find you've let a spy into camp ..." he snarled ... "I'll shoot you myself, then hunt the vermin to make terrible work of his stinking body."

Christopher winced.

The sergeant turned, stared at Christopher, and waved his weapon in Christopher's direction. "What's your excuse, fella? This is a military camp. What business do you have coming here?"

Christopher tried to capture the sergeant's eyes in his own—for who could resist his kind eyes, his gentle demeanor? He chuckled at his own self-effacement, but the man's glare defied kind intentions—real or unreal. His eyes were dark, his scowl a scary thing, and as he took three steps closer, his body odor was disgusting. Swampish even.

Christopher looked over the sergeant's shoulder at the camp. A muddy place, paths stretching in different directions, all containing puddles of water rutted by wagon tracks. Six-man tents stretched shoulder to shoulder into the distance.

Soldiers scurried in all directions, appearing to have taken baths in dirt and mud water.

Maybe the sergeant had taken a mud bath at low tide.

Officers hollered orders—no one in a good mood. Yes, war tended to temper a person's kindness. Especially when you were far from home. Especially when the weather was nasty. Especially ...

"Mister!" The sergeant broke Christopher's musings. "What's your business, and what's in the sack?"

The private answered for him, blurting out, "Says he's bringing his nephew food of some kind."

"Shut up, soldier," the sergeant said, keeping his gaze on Christopher. He squeezed his eyes and his eyebrows met in the middle. His stare would sizzle an egg. "I'm asking you, sir."

Finally, Christopher managed, "My nephew, sergeant. I believe him to be here. He's German. We're German, his aunt and I. He'd be among the Hessian forces."

The sergeant pointed his rifle at the sack. "Open up. Slowly. We've already had one of our sentries gutted by a 'visitor.' A man pretending to be a friend, a loyalist. We hung the scum from the nearest tree."

A shiver ran along Christopher's back.

He bent, pulled out a cloth wrapping, opened it up, and pulled out two pieces of gingerbread, each the size of his palm and shaped as a king's crown.

He looked with anticipation at the sergeant, half expecting the man to shoot the delicacy out of his hand—hoping he'd scoop it out.

No bullet was fired, so Christopher handed a piece to each soldier.

The sergeant grunted, examining his piece of gingerbread as if searching for a hidden pocketknife.

After his examination, his peered at Christopher, his face shifted to a milder look, and he took a bite. At first taste his eyes opened wide in enjoyment. The private followed suit, with the same results.

The sergeant devoured the rest of the treat. His voice now a soft growl, "You should find your kin about a kilometer." He pointed to the northeast. "Their encampment is on the path to the right. You'll pass a pasture, then you'll smell the 'surgery,' such as it is, off to your left. Then all the Hessians are camped together scattered through a mammoth grove of pine trees. A ten-minute walk—" He assessed Christopher's rotundness. "Maybe fifteen for you."

The wonders of gingerbread.

As Christopher grabbed his satchel, the sergeant added, "If your nephew survived the rebels' cannon fire when he sailed into harbor a couple days back and then the last two days of battle." He snarled. "Drove the rebels out of the forest, we did. Tore 'em to shreds. We'll continue to until they grovel at our feet. Might take a week or two."

Christopher struggled to affect a smile.

Tore 'em to shreds, he'd said. He held back a sigh of pity.

★★★

As he strolled through the camp, Christopher tried not to look guilty. Husky commands, followed by murmured "Yes, sirs" echoed around the camp. Draft horses pulled wagons filled with bags of grain and other goods. Others hauled cannons. Oh, so many cannons! From the northwest toward the northeast. The Redcoats had commandeered an American house or two to use as their command. The generals would be sleeping comfortably, while the troops ... well, the troops.

Wails of pain pierced through the camp's noises. The anguish gutted him. The surgery was nearby. A soldier was under the knife. Christopher recalled the doctor stitching the bayonet wound to his side. He bent forward at the recollection. His own blood and gore hadn't been his problem. the needle's every piercing through his skin had been. Biting on a stick of wood hadn't helped dull the pain, only kept him from biting off his tongue.

He struggled to straighten his back, to continue on his way. Then another screech brought the same effect.

These were the shrieks like sometimes still woke him in the middle of the night.

Wagon wheels rattled behind him. Horses sniggered.

The military is dominated by periods of hustle-bustle-wait, hustle-bustle-wait. But the "wait" was too soon followed by fight. Fight for your life. Fight not to die. Equal slices of fear, faith, timidity, and bravery.

Christopher wondered if war might be more bearable if there were fewer intervals of peace, not more. Such a notion seemed irrational, but "down time" gave a soldier time to think. Ponder the possible outcome of the battle ahead. The dark hole of death. Wives, lovers, friends they might never see again, let alone kiss, laugh with, hold again. Or surviving, but with a debilitating injury—a lost leg or arm. Or games they might never again play, plays they might never again watch, favorite meals they might never again eat.

At the moment, he knew this prefight time was sure to be short, but he hoped it was giving the Hessians the opportunity to consider for what they were fighting.

Christopher had learned going to battle for excitement's sake was a short-lived attainment. Because there was always the next battle and the next battle—until there wasn't.

Then there was the next war—until there wasn't. Until your mind and body were so fatigued, so worn out it didn't matter if there were an honor to win, a ribbon to wear, a note from King Frederick or King William reading: "Thank you for your dedication."

Consequences. Yes, war had consequences. Perhaps these points would reach the mind and spirit of most every soldier to whom he was about to speak. Lower your arms, give your heart to a greater King.

Here he was, trying to achieve calm in the midst of the storm. All he had to do was wear the appearance of a Royalist. He tried to convince himself of this, as he hurried to where he no longer heard the cries of the wounded.

He readjusted the satchel over his shoulder. The weight was starting to be a bother.

Ahead, he spotted Schäfer and Blum. He blew out a sigh of relief. They were standing together, speaking to a couple of their fellow Jägers. Captain Wreden's troops, most likely. Besides their green uniforms, atop their heads were those blasted hats, the one thing which had always made him feel encumbered when in battle.

The men's presence calmed Christopher's nerves. He threw back his shoulders, placed a broad smile across his face, then proceeded at a jaunty pace. When he neared, he called out in an upbeat voice, "Hallo! *Guten nachmittag, meine Freunde!*"

Heads spun, questioning who might this stranger be?

Blum and Schäfer turned from the officers to whom they were speaking and—as planned—acted as if they didn't know him. Blum raised his hands in a gesture of "who's this?" while Schäfer spoke the words, "Who's this?"

But Rudolph, standing nearby, sprang into action.

"Onkel Christoff!" he exclaimed.

"Rudolph!" Christopher stepped toward him, lowered his satchel to the ground. He embraced the lad in a bear hug. "Years, my boy, since we've seen you. Years. How you've grown!"

Rudolph chuckled at the statement, gathered himself, and asked, "How is Tante Catharine?"

"Fine but missing you, longing for the family back in the Old Country." Christopher stepped back, examining the young man. "Have you seen battle?"

"Battle? I've been captured and escaped. Eight of us here, including our two Jägers, to whom we owe our lives." He motioned toward Blum and Schäfer.

Christopher nodded at the two. "Danke. Danke. Our nephew is more than blood to us. We can't lose him."

Rudolph peered at Christopher's satchel. "What do you have there, Onkel?"

"Lebkuchen. Gingerbread." Christopher pulled out the square-shaped cloth wrappings and held them high to see. King's crowns, soldiers, German emperors, Christian crosses. His best molds.

In a hurry, he was surrounded by soldiers, hands extended. Their faces were dirty, their hands filthy, their bodies tired, but their smiles were broad. Among them, he spotted Johann, Emil, Bernhard, and Heinrich. Hans was missing. But no worry. Marta so enraptured Hans that his decision was solid.

"Lebkuchen. God's manna," he announced again in German. "I supposed you'd appreciate a treat to remind you of home."

A minute later, scores of Hessians sat on tree trunks and benches all around in a great circle, with Christopher in the middle.

He regaled them with stories of his childhood. How he rose early with his *vater* in *Gießen* to bake bread at his bakery. "Gingerbread is in our blood, Freunde!" The soldiers cheered.

How he climbed the Zugspitze in the Alps with his cousin Zitti, wandered off the trail, got lost, and when he took off his shoes to rub his sore toes, one shoe fell over a cliff, and he hobbled all the way home leaning on his cousin's shoulder after they'd been found by an elderly couple. His rescuers? "Dressed as immigrants from Poland, their first time over the mountain. As clueless as us."

Christopher paused until the laughter changed to chuckles, then faded.

How he caught a fish in a tributary to the Rhine so big it yanked him off the riverbank into the river, where he lost pole, line, and fish. "Not to mention my dignity."

Emil and Hans led a row of young men their age in laying on the ground chortling.

How he sang in the church's choir when a teenager, trying to sing loud enough so everyone would recognize his adoration for the Savior. But then, after his first rehearsal, the choir director took him aside, saying, "Christoff, I admire your zeal. You can show your love for the Lord by one thing."

"What?" Christopher had asked.

"By mouthing the words."

A round of hoots and clapping hands greeted this admission.

Thus, Christopher became as good as family. He had a captive audience which was enough for his first day behind enemy lines. At least he hoped so, though a sense of impending—something—clouded his mind.

"You can spend the night here with us, Herr Ludwig," Blum announced afterward, making sure everyone heard. His excuse to remain at the camp.

He nodded his assent. "Danke. Danke."

The mood was broken when a man on horseback rode into camp, mud flying from the hoofs of his horse. He was in a fluster, calling, "Kapitän Wreden! Kapitän Wreden!"

Someone pointed him toward the Jägerkamp's commander. Moments later, a solid plume of cuss words filled the air from Wreden's direction.

Rudolph drew close to Christopher. "The commander," he said. "He's a man of extreme emotions. One of the reasons his troops love him—and sometimes hate him."

"Not to be fooled with then," Christopher said.

Rudolph's clear eyes twinkled in mirth. "Not if you want to keep your rank."

As well as your back free of scars, Christopher guessed.

CHAPTER 17

A minute later, Blum and Schäfer, along with other Jägers, were ordered to meet their superior officer. When the two men returned, Christopher couldn't read their expressions. He expected distress or dismay, but wasn't what he perceived in their demeanor closer to nonchalance?

Schäfer stepped on a log. "Men! Attention!"

The company gathered around him.

"We have news from the front," Schäfer said. "From General Von Hester."

The men stepped closer to hear their Jäger's pronouncement.

"When the fighting stopped, Washington's troops were trapped. The British had warships in the harbor and river, while the British, German, and Scottish troops had them in a vise, a blockade by land."

Christopher felt a heavy evil surround him.

But God, I was so certain. Was I wrong?

"Siege, or annihilation by force," Schäfer said. "Either way, they were in the hands of the British. With the American military leader in hand, with his troops under guard, the revolution would most likely be over."

The word "würde" (for "would") hung in the air. Men held their breath.

Blum cut in. "But—the fog!"

Gasps and curses met the statement as every Hessian grasped what had transpired.

"The fog," Schäfer said, "was so thick—the winds so strong—they kept the British ships grounded. Every American escaped across the East River. The British were within eight hundred meters but didn't see a thing, didn't get an inkling of the escape. We estimate twenty thousand men. Not one remains."

Christopher fought to contain his joy, but he must not show relief. He must act dumbfounded, discouraged. But, as he struggled to look downcast, he recalled Psalm 18 wherein King David spelled out the ways God used His creation to help him escape capture and death. God had bludgeoned with earthquakes, hailstones, and coals of fire. He had confused with thick clouds and darkness. He had deafened and blinded with astonishing thunder and lightning.

And last night—fog!

No one ought to ever put the Lord "in a box." Not the Redcoats. Nor the Hessians.

Christopher thanked God for saving his friend, George Washington, and all the good men with him. How many wives would have been left widows? How many children would have been fatherless? How many livelihoods destroyed?

Rudolph drew next to Christopher. "Herr Ludwig, perhaps this is even a less safe place for you right now. You ought to leave."

Christopher observed the men around him—part of an eight thousand-man contingent of his countrymen, everyone a possible "recruit"—a conscript not to fight, but to abandon fighting. Everyone a man who, if they left, would mean at least one less musket ball aimed at an American.

Christopher placed a hand on the young man's shoulder. "Leave you, nephew? And our friends to run from my appointed task? You will learn to know me better."

"What I'm hoping for," Rudolph's voice was so low only Christopher heard, "the ability to get to know you better, after this war!"

"Aha!" Christopher leaned back, locking his eyes on Rudolph. He whispered, "Young man, you are destined to be a citizen of our country. I know a pretty *mädchen* named Gretchen who I believe would be pleased."

Rudolph's face lit up?

"Truly?" he asked.

"I'm relating what my eyes saw."

Schäfer, still within earshot, was outlining how the battle had played out the last couple of days.

"Lieutenant Rueffer of the Mirbach Regiment said the enemy were hidden in the thickest bushes. No one would have known where they were if they hadn't fired on his men. Then he said something interesting—'the Americans would almost sooner be shot than surrender.'"

After the Hessians had disassembled, Blum and Schäfer summoned Christopher, then gathered the contingent who had traveled to Philadelphia. They huddled together.

"The Americans would almost sooner be shot than surrender," Schäfer repeated. "Very enlightening."

"Sure is," Blum echoed.

"It's our cause," Christopher said. "Freedom for your family, your country is worth dying for. At least in our case.

Last year a brave American, Patrick Henry, declared in a public place, 'Give me liberty or give me death.' His speech swung the balance in convincing Virginians to deliver their troops for the Revolution.

"Taking Henry's statement to heart, tens of thousands have set aside their immediate aspirations for personal success to fight for a future worthy of a free people."

Johann stepped beside them. "Two of our friends from back home are interested. They grew up together in an orphanage near us."

"They've nothing to lose, everything to gain," Christopher said.

"Recruiting might be more difficult than before," Blum said. "Despite Washington escaping, the British are still claiming a major victory. They did capture an American general by the name of Sullivan."

Christopher recoiled. He knew John Sullivan, a good young man. In his twenties and a general!

My, how military rank progresses during war.

John had lived in one of the Ludwicks' homes a couple of times while staying in Philadelphia. First, he roomed at the Sixth Street house, along with Nathanial Folsom, two years ago when they were sent to represent New Hampshire in the First Continental Congress. Then, last year, with a fellow named Langdon, when he told the Second Continental Congress the British had started the war at the Battles of Lexington and Concord, and the colonies should proceed with revolution.

John was relentless, so adamant Washington had named him a brigadier general before he left Philadelphia to join the army at the siege of Boston.

Catharine was distraught at his destination, having grown fond of the dark-haired, handsome young man.

As Sullivan rode off after saying his goodbyes outside the Ludwick home, Catharine had turned to Christopher and said, "His wife, Lydia, and poor mother."

"Poor mother?"

"Yes. If I'm this upset, how must she feel? She has already lost one son, Benjamin. And John is unaware of his mortality."

"Or assured of his immortality," Christopher rejoined. "He is a Christian."

Schäfer interrupted Christopher's recollections, declaring, "Sullivan is foolhardy."

"What do you mean?" Christopher turned his gaze on the Jäger.

"Van Hester said the man charged our ranks at a place called Battle Pass with only a pistol in each hand. Pistols!" Schäfer said this with admiration.

"One shot out of each," Blum inserted, "and he was met with a blade to his chin. End of fight. Would have been shot if not for the star on his bar."

"Mad," Schäfer said.

"Exuberant," Christopher countered. "And a friend."

"A friend of yours?" Blum asked.

Christopher told them of Sullivan's stay, his fastidiousness in taking good care of their rental house, his sharing meals at the Ludwick home with Catharine, Christopher, and George Washington, discussing the imminent war and his determination to take part in it. Serving on the committee preparing the defense of Philadelphia in case of British attack, Christopher shared his concerns with Sullivan. He was impressed at the young man's wisdom—perhaps because of his law studies, or, as Christopher joked, despite those studies.

Christopher hesitated, then asked, "Do you know where they're holding the general?"

"In a barn not far from here." Schäfer pointed. "Scores of Americans."

Blum put a hand on Christopher's shoulder and turned him to face him. "Don't you dare go there, Christoff."

"But ..."

"The barn is so well guarded, there is no way you'd be able to speak to him. If you insist, the Brits will figure you out as a rebel."

"I must get a message to him, to encourage him, let him know we're aware he's not dead but captured."

"Write a note. I'll sneak it to him," Schäfer offered.

"I must speak to him face-to-face. Show him I'm here, directly involved, a friend."

Blum stepped in front of Christopher. "I'm pulling rank on you."

Christopher chuckled. "We're not in the same army, Karl."

"Yes, we are." Blum reached beneath the collar of his uniform and plucked out a small cross on a chain. "His army."

Christopher's eyes went wide at the sight. "Hide it, Karl. You'll get in trouble."

"Trouble is an obstacle we knew we'd face if we came back. You can't get involved, Christoff. If you do, Von Hester will know your coming here was a ruse. All of us who've played along with it will be shot."

Christopher reasoned it through. Involving Rudolph as his "nephew" did put them at risk. He had to be prudent, alert, discerning.

"Do you want me to leave?" he asked, gazing at Blum and then Schäfer. The Jägers exchanged looks, turned back to him, shaking their heads.

"Just be cautious in your conversations, my friend," Blum said.

Christopher went to his satchel, pulled out a blank parchment, then sat to write a note to Sullivan. When the phrase "prisoner exchange" came to his mind, he said a quick prayer for a swap.

Then, keeping his words vague and opaque, yet with a message decipherable to the general, he wrote:

> Remember we got the chicken out of the oven before it burned. I will talk to our mutual friend, G, about doing the same. Catharine and I will pray.—CL

***

Blum took the note and returned shortly after noon. As he walked toward Christopher and Schäfer, Blum gave a slight shake of the head.

"We Hessians do not beat defenseless captured soldiers, especially those of rank," he said. "We give them respect. We expect the same in return."

"Oh, no," Christopher responded in alarm.

"Apparently the British disagree with this notion. Or at least the ones guarding the prisoners of war do." His mouth twisted in revulsion. "Your friend?"

"Yes?" Christopher couldn't help anxiety at Blum's account.

"Let's say he has seen better days, though he may not see another. He's refusing to talk, to reveal anything about his troops, or Washington's, or some general named Miles."

Christopher hung his head.

"You know," Blum said, "all your captured soldiers are considered traitors. The reason the British aren't shooting or hanging them is fear of retaliation. They'll be putting them on the Whitby, a prison ship anchored in the bay off

Brooklyn. There, they'll be given two options—turn traitor to America or die."

Christopher shivered at the idea. Turn or die. They'd all be imprisoned in dungeons of death. If caught, he himself would suffer the same fate. Yet this was what he had volunteered for.

"Did you get my note to General Sullivan?" he asked.

"I was able to pass it to another American soldier through a broken board in the side of the barn. He promised to pass it along to Sullivan."

Christopher blew out a breath. With the Whitby nearby, time was not on the side of these captured patriots. If John refused to relinquish any information to help General Howe, then ...

He considered his options. Then decided. He'd stay the rest of the day with the Hessians, convince as many as he could, then—barring getting caught—stroll innocently out of the encampment tomorrow morning to get word to Mercer. Hopefully, the Flying Camp general could engineer a swap of captured men.

★★★

The rest of the day, Christopher walked the military compound in one-on-one conversations with young Hessians about the bounty of America.

"You should see my farm!" he'd exclaim.

"Forests full of game!" he'd say.

"Rivers and lakes teeming with fish!" he'd declare.

"Jobs abound!" he'd promise.

But the most effective declaration was "Free land!"

And then Christopher felt a hand on his shoulder. Rough. Squeezing. He turned to face a rugged Hessian of about forty years, five-foot-ten, his dark eyes seething, his left hand clenching, releasing, clenching, releasing. His right hand? Griping a knife that seemed the size of a scythe. When a ray of light glistened off the blade, it appeared as sharp as a razor.

Christopher visualized the advertisement—German steel. Made for a lifetime. He'd bought kitchenware made by this company. It cut through beef like—well, that thought was frightening.

Maybe he wouldn't have to worry about a firing squad. He took a deep breath to fight off fear. The man's uniform identified him as a sergeant in the artillery. Eyeing him, Christopher tilted his head and raised an eyebrow. His expression asked, What gives?

"You're contaminating the ranks," the soldier spit out. Actually spit out—spittle hung on his lower lip.

"Beg your pardon?"

"Desertion is a crime punishable by death. And you're encouraging it."

Christopher checked the man's rank, then, "Sergeant, I'm merely sharing my experience as a German in America."

"And I'm sharing my knife to your gut!"

He jerked the blade toward Christopher's stomach. But instinct—reflexes from ten-hour-a-day training forty years ago—kicked in. Christopher spun his left hip away, bent his right elbow and rammed it backward with full force into the man's throat. Hard bone against soft tissue.

The Hessian dropped his knife and fell backwards, gagging and grabbing at his throat. Several soldiers noticed the commotion and rushed to circle the two men. As the sergeant gasped for air, Christopher knelt to the ground and picked up the knife.

Standing and holding the blade, with the handle towards his adversary, he said, "Your weapon, sir—if you promise to holster it."

The sergeant staggered to his feet and jerked the knife away from Christopher, then, without apology, tottered away, not looking back.

Christopher threw up his arms as if to say, "Strange things happen in combat." Before he knew it, the crowd had dispersed. All except one young soldier, still a teenager. He looked Christopher over. "I saw what you did," he said. "It shocked me."

Christopher laughed. "Shocked myself. Old instincts. I was about your age when I joined the Emperor's military."

"Truly?"

"Truly."

An hour later Christopher was sure he had one more recruit.

***

Catharine Ludwick stood in her "happy space," preparing a meal in her kitchen for two guests—both widows. To her left, handling a bowl full of greens, was pretty, young Betsy Ross, whose husband, John, had died the previous summer in a gunpowder explosion while guarding munitions for the Pennsylvania Provincial Militia.

To her right was one of her closest friends, and closer to her age, Anna Maria Ott, who peeled potatoes while humming to herself—a familiar hymn. Catharine and Christopher often sat next to Anna in church. The Bibles and hymnals in the pews were obtained through her business, which specialized in German-language materials.

Betsy attended Christ Church a few blocks away from the Ludwick home. She had been walking home from there an hour earlier when the two women passed on the street. Catharine had asked her to join her and Anna for dinner, having already asked Anna to come over.

Right now, Catharine was whipping three eggs into shape in a bowl with a cup of milk. Each had their chore for their dinner.

Since arriving, the three had been sharing life and all its foibles and joys. Before the America declared independence, England had many times doubled down on its intransigence. Americans had retaliated with boycotts and speeches hot enough to start a mighty fire. But the king would not retreat. Once the Declaration of Independence was signed, all the faults had become starker. Instead of troublesome pebbles in your shoe, new laws and regulations became knives in the back.

Then Anna changed the tide of the talk.

"The amount we've raised is remarkable," she said, "largely due to Esther."

She referred to Esther de Berdt Reed, a transplanted Englishwoman, who was married to prominent lawyer Joseph Reed.

"Esther wants to form a Ladies Association of Philadelphia to raise funds to provide food and clothing to the Continental Army," Anna added, chopping one of her potatoes into quarters. "This fundraiser is a test."

"Esther's brilliant," Catharine said. "So enthusiastic and inspirational. I'll join with her, for sure."

"I too," Betsy said. "I believe we'll find plenty of ladies to form this She Business Association you mentioned, Anna."

"So many husbands off to war, leaving their wives to operate their shops ..." Anna said.

"As well as all the women who were already running their own businesses," Catharine added.

"Plus the variety and diversity which we all offer," Betsy continued.

Catharine turned toward Anna. "Who's on your list of potential She Business members?"

"Besides you two," Anna said with a twinkle, "foremost are Mrs. Redmond and Mary Eddy. Mrs. Redmond, because she sells everything from diamond rings and silver tweezers to snuff boxes and children's toys. Mary because, well, think of it. Her hardware business may specialize in ironmongery and cutlery, but she sells tools for joiners, shoemakers, and watchmakers as well as glassware, earthenware, metalware ..."

"I bought this set of knives from Mrs. Redmond. Many of our bakery's cutlery and pots and pans came from Mary," Catharine offered. "Who else is on the list?"

Anna raised an index finger. "The tea sellers—Cornelia Smith, Mary Gordon, and Mary Oswald."

Then a middle finger. "The molasses merchants—the Widow Penrose and Deborah Connolly."

Anna continued her finger count to both hands as she added the widow Sharpe, who sold furniture, dry goods, sewing materials, and parcels of drugs; Jane Kirk, whose shop stored a wide variety of groceries; Elizabeth Combs, who offered a range of common dry goods and textiles as well as the more unusual sailcloth and sortable shot.

"I'd add Charity and Lucy Leonard," Catharine said. "Few merchants sell exclusive items from Europe and East India."

"How about Mary Katherine Goddard?" Betsy asked. "She did print the first copy of Declaration of Independence. Her business was already prominent, about the size of Robert Aitken's."

"Both good ideas," Anna said.

"Along those same lines," Catharine offered, "I'd be happy to ask Ben Franklin's Deborah. She runs his shop whenever he's off on his other pursuits, which is often."

A moment of silence followed, then the women looked at each other and laughed.

"We have a beginning, ladies!" Anna exclaimed. "I saved one of the best for last—Cornelia Bradford."

Cornelia and her husband, William, operated the Sign of the Bible, one of the best-known bookstores in Philadelphia. She printed the *Pennsylvania Gazette* and sold English-language religious materials, along with spelling and arithmetic primers, writing paper and ink—all of which were used in the school Christopher and Catharine had established to teach immigrants.

"Your competitor," Catharine said.

"My sister in Christ," Anna answered.

"Indeed."

Anna looked at Betsy, "Will you be the first woman to sign up?"

"Unequivocally."

Since Betsy's John died, she had carried on their upholstery business with notable success. She and Catharine had become friends at various women's knitting and quilting bees and such.

"So," Betsy said, twisting a wisp of her long dark hair behind her right ear. "I've been working on something special."

"Yes?" Catharine turned to hear the news.

"It's exciting. It all started with the flags I made for the Pennsylvania Navy."

"Beautiful too," Catharine said, "the blue with red and white stripes."

"Well, General Washington, Robert Morris, and George Ross came to the shop last month not long before George joined the army in New York."

Impressed, Catharine raised an eyebrow. "And?"

"They asked me to make America's first national flag."

Catharine's mouth went wide, though she wasn't surprised, given Betsy's previous success.

"They brought a rough sketch of a flag with thirteen red and white stripes with thirteen six-pointed stars," Betsy continued. "I suggested the six-pointed stars be changed to five-pointed stars because they're easier to make. I folded a piece of paper into triangles and, with a single snip of the scissors, made a perfect star." She chuckled. "They all agreed to change the design."

"Good for—"

A loud, insistent knock at the front door interrupted Catharine.

"Excuse me," she said, setting the whisk on the counter. She walked to the door and opened it.

A young private stood before her. Too young to be fighting a war. Too young to die. Too young to ... what was he doing here?

"Yes?" she asked, hesitant.

"I come from General Mercer's Flying Camp," he said. "I promised your husband I'd bring this to you as soon as I delivered a post to headquarters."

Catharine took an envelope from his hand.

Her first impulse was—My man. He's still alive.

Then, what can this be?

She read silently.

She smiled at "My dearest Beloved."

She frowned at the past tense "What an adventure we've had!"

She smiled, then frowned with unease at "What a wife you've been!"

You've been! Been?

Her trepidation fought with optimism, then optimism won with the next sentence: "I believe we will find success."

She released a long-held breath when she reached "Please keep me, and all our military, in your prayers."

She chuckled at his amorous streak—"Until I hold you again in my arms."

You romantic.

Then she put a hand on the back of a nearby chair to steady herself when she read "Eternally yours."

Yes, eternity awaited them both. This was a startling reminder.

A shadow passed over her vision, and she settled into the chair.

Betsy stepped beside her. "Are you all right, dear?"

She showed Betsy the letter. "Christopher. From the Flying Camp." She gazed at her friends. "Will you pray with me?"

She needed to ask the Lord for an extra couple of decades before she and Christopher met eternity. She didn't think she'd survive widowhood as well as Betsy and Anna.

No, she felt a sense of urgency.

This is serious. This is imperative.

Their prayers reflected such urgency.

***

A formidable-looking Jäger appeared out of the wafts of smoke from a nearby cooking fire. All the men stood to salute, their backs straight, their faces stern and anxious. Christopher rose as well, compelled by the man's mere bearing.

Blum, standing next to him, whispered, "Von Donop! Commands four battalions of grenadiers as well as the Jägercorps. He's a count back home."

Tall, slim, with a high forehead and a determined look on his face, Von Donop stalked up to Christopher like he was approaching a troublesome cockroach. He didn't stop until his patrician nose was no more than a nose away from Christopher's peasant appendage. Then, he pulled a pistol from its holster and poked the muzzle into Christopher's provincial ribs.

A knife, now a pistol?

"I'm Colonel Carl Von Donop," he boomed. "You've overstayed your welcome, Ludwig. Our men need to be alert, not relaxed. You and your stories are a distraction. They tend to mirth, not concentration. We're at war, not dining in a social club."

"I have no awareness of social clubs, Colonel," Christopher replied, straining to restrain affront. "There were none I know of in GieBen, where I was raised. And I would have appreciated a bit of levity when the French and Bavarians held us under siege for month on end."

"Siege?"

"With the Austrians at the Siege of Prague," Christopher said. "Three thousand of us. A bit of levity would have been accepted, Colonel. Humor ... and gingerbread." He patted his stomach, forcing a smile. "As you see, I have made up for scarcity since sailing to America."

Von Donop feigned a chuckle himself, but his jaw was set while he kept his pistol stuck in Christopher's ribs. "I've heard whispers, Ludwig. Whispers you may be trying to sway our men to leave the war."

Christopher didn't respond. Admitting to the truth would find him a dead lump on the ground.

"Is this true?" Von Donop's eyes bore into Christopher's.

"I've told them how many in America live as Germany's gentlemen. Free, full and finding themselves with abundance ... if they're diligent, work hard. As well as the faith of our fathers."

Christopher tilted his head to see if this last bit touched the man. It didn't.

"Pshaw! 'Faith of our fathers.' Faith of your father, maybe. Mine was an abusive tyrant."

"All the more reason to meet the Father of all of us," Christopher said. "Was he the reason you joined the Jägercorps?"

"You mean to ask if he's the reason I kill?" Von Donop's glare was a dagger. "Frankly, yes. His is the face I see when I line up an enemy in my sights, when I pull the trigger, when I drive the bayonet home."

"Wouldn't you prefer to be free of such nasty business? This sort of memory steals your sleep."

"I might answer your question later. Right now, we're here for one purpose—not to get more sleep, but to kill Americans!"

There's anger. Defuse it.

"Then, you're here to kill me." Christopher patted his chest. "Once one of your countrymen, but now an American."

A snarl curled the lips of the Jäger. Christopher was uncertain whether the man was considering doing the deed any second.

"What's going on here?" The familiar voice of Karl Blum broke the tension and gladdened Christopher's heart. He took a breath of relief.

The last time he'd felt a pistol in his ribs, he was twenty-one years old. But he wasn't going to die today. Well, not at this specific moment.

Settling his pistol back in its holster, Von Donop glared at Blum.

"Your friend here needs to leave," Von Donop said. Determined. Unrelenting. Demanding.

Blum seemed to stand taller, straighter. "My friend here is no danger, sir—the uncle of one of our men." His eyes narrowed. "You need not worry, Colonel. I'll accept responsibility for him."

Von Donop's hands squeezed into fists. His face turned even darker.

The two men scowled at one another. Blum had bucked rank, and if Christopher remembered anything about the German military, rank even outweighed pedigree. Gentry notwithstanding.

Von Donop must have contemplated the consequences of a squabble over one overweight noncombatant and relented. "Your responsibility then," he said, spinning on his heels and striding away.

Christopher traded a look of relief with Blum.

★★★

In the Ludwick kitchen, Catharine sat straight, startled by how swiftly the ominous feeling had swept away. Like nutmeg and cinnamon, relief and elation mixed, sending a tingle down her spine. She might never know why she had been compelled to pray, but she was assured she was now free to carry on.

She gazed at Anna and then Betsy. "It's done."

CHAPTER 18

Christopher lay on the bare ground to sleep, his mind full of questions. Around him in a circle, were the pup tents of his Hessian friends. Their conversations were as restless as he was. He offered some encouraging words, followed by a story of some Quaker friends of theirs.

"Quakers are among those who help runaway slaves escape," he said. "Doing so is illegal. But if a lawman comes to their homes to ask about hidden slaves, they say, 'No slaves in our house.' How do they do so without breaking their vow to never lie?" Christopher hesitated a moment because he knew they had no answer. "Because they do not acknowledge slavery as an institution."

Exclamations of appreciation responded.

"So, my friends," he continued, "if you ever need a place to hide, and you can't find one of us Lutherans ... look for a Quaker."

Quiet laughter broke the tense atmosphere. Moments later, Christopher landed in a deep, overwhelming slumber.

In the midst of his slumber, cannon balls blasted the ground in the distance. The ground shook. He opened his eyes to see cannon flashes light the predawn darkness. Men all around him screamed each other awake.

"Zu den Waffen! Zu den Waffen!" called Von Donop's authoritative voice. ("To arms! To arms!")

Christopher rubbed his eyes and stumbled to his feet. Someone handed him a musket, longer and newer than he was used to. Attached to its barrel near the muzzle was a bayonet.

Oh, no! There'll be close combat.

He held the musket tight to his chest, gazing about him. Cannon balls rained through the darkness, ripping through tents in a thunderous display. Havoc! Men screamed in pain. Tents lit on fire, the flames billowing high as a wind surged through the encampment. A munitions depot exploded, sending a blinding light and shaking the ground. A nauseous odor filled the air. Gunpowder and something stinging.

Perspiration wetted Christopher's brow as he scanned about him. Blum and Schäfer were leading Rudolph and the others, all sprinting toward the north from where the cannon fire seemed to be coming.

"Fire straight, fire true," Schäfer hollered.

"Christoff!" Blum was looking straight at him, motioning for him to follow.

Christopher peered at Blum as the Jäger turned. They all disappeared into a veil of smoke. He looked around him. The camp had emptied. Campfires smoldered. All the soldiers were gone—into the battle.

Then, out of the smoke came a British Redcoat, charging at him with sword glistening as if oiled for the kill. Dumbfounded, Christopher stared at his musket and raised it in defense. The soldier was perhaps ten meters away, or less. In a dead sprint. With his eyes glazed in fierce determination, he aimed his sword for Christopher's chest.

Then the two met and at the same instant realized they were face-to-face with their doppelgänger. The non-Christopher dug his heels in, pulling himself erect.

They stared at one another in shock. Fear, panic, astonishment and bewilderment crashed down upon Christopher. And his doppelgänger, too, it appeared.

The man's left eye quivered as did Christopher's in times of extreme stress. In fact, he felt his own left eye quiver. His doppelgänger lowered his sword. Christopher lowered his musket. His doppelgänger bowed his head, turned, and ambled away as if deep in reflection.

A sharp noise from behind Christopher startled him awake. He was lying on the ground, drenched in sweat. Everyone about him was asleep, some snoring. There was no cannon fire, no tents on fire, no shouts of impending battle. No doppelgänger.

He'd been immersed in a dream. He remembered his father sitting at his bedside telling him the German folk tale about the Doppelgänger, the idea every living creature has a spirit double who is identical, but invisible. Not a ghost, which only appears after death. The Doppelgänger's appearance is often a harbinger of bad news.

In this case, the news had not been bad, no? Indeed, his doppelgänger had lowered his sword and spared Christopher's life. Christopher realized he had been fighting himself.

Always?

He sat forward and wiped his brow with his shirt sleeve. A breath escaped him and he decided he would leave even without breakfast in his stomach. After wrestling all his belongings together, he started a round of goodbyes.

First, he approached Blum. As he bent to touch him on the shoulder the Jäger's eyes opened wide, his hand flying to his sword.

"No, no, no," Christopher whispered. "I'm waking you to say, God willing, I will see you soon."

"Leaving so early without a proper goodbye?" Blum croaked. He was already awake, alert.

"A dream of warning," Christopher said.

"Ah." Blum nodded as if understanding, as if he'd had his own Doppelgänger confrontation in the past. He reached to shake hands. "Godspeed, mein Freund."

The voices awakened Schäfer, and he leaned on an elbow, trying to focus his eyes as the rising sun nipped the tops of the surrounding trees.

"You're away," Schäfer said.

"Away, but looking forward to seeing you again, Kristian. Mein *neuer nachbar*." (My new neighbor.)

Schäfer couldn't prevent a smile from crossing his face. Then he scowled. "That land had better be mine—I have plans for a potato harvest."

Christopher and Blum shared a quiet laugh, and Blum countered, "A bit smaller harvest than mine, but yes, a crop indeed."

The others were stirring around them now.

Rudolph was at his side. "Leaving?"

Christopher nodded. "I'll miss you all until I see you again. All you need to do is find the Flying Camp which may or may not be where it was when we left. They may have established camp further north along the river, closer to Washington's army."

The other Hessians—all stirred awake now—approached to say their goodbyes.

Christopher approached Hans, laid a hand on the young man's shoulder and said in a low voice, "Your father, Hans. Have you forgiven?"

Hans stepped back, so Christopher's hand dropped away. "Herr Ludwig, you know my feelings."

"You know God's."

Hans shrugged. "My whole life I've wanted to get away from him."

"So, now, you are away, you think distance is all you need? You can grow into your own man."

"Yes."

"Half-true. You can grow up, but you'll be the devil's man."

Hans's face screwed up. His face turned red.

"No!"

"Yes!"

"Have you ever been beaten with a belt so you can't sleep on your back?" Hans asked. Pain was evident on his face.

"No."

"Have you ever been locked out of your home by your father with no shoes on in the middle of winter?"

Christopher shook his head.

"Have you been belittled, told you were one level below a moron, a disappointment, a disgrace to your father?"

Feeling the sting of the young man's heartache, Christopher shook his head again. He could relate to none of these things and wondered how he would have coped if so.

"Emil's father has been more of a daddy to me than my father ever was," Hans said.

Christopher looked at Hans with sorrow in his eyes, drew closer, and again placed a hand on his shoulder. "I can't put myself in your place. I can't imagine how all such abuse must have affected you. I can't, but Jesus can. Imagine the King of kings lowering Himself to come to earth in the flesh, then being subjected to torture, being nailed to a tree, and, while dying there, forgiving His tormentors, His killers."

Hans lowered his head, eyes to the ground.

"Forgive, you will be forgiven, and our Savior will honor you for it," Christopher said. Then in a whisper: "If you do this for me, son, I'll leave you alone."

Hans looked up.

"He'll honor me?"

"Yes. God says in First Samuel and again in the Gospel of John, He honors those who honor Him."

As Hans considered this, Christopher continued, "Just as you dislike your father, pray for him. Entreat every day until you feel released from doing so."

"What do you mean, 'released'?"

"Ask God to soften your heart so you can forgive all the wrongs. Ask Him until you know you don't have to ask any more."

Hans shrugged, but a light had come on.

"Forgive and be honored, huh?" he said.

Christopher nodded.

"I can forget the man easy enough," Hans said, "so I guess I can forgive, too, since I'll be an ocean away."

"Good man."

The two exchanged hugs, then Christopher hefted his pack over his shoulder and walked away through an otherwise sleepy army. To a man, the Hessians waved goodbyes.

I hope this will be a temporary farewell.

★★★

As he approached the two sentries, Christopher called out in English, "Goodbye, men. I'm returning home. I wish you well for King George and the colonies."

"King George and the colonies," the younger soldier repeated in a half-hearted tone. He was the same as had been on guard when Christopher first entered the camp. "How was your nephew?"

"Alive." Christopher shifted his satchel on his shoulder. "And I hope to God he stays alive. You, too, private." He glanced at the sergeant. "You as well, sir."

"Thank you," both responded.

Christopher felt the men's eyes on him as he crossed the camp's invisible boundary line. He sighed in relief, hoping he'd find Hugo where he'd left him. He settled into a stride and sucked in the predawn air, not yet warmed by the certain heat to come.

Then "Onkel! Wait!" The voice sounded familiar. Christopher turned.

Rudolph was hurrying toward him. "Onkel," he called again.

He held out a folded sheet of paper.

Christopher couldn't help but smile at the young man who had claimed a place in his heart. Yes, he was wearing the Hessian uniform the sight of which struck fear into many a man's heart. But for Christopher, the sight of this man—and the tone of fondness—warmed his heart.

Rudolph passed him the parchment. "For Gretchen," he said, a tad of embarrassment in his look. "Can you get this to her?"

Christopher folded the paper and tucked it into a shirt pocket. "I'm not returning to Philadelphia, but I'll find a way to send it to her."

Rudolph burst into a broad smile. "You know, don't you."

Christopher mustered a nod., matching the smile with one of his own. "I sensed it," he said.

"Ha!" Rudolph spun on his heel and headed back to camp.

Christopher wondered how long it would be before the young sharpshooter was hunting for game on his own American land, with Gretchen burning the home fires.

★★★

Minutes later, a rain shower dampened his step, hurrying him along the road back to Flying Camp. In a short while he passed the farm's well-kept barn, then reached the field where he'd left Hugo. There was his stallion, standing in the midst of a flock of white sheep, enjoying the green pasture where Christopher had left him. Hugo turned as if sensing Christopher's presence. He appeared to be standing guard, protecting his friends against any wild beast looking for lunch.

Smart horse. Hugo oftentimes was hitched to the Ludwicks' carriage, taking them to one or the other of their farms. He knew the way so well Christopher could loosen the line and carry on a conversation with Catharine without concern for the road ahead.

Yes, smart. And a good thing. Christopher didn't covet the idea of walking all the way to camp. As he hustled to uncover the saddle from the branches he'd laid over it, Hugo meandered over to say hello and inspect what he was doing.

Gone!

Hugo nickered as if to chuckle at Christopher's obvious irritation.

Not funny!

Christopher looked around him, now tense, realizing his saddle had been discovered. Out of the barn strode an extraordinarily tall and ancient man, wearing well-worn overalls, a face of inquisitiveness, and carrying a musket. Aimed at Christopher.

Christopher took a step back instinctively.

"Lookin' for somethin'?" the man asked. The tone was hard as granite, but neither hostile nor friendly. Difficult to read.

Christopher put on his best smile. "Christoff Ludwig stands before you at your mercy, sir. I'm looking for the saddle I left here two days ago."

"Hid, you mean," the man said. He nodded in Hugo's direction. "So, them there's your horse? Such a handsome lad—left to forage for hisself. Standin' among my sheep. Eatin' my grass as if it were his own?"

Christopher weighed the statement. Again, the statement was testy maybe, but not antagonistic. Perhaps disguising jest. He hoped. Indeed, the farmer might be joking, pulling Christopher's leg.

Christopher stared at the musket, still aimed straight at him. Then, looking eye-to-eye, he replied with a half-smile—for he dared not offer a full one—"I must admit, Hugo's manners are lacking for not asking permission."

The man laughed. "'Askin' permission.' Ha! So, Hugo's his name. A good one."

Lowering his musket a trifle, he stepped toward Christopher. Slowly, as if sizing up a partridge in a glen.

"I left him here for I knew not what else to do," Christopher said. "I was visiting a nephew in the British camp."

The musket rose back the trifle it had dropped.

"Family among the Brits, eh?"

Christopher hesitated. The man's brow had creased, his eyes steely now. His index finger was tethering the trigger.

If Christopher were to guess, he'd say the farmer was not a loyalist. But such a guess could invite danger.

Wisdom, Lord, he cried out silently, discovering the answer in an instant.

"Sir, I am a friend of General Washington. Of Benjamin Franklin and Thomas Jefferson. I serve on several of the Philadelphia committees forming a government."

Might be overkill to mention he helped draft a proposal to the First Continental Congress, was a member of the Philadelphia Committee of Correspondence, deputy to the Provincial Convention, and procured muskets and gunpowder for the Continental Army.

He waited for a reaction—a gunshot to the chest, or an offered handshake. He took a breath until ... the farmer lowered his musket and offered his right hand. With gladness, Christopher shook hands, exhaling.

"Why, may I ask, were you in the enemy camp then?" the farmer asked.

"Recruitment," Christopher said, "plus a bit of reconnaissance."

He relayed Congress's offer to the Hessians and what he had accomplished so far.

The farmer shook his head in incredulity. "You're a brave man, going into the Redcoats' camp. I sit here two miles away and when I have to, I pretend to be a Royalist. General Howe's men rode in here, brandishing swords and swagger. Thieved a dozen of my best sheep to feed his troops. A mere lunch for them, a livelihood for me, but I didn't object."

Christopher shook his head. "I'm sorry for your misfortune, sir."

"Malcolm," the farmer said. "Malcolm Holmes. Came here thirty years ago from Wales to escape the crown's interference with my religion. Seems I didn't emigrate far enough."

Christopher raised an eyebrow.

"England's calling this a Presbyterian Revolution, you see," Malcolm said, "so when they arrived here, they seized our church for their headquarters. They're quartering their troops all around the building. Howe himself is sitting at our pastor's desk in our pastor's office, commanding the killing of our people—those who've taken arms against the king, anyhow. Most of our congregation support the Revolution, though a few differ. We're a family regardless. None of us would turn on another. Since everyone knows my two sons are fighting the war somewhere. Connecticut, I understand."

Christopher nodded but wondered if such loyalty to one another would stand the test of war.

"Ours is a large, large congregation," Christopher said. "Lutheran. We are one hundred percent behind the Revolution. Christ is our King ... today and forever."

"Amen," Malcolm said, then, "So you need to be on your way to the Flying Camp."

Christopher nodded.

"Let's get you saddled up."

Malcolm walked him to Hugo, and they followed him to the barn, where Malcolm had stored the missing saddle on a sawhorse in a room filled with sheers, ropes, saws and tools of every sort. Christopher looked about in admiration of the man's orderliness.

Settling his satchel next to the saddle, he pulled out a cloth containing the last of his gingerbread slices.

"From my Laétitia Court bakery in Philadelphia," he said. "If ever you come to the city, please visit for a complimentary meal—my payment for Hugo's 'meals' at your expense."

Malcolm laughed. "No need, Christoff."

"Please."

Malcolm acquiesced, taking the gingerbread. "Thank you."

"The best gingerbread in America." Christopher winked, the men exchanged handshakes, then he was off.

CHAPTER 19

SATURDAY, AUGUST 31, 1776
PERTH AMBOY, NEW JERSEY

A half-hour later, Christopher arrived at Flying Camp. At least it had been the Flying Camp. The army had moved on.

Ruffled Hugo's main. "I guess they've marched north to bivouac somewhere along the Hudson River—at Woodbridge, or maybe even Elizabethtown."

Hugo snorted and Christopher decided to follow the most-trodden trail. In fact, he'd call it Trampelpfad (Trampled Path).

As they rode northward, two things were on his mind— the Hessian friends he'd left behind and informing General Mercer of General Sullivan's capture, asking the odds of negotiating a prisoner exchange.

Beyond this, he needed to connect with Washington to begin his duties as Baker General of the Army, Superintendent of Bakers, Master Baker—whatever they were calling his position. Oh yes, and getting Rudolph's letter to Gretchen, along with a note he intended to write to his beloved Catharine.

Christopher fluctuated between exhilaration and depression.

He couldn't have dreamed of the success he'd had with the Hessians, the initial eight as well as those he'd spoken with behind British lines. Besides what he was now calling the Great Eight, he envisioned many others deserting the Redcoats—leaving behind the drudgery if they returned to Germany—for the promises of a wonderful life in America.

But then there was the matter of John Sullivan's capture. Think of it ... a general in chains. What leverage the British had!

He felt the high spirits of Blum, Schäfer, and the others of the Great Eight in anticipation of fresh starts. But then he recalled the apparent overwhelming defeat of the Continental Army in the Battle of Long Island. If Washington's forces had been captured? The end of the Revolution. A return to domination by a tyrant "parent." Even more brutal and intrusive, burdening taxes and regulations. America would continue as a "possession" of Great Britain.

Then the miracle of Washington's Army's escape in the middle of a night of dense fog returned to his mind, bringing a smile to his face and a raised arm to the heavens.

Hugo had sniffed the scent of the Flying Camp from the horse manure they passed. His ears going up, he nickered. Turning a corner around a stand of trees, they came upon a small company of perhaps a hundred soldiers. They had reached Woodbridge, Christopher presumed.

The sentry was a young man who frequented the bakery—Monroe Hanson, whose parents hailed from Sweden. Monroe lowered his musket when he recognized Christopher.

"We've been hoping you'd make it out of the Redcoat camp," he said. "Everyone's telling the tale of how our baker became our spy."

Christopher laughed despite himself.

Spy. Sounds too close to "hero."

"Well," he said, "this baker is trying to find General Mercer."

Monroe pointed north. "Most of Flying Camp is heading to Fort Lee," he said. "The general is leaving a company at various spots along the way. Not certain where, but if you follow the river, you'll find them. There's a company or two at Elizabethtown."

"Thanks, Monroe. Stay safe. Your mother loves you dearly, I'd dare say more than she fancies the idea of a new country."

"Yes, sir, Mr. Ludwick." Monroe hesitated, then, "Oh! Did ya' hear about General Washington's escape?"

"Indeed, I did."

"Did ya' hear they were all gone off the island before the Brits even knew they were leavin'?"

"Indeed, I did."

Monroe chuckled. "Foggy night. Foggy brains, them Redcoats."

Christopher smiled. "But not a foggy God, eh?"

He tapped the tip of his tricap, snapped the reins and rode off. Several men waved to him as he passed.

An hour later, he came to another camp and, yet again, this sentry knew Christopher.

"Mr. Ludwick," he exclaimed, "glad for the sight of you!"

Christopher settled Hugo by a brook. The day was heating up.

"Glad for the sight of you, too, James," he said. "I'm riding to Fort Lee."

"To catch up with General Mercer," James Gordon guessed. James's father was another Scotsman who'd fought against the British in Scotland before emigrating to America.

"Yes."

"My Dad's with him."

"So, your mother has two men to worry about."

"Suppose so."

"Keep yourself safe, my boy."

James nodded, then, "Hey, did you hear about General Washington's escape?"

"It's the talk of the day," Christopher replied. "Do you know anything more than they rowed across the river in a thick fog in the dead of night?"

"Every last man reached this side of the river by six in the morning. The river is a mile wide where they crossed. It was the only night in forever when warships couldn't patrol the rivers and bays."

Christopher smiled. The story got better, more exhilarating.

After another two hours riding north, Hugo whinnied, "We're there!" and they reached a third camp with what appeared to be another hundred soldiers busying themselves raising tents and stacking rocks for campfires to cook by when the time came.

Christopher waved to the guard, this one every bit his own age. The man possessed a look of keen anticipation, as if a hoard of the enemy were to ramble over the hill at any moment. As long as his trigger finger didn't have a hiccup, Christopher was fine with his preparedness.

"No enemy will be coming today," Christopher announced. "Just me."

"As if I didn't know you," the guard said. Christopher took a closer look at the sharp-featured man before him.

"If it isn't Samuel Ladd!" he exclaimed, dismounting Hugo as fast as his aching bones would allow. He settled the horse along with a score of others tethered alone a rope drawn tight between two trees. A water trough kept them happy.

Christopher walked up to his old friend—"old" in the sense he hadn't seen the man in a decade. Extending a hand in greeting, Samuel walked through it, giving Christopher a hug meant for a bear.

After a few moments, Christopher was able to breath. He let loose a laugh.

"I didn't see you when I was in the Flying Camp back at Perth Amboy."

"Wasn't there," Samuel said. "Joined the other day. Martha couldn't stand me stewing for being too old to fight. So, she shooed me out the door. 'Go fight, but don't die, or I'll kill ya', old man,' she said." Samuel chortled. Christopher joined him.

The Ladds had been neighbors of the Ludwicks for a dozen years or so, before moving to farmland somewhere in northern New Jersey.

"I told Martha I related to Caleb in the Bible. Eighty years old and, when given the choice of which land to conquer for his clan, he said, 'I'll take on the giants, the Amalekites.' Well, Christopher, I'm closing in on eighty, and I'd compare America fighting the behemoth England to Caleb taking on the Amalekites."

An appropriate comparison.

"And as did the Israelites," Christopher said, "we have God on our side in this war, Samuel."

Samuel nodded, then eyed Christopher. "How is your Catharine?"

"Finest wife I'd ever ask for. She's running the bakery, the farms, and our other homes while I'm off to war."

"Farms and other homes?"

As the two men joined a handful of others for a lunch of bread and cheese, Christopher updated his friend on his bustling business ventures, then related his dealings with the Hessian soldiers."

Samuel looked incredulous.

"Are you telling me these hardened mercenaries, these Hessians, may desert the army?" he asked.

With a growing crowd of Flying Camp soldiers around them, Christopher expounded on the bleak state of life in Germany, and how many of the Hessian soldiers had been conscripted into the ranks of the military to fill the emperor's coffers.

"Don't we have jobs to offer?" he asked. "Don't we have forests to hunt, pastures to plant, rivers to fish?"

Not one "Nay" came forth.

"For every Hessian soldier who deserts the British, a musket shot won't wound or kill one of our soldiers— meaning at least one of us Americans will live a full life," he said. "King George hired them because of their expertise. What do we know of war, most of us?"

As he asked this last question, Christopher realized the most crucial shortcoming General Washington faced—lack of training. Preparation must be addressed, but when and how? When he saw—if he saw—Washington, perhaps he would ask.

Before leaving camp, he asked the men, "What can you tell me of Washington's miracle besides every man escaped before six in the morning with the Redcoats never having a clue?"

"Not only the men escaped, Mr. Ludwick." Christopher recognized the speaker. He was Major Hays, who he had met under Mercer's headquarters canopy when the general introduced Christopher to his leaders. "Our equipment got out as well. Every piece of field artillery, every tent, the baggage—all of it. We didn't leave a single musket ball behind."

"Nothing but a full latrine," muttered a private to camp-wide laughter.

***

Christopher ended riding right past the troops in Elizabethtown and stopped to rest Hugo when he reached the next company north, in Newark or Hackensack, he didn't know which. The men were a mixed bag of exhilarated, fearful and irritated—exhilarated at the news of Washington's escape, yet fearful about the consequences of the major defeat in what was being called the Battle of Long Island. Perhaps, they were most irritated because they had left family behind to fight this war, and they had not been paid.

Did hunger play a part? Well, yes. Hunger always exacerbated vexation and weariness.

Christopher soon remedied the appetites, baking a storm over two fireplaces. He won friends along the way.

Still, he wondered, if a Redcoat had fed them, would they be patting the Brit on the back? Perhaps so, for hunger held powerful control on a human being. One of the reasons—fellowship over meals is such a powerful function of friendship. And feeding soldiers was to be Christopher's next challenge. Or so he thought.

CHAPTER 20

They'd arrived—a fact supported by Hugo's ears perking up. The stallion, though lathered a bit, was getting frisky. His hearing was as astute as his sense of smell. So, when the horse sidled sideways a couple steps, whinnied, and attempted to transition into a trot, Christopher knew they'd about reached their destination—Fort Lee.

The sun was halfway its downward slide, which meant they'd made good time.

Several minutes later, shouting sounded ahead. As he drew closer, the shouts became distinctive. Closer still, he could comprehend the words. Finally, he reached several sentries standing in front of a bustling camp at the bottom of a bluff. This he recognized as the Palisades, a twenty-mile-long hilltop with a precipitous drop to the Hudson River. Fort Lee sprawled along the southernmost section, overlooking a ferry landing below—Burdett's, if Christopher recalled correctly.

Today, this was perhaps the most important parcel of land on the entire American continent.

If the British controlled the Hudson River, they'd separate the colonies from one another, quashing the rebellion—a reality even the people in Philadelphia understood. Therefore, Fort Lee and, across the river on the east side, the larger Fort Washington, were essential to the Revolution.

He hailed the four sentries. "Christopher Ludwick, gentlemen, with good news for General Mercer."

Two of the soldiers stepped forward, awaited his approach.

"Ludwick, you say?" asked the older of the two, a corporal.

"Here to see General Mercer," Christopher confirmed.

"Better come with me," the corporal said.

Christopher dismounted, hitched Hugo to a poplar, patted his exquisite nose, and followed the man through the camp, along the incline to the top. There, hands on hips and scanning the horizon to the east stood Mercer, bracketed by Colonel Henry Haller and Lieutenant Colonel Lawrence.

"Christopher!" Mercer exclaimed. He pointed across the river. "The general wants to see you right away."

"Washington?"

"Yes. The general," he said.

"Don't you want my report first?"

"He takes precedent—always."

"So-o ..." Christopher stumbled, wondering what was next.

"I'll have Colonel Washburn escort you over Burdett's Ferry," Mercer said, motioning toward a nearby soldier.

Washburn stepped forward. "Follow me, Mr. Ludwick."

Christopher wondered about the urgency as they hurried over the hill.

Soldiers were bustling all around, many of them carrying planks of wood to the top of the bluff.

"We're building on both sides of the river," Washburn said as they neared the long, broad ferry. "Expecting Howe will be coming before winter hits us."

Christopher blew out a whistle and followed him onto the ferry along with a dozen others—some looking official, some dazed, two privates hefting a long box onto the barge.

As they started across the Hudson, something grabbed Christopher's attention—something sunken below the surface about twenty yards downriver.

He pointed and called out, "Did anybody notice something's in the water?"

Washburn put a hand on his shoulder. "A boat," he said. "We've sunken a few between the two forts to prevent the Brits from patrolling the water upstream."

Christopher chuckled. "Good idea, I'd say. Let's hope they never get this far."

"Oh, they will. But no farther. Hopefully, they won't see the boats but will ram right into them and sink."

They disembarked on the east side of the river. Washburn stepped off quickly, motioning to Christopher. "Right this way."

They walked straight to a large log building, which appeared to become larger still as dozens of men carried logs, two-man saws, and nails larger than any Christopher had ever seen.

Stepping around the bustling soldiers and wagons, and cannons and horses, they entered the building, which appeared to be the home of Peter Burdett, who Washburn told Christopher operated the ferry.

Washington stood straight-backed, the full six-foot-two of him. His tricap lay on top of his uniform coat, which was draped over the back of a chair. Before him was a large table covered with papers. Across the table stood a man a good six inches shorter and the same width.

Christopher did not recognize him. His face was red, his forehead sweating, his mood disturbed—as if a bevy of torturers were drubbing him. Yet, he and Washington alone occupied the room.

Hearing Christopher and Washburn enter, the general turned to look. His brow was furrowed, his eyes dark. But the instant he saw Christopher, his face brightened.

"My old friend!" he exclaimed. He stepped over to shake Christopher's hand, then motioned toward the paper-filled tabletop. "It's a disaster, Christopher. An absolute muck-up!"

Some people had declared Washington a stoic, unapproachable individual, but from their first meeting, Christopher had found him fun-loving, outgoing. He had won Catharine's favor, finding time to dance with her at balls in Philadelphia—once at Robert and Mary Morris's home, once this spring at Benjamin and Julia Rush's wedding in the neighboring Township of Byberry—to which Washington and his wife, Martha, had traveled far from their home in Mount Vernon.

Washington possessed a special grace accompanying his physical presence—an attribute his faith accentuated. Though he had his detractors, the man had distinguished himself in battle before this Revolution, assigned command of the Virginia Regiment for the Brits during the French and Indian War.

Christopher had been at the Second Continental Congress in May 1775 when Washington was made commander of the rebel army despite knowing there was no actual army. Accepting the appointment itself took courage, knowing the microscope he'd be under.

Though he wouldn't tell the stories himself, men who had fought beside Washington were amazed that, although he led them into battle, he never had a flesh wound from the skirmishes.

At the Battle of Monongahela in 1755 during the French and Indian War, with General Braddock dead, and soldiers being shot down all around him, Washington took charge of the collapsing lines, encouraging the men. Two horses were shot out from under him. Four bullet holes shot through his coat. Was he wounded? No.

Have a question about that? Ask God.

"You're the man for the job," Washington said, interrupting Christopher's musings. "Logistics are killing us. Not only in the battlefield but keeping the men healthy. They're sick, they're hungry, yet they're called upon to fight a war. This can't be. I need your help. I need you to take charge of feeding the troops—all of them.

"I hear it from the men," he continued. "I hear it from the officers. This morning, I received a letter from Dr. Rush, describing 'bad bread, the absence of order, and universal disgust.' I accept the blame. I'll take charge of training the troops, of planning the military operations. Will you take care of the 'bad bread'? Will you be my Baker General?"

Christopher didn't have to think it over. He'd been contemplating what and how he would do since General Mercer told him of his coming assignment.

He nodded. "Of course. I have plans—for bakers, for ovens, for food distribution. But first, sir, I need to alert you to something of immediate importance."

Washington raised an eyebrow. "What?"

"General Sullivan has been captured. A number of them are being held prisoner in a barn in Howe's camp on Long Island. I hope you can negotiate a prisoner exchange."

Washington cupped his chin with his right hand and smirked. Smirked!

Christopher was at a loss as to how to react.

Then Washington called to the soldier standing guard at the door, "Corporal, will you find General Sullivan and tell him I need him here?"

"Sir!" The corporal scooted away, leaving Christopher in astonishment. He was pondering what must have happened when Sullivan entered in.

"John!" Christopher exclaimed.

"Christopher!" Sullivan said.

"You're here!" both said in unison.

Sullivan's face was bruised black and blue. A cut over his left eye was bandaged.

They stepped toward one another. Sullivan winced as he extended his arm to shake hands.

"I heard of your ill treatment," Christopher said. "No gentlemen there."

"Agreed."

"How on earth did you escape?" Christopher asked.

Sullivan shrugged and motioned for Washington to explain.

"I've been in contact with General Howe several times," Washington said. "Always by courier carrying a white flag. Today, Howe's courier was General Sullivan."

Christopher shook his head in incredulity.

How many times? How many times have I stuck You in a box? Will I never learn to expect the unexpected?

His brow knit. "What does Howe want?"

"He wants us to give up, give over, end the war, admit we're undermanned, underequipped and haven't figured this revolution through to the final consequences of our revolt. He wants to meet with members of Congress. I'm sure he felt giving us back one of our own, in particular one as treasured as General Sullivan, we would acquiesce to a conclave."

"I was in the British camp two days ago and discovered you were a prisoner," Christopher said.

"I know. I received your note. You thought I'd find myself festering away in the bowels of a dungeon ship," Sullivan said.

Christopher and Washington both nodded, then Washington turned to Christopher, "Indeed, I was told a story about you—one I believed a wild fabrication, at first. But then, remembering your service to your emperor, your love for your old countrymen, I reconsidered. 'Of course. Christopher Ludwick for you.'"

His chuckle gladdened Christopher's heart.

Christopher smiled, then briefed Washington and Sullivan on his time with his eight Hessian prisoners, their commitment to convince their comrades to dessert the British army with them, and his return to Flying Camp.

As Christopher told the story, the two generals smiled, encouraging him to continue.

When he finished Washington said, "Extraordinary."

Then he turned his gaze on Sullivan. "Well, John, off to Congress with Howe's request. I'll write a note to accompany the general's missive."

Washington stepped away to a table where he drew stationary out of a drawer to write a note.

A minute later, he waved to a major who had entered the room. "Have six men accompany General Sullivan to Philadelphia," he said. "John, take this letter to Congress with you."

"General," Christopher said, "will you send these two letters along as well? One is to my wife, the other she can forward to a young lady from one of our Hessians, who is soon to leave the Redcoats to be an American."

Washington smiled. "How is Catharine?"

"Tending the business." Christopher smiled. "Better than I, I'd wager."

His face turning ominous, Washington spoke in a soft voice to himself but loud enough for Christopher to hear. "What will Howe ask of Congress? A surrender. Capitulation on his absolute terms?"

Aloud he said, "Congress will send Franklin and Adams."

"Maybe Rutledge and Jefferson too," Christopher offered.

"Brilliant minds. I pray they'll decline."

Sullivan chuckled. "Ben will say to Howe something like, "Billy, don't you know he who lays with dogs shall rise with fleas."

"And," Washington said, "he'll add, 'Bad relationships are cracked with ease, but never well mended."

"True," Christopher said. "I know this—whoever goes to represent America will not let what happened on Long Island determine the future of our endeavor. They feel, as we do, God bestows on us the right of freedom—it is not man's gift to give."

His eyes looking upward, Washington nodded. "True."

"I'm off, then," Sullivan said. "To return as soon as I can."

"Godspeed," Washington said and as suddenly as he had appeared, Sullivan was gone.

★★★

Turning back to the table, Washington blew out a breath and stared darts at the fellow who was there when Christopher entered the room

He glanced at Christopher and said, "Before you, Christopher, stands Isaac Hancock, who owns a mill in Reading, Pennsylvania, that provides us flour."

Christopher nodded a hello.

"Now to the order of business for which I need you." Washington heaved a sigh. "These are all bills of lading, accounts dealing with soldiers' rations and salaries. You need not take notice of the salaries, which we cannot afford, but the rations. Make sense of the lot, Christopher. Put things in order."

Washington picked a paper from the table and waved it. "John Hancock sent me this letter. 'I make no doubt Christopher will do to the entire satisfaction of the troops, in such a manner as to save considerable sums to the public.' Meanwhile, Congress has given you 'power to license all persons employed in this business, using your best endeavors to rectify all abuses in the article of bread.'"

Phew! Christopher had believed the choice of him to head the baking was Washington's idea alone. To think the entire Congress had given it support—indeed, a blessing, was a bit overwhelming.

Christopher breathed deeply, looked at the mass of paperwork, then at Washington. He nodded. "At your service, General."

"Tell me what you need to get the job done. I'll move heaven and earth to do what's needed." Washington pointed to a hallway. "First room on the right is yours to use. Sleep there. Work there." He waved toward a soldier who had been standing guard at the door. "Private, help the Baker General with these papers, will you?"

Christopher thanked Washington, then asked, "Manpower, sir. And equipment."

"Tell me what you need. We'll see to it." He motioned to the private. "Do whatever he says." He peered ever so briefly at Isaac Hancock. "You're dismissed, sir. You'll be hearing from Baker General Ludwick, I'm sure."

Christopher didn't know what Washington meant but was certain he'd find the answer."

Washington spun on his heels and walked out of the building.

Christopher watched the general march off, Hancock skulk off, and the private remain in his spot, standing at attention, looking baffled.

"What's your name?" he asked the private.

"Gilmore, sir. Dickie Gilmore."

Christopher looked him over. Young. His dark hair spilling out the sides of his cap. Trying to grow a beard without success. Eagerness in his eyes.

"Well, Dickie, it appears to be you and me ..." Christopher stared at the papers piled on the table ... "along with a bit of examination and research."

"Yes, sir."

"First, please fetch my horse, Hugo. He's the Narragansett Pacer at Fort Lee under General Mercer's charge."

"Sir." The private saluted and hurried out the door.

Christopher wondered how he was going to deal with this saluting thing. He'd always been the one doing the saluting.

He pulled a chair to the table, peering at the stack of chaos he'd been given to make sense of.

Lord, give me wisdom.

One piece of paper stood out to him, perhaps because of the word in bold capital letters—RATIONS.

As Christopher read the document, his eyes widened in near disbelief of the immensity of his task. The Continental Congress had dictated rations be comparable to the British provision. Every day—one pound of beef or three-quarters of a pound of pork or one pound of salt fish; one pound of bread or flour; and one pint of milk.

The week's ration included three pints of peas, beans, or other vegetables, and one-half pint of rice or one pint of Indian meal.

In addition, he needed to provide either one quart of spruce or malt beer or cyder per man per day, or nine gallons of molasses per company of one hundred men per week.

The Massachusetts Provincial Council had done Congress one better, adding weekly allowances of six ounces of "good butter," half a pint of vinegar, and one pound of "good common soap" for six men per week. Good thing he wasn't in Boston. He released a rueful chuckle. But, indeed, vinegar was a good idea—one he'd implement. Not only did vinegar add flavor to food, it made the water from rivers and lakes more potable.

Christopher flinched at the cost of it all, wondering how far his own contributions, though considerable, would go. The Ludwicks' farms provided most of their needs, so they didn't pay for a lot, but the last he checked, peas and beans cost about one dollar per bushel, and a pint of milk was something on the order of eight cents. Who knew the cost of rice and butter?

Then, he considered the British, an ocean away from their homeland. He doubted they were able to provide such provisions to their troops, even with their supply ships and the number of loyalists in the country. He wondered, too, whether he could meet the effort. Many American farmers were shouldering weapons, not spades, right now. Even if they were indeed farming, think of the transportation!

No. No. He had to focus. He must figure out this problem. He wished Catharine were here; they worked so well puzzling complications together.

★★★

Christopher found himself burning not one candle but two deep into the night. At some point, he sent Dickie to bed down Hugo and catch some sleep.

At another moment, Washington walked past on the way to his quarters and asked how he was progressing. Christopher didn't realize until his head hit the pillow in his upstairs room that he had acknowledged the Commander of the Armies with a half-salute.

Private Gilmore had proven helpful, delivering Hugo to the headquarters, brushing him, and settling him for the night with plenty of hay and water with other horses, including Washington's Narragansett Pacer, Nelson, in a nearby barn. Christopher fancied Hugo was making friends with a general's horse as he sat here.

Later, Gilmore had delivered a plate of food, including a fist-sized portion of beef, a cupful of string beans, and tea. At least Christopher supposed it was tea—perhaps it was a few drops of molasses in hot water.

Gilmore, insisting on being called Dickie, had told Christopher that, as Baker General, he was to receive two rations a day. He'd scoffed, patting his stomach. "They want me to gain weight? No, son. One will do."

"Well," Gilmore had scuffled his feet, "at least you'll be paid well. Seventy-five dollars a month, I heard."

Christopher had leaped to his feet. "No! Christopher Ludwick will not profit from the war."

Gilmore had retreated, feeling admonished it appeared, something Christopher hadn't intended at all.

He determined he would write a report in the morning, listing the procedures he intended to feed the American troops, which were bivouacked everywhere from New Hampshire to Georgia.

Christopher had sifted through reports from Generals Horatio Gates, Nathanael Green, Henry Knox, Benedict Arnold, and his friend John Sullivan. He'd dug himself out of an avalanche of complaints about the bureaucratic quagmire of the Commissary Department and Quartermaster Office, the taste and quantity of the food, the lack of ovens to bake bread, on and on.

When his head was about to hit the table from exhaustion, one fact woke him, turning his irritation into fury. He couldn't control himself. He stood, hurried to the stairway to the second floor, and climbed the stairs with abandon. A stream of seething words escaped his lips as he strode along the dim hallway lit by one lantern on a wall to a door, which he guessed was Washington's. He was about to put fist to door frame when a concern struck him. Perhaps waking the commanding general in the middle of the night would not be appreciated.

He stood in place, put his hands on his hips, and stared at the floor, trying to contain his rage. He breathed deeply, then again and again until a certain calm settled upon him.

Bit by bit a plan formed within him, he nodded to himself and returned downstairs. He stacked the papers in a methodical fashion—invoices here, farmers and other food provisioners there, operations and procedures over here, plus three piles of problems gauged by severity. Laying alone was his latest discovery, one that would create not a few enemies.

When he lay his head on a pillow for the first time in what seemed to be a month, Christopher fell sound asleep.

CHAPTER 21

SUNDAY, SEPTEMBER 1, 1776
FORT WASHINGTON, NEW YORK

The bright flare of the early-morning sun streamed through the window, hitting Christopher in the eyes. He grumbled and pulled his pillow over his head. Then horses whinnying nearby and wagon wheels rumbling outside his window made sleep impossible. When dressed, he descended the stairs in search of Washington.

A soldier stood guard in the door.

"Where is the general?" Christopher asked.

The soldier pointed upwards. "Still in his bedroom, I'd guess, sir."

Christopher climbed back up, made his way to Washington's room, and tapped on the door.

"Enter."

Christopher opened the door. Washington was rising from his knees to his feet. The general offered a half-smile. "My morning sacrifice, my prayer to our Maker."

"I see."

"If we are to make a happy nation, we need God's holy guidance and protection."

"I agree."

"I've been given these heavy duties I can't discharge on my own wisdom. I know. And so, I begin and end every day on my knees before our Creator and with His Word." He grasped a Bible from the chair at which he had kneeled.

"A worthy undertaking," Christopher managed, wondering why he himself hadn't pursued such a trail. Perhaps he should. Indeed, he should. With Catharine—both on their knees. Put your slippers beneath the bed, so when you wake in the morning you have to get on your knees to dress your feet. And when you're there, well ...

"And today being the Lord's Day, we'll have a sermon at the river."

"Oh?"

"The Reverend James Caldwell," Washington said. "A Presbyterian from Elizabethtown, New Jersey. The men are already calling him 'the fighting parson.'" Washington chuckled and sighed. Then, he added, "I'm going to write Congress, asking for appointment of one chaplain to each brigade, with the same pay and rations as a colonel."

"Perhaps the best idea I've heard in a long time," Christopher said. He remembered of all the great preachers who had sailed to America to spread the gospel, only to get recalled to England and Europe when war broke out. Methodist Francis Asbury alone had refused the call and remained here. He knew of Caldwell, who preached in the town across the Delaware River from Philadelphia.

"I know this, Christopher," Washington said, "today we need to give the Lord humble and hearty thanks for preserving our army from extinction or capture on Long Island. The fog aiding our escape? The drenching rain? The ebb tide keeping British warships from sailing upriver?"

He placed the Bible on a bedside table. "Once we stepped aboard our boats, we couldn't see land until we bumped into it." He laughed. "The path we took from one shore to the other was squirrelly, no matter how professional we believed ourselves to be."

Washington motioned for Christopher to follow him out of the room. As they walked along the hallway and to the stairs, he continued his story.

"And the boats?" he said. "We had not one more nor less than the exact number required for all the troops. No happenstance there. No coincidence. The Lord saved me from the danger of the night past and brought me to the light of day."

Hearing the story from the mouth of the Commander of the Army himself brought a chill to Christopher.

"I'm reminded of the story when Elisha asking God to blind the Syrians who had surrounded the Israelites with an army of horses and chariots."

Washington acknowledged the comment with a nod. "So be it for us as well."

They reached the bottom of the stairs and were met by a handful of officers, all wearing expectant looks.

Christopher turned to Washington. "You have more important things with which to deal, sir."

"Christopher," he said, "we face fierce enemies. Two cunning brothers. General William Howe, commander of all the British ground forces, and Admiral Richard Howe, commander of the entire British naval fleet. You know what they call Richard?"

Christopher shook his head.

"Black Dick. They say the nickname's derived from his complexion. But I believe it a description of his heart, or lack of one." Washington scowled. "All for the king! is how they live."

"But we have the real King on our side," Christopher said.

Washington pushed a smile to his face. "And in Him lies our greatest hope."

The general glance toward the officers awaiting his attention.

"Once we've finished here, I want to hear all you have learned and have to say. Why don't you find some breakfast and come back in an hour or so?"

***

Christopher took the opportunity to jump on the ferry across the Hudson to find Mercer.

He found the general busy at two things—dispatching men to oversee strengthening Fort Lee earthen fortifications for the sure-coming assault, and mapping a plan of defense, placing cannons in strategic places along the Palisades to fire upon British ships attempting to penetrate beyond the two forts.

Mercer seemed at ease in all he did, but Christopher wondered if his men had as difficult time as he did in understanding the tall red head's strong Scottish accent. Something about the "r's" and "o's" and a few other pronunciations besides.

Christopher stood back and waited until Mercer was free to speak with him.

A few minutes later, the general dispatched all his charges and turned to Christopher.

"Whatever comes our way," Mercer said, "overwhelming firepower from one side or the other will determine the victor. We need more munitions, more cannons, and adequate food. And I swear I had a better supply of medicines in my apothecary back in Fredericksburg than we have here."

"There are many needs, for sure," Christopher said. "Me, I've been praying for confusion in the enemy camp."

Mercer smiled. "Amen," he said, "and now I want to hear what happened behind British lines."

"Better than I'd dreamed possible."

"And you didn't get shot," Mercer said.

"Right, too, though at one or two moments I was certain Catharine about to be a widow." Christopher drew a breath. "Instead, I experienced miracle upon miracle. Open hearts, open minds."

"And your eight friends?"

"Persuading their comrades. In the midst of danger—getting shot for conspiracy—they're convincing, inducing, coaxing. Rudolph pretended to be my nephew." Christopher's chest puffed out. "What a young man! I may adopt him, indeed."

Mercer smiled broadly.

"And then Schäfer—of all people—he and Blum saved my life." Christopher shook his head at the memory. "This Colonel Von Donop ..."

"Von Donop?!" Mercer's voice took on an air of danger.

"Yes."

"You're certain?"

"Yes. Why?"

"What happened?"

Christopher recalled the metal touch of the pistol's barrel to his ribs and flinched despite himself.

And he recalled Von Donop's words: "We're here for one purpose—to kill Americans!"

As Christopher retold the incident, fear welled up stronger than when it happened. He had indeed escaped a spy's death. Had he been thankful? Was he ever sufficiently thankful? For anything good? For all he considered good? He'd have to think it over.

When he finished, Mercer said, "We need His holy protection—always. And I fear it will be indispensable in the months ahead."

No doubt.

***

An hour later found Christopher back at the ferry landing on the Fort Washington side of the river, crowded in on each side by men eager to hear James Caldwell. Christopher hadn't experienced a Sunday without church in memory, so this was a welcome time. For the others, too, because it was apparent by their rapt attention these men held the pastor in high esteem.

They were all far from home, far from family, far from safety.

"Friends. Colleagues!"

The call came from a man standing alone on the ferry tethered to the dock before them. Christopher had an image of Jesus preaching from a boat to crowd on the shore of the Sea of Galilee.

Wearing tricap and wig, this must be Caldwell. Though appearing to be still in his twenties, he stood tall, erect, and in charge.

"In the days ahead—perhaps even today," he said, "we may be shedding our own blood and we may shed others'. Remember one thing. The One whose shed blood changed the world was our Lord and Savior, Jesus Christ. He died on the cross as a sacrifice to cleanse us of our sins."

Christopher's fingers fiddled with his grandfather's coin in his pocket. He pulled out the silver and reread its inscription yet again—but this time with even more poignancy, since he was standing on ground which could soon be a field of blood.

"The blood of Christ cleanseth from all sin." So profound.

"I said unto thee when thou was in thy blood, live." So clear.

Yes, a field of blood.

"Whether we live or die in this war," Caldwell continued, "all who believe have a bright future. Here on Earth or with Him." He pointed heavenward. "Always remember this from Psalm 27. 'Though an army besiege me, my heart will not fear; though war break out against me, even then I will be confident.'"

Christopher let his eyes scan over the men around him. Men's lips were pressed tight together. Many eyes were on the ground before them. Many feet were shuffling.

Caldwell raised his voice an octave, perhaps to project it to those on the periphery of the crowd. "The Lord said, 'Trust I will not fail you nor forsake you.' He is God and He does not lie."

He protected me in two wars. Christopher remembered. *He kept me alive on a torturous trek during which many friends died. Yet even if He hadn't, I would still trust in Him.*

"Did we not just experience this? Didn't we see the extraordinary hand of God? The fog, the rain, the blinded enemy ..."

"Yes!" came the reply from many as men forgot this was a sermon, not a rally.

"Then how can one man among us—even one—doubt our Creator is on our side in this battle?"

Men shook their heads. This statement stood as an undisputed fact—a living, walking being—among them.

"Whatever transpires," Caldwell, said, "in the end, His will is loving and His plan is perfect."

Christopher returned his coin to his pocket, bowed his head, then raised it with glistening eyes.

Caldwell gave his blessing, quoting the Scripture from Numbers. "The Lord bless thee, and keep thee. The Lord make His face shine upon thee and be gracious unto thee. The Lord lift up His countenance upon thee, and give thee peace."

Christopher struggled through the throng toward Caldwell. When he reached him, he extended his hand and said, "Christopher Ludwick thanks you for your inspiration, sir."

"Christopher Ludwick," Caldwell responded. "I know you. I've eaten at your establishment."

Christopher's brow knit.

"Marvelous." Caldwell's one-word assessment was all Christopher needed. His face beamed.

"I must be off," Christopher said, "but please, Pastor Caldwell, stay safe. The republic needs you and other people with your level of faith."

"Thank you," Caldwell said. "I will."

★★★

A few minutes later, Christopher was face to face with General Washington.

"You may want to sit for this discussion, sir," he suggested.

Washington frowned and took his advice. They were alone in a receiving room located off the side of the main room where Washington was doing all his planning and where Christopher had taken on the pile of papers and ledgers the day before.

"There has been major deception in flour consignments, General," Christopher said. "And I'm not talking about one man or two. Besides the gentleman with you yesterday, Isaac Hancock, I've listed merchants profiteering from this war." He tapped a page where he had written several names. "These men, and more than likely others, have been serving our soldiers a diluted product, and my guess is so they can sell the surplus flour for profit."

Washington frowned a question.

"Sir, you ask for one hundred pounds of bread for every one hundred pounds of water."

"Yes."

"When making bread, a baker adds thirty percent water. Every hundred pounds of flour produces one hundred and thirty pounds of bread. Hancock and the others are pocketing thirty-percent profit."

Washington's face reddened, and he put hands to hips in rigid attention.

Christopher continued, "I noticed, also, many soldiers pool their resources and rely on one baker in the camp. I'd evaluate each of these bakers as I'd appraise anyone I'd hire in my business."

Washington nodded approval, then said, "There are reports some of the men are taking their flour supply and trading with the local citizenry."

"I don't doubt the accounts."

"I have long been assured many abuses have been committed for want of some proper regulations, Christopher. Now you've uncovered them, what do you suggest?"

"I'd say, first, you declare harsh punishment for any bakers swindling the military and stiff warnings against men trading rations. Second, something else bearing a great deal of initial investment but that will pay major dividends in the months ahead."

"What?"

"Bake ovens, general. Ovens small enough to be transported along with the troops aboard wagons. Also, large ovens and several of them, strategically placed, to bake huge amounts of bread to distribute by wagon to our encampments. This will centralize baking operations to lessen the reliance on those field ovens.

Christopher drew a breath, then, "Meanwhile, security has been an issue, and this would allow us to hold the flour and bread under lock and key. So far, nobody seems willing to take control of the bread once it leaves the ovens. I recommend the Quartermaster Office be made responsible for transporting the bread."

Washington's eyes widened at the idea. "Go on."

Christopher raised his hands to stave off any objections. "I understand, because of the vagaries of war, our plans for food supply and baking must be fluid. But at the same time, we need to prepare some stationary places—places we're certain will be secure from the enemy."

He beckoned for Washington to follow him as he walked into the front room and to the table covered with maps.

Motioning at those maps, he asked Washington, "Where must we begin?"

"You're asking, if we can secure funding from Congress, where would I place these baking ovens?"

Christopher nodded.

Washington bent over the maps and blew out a breath.

Christopher waited.

Washington's right hand wandered over the map and went west, away from New York City, away from Fort

Washington and Fort Lee, past Newark and then stopped. He pointed an index finger at Morristown.

"Between New York and Philadelphia, so it ought to be secure," Washington said. "A center for farming, mining, and timber, so it has the resources for fuel and to build winter shelters. A good water supply ... As a matter of fact, if things don't go well, we may have to winter there."

Christopher grimaced, then squared his shoulders.

Washington asked, "Do you have any idea the best manufacturer to buy them from?"

"Two places," Christopher said, "and both are in Chester County. Anna Nutt and Company in Elverson is one. She is considered the first woman industrialist in the country."

"Excellent choice," Washington said. "Since taking over the operation, Samuel Potts and Thomas Rutter have been producing munitions and cannon for the Pennsylvania Navy and for the Army. Ardent patriots!" He looked at Christopher. "You said there are two?"

"The other is Redding Furnace in Warwick. George Taylor and their ironmaster, Samuel Flower, run the company."

"I know George," Washington said. "One of the men who signed the Declaration of Independence."

Christopher nodded. He, too, knew the man, and trusted him to do well for the army.

"Samuel," he said, "has been making Jamb stoves for years."

"Jambs, huh?"

"Well, I'm enamored with Jambs, since they were invented in Germany and many of our settlers in Pennsylvania use them. You've seen them yourself."

Washington raised a brow.

"In our house," Christopher said. "The stove with the tulips and the Scripture about the dangers of evil."

"Oh, yes!" Washington smiled broadly. "Two good choices. If you can give me the cost, I'll write off to Congress right now requesting the money."

Christopher had written an estimate and handed the general the paper.

Washington's eyebrows raised. "So much?"

"In the vicinity."

"All right."

"When can I begin the process?" he asked.

"As soon as I receive permission from Congress. I'll send off the request right now, with our fastest rider." He motioned to a soldier nearby. "Bring Corporal Wright to me, Private."

The private saluted. "Sir."

"I want to begin recruiting bakers," Christopher said.

"You have my approval. Are you satisfied with Private Gilmore?"

"Dickie?" Christopher couldn't stop a smile from forming. "He'll do fine."

"Then, he will help, and if you want other assistance let me know your procedures. Hancock, Congress, and me, Christopher—we all have the utmost confidence in you."

Christopher smiled a thank-you, nodded, and said, "At your leave, sir. I'll start making arrangements in anticipation of Congress's approval."

He turned on his heels and hurried from the building, excited to begin this challenge. His mind turned to involving Catharine in the endeavor. She had struck a friendship with Anna Nutt, when they had traveled out to Warwick to investigate an oven purchase. Anna had since retired.

Catharine was drawn to other women of substance. And Anna? Well, Anna had passed her test without doubt. A snippet of a lady, but the spark she carried could energize someone twice her size. Small wonder the ironworks had flourished under her and her daughter Rebecca's guidance until Englishman Robert Grace arrived and took control, further ensuring its success.

Warwick Furnace required timber from the Nutts's more than two hundred acres of forest. A large waterwheel on French Creek powered the bellows required for iron production. The ovens Christopher wanted would be no problem, and he expected a "deal" from such a patriotic family, despite the price he'd submitted to Washington. Perhaps his vision of ovens in other strategic locations would be affordable to the money-strapped Congress.

★★★

Catharine was on her way out the door to church service when a military courier dismounted his horse in front of her and asked, "Mrs. Catharine Ludwick?"

"Yes," she replied.

He handed her a letter, and she snatched the missive from his hand with excitement. News from her husband.

"Thank you," she said, then, as the courier rode away, she stood right there as she read:

My dearest Catharine,
What we have hoped and prayed for has happened. I spent a bit of time behind British lines, met with our eight friends, and was able, I trust, to persuade several others to accept America's offer. Indeed, I believe our friends are becoming even more successful in this regard. Please continue to pray daily for their safety, for who knows if they may be discovered? If so, death awaits. And perhaps their death may come after a period of torture to discover any co-conspirators.
With so many accepting our terms, I do hope our community, indeed our country, will welcome them as

friends and neighbors, as employees and even employers. Beloved, I am about to accept Congress's offer to become Baker General of the Army. I even had a young private salute me today. What do you make of such a rank? Ha! I'm not sure what lies ahead, but I have plans, grand plans for this endeavor. It is far more complicated than I first supposed. Logistics! How not only to bake the necessary food but distribute such massive rations to so many men in so many diverse places. If only man flew like the birds!

We will have small ovens to transport from camp to camp and day to day, and I hope to have larger ones built in various safe cities around the country.

How I wish you were here at my side, with your acumen for this sort of thing. We will need to find the best men and women to help with the job, and you are such an astute judge of character.

Keep me in your prayers as you are in mine, my Love.

Your Christopher

Catharine smiled to herself. Christopher had always gone out of his way to include her in everything important in his life—so unlike many men today. Many ruled their households as they managed their businesses and employees. If they had no business and employees, they compensated by controlling their homes and wives as such.

Indeed, she reread her husband's letter and wondered if he had dropped a hint. "With so many accepting our terms, I do hope our community, indeed our new country, will welcome them as friends and neighbors, as employees and even employers."

She started off to church, thinking through the message. The germ of an idea was forming. The notion blossomed as she strolled along North Fifth Street, then bloomed as she walked through the church doors with a crowd of people exchanging hellos.

Catharine hurried through the vestibule, along the pews in the sanctuary, past the choir singing a Psalm, and through the west deacon doors. She knocked on the door of the vestry and heard a hearty "Come in."

Inside, Henry Mühlenberg and two assistant pastors were putting on their vestments—white tunics for the season, Henry's more ornate than the others.

"Catharine," he said, his face bright. "Come in, come in."

She excused herself for the intrusion and told Mühlenberg her idea.

"Splendid!" he said. "Brilliant! I'm sure all will agree. Leave it to me."

She gave him a sisterly hug, nodded to the others, who nodded back, and left to find her seat in the fourth row, right side, her usual place sitting next to Anna Maria Ott.

***

The choir sang beautifully, the congregation joined in stirring hymns, the liturgy was comforting.

Catharine tried to pay attention, but her mind kept whirring with ideas of how to help the cause of the Hessians not only escaping the British forces but avoiding prosecution for doing so if the Redcoats came searching for them.

Here she sat in a German-language congregation—a secure place with no "outside ears" listening in. And Henry said, "Leave it to me." So-o she would.

Then Mühlenberg took his place behind the lectern and proclaimed: "Inconvenient!"

The word grabbed everyone's attention—even Catharine's.

"Life is so often ill-timed, isn't it?" Mühlenberg said. "Annoying."

He looked over the sanctuary. "How often do we decide upon something with the reasoning: It's inopportune. It's tiresome, so I won't do it"?

"Or it's more convenient for me to do this and that, than to do what is best for everyone. Of course, we can view circumstances in shades of gray, but I ask you, does God have shades of gray?"

No, He doesn't, thought Catharine, and it is inconvenient to do the myriad things necessary to help some people in need.

But we must.

Mühlenberg stepped away from the lectern, raised his eyes to the ceiling, and said, "Tithing is difficult. Praying is too time consuming. Helping our neighbor is an intrusion on our time. Tending to the sick and needy carries germs."

His eyebrows raised in exaggeration, his sarcasm obvious, he exclaimed, "How inconvenient!"

Laughter met his animation.

"But ..." he said, pointing an index finger skyward, "... God has a set of rules. Inconvenient or not, love your neighbor as you love yourself. And how often does God want us to go outside our life's convenient?"

Prepare their hearts, Lord, Catharine prayed.

"We must weigh His commands, His desires, His directions above any aggravation or bother—even danger," Mühlenberg said. "Was it a happy decision for Jesus to suffer and die on the cross? But He made his choice: God's will ... the world's salvation.

"Was it a problem for Peter to leave Jaffa and travel to the centurion's home? Or too much to ask of Paul to sail the seas time and again?

"We may not have such drastic choices, but we do face decisions. And when we do, we ought to check the whole notion of convenience. We should rejoice if God deems it good to choose us for a chore. Isaiah was thankful God chose him."

Mühlenberg stepped back behind the lectern, opened the massive Bible, turned the pages. "Isaiah wrote in chapter sixty-one: 'The Spirit of the Lord is upon me because the Lord has anointed me to bring the good news.'"

Catharine and others all around her gulped a breath as their pastor took a half-step backwards and removed his vestments. First, his stole, folding and placing it upon the Bible. Then, his alb. Then his cassock and vest. Each one, he folded with care and placed upon the other on the Bible until he stood before them in simple white shirt and trousers.

Catharine and the others had become less and less shocked over time at Henry Mühlenberg's unique ways of sharing a message. But this ...

She leaned ever so close to the edge of the pew.

Oh, Henry. What now?

"I stand before you as one of you ... in heart and mind and spirit," he said. "As a brother. The Bible says all believers are co-heirs of Christ, so we're family."

Rumbles of confirmation came from every corner of the sanctuary as well as the two assistant pastors who sat behind him.

Henry crossed his arms and peered across the congregants.

"Friends," he said, "we have countrymen who need our support and perhaps even our protection."

Around Catharine, people sat forward in their seats. Beside her, Anna murmured a surprised, "Oh?"

Catharine reached for her hand and held it. For her own support or Anna's?

"You may have heard Christopher Ludwick brought eight captured Hessian soldiers to our city to convince them to leave the British army and come and live among us. Catharine reported to me this morning Christopher's attempts have been successful. Indeed, our friend put his life in peril and crossed enemy lines to convince other German soldiers to do the same."

Several people gasped at Christopher's daring. Catharine guessed some among them gulped, considering it foolish endangerment. Some might agree. But what do you do with a man like him? Others first, always. Sometimes an exasperating "always."

"These are fellow countrymen from the Old Country," Henry said. "Fellow Lutherans—well, most of them."

Scattered chuckles met this remark. For Germany was Lutheran, surely.

"You may have noticed them in this church last week. If, and when, they come—and I pray they survive the war—they will need shelter and work. Yes. But more. I'm speaking about friendship ... community ... a sense of being welcomed and belonging."

Catharine glanced around. Rapt attention. Even more so than the sermon. *Henry, you read my heart—and God's, too, I believe.*

Mühlenberg's eyes roamed around the sanctuary, then he smiled.

He must spot a lot of "welcoming" faces.

"My hope and prayer is we in this church will be foremost in the forefront of their acceptance. A refuge, each of us, for these men."

He stepped away and motioned to the organist, who played the instrumental introduction of "We Gather Together."

Catharine broke into silent prayer as the choir and congregants around her sang the beloved old hymn.

When all was said and sung, and the benediction done, she remained in her pew, letting go of Anna's hand to remain in the quiet. She knew many friends wanted to speak to her about Christopher, to ask if she needed any help around the workplace or home, or any myriad of things, but she wanted a time of peace and quiet with her Lord. This church—with its sturdy oak and mahogany, with this late-morning light pouring through high windows, with an atmosphere for reverence—afforded her comfort.

Peripherally, she heard people walking along the center aisle toward the front entrance, the hushed voices of Henry Mühlenberg and others perhaps speaking of what they were capable of doing in response to Henry's call to action. Then minutes later, shuffling of feet, doubtless Henry's and his assistants', back toward the presbytery. She was thankful they continued past her. For, more and more, she saw the steps she was to take next. Some schemes came so quickly she scarcely grasped them.

The farm in Lancaster. The farm in Germantown. The Ladies Association of Philadelphia. *Freischule*, the free school. Her "girls"—Gretchen, with whom Rudolph was so infatuated and vice versa; Marta, Hannah—all those who may-might-could make marriages with these men. Christopher, perhaps because she may-might-could be able to get away from Philadelphia to help him in some way.

And then, there was tomorrow's task.

CHAPTER 22

Catharine had risen early, hurried to the bakery to help get the work started, and then left Martin to run the business. Now, she was off to put her plan into operation.

She hustled down Front Street and turned west on High Street on her way to the offices of the *Pennsylvania Gazette*. Along the way, friends and acquaintances tipped their caps or said, "Good morning." She smiled and hoped the hurry in her step was an excuse-me-but-I-must-run reply.

As she reached for the door handle at the *Gazette* office, the door opened before her, and she was face-to-face with Robert Aitken.

The publisher of Thomas Paine's *Common Sense* and of the Continental Congress's *Congressional Journal* as well as the *Gazette*, Aitken was a stalwart of the community. The Ludwicks were weekly advertisers in both the *Gazette* and the *Staatsbote*, which was located a couple of blocks away on Chestnut Street.

Robert greeted her with a wide smile, a nod of the head, and a "Good morning" with a Scottish accent so strong she always had to concentrate when speaking with him. Behind him stood a young man whom Robert had hired to replace Paine when the emerging author left his job as editor-in-chief of the *Gazette* to take up arms in the Revolution.

Robert and his wife, Janet, had moved from Scotland several years ago and become friends with the Ludwicks. They shared a faith, though they were staunch Presbyterians. And they sometimes shared a dinner table—Christopher making certain the couple brought their uproarious three children with them.

What a menagerie!

"I've an idea," Catharine blurted without even a 'good morning.'

"Nothing unexpected from you," Robert quipped.

Catharine smiled. "An idea with which I need your help, Robert."

Robert tilted his head in curiosity. "Share away, my dear." He motioned for her to follow him to his desk several feet away. Aitken's offices were unpretentious, all business. Voices coming from a room at the rear seemed harried.

They each took a seat, Aitken behind his desk, Catharine before it.

Robert spotted her noticing the sounds. "Getting out the latest *Gazette*." He spread out his hands. "How can I help you, Catharine?"

She spoke in a rush. "Congress has agreed to give free land to any Hessian soldier who deserts the British and comes to live here as an American."

"I'm aware," Robert said. "The *Gazette*'s front page contains an article about it—coming off the press in about an hour." He pointed a thumb in the direction of the back room.

Catharine lit up. "So, my idea is a follow-up."

Robert's eyebrows rose. "I'm listening."

"What few people know is Christopher has gone behind enemy lines and into the Hessian camp to convince them to accept Congress's offer."

Robert leaned forward, concern covering his countenance. "Christopher?"

She nodded.

"Is he back? Did he get out?"

Catharine nodded again and didn't contain her smile.

"He might have been shot as a spy, Catharine!"

"But he wasn't," She knew her smile was smug, but she couldn't help it. "He believes he has convinced a number of them to do so—he and the eight Hessians he escorted through the city a week ago."

"I heard," Robert offered. He waited for her to continue.

"This is where I hope you can help," she said. "I received a letter from Christopher saying he hopes our community will welcome them as friends and neighbors, as employees and even employers."

"A-ha." Robert raised an eyebrow. "This is where I come in."

Catharine struggled to contain her excitement but knew her expression did little to hide the emotion. "My first idea was an article, interviewing various businesspeople, Mr. Hancock, et cetera. But in church yesterday, I believe the Lord revealed to me we need to reach the German population in particular. There are others here in the city who would rally against our efforts. Who would see this offer as being to 'enemy' soldiers and therefore a bad idea. Who would not realize such a thing will save the lives of our own men, our friends who are in the battlefield."

Robert cupped his chin in his right hand. "So, what is on your mind?"

"If I can persuade Herr Miller at *Staatsbote* to publish a flyer in German to distribute to their readers, and also print enough extra copies, would you distribute them to your readers?" She was referring to Heinrich Miller, publisher and editor of the newspaper.

"My competition, huh?" Robert formed a crooked smile, a twinkle belying any displeasure.

Catharine returned a demure look of her own. "Your friend, Robert. I know you and Heinrich are secret comrades in arms."

He narrowed his eyes, raised one eyebrow, lowered the other. Catharine was familiar with the look. How does he do that?

"It's a deal," he said. "And no cost on my end. My one question is what about street copies—those my news boys sell?"

"Better not," Catharine said. She leaped to her feet and extended her hand. "Thank you, Robert. Thank you. Thank you!"

She spun around to leave.

"Off to *Staatsbote*?"

She smiled ear to ear, nodded, and waved good-bye.

Two blocks further, on Chestnut Street, Catharine walked into the offices of *Pennsylvanischer Staatsbote*.

A young woman stood from her desk and welcomed her with a wide smile. "Catharine!"

"Good morning, Tildie. I need to see Heinrich."

Tildie Becker, who had worked for Miller since he started the newspaper more than ten years before, rolled her eyes as if to say "the tornado you seek is ..." She pointed to a room off to the side of the reception area.

Miller was a humorous and humble man in his mid-sixties, who never seemed to relax. He published Tuesdays and Fridays, unlike most papers' weekly Tuesday editions. He was hectically busy, setting type and doling out instructions to two young apprentices.

Miller too was born in Germany. And he too had emigrated to America, but in 1741, a good dozen years before Catharine's husband. The two men shared a cultural and language bond as well as spiritual. Christopher called him "Müller"—his given name—and Miller called him "Christoff."

After church services, the two men would greet each other this way, laugh, clap each other on the shoulder, and be on their way. A silly ritual, but a ritual, nonetheless.

When the *Staatsbote* beat the other five newspapers in the city to reporting the signing of the Declaration of Independence two months ago, no one was surprised. Heinrich was diligent, professional—and by appearances didn't sleep.

He also published on July 5, a Friday, four days before his competitors.

With caution, Catharine walked into the room where all the action was happening. They were on deadline, after all.

When Heinrich spotted her, he stepped away from his work, wiped his hands on the brown apron hanging from his shoulders, grinned, and offered, "*Guten Morgen*, Fräulein Ludwick! I hear congratulations are in order for your husband."

"You know already?"

"Yes. Baker General. Impressive. Good choice."

"How did you find out?"

He furrowed his brow. "You need to ask?" He stepped toward her and took her hand with gentleness in both of his. "I would have approached you about it after church service, but you looked deep in prayer."

"I was," she said with a smile.

"To what do we owe the pleasure of your visit? An advertisement?"

Catharine shook her head and proceeded to tell him her idea. "But it's too late, I'm sure, for this edition."

"Late? Too late?" Heinrich harrumphed. "I am a writer of blistering speed. A gazelle among a herd of elephants."

Catharine chuckled. He raised an eyebrow. "You think this a joke?" Then, he laughed, though lightly.

He motioned for her to follow him and led her to a desk in the rear corner of the front room. Papers were stacked what seemed willy-nilly. A waste basket beside the desk overflowed with notepapers. He dipped a quill in an inkwell, snapped his eyes to hers, and pelted her with questions, jotting down her answers. Dipping in the inkwell and writing.

Where are these men going to be located?

Can these men speak English?

Can they do the jobs colonists are now unable to perform because they're fighting the war?

Are you encouraging people other than German Americans to engage with them?

Have you met any of these Hessians yourself?

Every once in a while, he'd stop her as an impression came to him, write a person's name, say "a good quote from him," or "he always has something to say."

Soon he looked at his watch, peered at her with twinkling eyes. "Lucky man, Christoff. This will do well. We'll have an article in tomorrow's edition, not Friday's. And I'll print a flyer both for our readers and Mr. Aitken's. Of course, ours will be distributed with Friday's edition. We'll get enough to Robert for his paper next Tuesday."

Catharine stuttered a "thank you" and left, feeling elated. The two most prominent newspapers in the city—one English, one German—and both were supporting the cause. She was excited to get word to Christopher.

***

Christopher, Private Richard "Dickie" Gilmore, and a corporal, Jonathan Pauley, were on the move. They'd left Sunday for the two-day ride to Morristown, and Christopher was anxious to begin the work of Baker General. An ominous job, he knew. A heavy weight needing to be shared with many. How many? He wasn't sure.

Not like catering a party of thirty at the Franklins' or Morris's.

Before leaving Fort Lee, Christopher had dispatched a letter to the Supreme Executive Council of Pennsylvania, asking for assistant journeyman bakers from within the state militia.

Argh! Bureaucracy! The foul stench of mediocrity when superiority was needed.

Between the Supreme Executive Council of Pennsylvania and the Continental Army's Commissary Department, operating your own company was more efficient by any measure. No committees, no boards, no ill-informed quarrels.

Christopher's plan was to establish two ovens at Morristown, baking seven hundred pounds a day. Another two ovens would be built for Pitts Town, three in Trenton, two in Valley Forge, one in Reading, and possibly, one in Elizabethtown—though the last might be chancy since Elizabethtown was in the middle of considerable potential action back and forth.

He also envisioned fabrication of portable ovens small enough for two of them to fit on a wagon.

This way, the army's food supply would have stability, with stationary ovens for extra-large output and mobility too keep astride the troops.

Hopefully, Anna Nutt and Company and Taylor and Flower's Redding Furnace could handle the output.

This was his plan, but wars are fluid things—a lesson he'd learned from bitter experience.

Man plans. God laughs.

He reached forward and stroked Hugo's cheek. He had had little need for horses over the years but had gained an appreciation after seeing their immense prominence in the war effort.

Anna Potts Company's buildings came into sight, and the three men tethered their horses outside an immense brick structure. Christopher smiled to himself. This was no "country" operation.

Minutes later, Christopher met an elderly man in the reception area in the front of the brick building. He introduced himself, Gilmore, and Pauley, and asked to speak to either Thomas Rutter or Samuel Potts.

The old man nodded generously, to the degree Christopher supposed his head might pop off, motioned to several chairs nearby, and said, "Have yourselves a seat."

Five minutes later, two other men stepped through a doorway and strode up to Christopher and the others.

"Thomas Rutter." A tall, thin man in his forties extended his hand. "This is my partner, ironmaster Samuel Potts."

Christopher shook the men's hands and introduced his assistants as he assessed the forge owners. Dressed as a banker, Rutter was dark-haired, dark-eyed with whiskers to brag about. His smile was wide, his eyes twinkled merrily, and he appeared familiar. Christopher had seen him somewhere, he was sure. Perhaps at one of the Pennsylvania commerce meetings.

Potts was a solid man in his mid-thirties, standing five-foot-nine, blond-haired, blue-eyed, broad-shouldered. His calloused hands revealed he was used to hard labor, and he looked as if he'd handle a half-dozen men in a wrestling match.

A leather apron accentuated the fact he was an ironmaster. Christopher wondered if Potts knew his friend Douglas Bradford.

Christopher told them his mission, spelling out his needs, and asked if they were able to handle the work.

Rutter raised an eyebrow.

"When were you last here, Mr. Ludwick?"

"About ten years ago."

"Let me show you our capabilities."

Rutter and Potts led the way outside, where the five men climbed into a large carriage and headed north along a creek. About a mile along the road, they came to an impressive complex of buildings.

To their left stood a large three-story wooden barn and several other structures, all stone.

Pointing to each structure, Rutter identified them. "Our smoke house, two blacksmith shops, cider press." He pointed down the hill to a wooden-framed home they had passed, "For employees to use until they can find permanent homes."

"However, gentlemen," Potts cut in, "this is what you're here to see. He pointed to their right, to a mammoth stone structure. "The foundry."

An extraordinary bell stood in a small patch of greenery in front.

"A lot of bullets could be made from the bell," remarked Pauley.

"True," said Potts, "but we ring her to call the men to work."

"We'd prefer they take all the clock weights before our bell," Rutter said, stroking his whiskers. "Those and whatever cannons we've found inferior for the battlefield."

"But we're here to show you are capabilities, are we not?" Potts said, his voice revealing an element of excitement.

Christopher nodded, catching a bit of enthusiasm himself.

Before they entered the building, Potts pointed to the wide stream rushing alongside an enormous building.

"French Creek," he said. "More than enough power."

The stream flowed at what Christopher guessed was a twenty-degree grade, and the building was built right into the side of the slope.

They entered a cavernous structure and three things struck Christopher at once—the blazing glow of the furnace, the heat's shimmering causing the room to seem out of focus; the intense, intermittent roar of its forced blast; and the heat itself.

"We built the place into the side of the hill, so we can load ore, limestone flux, and charcoal from the top with little trouble," Potts said against the noise, pointing toward two workers about thirty feet above them. An occasional stream of sparks whistled into the air toward the high ceiling.

An immense water wheel churned along nonstop, with the sound of a wet rope being tightened.

"Liquid metal," Rutter said, his voice an octave higher to be heard.

"Liquid gold," Potts added. "With the water running as it does, operating those enormous bellows," he pointed, "our weekly production amounts to twenty-five tons of iron, comprised of both pig iron and castings for ovens, stoves, pots, kettles, andirons, smoothing irons, clock weights and more."

Christopher spoke up. "So, you're saying you can meet our needs."

"Yes, and we'll do so without taking a profit," Rutter said. He looked at Potts for confirmation.

The ironmaster smiled affirmation and said, "Full stomachs make for good soldiers. All we need from you, Mr. Ludwick, is the dimensions you'll require for the ovens."

Christopher dug into a pocket, retrieved a folded paper on which he had drawn his dream oven, and handed the parchment to Potts.

"How soon?" Potts asked.

"Yesterday."

CHAPTER 23

Two months later, Christopher's outreach was successful, his operation fully manned, the large baking ovens in place, the mobile ovens being produced and delivered to where they were needed.

Weather had turned from hot to cool to the edge of cold. Two days before, Christopher had received a letter from General Washington summoning him to Fort Washington, post haste.

Christopher, Pauley, and Gilmore, now known as Christopher's Kitchen Crew, arrived at Fort Washington in the late afternoon. Christopher hastened to Washington's headquarters, asking his two assistants to bed the horses and stay nearby.

Led into the headquarters by a corporal, Christopher spotted Washington straight away. Standing with three other officers, he was pointing to a spot on one of his many maps. Hearing Christopher enter, he turned. "Christopher, my old friend. You made good time!" he said, then he moved his gaze to a nearby desk, where a pleasant surprise awaited Christopher.

Christopher had written to Catharine and had asked her to send his bowl to Fort Lee, and indeed, here stood the precious possession. This was not any bowl. When sailing on the Royal British Navy's *H.M.S. Duke of Cumberland*, they came to the East Indies and then China, where he purchased the luxurious silver-chased china bowl. Later, in London he had his name engraved upon it.

By the look on Washington's face, the general himself remembered it, for whenever Catharine and he hosted guests for dinner, he would raise the bowl with the toast: "Health and long life to Christopher Ludwick and his wife."

Washington had been one of those guests and had remarked on the bowl's unique beauty—so unique.

As Christopher smiled and took in the scene, he fingered the special coin in his pocket.

No wonder the pharaohs ensured their most treasured possessions were entombed with them in their pyramids. Sad, for them, there was no paradise. For Christopher and other believers, their paradise needed no "treasured possessions" to keep them company into eternity.

Washington broke his reflections.

"That, my friend, is not why I asked for your swift transport here."

Christopher raised his brow in question.

The officers around Washington appeared to know the reason. The general went to the desk, where he removed and handed a parchment to Christopher.

The letter was official-looking and written in a hand with which Christopher was familiar. John Hancock, president of the Continental Congress, possessed a most commanding signature and this was an official request, a specific entreaty, an appeal about Christopher.

He scanned the message, then studied it more slowly. English was still his second language.

He looked over at Washington. "General, do I understand Congress wants me to arrange the exchange of Hessian prisoners for some of our men and do so in Elizabethtown?"

Washington nodded. "And I agree with them, Christopher. You are the perfect man for the assignment."

"Because?"

"Because you're German, you speak German, the prisoners are German, and whoever is handling our men for the British is German."

Makes sense, indeed.

"Hammer geil," he said. "Outstanding."

What's another ball to juggle?

Christopher straightened his back, then his shoulders. "Where are the Hessian prisoners now, and when does the exchange happen?"

"They're being held in Hackensack, and the exchange takes place at twelve noon the day after tomorrow, Friday," Washington pointed to one of his officers. "Lieutenant Colonel Walter Lawrence here, will be your right hand, Baker General."

Lawrence was among the officers Christopher had met at Flying Camp. All six-foot and two hundred pounds of him stepped forward to shake Christopher's hand. "Glad to be working with you, sir."

Christopher shook his hand and again looked at Washington. "Then, General, I propose two things."

"Yes?"

"I will cook a meal for you and your immediate officers here tonight, and I will do the same for the Hessian prisoners tomorrow."

Washington shot him a questioning look.

"The dinner tonight will celebrate the imminent release of our soldiers, praise the Lord. The dinner tomorrow will give me a chance to persuade more Hessians to abandon the British army."

"Ah-ha!" Washington exclaimed, and all the men around them laughed in agreement.

***

Dinner! Christopher enjoyed the preparations. Cooking was an art, and he embraced every nuance of it—experimenting with this spice, that herb, this type of potato, that type of squash. The Pottses had been perfect hosts and had allowed him to prepare meals for them when staying in Morristown. But those occasions were not enough for Christopher to fulfill this vital part of him. Call it a "need."

Der Küchenchef Ludwig.

Did husbands the world over appreciate their wives' efforts—not solely around the house but in the kitchen, in particular? He did. Doing so with Catharine was a "bonding."

So, he put his heart into a celebratory meal. He even ordered a barrel of ale.

The order of the day was *Badische Schupfnudeln*, or potato noodles, alongside *Rouladen*, thin slices of beef, browned, then braised. Simple, delicious, German. He would cook the same meal for the Hessian prisoners before sending them away—at least those he couldn't persuade to stay.

The ingredients might be a challenge to the commissary—the pickles, onions, celery and carrots, in particular. But there was always beef for an army's officers, was there not? And eggs and potatoes and flour?

As the night sky encompassed Fort Washington, Washington and two other generals, along with a handful of other officers and the Presbyterian pastor, James Caldwell, sat around the dinner table, chatting informally.

Christopher stepped into the room from the kitchen and all the faces looked expectant.

"Reverend Caldwell has joined us," Washington said. "Since his home is in Elizabethtown, I asked if he'd accompany you and Lieutenant Colonel Lawrence, and he has agreed.

"Good." Christopher nodded at the pastor. "Perhaps you would say the grace too?"

Caldwell did so, Christopher took a seat in the middle of the long table, Pauley and Gilmore had volunteered to serve the meal and did so with special aplomb, drawing a smile from the head of their Kitchen Crew.

The Badische Schupfnudeln and Rouladen drew raves all around. The conversation ranged from families to farms, fishing to wild game—it seemed avoiding the imminent danger so close in distance and time.

Christopher had found human nature seemed to tend toward one extreme or the other—focusing on either the good or the bad. Tens of thousands of Redcoats and Hessians were bivouacked no more than a few miles away. Each possessed a musket, black-powder cartridge boxes, and pouches of lead balls. Some had a cannon and cannon balls. A number with a blade and an itch to draw blood with its tip wet-stoned as sharp as a razor. Some kept track of their "kills" to secure bragging rights back in camp. So proud.

The best warriors fired off three or four shots in a minute. In his youth, Christopher managed perhaps three, if he fumbled his way through the process at all. If he could take a life at all. Those were days he fought to forget. Perhaps this was one reason discussions of battle were verboten this night.

As Pauley and Gilmore were about to deliver peach kuchen, Washington, sitting at the head of the table, looked at Christopher. "Thank you, old friend. This was a most delicious meal and celebration of God's deliverance."

"Hear-hears" around the table met this remark.

Christopher nodded his acknowledgment, then proceeded to pull his china bowl to him, poured in a pint of beer and toasted, "Health and long life to Christopher Ludwick and his wife."

"To Christopher Ludwick and his wife," the men all repeated as they joined in the salute.

The response brought a broad smile to Christopher's face.

What a difference in wars, eh? Prussia and America—two unalike landscapes, so diverse the motives, so dissimilar in so many ways. And hopefully, prayerfully, so different the outcome for those I love.

The peach *kuchen*, which consisted of peaches, custard and a shortbread crust, ended the evening with utter contentment.

Christopher hoped one of the results would cement friendships, but also when these officers heard of a Christopher Ludwick request—to the Commissary or Congress—they would support him. Soldiers needed strength to fight. And for strength, they needed nourishment. "Baker General" might sound trite, but the extent of his success could win or lose wars.

★★★

Christopher rose early the next morning, Thursday. He felt he needed to prepare "inside" as well as outside for the upcoming task. He was in the same bedroom he'd occupied the last time he slept in the headquarters. Further along the hallway, General Washington must be kneeling in prayer before starting his long day. What better routine to imitate?

So, he did. And when he did—kneeling and remaining quiet, for God wasn't uninformed of anything he might share—his design for this day became clear as the Irish crystal vase Catharine cherished in their downstairs sitting room.

First, he sent for Lieutenant August Fischer—the perfect right-hand man for the endeavor.

Having lived the life of a Hessian soldier, Christopher knew a bit about the Hessians he would meet later. He knew, when fighting a war away from home, you build a family to replace the one you left behind. This was an instinct dating back to Adam and Eve. The man next to you becomes your brother the same as you become his.

When one of those brothers dies, well ... the trauma, the depression. The physical and emotional tearing of the soul. Psychological and emotional distress piled upon physical stress. A man needed good news, hope, light in the darkness.

Yes, Christopher's strategy was good news, indeed, for these Germans. Darned if there weren't enough Germans over here, if you brought them all together, they could form a country on their own. They already had Germantown. Deutsch Land sounded plausible.

Ha!

Pushing himself to a standing position, Christopher considered how fortunate he was in this war compared to the thousands of soldiers sleeping on the ground in tents, if indeed they had shelter at all. All during this Revolution, except for a few times, he had spent his nights in a house in a bed, comfortable, sheltered from the elements.

Congress had extended Christopher an extra portion a day of food, but he had refused to feast while his equals had left homes, families, and jobs for little but a "thank-you-so-much" and "we'll-pay-you-when-we-can."

He quickened to dress, leave the headquarters building, and find Pauley and Gilmore, who'd become blood brothers to each other and sons to him. Pauley and Gilmore relied on the other's strengths, and both building on their potential as Christopher made demands on them forcing their knowledge and growth.

If not for this foray into Baker Generalship, who would have known Pauley's mechanical skills, or Gilmore's tenacity in finding needed parts for all sorts of equipment? Not to mention the persuasive skills of both men—for, before war erupted, when men went about their ordinary daily lives, who in the world even considered the necessities of baking for sixty thousand troops scattered across thirteen colonies?

This venture these two men shared with him was profound, and they had met every demand with an attitude Christopher wished he witnessed more often in those "conventional" times.

Surely, someone had written about such odd discoveries of wartime.

Christopher knew this, and he agreed with Ben Franklin when the latter said even peace may be purchased but at too high a price. A large part of the price had nothing to do with money. Instead, the accomplishments that would have been achieved by the thousands of men who died on the battlefield. The inventions. The books and art. The children and children's children for generation upon generation.

What price those?

Christopher pondered these questions as he grabbed a bite of bacon here, a slice of warmed bread there while looking for his two assistants. He found Gilmore and sent him to find Lieutenant Colonel Lawrence, then discovered Pauley and dispatched him to find Pastor Caldwell. Elizabethtown awaited them.

He was thinking now as a commander of troops, not the civilian recruit he had considered himself when he left Catharine's arms to join General Mercer's Flying Camp. Perhaps this was the mindset he had begun to assume when Congress requested Washington to name him Baker General. This job was no bake shop with six or eight employees, nor farm with a half dozen workers. This was perhaps comparable to a military company with three or four platoons.

Each regional oven would serve as a hub from which his men would drive wagons to transport the baked goods. Armed guards would travel with them.

Communication was crucial—from the various armies to Christopher and his "hubs" ... and vice versa.

This war was more fluid than perhaps any in any land the world over, and the changing locations and needs of the troops would need to be reported as "immediately" as possible.

Today, the Continental Army controlled Forts Constitution and Lee, but tomorrow might tell a different story. The future of Boston had changed one hundred and eighty degrees after the Battle of Bunker Hill, so might the future of Philadelphia flip to turmoil if the Redcoats were to charge the city.

Imagine a wagon-full of bread and other food goods being driven to a position having been taken by the enemy!

Soon Christopher, Lieutenant Colonel Lawrence, Lieutenant Fischer, Pastor Caldwell, and the rest of the contingent of about fifty men were on their way to Elizabethtown. Christopher pulled Hugo alongside Fischer, who rode behind Lawrence.

Fischer looked at him.

"Same as in Philadelphia, Gus," Christopher said.

Fischer regarded him for a few seconds, then his face brightened. "Yes! "Worked well, didn't it?"

"With prayers, it will do so again, though we'll have only one evening with these men."

"Understood."

Christopher nodded then held Hugo back until Caldwell, riding behind on a handsome Morgan gelding, drew alongside him.

Christopher regarded the churchman. Forty-ish, handsome in his pastoral apparel, wearing a wig under his tricap. Even by appearance, he it was easy to believe him a captivating speaker.

Finally, Christopher said, "Pastor Caldwell, you live in Elizabethtown."

"First, please call me James. And, yes, my wife, Hannah, and I live there."

Christopher smiled. "Every man needs a wife. A minister, in particular."

"In particular."

"What does Hannah think of your involvement in the Revolution?"

Caldwell reached behind him and patted a satchel hanging on his horse's rump. "Bibles," he said, "for our men."

"Aha."

"She's pregnant with our first child. Nevertheless, she does, with reluctance, agree with my involvement in the war. Although she insisted if I left, I must take with me a supply of King James Bibles." He hesitated at a notion, then said, "Ha! I ponder what King James would think of this war, good Scotsman and Christian as he was."

"He might even fight for our side," Christopher said with a chuckle.

Caldwell laughed along with him, and they settled into comfortable silence for a while.

Christopher considered of the clergy's sacrifice for this Revolution. The Presbyterians had Caldwell and William Marshall of the "Seceders" Church in Philadelphia. The Methodists had Francis Asbury, who traveled from Georgia to Maine. The Congregationalists had Jonathan Mayhew in Boston. The Baptists had Reverend Samuel Cooper in Boston. Episcopalian Samuel Seabury was based in Connecticut. Anglican Myles Cooper preached in New York. And, of course, there was Jacob Duché, chaplain to the Continental Congress and rector of Christ Church in Philadelphia, a casual friend of Christopher.

Caldwell seemed to read his mind.

"I think," he said, "not King James, but this king deceives his subjects and himself as the Church of England's 'ambassador to God.' Ambassador of who? I see no morals in the man."

Christopher couldn't object. "What of the others of his denomination?" he asked.

Caldwell shook his head in sadness. "Well, most of the Loyalist clergy I know are Church of England, and many of them were remaining mute—either to prevent rebellion among their own ranks or retain their own skins."

Their own skins.

Christopher recalled the news article he'd read in the *Philadelphia Gazette* proving tar-and-feathering had been taken to a whole unthought-of art. Customs officer John

Malcolm, who was first tar-and-feathered by Mainers, met a worse fate when he proclaimed the Mainers had done a bad job of it. Boston's Sons of Liberty had taken him at his word, stripped him naked, and used hot tar in the process. Malcolm had returned to England, possessing a jar of his skin, torn off when he had removed the tar.

Christopher cringed at the idea of such a brutal attack. Yet, the Bostonians' fierceness did not make the cause of freedom any less righteous.

Several of Christopher's fellow Philadelphians were Loyalists but keeping quiet about their inclinations. In Philadelphia, as elsewhere, wherever Patriots controlled land in the thirteen colonies, royal officials had been expelled. No one in those areas, who proclaimed their loyalty to the Crown, was allowed to remain, so Loyalists fled or kept quiet. Mum was the norm and would remain so—until the tide turned. Christopher hoped and prayed such a change would never happen.

He steadied his gaze on Caldwell. "Besides your wife, what of the others in your church regarding the Revolution?"

Pride filled Caldwell's voice. "We have thirty-six commissioned officers in our congregation, as well as many noncommissioned officers and enlisted men."

This was a good sign. Many in the church would be praying for the upcoming endeavor.

★★★

Soon they arrived in Elizabethtown, a beautiful village awash in white. A town square, complete with raised gazebo, stood in the midst of the wooden First Presbyterian Church on one side, a brick courthouse on the other, a forge at one end, what appeared to be a hardgoods store on the other, and several shops besides.

Women, children, and elderly men were bustling about and raised their eyes in alert at the sudden appearance of the troops. Seeing they were Continental Army, the people went back to their own business. But something was astir.

"Our townspeople are ever vigilant," Caldwell said. "Sitting on Newark Bay, which flows into the Hudson, and being so close to Staten Island and Manhattan, Elizabethtown will see considerable action in this Revolution."

At the front of their troop, Lieutenant Colonel Lawrence raised a hand, motioning for everyone to stop. He looked back at Caldwell and called. "Some help here."

Caldwell responded quickly, sending his horse into a gallop, and Christopher followed him to Lawrence's side.

"Can we bivouac around your church?" Lawrence asked.

"There and around my manse as well—the home on the street beside the church."

Three Continental soldiers appeared, walking briskly toward them from around a barn on the far side of the square. In front was a burly, middle-aged man, his long sleeves rolled up to reveal bulging biceps. "Authority" dripped from his pores. His long mustache twirled on each side. An extraordinary achievement.

At either side of him was a strapping young soldier, taller than him and athletic-looking. Christopher wondered if the younger men were chosen to lend even a thicker air of power.

"Lieutenant Colonel!" the mustachioed man called.

Lawrence nodded.

As the man drew nearer, he saluted—sharp. All military. "Sargent Roger Mallet at your service, sir. And to help with the prisoner exchange."

He strode right up to Lawrence. He reminded Christopher of the soldier who'd trained him and his fellow recruits thirty years ago outside Frankfort, Germany.

"We've received a message from General Howe," Mallet said. "He's moved the exchange to eight o'clock tomorrow morning."

"No objection here," Lawrence said, "Where are the prisoners?"

"In a barn yonder." Mallet pointed southeasterly.

"I've brought General Ludwick here," Lawrence motioned toward Christopher, "to serve as a liaison. He's a German speaker."

"Good, 'cause we're having a problem with the language. I don't know how the Brits communicate with these men."

Christopher had to chuckle. Germans were obstinate by nature and, he knew firsthand, they enjoyed being the boss, not the bossed. They were meticulous and methodical and considered disorder a lack of discipline as well as intelligence.

"We'll have no problem," Christopher said.

"Yes, sir, General Ludwick."

There it was again. Being addressed as "general" and saluted.

Robert Morris's Jewish friend, Haym Salomon—a witty man whom Christopher had met at the Morris home—would say, "Oy vey." So, he said to himself with a chuckle, in his Polish accent, "Oy vey."

***

While the troop was erecting a half-dozen six-man tents between the Presbyterian church and its cemetery, Caldwell led Christopher, Lawrence, and Fischer to his home.

Hannah Caldwell met them at the door. Dark-haired, bright, and beautiful, she hurried to her husband's arms—or as close as she her protruding stomach allowed.

After a prolonged hug, Caldwell drew away enough to introduce her to the two men.

"When is your baby due?" Christopher asked.

"January, perhaps February," she replied. "I hope I'm ready."

"Treasure your little life," he said.

"We will," she said.

"We do," her husband added. "The Lord knows us when we're in the womb, so we treasure his or her life even now before we meet."

Christopher smiled.

"You have children," Hannah said.

This brought a sting, because their little boy had died young.

He shook his head slowly.

Caldwell sensed the hurt and tried to turn the tide, adding cheer to his voice. "Let me show you rooms upstairs while you're here."

Christopher appreciated the pastor's sensitivity.

"I'll cook dinner for you tonight," Hannah offered, her voice as bright as her face.

Christopher shook his head. "Thank you, dear lady, but Christopher Ludwick has other plans. Plans for our Hessian friends."

He proceeded to fill them in on his strategy for the evening.

"Is there a place I can use to cook a meal to serve our prisoners?" he asked.

"Our church has a kitchen and large dining room," Caldwell said. "We use it for special functions as well as feed the poor."

"Yes, and I can have some ladies help serve," Hannah said.

This was all coming together.

"Any German-speaking ladies among them?" Christopher asked.

Hannah considered this.

"How about Fran Becker and her daughter—Sadie?" Caldwell asked. "They both speak fluently."

"Yes." Hannah looked at Christopher. "But I can recruit others to serve."

CHAPTER 24

The church was the perfect spot for the evening. First, God was present. Second, the kitchen was more than sufficient. Third, there were tables enough to seat a hundred, let alone the dozen Hessian prisoners along with Lawrence, Fischer, and Christopher's Kitchen Crew—for Pauley and Gilmore deserved a treat after being the servants the day before.

The order of the day was Badische Schupfnudeln and Rouladen—the same as he had cooked for Washington and the others. Potato noodles alongside thin slices of beef, browned, then braised.

"We need to inform the Hessians 'home' is where you make it—whether Stuttgart or Philadelphia, Düsseldorf or Boston" Christopher told Caldwell. "'Home is where you share your roots or grow new ones. A place where you are able to remake yourself—no preconceptions, no limitations except those the self-imposed, no expectations from those who knew your vagaries when growing up, or your sins once you were grown.

"Christoff Ludwig," he continued, "is himself a prime example, and he isn't shy in sharing the fact—if possible, over a strudel at his kitchen table. But this church in distant Elizabethtown, New Jersey, will do fine, Pastor."

Bustling around them, Pauley and Gilmore were their efficient selves. They had learned what Christopher desired when large gatherings were taking place. They'd put all the food provisions in their place, setting the stage for a meal. Christopher would want the two available tables alongside each other as though the Hessians were among comrades and equals.

Christopher checked his pocket watch. Five o'clock. Six o'clock had been his favorite watch while out at sea. He'd survey the ocean and behold the days pass into sunsets so stunning they would light a fire in your soul. The beauty was still there, even on evenings whose chill winds wanted to invade your wool coat, even when rain blistered down in blankets, even when the waters roiled in a storm.

So, yes, six o'clock through midnight? They had been his treasured hours while at sea. He prayed he would muster words sufficient to shine the glories of this fledgling country for these men to see.

Christopher gazed about the room. He exhaled in relief and anticipation. The Kitchen Crew had one hour to get about its business, preparing the meal. A meal so delicious would change these men's lives—or some of them at least.

"Ready, General?" Pauley asked, motioning toward the potatoes, onions, carrots, and celery spread across the countertop waiting to be prepared. He smiled ear to ear because he knew how Christopher frowned on the title. Congress had suggested Superintendent of Bakers—a salute-less title he preferred. No contract had been offered designating either title, so he had simply gone about his duties.

Christopher nodded. An hour later, Lieutenant Colonel Lawrence, Lieutenant Fischer, and Sargent Mallet strode through the doorway, leading a single-file line of Hessians and another four soldiers with muskets at the ready. Two of the prisoners were Jägers, wearing green jackets with crimson facings. The blue jackets of the others described them as infantrymen.

Christopher counted them. Eleven all together. He looked at Mallet. "I was told there were a dozen prisoners, Sargent."

Mallet snorted. "One of the Jägers spit on the floor and snarled something sounding like a cuss word."

Christopher shrugged.

To be expected, honestly.

Christopher roamed his eyes over the Hessians. *"Siein Sie sitzende,* Freunde," he said. (Be seated, friends.)

He continued in German, "Christoff Ludwig, your former countryman from Gießen, welcomes you to the best meal you've eaten since leaving Germany." His eyes flashed a smile. "Perhaps since you ate at your momma's table."

A few of the men snorted an I'll-believe-it-when I taste-it, but they all pulled back chairs from the two side-by-side tables and sat, backs rigid as if they were in mess hall with a general present.

Christopher motioned for the American officers and Pastor Caldwell, who had entered from another door, to sit at a third table, where the Kitchen Crew joined them.

Hannah Caldwell had done as she'd proposed, recruiting several of her church ladies to serve the meal. There were glasses of ale before every setting. The women began serving the Badische Schupfnudeln and Rouladen.

Christopher examined the expressions of the Germans, looking for the leaders who were sometimes not the Jägers. The men exchanged looks, and one of them gave the slightest of nods. "Sure. Go ahead."

Christopher wondered how anyone could resist the meal. The aroma itself brought joy to his own heart. Every time he ate this specialty, he relived one of the last memories of his mother before she died. Badische Schupfnudeln was her specialty. His vater always cooked it in her memory on her birthday.

Knowing Pastor Caldwell did not speak German, Christopher bowed his head and spoke in his native language: "Come, Lord Jesus. Be our guest. Bless the gifts You have given us."

A couple of the Hessians mumbled *"liebe"* (amen) while the Americans did, even though they assumed he'd said grace, then everyone dove into the meal.

Christopher stepped toward Millet. "What's the name of the Jäger who refused to join us?"

"Hoffman," Mallet said. "Why?"

"We'll see," Christopher said. "Enjoy your meal, gentlemen."

He turned on his heel and walked to the door leading outside. A private and a corporal stood guard there. He gazed at the corporal and said, "Take me to the prison barn."

"Sir?" His face was one big question mark.

"To the barn, Corporal." His voice was one of authority. He no longer felt otherwise.

They made the walk in about three minutes, enough time for Christopher to question whether this was a good idea. Was it?

"**You're called.**" He heard the words as if they had been spoken by someone behind him. He turned to look. No one was there.

"**Do it. Trust Me.**" He turned again. Still, no one was there.

Sentries stood at the corners of the large barn, another at a double-door in the center of the southernmost wall.

"Open up!" Christopher called.

The guard at the door looked a question at the corporal, who nodded approval.

Christopher stepped inside. The place was cavernous, filled with the mixed smells of cut hay—pleasant—and buckets in a corner used as an outhouse—foul. Topside, the unbaled hay spilled over a railing. The floor below was swept clean, mostly. Clothing was strewn around, where men had stripped in the heat.

Christopher eyed another American soldier, standing guard over a single man, who stood leaning back against a pillar, chewing a stick of green hay, his green coat tossed over his shoulder. He looked at Christopher lackadaisically.

"*Entschuldigung,*" Christopher said. (Excuse me.)

The Jäger dismissed him with "*Es ist niemand zu Hause.*" (No one is at home.)

Nonplussed, Christopher continued in his native tongue. "I see someone of note. I see someone of the courage to refuse to go along with his comrades, to look the enemy in the eye and say, 'Keep your food!' But we are not your enemy, Jäger Hoffman. We are more so your 'targets.' Aim, fire, reload. I know the drill.

"Yes, Jägers are the bravest fighting men the world over. But even brave men must eat, no?"

The response was a disinterested "*Jein.*" (Yes and no.)

"Jein as in yes when offered by a friend, nein when from an enemy? But, again, I am not your enemy, Jäger Hoffman. The Badische Schupfnudeln and Rouladen were made by my own hands—the hands of a humble baker from Gießen. Christoff Ludwig."

Christopher walked straight to him, extending a hand.

Hoffman turned to the side, facing away from him.

"We wanted ... I wanted to offer, in friendship, a fine meal before you return to the British for whom you fight."

"Rückgabe?" (Return?) Hoffman asked. *"Hast du alle Tassen im Schrank?"* (Do you have all your cups in the cupboard? Are you nuts?)

Christopher smiled. He hadn't heard the expression in two decades.

"Nein," he said. "Tomorrow morning, all you men are being exchanged for American prisoners. If you want, you can return to your commanding officers, to serve your emperor. To fight for England."

"England!" Hoffman scoffed. "I fight for Germany."

"What will Germany gain from an English victory in America?" Christopher asked. He addressed the question not as a challenge but a simple naïve query.

Hoffman was stumped. "Germany gain?"

Christopher nodded innocently. "What do your countrymen gain by killing Americans for the king of England?"

Hoffman shrugged.

"You and your comrades," Christopher said, "are chattel. Your bodies for rent to the highest bidder, the proceeds going into the pocket of our emperor."

He used the possessive "our" to drive home his German heritage.

"What do you know?" Hoffman dragged out the words, acid dripping off each one.

Christopher lifted his shirt to reveal one of his wounds.

"I too fought for the emperor," he said. "Two wars. Lured by the promise of excitement, adventure. Were you not as well?"

Hoffman scowled, but Christopher had him thinking.

"More than a few Jägers have spilled their lives' blood next to me," Christopher said. "Then, on our march from Turkey to Vienna, more men died of starvation and the elements than had from bullets and cannon fire."

Hoffman raised an eyebrow. He was beginning to take interest, perhaps.

"I ask myself," Christopher said, "was it exciting? Was it adventurous?" He scoffed and glanced at Hoffman to gauge his reaction. The man's mouth was twisted in a knot.

"America," he continued, "is offering free land to all Hessians who leave the employ of their emperor and choose to live with us. Our land, Jäger Hoffman, is rich, bountiful, full of lakes and rivers teeming with fish, forests abounding with game."

An eyebrow rose, eyes opened wider.

"Join us, please," Christopher said. He motioned for Hoffman to follow him. Turning, he ambled toward the door. Hoffman didn't follow. Christopher continued his pace. Hoffman didn't follow. Christopher reached the door, constraining himself from looking over his shoulder. Hoffman didn't follow.

Then, as he opened the door ...

"Herr, Warte." (Mister, wait.)

★★★

All eyes turned when Christopher and Hoffman, with the corporal behind them, walked through the door of the church. The German ones were unbelieving, most of the Americans surprised, Sargent Mallet staggered, by the looks of him.

The only ones not startled were Pauley and Gilmore. Those two doubtless expected Christopher to return with the recalcitrant Hessian.

Christopher led Hoffman to an empty seat, then strode to the table where the Americans had emptied their plates and were enjoying seconds.

"Gus," Christopher acknowledged Fischer with a wink.

"Christopher." Fischer shook his head in admiration. "Unbelievable."

Christopher glanced over to gauge what was transpiring around the Hessian table. Were they at ease? No. But the meal had satisfied his "guests," it appeared.

One of the church ladies was serving Hoffman, who grumbled some acknowledgement and dug in. All along the table, the Hessians were keeping their eyes on the Jäger. Anxious, it appeared. Between the barn and the church, Hoffman had donned his green jacket, a symbol of superiority to everyone at the table except two other Jägers.

But once he put fork to Badische Schupfnudeln, the atmosphere appeared to shift. Moments later, when he tasted the Rouladen, the temperature in the room seemed to drop ten degrees.

Christopher released his breath.

A minute later, the serving ladies delivered the finishing touch—Christopher's famous gingerbread. In the shape of a crown.

The perfect allegory.

Christopher touched Pastor Caldwell's shoulder. "Pray for me, James," he whispered.

Caldwell gathered Christopher's eyes in his own and nodded with a firmness meaning business in God's throne room.

Christopher glanced at Pauley, giving him a look they'd shared before. Pauley reached into a satchel hanging on the back of his chair, pulled out Christopher's bowl and handed him the treasured possession.

Christopher poured a cup of ale into the bowl. When he raised it in front of him all eyes noticed and turned to him.

"Gesundheit und langes Leben an Christoff Ludwig und seine Frau, Catharine!" he said with aplomb, then repeated in English: "Health and long life to Christoff Ludwig and his wife, Catharine!"

The men at his table raised their glasses, repeating, "Health and long life!"

The Hessians appeared perplexed, but one by one raised their glasses, drinking what remained of their ale.

Then Christopher turned serious. He stood, stepped closer to the table of Hessians, and motioned toward the gingerbread crowns.

"Ihr seid Könige," he said. (You are kings.) He continued in German: "Each man is the monarch of his own castle. His wife is his queen. We Germans don't know this concept in Germany, but we learn it well here. There is no king in America. There never will be one. All men will be equal under the law with equal opportunities to succeed.

"I've been where you are—away from home fighting a war. Months, even years, away from our families, we may feel the urge to develop the same family ties with those closest to us. I did. You do. When one of those family members dies, well ... the trauma, the depression."

Christopher struggled to hold back tears from memories still vivid to this day. He squared his shoulders, waiting to keep his emotions in check.

"The physical and emotional tearing of the soul. The trauma. Stress and distress. Psychologically, depression is sometimes tantamount to defeat. Physically, we return home missing a leg, an arm." He shrugged. "One way or another—usually both—war destroys."

Christopher looked at the faces around the table.

Not one Hessian murmured opposition to what he said. One face was filled with consternation—Hoffman's.

He reminded Christopher of Schäfer, at first.

There's hope.

He marched on, with the idea that words, spoken well, were sometimes as powerful as weapons—sometimes more so. "America is going to win this war, you know."

Lord, keep my thoughts clear, my tongue from twisting.

"How do you know this?" The question was firm, doubting and it came from one of the other Jägers at the table.

Christopher peered at him—a rugged man with bushy eyebrows, calloused hands, with a demeanor to match. "I know, because we're fighting for something belonging to us, not someone else's possessions."

He turned to the table of Americans, then back at the Hessians. "By our own brawn and brains, we've built this country. She is ours now, not belonging to some king or Parliament an ocean away. These are our homes. These are our churches, our businesses. This is our land.

"When you fight for your own home, you fight to your dying breath. This is why I'm certain America will defeat the British, whose soldiers have no personal stake here."

He stepped closer now, standing no more than two feet away from the soldiers at the end of the table.

"We're offering a portion of our land to each of you who are brave enough to leave the employment of the emperor, abandon the British army. Up to twenty hectares, yours free and clear. You can both enrich yourselves while being an enrichment for your countrymen."

He noticed several deep breaths taken. Gulps of air. Unbelief.

"As soon as the war is over, a promise of our Congress."

To a man, the Hessians looked at each other, incredulity in their eyes. This was food for thought, for debate. Christopher prayed he would see the same results as he had with Blum, Schäfer, Rudolph, and the others.

"How do we believe this?" asked one soldier between bites of gingerbread.

"Christoff Ludwig tells no lies. Not since I left behind a life of despair in Germany when I determined to build a life of prosperity here in America. No lies. No debts. No life controlled by a sovereign I do not know, have never seen, nor will ever meet."

"Wir kennen dich nicht Von Adam," said one soldier. (We don't know you from Adam.)

"No, you don't, but I have an honest face." Christopher chuckled. No one else did. "I suppose I'm trusting you to trust me."

His remark met with mixed results, more negative than otherwise.

This is the moment.

He pulled a letter from a breast pocket, unfolded the page and read:

"My dearest beloved Christopher—" he winked and displayed the twinkle in his eye, which met with scattered chuckles, then continued.

I am overwhelmed with the response we have received from Philadelphians the city over as well as from many in Germantown and out in Lancaster. People from all walks of life are telling us they will welcome any German soldiers who have departed British ranks. A number have offered jobs, among them Mr. Potts and Mr. Rutter from Anna Nutt Co. and Samuel Flower from Redding Furnace. Both are missing men who have gone off to war, and as you know, the demands on their manufacturing are extraordinary—what with all the ovens you've ordered as well as cannons and cannon balls. Many farmers are also in great need of help, with the late-summer and fall harvests either here or approaching.

Christopher hesitated. looking over the table to gauge the men's attention. Maybe yes, maybe no. He continued.

Mrs. Redmond and Mary Eddy of the She Business Association visited me at home to offer their support, though most of their members are self-employed. Deborah Franklin also stopped by on a stroll, sharing that she and Benjamin have high hopes this strategy of Congress may help swing the war in our favor.

Christopher stopped there, not mentioning the rest of the letter. Catharine related she had procured the promise of the one hundred acres adjoining their Germantown farm for Jägers Blum and Schäfer. Also, Douglas Bradford had inquired when Johann would arrive to help with the livery. Besides, her "girls," Gretchen and Marta, in particular, were asking about Rudolph and Hans. Catharine's amorous closing was a particular secret between them.

He turned to catch Fischer's reaction, the lieutenant being the one person besides the Hessians who understood a word he read.

Gus offered a crooked smile which Christopher interpreted as "well done," then he returned his gaze to the table of prisoners.

"I pray," he said, "this gives you plenty to consider before we return you to the Redcoats tomorrow morning, my friends."

The expressions he met ranged from disinterested to perplexed, but at least a couple would find sleep difficult tonight.

CHAPTER 25

THURSDAY, NOVEMBER 21, 1776
ELIZABETHTOWN, NEW JERSEY

They were to meet at eight o'clock in the town square, which was a fifty-one-hundred-yard grassy rectangle.

Before they assembled, Sargent Mallet hurried into the Caldwell house, where Christopher, Lawrence, and Fischer had spent the night.

Pushing through the front door with hardly a knock, he gasped, "Lieutenant Colonel—" His eyes were wide, his voice cracking, an odd sight for a man in such control.

Lawrence nodded. "What is it, Sargent?"

"Two of the Hessians approached me. They want to stay, sir. They want to desert, to accept Congress's offer."

Lawrence straightened in surprise.

"Aha!" Christopher exclaimed. He smiled as though he were about to meet a long-lost relative.

Caldwell entered the room. Christopher spotted him. "Your prayers, James. They were answered."

He shared the news.

"What do we do?" Mallet asked.

Lawrence answered, "Keep them back. After the exchange, bring them to me. Then we'll deal with the matter." He turned to Christopher. "Do you have a procedure for these men?"

"Congress does," Christopher said. "First, we're to escort the Hessians to a barracks in Philadelphia—the one on the west side of the city at the far end of Filbert Street. There they will be asked to sign a 'parole,' an agreement to not take up arms against us again, or be an obstacle to the army in any way."

"We're to take them on their word?" Lawrence asked.

Christopher nodded. "Afterwards, they will pretty much be given free rein—basically released on their own recognizance." He pulled at an ear. "We hope they'll head to Lancaster County, being beyond the battles. Lancaster's our preferred destination. Several farms there, and elsewhere outside the city, are offering jobs, including my own. Businesses, also, have promised positions. Many of the officers will have the choice of going to Virginia. If so, we'll lead them there."

Lawrence shook his head. "I sure hope this works."

Gus Fischer weighed in. "Back at Fort Lee, I heard General Washington is going to publish a proclamation stating the Hessians are not our enemy—they are forced into the war and should be treated humanely."

Christopher had not heard this but wasn't surprised.

Lawrence checked his pocket watch. "Seven fifty-five. Time for the exchange."

A minute later, at the west end of the town square, all on horseback, Christopher and Fischer bracketed Lawrence at the front of the American party. Behind them, Sargent Mallet and his men surrounded the ten Hessian prisoners. Lawrence's forty-soldier platoon was in the rear.

Assembled at the east end of the square were a similar number of the Redcoats and a few Hessians along with the American prisoners.

All these Hessians for a mere two Americans.

What gives?

Christopher found his answer when he studied the two Americans.

General Sullivan's right-hand man—you might call him Sullivan's actual right hand, Major Ebenezer Swift—stood erect, chest out, his hands tied behind him. He appeared beaten and abused, similar to his comrade beside him.

Thrashed. Mistreated. The British are living up to their reputation.

Six Hessians in excellent health for every one American needing medical attention.

What a delegation of importance. Our men are more significant to us than yours are to you.

"Follow me, gentlemen," Lawrence said. He snapped his reins and trotted forward. Christopher and Gus followed suit.

At the same time, a British soldier who appeared to be a full colonel rode forward alongside one of the Jägers.

The two contingents met in the middle of the square.

Christopher took a closer look at the Jäger. He seemed familiar. In fact, he was very familiar.

Von Donop!

The colonel, the count, commander of grenadiers and Jägercorps. The man who had confronted Christopher at the British encampment on Long Island.

The man stood tall and regel atop an Arabian.

The memory returned fresh—like a frightening dream. Von Donop striding up to him as though Christopher were some loathsome creature impeding his passage, then jamming a pistol into Christopher's ribs.

Christopher remembered Von Donop's precise words: "I've heard whispers you may be trying to sway our men to leave the war."

Thank God, Blum came to the rescue, or this confrontation might have been the end of Christopher before his war had even started.

Christopher adjusted the front of his tricap downward, trying to prevent Von Donop from recognizing him.

The British colonel broke the silence, speaking in English. "You have our men," he motioned behind him, "we have yours. The letter we received from General Washington said there were a dozen."

"Ten," Lawrence said. "Two have defected from your employment."

The colonel looked aghast—feigning astonishment, Christopher guessed. His look changed to one of disgust and disbelief.

He turned and spoke in German, interpreting for Von Donop, who exploded with "You beat them to death!"

Lawrence glanced at Christopher, who repeated the accusation. Christopher held up a "I'll-handle-this" motion to the lieutenant colonel.

Christopher knew his face had turned crimson as he peered from under his tricap. "Take a look at our two men, Colonel, then gaze upon the well-fed, well-cared-for Germans behind me. Last night, their meal was Badische Schupfnudeln and Rouladen. Now look at our men behind you. What was their meal? They can barely stand!"

Von Donop's brow wrinkled, then he looked at him quizzically. "Do I know you?"

"No."

I may have run out of time. Christopher decided to hurry negotiations along.

"We're still exchanging ten of your men for two of ours. More than an even swap, I'd say."

"I'm certain I've seen you," Von Donop said—his mind more occupied with the mystery than what Christopher had said.

Beside Christopher, Gus was informing Lawrence of the dialogue. An odd diplomacy, this.

"Do we have an agreement?" Christopher pressed.

Von Donop settled back in his saddle, scowling. After a moment, he glared over Christopher's shoulder. "Bring Jäger Hoffman to me."

Christopher turned and waived to Sargent Mallet. "Escort Jäger Hoffman here, will you, Sargent?"

Moments later Mallet and Hoffman stood in front of Von Donop. Peering past the horse's Arabian nose, Hoffman saluted. "Colonel Von Donop."

"How have you been treated?"

"Respectfully, sir."

Von Donop rubbed his chin. "Tell me, Jäger, what was your last meal?"

"Badische Schupfnudeln and Rouladen, Colonel."

Von Donop shot a look at Christopher. Inscrutable. Christopher envisioned the man's mind churning, but he was indecipherable. Christopher again felt the cold prick of Von Donop's pistol to his ribs.

Indeed, Von Donop placed a hand on his pistol grip, causing Christopher to flinch. Several moments passed, then Von Donop and his British counterpart exchanged nods.

The Redcoat faced Lawrence and said, "We'll make the exchange, your two for our ten."

Mallet turned a gave a nod to his men, who escorted the Hessians forward as Major Swift and his companion were brought to Lawrence and Fischer.

While this was going on, Christopher bowed his head and turned Hugo away to head back to the American forces. Passing Hoffman, he uttered in a low voice, "Remember what I said, Jäger."

Hoffman nodded but kept silent.

Seconds passed while Christopher kept his back toward Von Donop. Then he heard Fischer say, "Major Swift, take my horse. I'll walk."

Christopher glanced back to watch. Von Donop was gazing straight at him. His eyes shot wide, and Christopher knew the man had remembered where they'd met. If so, he'd remember Blum and Shäfer had interrupted Von Donop's interrogation of him.

And if he remembered that, then all Christopher's friends were in imminent peril. Rudolph, having posed as his nephew, for one. The others as well—every one of them having returned to the Hessian camp on Long Island after being missing for several days, reporting they had escaped capture.

He turned back and snapped the reins. His mind was racing faster than his horse.

How would he get word to his Hessian friends before Von Donop returned to camp? Impossible!

Lord, Your help, please!

★★★

Malcolm Holmes had brought his sheep into the barn the previous night to get them out of the way while he scythed his way through a back pasture this morning. He was storing his second cut of hay for the winter. Old age was slowing him, true, but not winning the battle. Not yet. The grim reaper would have to wait for this old Welshman.

Having raked the cut hay into piles, he headed back to the barn to harness a couple of horses for his hay wagon. Normally, he'd have a couple young men to help him, but they were joining the battle somewhere. Anywhere safe, he hoped. As he walked, he sang a favorite song of his beloved wife, Alaw, who had passed the previous winter. She had taken with her as melodious a voice as her name implied— "tuneful."

"Arglwydd, arwain trwy'r anialwch" or (Lord, Lead Me through the Wilderness)

"Arglwydd, arwain trwy'r anialwch, Fi, bererin gwael ei wedd..." Malcolm sang. (Guide me, O thou great Redeemer, pilgrim through this barren land ...)

"Nad oes ynof nerth na bywyd; Fel yn gorwedd yn y bed." (I am weak, but Thou art mighty; Hold me with Thy powerful hand.)

Malcolm hummed the second verse as he reached for the double-wide barn door, then stopped. There was a noise inside. A man's voice muffled but German.

In my barn? In my barn! The Redcoats steal my sheep. Now the Germans!

He hurried into the farmhouse, reached inside the side door, and drew out his trusty musket, always loaded. The weapon used to shoot wolves and coyotes out to kill his sheep; now it was men.

Except maybe the fellow who put his horse in the pasture. Ludwick, the baker.

Malcolm returned to the barn, put musket to shoulder, prepared to do his worst.

I may be ancient of days, but no more so than Caleb when he volunteered to take on the giant Amalekites.

He burst through the door and there before him stood five, six, eight men—maybe a dozen besides. All Hessian soldiers, all in the throes of removing their blue or green coats. A pile of Hessian hats laid on the ground in the corner of the barn to his left.

When he barreled into the building and the Hessians saw his musket, several raised their arms in surrender, but a couple rushed to their weapons set aside here and there.

But one of them—a tall, broad man—raised his hand and said, "Halt!" The one German word Malcolm knew.

All the Hessians then stood still as scarecrows, their faces revealing concern if not fright. The one who had told them to stop turned to another soldier nearby and murmured to him in German. The man stepped forward and spoke English.

"Sir, we mean no harm." The accent was strong, but Malcolm had dealt with stronger back home in Wales from the men living in the mountains.

"No harm?" Malcolm said. "Your friends, the British, have squandered off with half my flock of sheep to feed their bellies."

The soldier raised his hands in a stopping motion. "My name is Carl Richter, sir. I promise we came here not to take any sheep. Rather to change out of our uniforms and make our way to an American military camp somewhere to surrender. We want to live here—in America."

The Hessian of apparent authority tapped Richter on the shoulder and spoke to him for a good ten seconds. Then Richter turned back, holding out his hands, palms skyward.

"Our friend Christoff Ludwig said your government would welcome us if we were to leave the British."

"Christoff Ludwig? Ha! Christopher Ludwick." Malcolm couldn't believe his ears. Christopher Ludwick, the man he'd met a few days ago. The one name in all the colonies these fellows shared with him.

"You know him?" Richter asked.

Malcolm told him about the one time he'd met Christopher, and the mission on which he was sent to the British camp.

Richter motioned to his superior. "This is Captain Blum. He says to tell you we rose before dawn to escape, but as we passed over the lines, a troop of men rode out. Yours was the nearest place for us to hide. We wanted to use your barn to remove our uniforms, so we won't be recognized."

"I'll do you one better," Malcolm said. "My two sons are gone to war. I've a closet full of their clothes in the house, along with a load we keep for the men we hire to help with harvest. Brawny men, they are. Come into the house, all of you. You can find some shirts and trousers to wear."

An hour later, the Hessians all appeared to be farmhands.

As they prepared to return to the barn with the plan to escape in the darkness once nightfall came, Richter said to Malcolm, "The word has spread. We expect many, many more of our comrades to desert. They may be passing your way. Ludwig was persuasive."

The revelation surprised Malcolm. He considered the Hessians hardened killers. But this?

He straightened his shoulders. "I'll be prepared. How can I help?"

"The same way you helped us." Richter met Malcolm's gaze with a smile. "Next to Herr Ludwig, you're the first person we meet from this country, and you welcomed us with open arms, even giving us civilian clothing." He patted a satchel hanging over his shoulder. "Plus, plenty of jerky and apples to see us on our way."

Jägers Blum and Schäfer were about to lead the men to the barn when the sound of hoofbeats alerted them. Malcolm looked out a window while the others out of sight.

A troop of about thirty or so British and Hessian soldiers rode by, heading to the British camp.

"Wir sollten uns beeilenin die Scheune," Blum said.

Richter grabbed Malcolm's elbow. "We're hurrying to the barn and will hide out there until dark."

Malcolm nodded. A good plan. His wife, Alaw, bless her name, would argue they must stay and sit for one of her famous meals. But no. This was for the best. He'd done his part and would be prepared for others in the days to come.

***

Colonel Carol Von Donop rode ahead of the contingent he'd led for the prisoner exchange, driving his knees into his Arabian's ribs, slapping the reins in fury.

He didn't slow one bit as he rode past two sentries, but he heard one, a Hessian private, exclaim, *"Dunkelflaute!"* referring to a dark, sunless weather pattern.

The other dropped his jaw, knowing someone was in danger—and it wasn't the crazed German.

Von Donop rode straight to the Hessian encampment, pulling his pistol from its holster as he leaped off his horse.

This time he was going to use it. No! A bullet was too good for the slime. He yanked his sword from its scabbard. This blade will do better. The traitors would watch their comrades die one by one!

"Blum! Schäfer!" he screamed. He couldn't muster the title Jäger for either one of them. They didn't deserve the recognition. The others? The regular troops? The co-conspirators? They, too, would die a coward's death. Blum

334

and Schäfer's past heroics flashed through his mind, but he dismissed them as he would dismiss the men when he saw them.

Heroes? Deserters!

Von Donop looked with ferocity about him, waiting for some response.

He pointed to one of his lieutenants. "Get me Blum and Schäfer. Put your sword to their throats and drag them to me if you must."

"Sir," he responded, "since you left this morning, we discovered Jägers Blum and Schäfer and maybe a couple dozen others are gone. We can't find them. Soon after you left this morning, Captain Wreden led a troop out of the camp in search of them. We haven't seen them since."

Von Donop's jaw quaked, and he drove his sword into the ground where it quivered as he stormed off in the direction of headquarters. Would he, Wreden, and Von Bardeleben have to answer for this? Envisioning his emperor, he lowered his eyes. Yes, they would.

This was a disaster. An utter humiliation.

CHAPTER 26

Monroe Hanson yawned. For a war, this was becoming ever more tedious. Instead of out killing Redcoats, he'd found himself his sergeant's favorite sentry, so here he was again. He'd discovered he hated mornings. He abhorred watching the sun rise. He despised not seeing action. How was it possible to rise to corporal or higher without accomplishing anything?

Heck, Tommy Hayes was in on capturin' a couple of Redcoats and had received a commendation along with the rest of his troop. A couple of Redcoats ... Ha! What luck. Here was Monroe, not getting recognized for nothin'. For certain not for seein' the sun comin' up.

Tosh!

Monroe leaned back against an old oak tree. He ran his right shoulder up and down its rough bark, scratching an itch. He'd wouldn't mind scratchin' an itch on his trigger finger, for sure.

He looked toward the horizon to check on the sun rise. It would have to rise sooner or later, right?

Sure enough, the red orb was sending rays across the tops of the tree line to the east.

Monroe shook his head. Time moved so slow. S-L-O-W.

His mom's pancakes came to mind and made his stomach rumble.

A sudden movement about fifty yards out drew his attention.

A person stepped out of the woods into the clearing.

Monroe narrowed his eyes, looking more closely. Not one man. Men. Men with rifles!

His pulse quickening, Monroe took the bugle hanging on his hip, turned toward camp, and blew the warning signal.

Turning back toward the oncoming men, he put the handle of his musket to his shoulder.

Action at last?

He heard the commotion of men behind him, scrambling from their tents. Part of a Flying Camp, they knew how to hustle.

Monroe was ready to bend to one knee, but first called out: "Who goes there?"

The man in front hollered something but Monroe couldn't make out the words.

Again, he called, "Who goes there?"

"… coming to *aufgeben*."

"Coming to what?"

"To aufgeben. Surrender."

"Stop there!" he ordered.

All the men appeared to be wearing civilian clothes. Perhaps they were recruits, come to join the fight.

The man in front turned to his comrades, who must now number more than a dozen, and was speaking to them. In a moment, they all stopped in their tracks.

Monroe almost keeled over at the sight of obeyance.

★★★

The Flying Camp's commanding officer, Cedrick Glidden, had been among the first to leap from the ground at the warning blast.

Pulling his suspenders over his shoulders, he'd grabbed his coat, musket and paraphernalia, and hurried to the sentry point.

In a moment, a good twenty of Glidden's men were scurrying to either side of him as they reached Private Hanson. He put a hand on the young man's shoulder. "Good job, Monroe. You've done well. I'll take it from here."

Monroe nodded, smiling.

Cupping cupped a hand to his mouth, Glidden bellowed, "Put aside your muskets!"

Again, the lead man turned to his comrades. A moment later they dropped their weapons to the ground.

"Approach slowly," Glidden commanded.

The contingent raised their hands high and walked forward.

When they were within a few yards, Glidden commanded, "State your name and your intentions."

The man in front spoke up. "Sir, my name is Carl Richter. I'm a corporal in the Hessian army. We have come to surrender. To accept America's offer."

"America's offer?" Glidden said.

"Our acceptance as Americans and a ready start in your country."

Glidden studied the man. While he did so, a tall, broad man behind Richter spoke to the Hessian in a foreign language.

Richter nodded agreement, then glanced back at Glidden. "Our friend Christoff Ludwig gave us these assurances."

"Mr. Ludwick?!" Monroe blurted out.

"Yes," the big soldier replied. "Christoff, our Freund."

Sure sounded like "friend."

Glidden had read General Washington's communiqué about Hessian deserters.

So, this is the beginning, he thought.

He rubbed his chin, then, "Right. Corporal Richter, we will transport you to Philadelphia. From there you will sign some paperwork and be allowed to go wherever you want. I don't know how the land will be dispersed. Congress's decision, I suppose."

He motioned for the Hessians to follow him into camp, then got the attention of several of his men.

"Jake, Tate, Rupert, you all go out there and retrieve their weapons. Malvern, you take a few men, ready two carrier wagons. You and Sargent York are going to take a contingent of men to escort our German friends to the Filbert Street barracks in Philly."

"Yes, sir."

★★★

As they passed into the American encampment, Jäger Blum turned to face Schäfer walking beside him.

"Do you believe we're doing this?" he asked.

"I do now," Schäfer said. "Appears our faith in Christoff wasn't mistaken."

"Who in the world does not know Christoff?" Blum shook his head in mirth.

Rudolph spoke over their shoulders, *"Hammer geil!"* (It's amazing!) Gretchen, here I come."

"You and women, Rudolph," Blum said with a shake of his head.

"No," Rudolph responded. "Me and Gretchen. Only her. My first stop after we're released."

Walking along beside Rudolph with an expectant look on his face, Hans muttered, "My first stop? Christoff's bakery. Marta."

"We came to fight a war ..." Blum said.

"And we stay to plant a field," Schäfer finished.

"Plant a family," Rudolph added.

CHAPTER 27

Christopher and Hugo, old friends now, rode the King's Highway west toward Philadelphia. A week ago, after witnessing General Charles Cornwallis's capitulation of the British Army to General Washington's troops, Christopher had supervised the baking of six thousand pounds of bread, so the troops were able to celebrate with their French allies.

Sitting among the men, Christopher had lifted his china bowl high, repeating his now-familiar toast. "Health and long life to Christopher Ludwick and his wife." Cheers had followed from one and all.

In the last of his many meals together with Washington, when they would spend an hour or two at a time in each other's company, the general had regaled him and others about the miracles which, in the end, had brought the British to their knees.

In the spring of 1776, with the British controlling Boston, and Washington having ordered cannons brought three hundred miles through snow from Fort Ticonderoga, a fierce hurricane, or Nor'easter of gale strength, forced General Howe to call off his amphibious assault.

When Washington launched a surprise attack on the British in Trenton at sunrise on December 26, 1776, a driving snowstorm brought the wind at their backs, into the faces of the Hessian troops who were drunk from celebrating Christmas the day before. In less than an hour, the Americans captured a thousand Hessians at the loss of a few men.

The next month, with Washington's troops trapped in Trenton, an extraordinary drop in temperature froze the ground, so his troops were able to escape from Cornwallis's men in the middle of the night.

In the summer of 1777, British General John Burgoyne's troops, attempting to retreat up the Hudson River toward Canada, were trapped and six thousand soldiers captured when a torrential rain turned the roads into a slimy bog.

When this last January, after the Battle of Cowpens in South Carolina, American General Daniel Morgan had to flee northward, the British forces were stopped not by one, nor two, but three unexpected storms. First, Morgan's men retreated over the Catawba River mere hours before "a sudden storm made the river impassable." When his men crossed the Yadkin River, again rains flooded the waterway. Finally, a flash flood at the Dan River blocked the British, allowing Morgan to cross into Virginia, a friendly territory.

Time and again, Washington said, Providence sent raging floods or other weather at the perfect time for the Americans, both on land and at sea once the French sent their naval fleet.

"How our brave, but feeble, troops have fought all these years, through every possible suffering and discouragement, to defeat such a force as Great Britain is little short of a standing miracle," Washington said.

Privately, Washington had patted Christopher on the back. "I have an idea what you have suffered and sacrificed. You are a true, faithful friend and servant to the public. Without you, and with the Sovereign as your Guide, we would doubtful have won this Revolution."

After the victory meal with the troops, Christopher had dispatched a letter to Catharine, asking her to pray Congress would accept his resignation.

Nine months earlier, the Board of War had refused to accept his attempt to resign, promising him more bakers as well as a pay raise. So, he had soldiered on.

But now, he was even more worn down by the relentless demands of his job. He had also received word the British had ransacked his Race Street home during the Redcoats' occupation of Philadelphia and had plundered his Germantown farm of furniture, dining ware, and even clothing. Meanwhile, his fortune had dissipated through paying for a lot of his supplies as well as his assistant bakers. He hadn't asked Congress for reimbursement, but he might have to make such a request.

He adjusted the eye patch he'd worn since losing his left eye in a mishap a year earlier. He chuckled at the thought of how much weight he'd lost—ever tightening his belt. One more reminder—he wanted to come home, no more. Yes, five years ago, the war had again found him. And, yes, he had answered the call of his adopted country.

More than anything else, Christopher was eager to see his beloved wife, rebuild their life, and discover how his Hessian friends were progressing. Catharine had sent him word four years before that the first group of Hessians had arrived. Rudolph had wooed, then married Gretchen.

Hans and Marta were courting. Emil and Lucretia had sent Germantown into a gossip town with their interracial marriage. Johann was working with Douglas at the livery and was close to being adopted by the Bradfords.

Just as exciting—hallelujah!—Karl Blum and Kristian Schäfer were now neighboring farm owners, distancing themselves from the moniker "Jäger."

Christopher had left Pauley in charge of the army's mess needs. A talented, intelligent man, Jonathan. Not to mention a lot younger and more vigorous than Christopher. Gilman, having proven himself diligent and trustworthy, would serve Pauley well as his right hand.

His mind whirling, Christopher almost missed "his tree."

He was passing over the bridge across the Lehigh River. The sturdy little eight-foot-high maple stood upright in the midst of the waterfall to his north.

He brought Hugo to a stop in the middle of the overpass and peered upriver at the phenomenon.

"How in the world did a tree grow way out in the middle of the quarter mile-wide waterfall?" Christopher asked his horse. "How did a tiny seed make it so far and become embedded in the rocks, take root, grow, and continue to flourish in the middle of the Lehigh?"

Hugo whinnied,

"The spectacle defies reason," Christiopher continued, as if speaking to a circle of friends at church. "It flouts nature. But obviously, it does not defy God."

In fact, Christopher believed God made it all happen so people, even nonbelievers, would ponder the mystery and the miracle of such a specimen.

With God, a seed doesn't need rich, soft soil. With God, a seed doesn't need sun to sprout. In fact, that tree had withstood floodwaters broiling right over its tip.

"With God, anything is possible," he finished.

At times, the last few years—in particular the bitter, deadly winter at Valley Forge—Christopher had felt overwhelmed and contemplated this tree.

When the odds of victory seemed insurmountable, he'd reflected on this tree.

God can accomplish anything. After so many years of withstanding the impossible, Christopher imagined if his tree had a mind it would think, "Nothing, but nothing, can knock me over and destroy me. Experience has proven so. Ice storms in the winter, floods in the spring, drought in the summer. No, I have nothing to fear. My God, my Creator will protect and deliver me."

The same as He had delivered myriad enemy defeats in mysterious ways, helping America's tiny underprepared army, with its meager war chest, defeat the world's greatest power and its Hessian enforcements. Americans had driven the "all-powerful" British military to its knees.

Somehow Christopher had escaped capture as a spy, convinced scores of Germans to defect, then overseen feeding the entire Continental Army, strengthening and sustaining all those soldiers for this long war.

Pulling his coin from a pocket, Christopher twirled the treasured possession in his palm. Yes, he had sacrificed an eye. Yet, peering at his coin, he recalled the larger, the eternal sacrifice of his Lord and Savior.

One more circumstance came to mind. Catharine's last letter, sent from their Germantown farm, revealed the war had ended, but British troops had still to leave Philadelphia. Among their troops were hundreds of Hessians.

Opportunity!

Christopher clapped his hands—his face shining, his eyes filling with tears of gratitude.

HISTORICAL NOTES

Chapter Two

1. On February 2, 1776, the Philadelphia Society for Assisting Distressed Prisoners was created, with Ludwick serving as one of twelve managers. Focused, in particular, on reforming the penal system, the organization survived nineteen months and was dissolved during the American Revolution.

2. In March 1775, Ludwick joined the managerial board of the United Company of Philadelphia for Promoting American Manufacturers. Organized by Dr. Benjamin Rush, the company focused on expanding the North American colonial economy through woolen, cotton and linen manufacturers.

3. Ludwick's efforts in the German Society of Pennsylvania and with Hessian prisoners were focused on education and employment, so German-Americans could have the same opportunities as he had.

4. Ultimately, the Philadelphia Society for the Establishment and Support of Charity Schools earned the honor of carrying forth Ludwick's design of educating Philadelphia's youth. In 1872, the Society was renamed the Ludwick Institute, and again in 1995 to its current

status as the Christopher Ludwick Foundation. Over time, the organization has transformed its mode of educating Philadelphia youth; yet, it has always maintained Ludwick's original intention. Currently, the Christopher Ludwick Foundation, based in Bryn Mawr, awards annual grants amounting to $250,000.

HISTORICAL INFORMATION

In 1763, the native German became a naturalized British subject, following an act of Parliament in 1740, which allowed foreign Protestants to achieve naturalization once the individual had lived in the colony for seven years, taken the necessary oaths, and provided certification of receiving the Holy Sacrament.

Ludwick was active in St. Michael's Church of Germantown, the first Lutheran church founded in the Pennsylvania colony. Following its completion on May 16, 1766, he also supported the Zion Church in Philadelphia.

When Philadelphians were fleeing the city to escape the killer yellow fever in 1797, Ludwick stayed in the city and baked bread for the needy.

Dr. Rush wrote of Ludwick: "Of the domestic virtues of Mr. Ludwick, the surviving branches of his family are the affectionate and grateful witnesses. Of his patriotism and integrity, the testimony of General Washington will be a lasting record. Of his liberality, there is scarcely a public institution in Philadelphia, established before his decease, that does not possess some monument. Three Africans, whom he had emancipated, proclaimed in tears over his grave, his regard to justice and the equal rights of man; while more than fifty persons who had been taught reading, writing and arithmetic at his expense in different schools in the city and its neighborhood summed up the evidence of his uncommon public benefit. His private charities were like the first that blazed perpetually upon the Jewish altar."

Ludwick's will included financial support to the German Reformed Church in Philadelphia, the German Society, the University of Pennsylvania, the Lutheran Church at Beggarstown to be "employed in educating poor children," the Pennsylvania Hospital for relief of poor patients, and the Guardians of the Poor.

In his elder years, while socializing in the city streets, he was often greeted with "There goes the general!"

ABOUT THE AUTHOR

A veteran of journalism for thirty years, during which he won seven national magazine writing awards, Mark Alan Leslie has written fourteen books, including *Publishers Weekly* Featured Book, *True North: Tice's Story,* and the American Family Association choice as Novel of the Year in 2022, *A Cause Most Splendid: The Battle for the Bible.*

His works range from contemporary adventure (*Chasing the Music, The Three Sixes, Operation Jeremiah's Jar,* and *The Last Aliyah*) to historical (*The Baker Was a Spy,*

A Cause Most Splendid: The Battle for the Bible, Midnight Rider for the Morning Star, The Crossing, True North: Tice's Story); the End Times (*Torn Asunder*); a devotional (*Walks with God*); a self-help book (*Fired? Get Fired Up!*); and the world of golf (*Putting a Little Spin on It: The Design's the Thing! and Putting a Little Spin on It: The Grooming's the Thing!*).

He and his wife live in Maine. They have two sons, four granddaughters and one great-granddaughter, Elliana, meaning "God answered." Elliana's mother was, according to doctors, not supposed to be able to bear children. Another miracle.

OTHER MARK ALAN LESLIE BOOKS